HAT GIRL

HAT GIRL

WANDA CAMPBELL

Signature
EDITIONS

Cover design by Doowah Design.
Photo of Wanda Campbell by Dune Campbell.

Acknowledgements
Ernest Hemingway's definitions of bullfighting terms are from the Explanatory Glossary of *Death in the Afternoon* (1932). The character of Will Murdoch is based on the life of British-born, New Brunswick artist Robert Percival. Though Percival did paint crucifixions including *Tormented Torsos* (1968) and *Crucifixion Collage* (1969), those described in the novel are fictional. Percival's descriptions of his medical condition are excerpted from an article by Douglas Hughes that appeared in the *New Brunswick Reader*, November 19, 1994. I am deeply grateful to my husband, without whom this book would not have been written, to my wonderful editor, to the Islanders who welcomed me, and to my friends who have kept the faith.

This book was printed on Ancient Forest Friendly paper.
Printed and bound in Canada by Hignell Book Printing Inc.

We acknowledge the support of the Canada Council for the Arts and the Manitoba Arts Council for our publishing program.

Library and Archives Canada Cataloguing in Publication

Campbell, Wanda, 1963-, author
Hat girl / Wanda Campbell.

Issued in print and electronic formats.
ISBN 978-1-927426-20-3 (pbk.).--ISBN 978-1-927426-21-0 (epub)

I. Title.

PS8555.A5439H38 2013   C813'.54   C2013-905422-7
C2013-905423-5

Signature Editions
P.O. Box 206, RPO Corydon, Winnipeg, Manitoba, R3M 3S7
www.signature-editions.com

In memory of Robert Murdoch Percival
1924-1995

For Dune

CONTENTS

PRELUDE:
DEATH IN THE AFTERNOON

> The great thing is to last and get your work done and see and hear and learn and understand; and write when there is something that you know; and not before; and not too damned much after.
>
> ~Ernest Hemingway, *Death in the Afternoon*

I am no stranger to death. After all, I am a Hemingway aficionado. I have taken courses on books he wrote, wars he fought, languages he spoke, art he admired, and I chose to be a journalist like he was. In the old days, you could get a job at the *Toronto Star* by sitting on a rusty radiator and telling exaggerated war stories in which you were the hero until someone took notice. It didn't hurt either if the head of the Canadian chain of Woolworth's department stores, who spent lots of money on newspaper advertising and whose crippled son you had been hired to turn into a man, put in a good word for you. At least that's how Hemingway did it. Then he proceeded to write articles about ether, war, canoeing, and how the pollution in Toronto was bad enough to kill trees. That was 1923.

Nowadays, of course, to be a journalist it helps to have education and experience, so I completed my degree in journalism from Ryerson while keeping body and soul together working as a cook at a restaurant called Carnivores that specializes in steaks, burgers, and wings. Experience is harder to come by. I did cover a Brownie Fly-Up for the *Ingersoll Times* one summer. "Get lots of pictures," the editor told me, repeating the golden rule of small-town reporting. "People like to see themselves." The Brownie leader said, "This is the last Fly-Up we'll have. Now it's not considered fair that the girls who earned badges get to fly up while the others have to walk up. Now everybody goes up to Guides together." I arranged the Brownies for a group photo, asking them to flap their arms as if they were flying. The picture appeared in the Saturday paper under the headline "Winging into History."

I can also say that, technically, I have written for the *Globe and Mail*. One of my salad dressing recipes appeared under "Creature Comforts" and I wrote a piece in defence of Hemingway that appeared in the "Facts and Arguments" section. In it I quoted Hemingway's bit about what newspapermen keep in their pockets. A cub reporter's pockets, he wrote, contain letters from his best girl, a street directory, stamps, receipts, a cigarette case he thought was silver, and, of course, clippings of articles he himself has written. *When the police find a dead body with a pocket full of clippings, they know it is either a cub reporter or an actor. As reporters never die, it is always an actor.*

I chose to study in Toronto in the first place because it was the only Canadian city where Hemingway spent any time. Throughout my four years at Ryerson, I took comfort in visiting the places Hemingway had lived. There was the Connable mansion at 153 Lyndhurst that had been at the northern edge of the city in 1920, but was now in the heart of it. It is still a graceful structure with its balconies, and arched windows and dormers, though it has been turned into upscale condominiums. I suspect the music room, the wine cellar, the skating rink, and the stables have all disappeared. Gone the glory. And then there were the far less glamorous lodgings on Shelburne and Bathurst Streets where Hemingway lived with his first wife Hadley. The Bathurst Street apartment was so tiny it didn't hold much more than a Murphy bed, but had a view that redeemed it for Hemingway. *Beyond the ravine you can see the open country.* Now there is no open country left in Toronto, as far as I can tell.

At some point the city started to worry me. I felt like I was inside a human body, the kind you see in old biology textbooks or encyclopaedias with the clear overlays showing the various systems moving over and under one another. The vascular system is transportation carrying a flow of life, a surging plasma of subways below and traffic above, red tramcars hurtling along like platelets. The nervous system is all the voices and digital information zipping through wires and cables and the air itself. Everywhere this intense buzz of process and mitosis. The CN Tower is like a giant needle penetrating the skin of the city and injecting it full of adrenaline, or some drug that speeds everything up, making the heart of the city beat faster and harder, fierce fluids rushing at a fever pace.

I had to walk through the U of T campus to get to Ryerson and had discovered a few quiet places like the campus chapels, or the cloisters at University College where the monastic stone arches echo with quiet, a soothing balm against the singe and hum of the traffic. But even there, more often than not, someone would be in the quadrangle doing performance art or tai chi or just talking. I also liked to wander in the Allan Gardens, especially through the old style conservatories where great green fronds press against a glass ceiling that keeps them from the sky. Everywhere in Toronto the green is contained. Even the trees in Queen's Park wear asphalt leg irons. There is a man in a kilt who plays the bagpipes in the park sometimes in the evening, but the plaintive sound of the pipes cannot compete with the roar of the city. When I walked there, I noticed how the pigeons defecate on the bronze shoulders of famous men, and found myself looking carefully at the bushes, as if one of them might be burning.

Hoping for guidance, I kept Hemingway's book on bullfighting, *Death in the Afternoon*, on my bedside table like a bible. I wrote down his descriptions of various bullfighting manoeuvres from the glossary on recipe cards and posted them around my apartment for inspiration. By the door: *Ver llegar: to watch them come; the ability to watch the bull come as he charges, with no thought except to calmly see what he is doing and make the moves necessary to the manoeuvre you have in mind. To calmly watch the bull come is the most necessary and primarily difficult thing in bullfighting.* Next to the bathroom mirror: *Natural: pass made with the muleta held low in the left hand, the man citing the bull from in front... It is the fundamental pass of bullfighting, the simplest, capable of greatest purity of line and the most dangerous to make.*

Ernest Hemingway is like Elvis Presley. Even people who have never owned a single album of his can sing a bar or two, have some notion of his life and how it ended. The same with Hemingway. People who have never read one of his books know about his safaris, his suicide, his old man and the sea. They have probably seen that famous Karsh photo. They are full of questions. And I respond, "Yes, he really did survive innumerable woundings, five wars, four marriages, three safaris, two plane crashes, and one revolution." No wonder Hemingway talked a lot about death. Death in the morning. Death in the afternoon. How "amazing" it was that the human body does not explode along anatomical lines, or how the unburied dead change from white to yellow, to yellow-green, to black growing slowly larger like a balloon, and how a man's head could be broken like a flower pot. Hemingway claimed there were very few people who could look at death without blinking.

All through high school I saved up to head off to Europe to see the places Hemingway loved: Paris and Madrid, Pamplona and Milan. I didn't stick around for prom or graduation, heading off the moment I was done exams. I actually made it as far as Pearson Airport. I had gone through security and was ready to walk down one of those passageways that reach out from the terminal toward the waiting plane like octopus tentacles when I heard my name on the intercom. I set down my backpack with the maple leaf sewn on it, and took the phone they handed to me at the boarding gate. It was my mother, June, calling from Ingersoll to say that my father had died suddenly.

He had been at work as usual in the library under the hum of the fluorescent lights. When he wasn't upstairs putting books back on shelves, he was downstairs in the library basement, archiving, filing newspaper clippings and other stuff related to local history into categories and boxes. That's where he was when he died. There was no visible sign that his heart stopped except this. When he slumped forward on his desk, the weight of his head warped the wings of his glasses. Suddenly, the elaborate house of postcards I planned to send from exotic places came tumbling down. I wanted so badly to just keep going, onto the plane, across the sea, and into the arms of Paris, but I knew I would have to stay in Canada, go back home to Ingersoll, attend the funeral, comfort my mother, sort things out. There was no one else.

At my father's funeral, I overheard people saying how natural he looked because they had fixed his glasses and placed them over his closed eyes. But to me he looked as grey as the ashes he would become. I had seen him looking this grey only once before. In an attempt at father-daughter bonding the previous summer we'd rented a canoe, which Hemingway called *that frail, tippy, treacherous and altogether delightful craft*. There is only one photograph of me on that trip, taken by my mother before we paddled away from shore. It is out of focus and from the back. I am stretching, arms held up like the Y of a slingshot, red curls falling down the back of my green shirt.

The first day of paddling went well and we slept soundly in our tent with the rush of water all around, but then my father got sick, as he often did when he was away from work. There was no need to panic really. This was southern Ontario. A long walk in any direction would lead to a road, and we weren't far from where my mother planned to pick us up. It was up to me to navigate the final head pond, while my father half-lay, half-sat in the bottom of the canoe, too sick to paddle. I wasn't used to being in the stern and it was hard keeping the canoe straight by myself. Deadheads from old log booms lurked treacherously just under the surface. The wind pushed at us like a bully. I did something I had not done since I was small. I prayed. I prayed the wind would go away and paddled like hell.

And the wind did go away. It died, suddenly and completely, whitecaps dropping out of sight like stones. The water became still enough to show the trees their own reflections. As I dragged the canoe ashore, the keel scraping the stones, I told my father what had happened. "The wind usually dies down this time of evening," he said.

He was probably right, but it made me angry all the same. He had a way of blowing out your candles before you had a chance to make a wish. Looking down at his grey face against the white silk lining the casket, I realized I had never forgiven him for that moment. And when you don't forgive one moment, you don't forgive those that follow.

That morning on my way to work, I grabbed my mail to read on the subway like I always do, and merged into the flow of people rushing along the sidewalk, some armed with coffee cups and cell phones, others with briefcases and assorted bags and packages. Halfway between my apartment building and the subway station, an empty plastic bag suddenly billowed upward from the sidewalk on a gust of wind. When I looked up to follow its progress, I saw a man fall out of a fourth-storey window. One moment he was seated on the ledge of the window facing inward. The next he was tipping backwards like a scuba diver off the side of a boat. Even before I could cry out or move toward him, he stopped falling. He never reached the sidewalk because the flat overhang above the front door of the building intercepted his fall. I could see the back of his head where it had struck the metal edge of the overhang, and before I would have thought possible, blood was dripping down on the sidewalk, probably making no sound at all, but in my mind, exploding. A child stooped down and stuck his fingers in the blood before his horrified mother could yank him away.

I wondered for a moment if the man had been pushed, if a crime had been committed and I had been a witness. But there appeared to have been a deliberate motion on the part of the man, a clear willingness to descend. It had been there in the thrust and heave of his shoulders. I looked and then I looked away. I once saw a photograph from *LIFE* magazine of a woman who had leapt to her death from the Empire State Building. The photographer had caught her cradled by the crumpled steel of the car she had landed on, looking serene, even beautiful, in her white gloves and dark lipstick. Only her nylons were torn. But this was different, because of the blood and the impossible angle of his head and the way I had seen it begin four storeys up. Soon there would be sirens and people would rush to the scene, though it would be too late. The police would arrive, and possibly reporters. But there was nothing I could do. Like everyone else in the city, I had other places to be, and so I moved away from the spot I had been standing when the bag billowed up and the man tumbled down.

I thought that perhaps I would read something about it in the paper the next day, but no words would be spoken about the spilling of a stranger's blood onto the ordinary sidewalk of an ordinary day. I had answered "yes" to the questions on the "Is Journalism for You?" website. (Do you regularly read at least one newspaper or consult an online equivalent? Do you regularly watch or listen to television or radio newscasts? Is it important to you to keep up with current events?) I knew newspapers don't generally cover suicides. If you kill someone else, that's news. If you kill yourself, that's your business, unless, of course, you were famous to begin with, like Hemingway.

Usually on the subway, I read my mail, but that day I just sat there wondering about the man who had chosen to fall. I was beginning to think I am not one of those few people who can look at death without blinking. I watched the other passengers who never look up, faces buried in hefty novels, or in the cleft between the ample breasts of the *Toronto Sun*'s "Sunshine Girl," or in official-looking folders filled with numbers and graphs. Some people were sleeping sitting up, swaying slightly with their hands clasped in their laps, their eyes closed, or hidden behind sunglasses. Only a man with a ponytail and a woman with lots of silver rings on her gesturing hands were looking at each other and talking. "How does the camera obscura work?" she asked. "How does a darkened room with a tiny opening to the outside world manage to bring in an image of that world and project it upside down on the wall?"

"I don't know," he said.

"What do you mean, you don't know? What kind of physics is that?"

"It took me years to be able to say, 'I don't know.' These are three valuable words."

I searched the maps above the flickering subway windows, as if there might somehow be a new destination marked at the end of the line, a new dot I could reach by refusing to get off at the last station. But I got off as usual at the station closest to Carnivores and climbed back up to the surface. When I first moved to Toronto from Ingersoll and started using the subway, I found it disorienting, coming up from underground and being expected to know which way was which. Actually being on the subway is easy; it was the getting on and off that seemed complex in the beginning. In time, though, it became second nature. I could stand with the rest of them, hardly swaying with the lurch, hardly noticing anyone or anything at all.

I walked the remaining blocks to Carnivores with my head down. The restaurant features the front end of a Hummer sticking out over the door as if someone had driven it through the wall. This is not an ideal place for someone who loves to cook because it is part of a chain that promises predictability. There is a book, pages laminated against spatter and spill, with complete step-by-step instructions and photographs, which tells you how to prepare and present each item on the menu. The goal is to make each Death by Chocolate dessert or each platter of Suicide Wings look and taste the same as the last one and the one to come.

The only opportunity for creativity I found was in the salad department. There were, of course, specific guidelines about what you put in the Garden Salad, two wedges of tomato, one slice of cucumber, and one carrot curl, but the customer could choose the dressing. One of the choices was House Dressing and, miraculously, it wasn't written down anywhere what that dressing should be. So I made my own, smuggling in ingredients and mixing them up, when no one was looking, in a special jar I kept for this purpose: Sesame Scallion, Citrus Ginger, Buttermilk and Cucumber, even one called Green Goddess made with avocados. You could be fired for this kind of thing—taking initiative—supplying your own unique and unapproved ingredients. But I did it anyway.

People chose the house dressing more often than not because Es Hébert always recommended it. Es is the waitress who befriended me when I first started working at the restaurant. We are the only two who don't smoke. I don't because, aside from being a colossal waste of money, it ruins the taste buds, and Es doesn't because her current boyfriend is a firefighter and on occasion she is called upon to dress up as Sparky the Fire Dog. She says she doesn't want to be a hypocrite, lighting things on fire when she's telling the children not to. She never smoked cigarettes, but she did smoke a pipe. I'd never met a woman who smoked a pipe. We take our breaks together inside instead of outside on the back step with the smokers. Other than the non-smoking thing we seem to be complete opposites. Physically, she's petite and olive-skinned, with long straight hair that changes colour from time to time but is always some shade of dark. I'm tall and fair with red curly hair that I always pull back in a ponytail to keep out of the way, and some *taches de rousseur*, as Es calls them, which sounds better than freckles. Es is French Canadian from a small town in northern Ontario, and I'm English from a small town in southern Ontario, and we're both here in the big city.

Her name, I discovered, is actually Esther but she shortened it to Es, which comes out sounding like "S" the letter, which adds a certain mystery to her, as if she's a spy or a code of some kind. Personally, I don't see what's wrong with Esther, which means "star" and smells of pomegranates and myrrh. I prefer it to my own name. I can't find out a thing about Pertice, no meaning or etymology. It's not in any of the books. And both Es and I have given up trying to get people to pronounce our last names correctly. McIlveen is pronounced MacIlveen, even though it looks like Mc. With Hébert, people choose to ignore the accent and say Hee-birt rather than A-bare, rhyming the second syllable with "squirt" rather than "rare."

We always talk on our breaks, but it wasn't until Es found me weeping in the washroom at Carnivores that we became friends. I never could cry delicately like people do in movies, with a single discreet tear rolling beautifully down one cheek. Instead my nose gets red and runny. I sniff and sob and tears gush out all over the place. That day, I couldn't even blow my nose because there was no toilet paper left, just a forlorn little wisp stuck to the empty roll. While the lights buzzed overhead and water gurgled in the pipes, I sat in my stall trying to recover until I heard a little knock from the one adjacent. "Are you okay in there?"

"Yeah," I said with a snuffle.

"Are you sure?"

"I think so…Is that you, Es?"

"Yes. What's wrong, Pertice?" Es sounded so genuinely concerned that I was disarmed out of the answers one might normally offer in such a situation—fatigue, a testy co-worker, or a cold coming on— and told the truth. "I'm afraid love won't find me."

"Where did *that* come from?"

I told her the story of Terence and my sweet sixteenth. In school no boys had ever noticed me except Terence. He was one of the "hicks from the sticks," as they called them at my high school. You could smell the poverty on him. He came up to me at day's end while I was packing up my books in the empty classroom. I remember the way the sunlight sliced through the chalk dust in the air and hit the blackboard erasers sitting upside down on their silver ledge like dead birds in their striped plumage. I was alone and then I wasn't. Terence was there in front of me, holding out a present—a book of science fiction classics with a picture of Saturn on the cover, the rings spinning like a rainbow that never meets the earth. "For you. For your birthday," he said.

It was obviously an expensive book, hardcover, with a beautiful dust jacket, a green ribbon for marking your spot, and heavy pages gilded gold at the edges. "I couldn't possibly keep it," I said, thrusting the book back into his shy, proud hands.

He stood his ground, with a hard look coming over his face. "Why?"

"I don't know," I said, and fled. Terence had noticed me, a silent knobby-kneed heron standing in the reeds a little apart from the flocks of schoolgirls that always flew together in a noisy V like geese. He had taken the time to find out that it was my birthday and that I loved books, and he had given me the best book he knew—stories that speculated about worlds better and worse than our own. I tried to justify rejecting his gift by saying that he couldn't afford it, that sci-fi was of no interest to someone who reads Hemingway, that who knew where such a gesture might lead. But I immediately realized that my arrogance could not easily be undone. The dandruff on the frayed black T-shirt that covered his thin shoulders resembled the stars that powdered the black space stretching beyond Saturn to the very edges of the universe.

At Ryerson, I threw myself into my journalism assignments and every moment that wasn't taken by school was taken by Carnivores. Occasionally there was a man who penetrated the fog of studies and work, but mostly they kept their distance wanting casual categories I had no time for, just friends, or friends with benefits, or just benefits. I had classmates who kept a running tally of men they'd slept with like fighter pilots painting kill marks on the tail of their planes, but that wasn't for me.

"I'm a lost cause," I said.

"What do you mean?"

"For God's sake, Es, look at our feet." I was wearing what Es called my *cauchemars*, my nightmares, practical orthopaedic shoes like the ones nurses wear, except in black, made for long hours of standing. Es, on the other hand, was wearing red leather sandals stamped with gold designs that must have come from one of those Indian shops on Gerrard Street East, with the coy little loop of leather around the big toe. She wore a slender gold chain on her right ankle and all her toe nails were individually painted in bright colours.

"Okay," Es said. "What do you do for entertainment?"

"I think about things."

There was an intake of breath, as if Es was conceding that the situation was more serious than she'd imagined. "Don't you have any hobbies? Besides Hemingway?"

I had not told anyone at the restaurant about Hemingway, though I'd put him in my application under hobbies because I couldn't think of anything else to say. I considered putting down films because I love movies of all kinds, but wasn't sure that sitting in the dark watching could be considered a real hobby. I could have put knitting because I once made a sweater, but the result was appalling, with a skinny chest, really long arms, and a neck hole for a pinhead. My mom said I should hang on to it, that I might meet a man who would fit it someday. "If there's a man out there who fits that sweater, I certainly don't want to meet him," I said, and unravelled it all. So I had put Hemingway. "How do you know about that?" I asked Es.

"I saw it on your application. Sometimes Stash gets me to clean his office." Stash is Es's name for the manager. She doesn't like moustaches. Either shave or grow a beard; none of this wishy-washy in between.

"Well, it isn't really a hobby. It's more of an interest."

"Well, there you go. And you can make Green Goddess from scratch, so in my books that makes you worthy."

I took a deep quavering breath. "Could you pass me some tissue?" Es's hand came under the stall divider with a huge wad of fresh tissue, way more than I could possibly need, and I took it gratefully.

As I emerged from my stall Es gave me a hug and said, "You need to fall for a man who isn't dead."

Some days I would stay after closing while Es counted her tips and cleaned up, then she would give me a lift home because I don't have a car. You don't really need one in Toronto; you can get anywhere you want underground, hurtling through a tangle of tunnels. A lot of the jobs waitresses have to do at the end of a shift, like filling up the condiments, are extremely tedious unless you have company. But it has to be done. People don't like to find a half-empty bottle of ketchup at their table. They don't like to think that anyone has used it before them. They prefer newness and fullness, as if they are the only ones in the world. I helped Es top up all the bottles of sauces, the salt and pepper shakers, the napkin holders and the tiny dishes of sweeteners, both artificial and real. Sometimes Es would wipe fingerprints off the brass railings with one hand and hold a newspaper in the other. She would read the daily horoscope out loud, prefacing it with comments like "Oh-oh!" or "This is your lucky day," even though, by that time, the day was almost over and whatever was supposed to happen had already happened. "Repairs are easier next week. So is love. Go in high style tonight," or "Outrageous remarks impress supervisors. Big news arrives at last. A move could increase your self-confidence." I'm not sure if Es actually believes that the alignment of the stars can influence your life. I certainly don't, but it's usually good for a laugh because the information is so vague. I once took a psychology course which I hoped would shed some light on the impact of Hemingway's mother's decision to dress him in girl's clothing early on. The professor passed out a horoscope to each student and asked us all to rate its accuracy. Almost all the students were convinced it applied specifically to them until they discovered everyone had the same horoscope. "Focus on one solid goal this afternoon and you'll have it by nightfall," Es read.

It was Es's turn to vacuum, so I helped her put the chairs upside down on the tables like we used to do at school. Then I sat down with an iced tea to open the mail I had been too upset to look at on the subway on my way to work because of the falling man. The manila envelope from the Ryerson School of Journalism was wrapped around the other letters and secured with an elastic band. It was probably my diploma. Much to my mother's disappointment, I hadn't even bothered to go to convocation. I'm not much for pomp and circumstance, and I didn't want to have to wear a mortarboard. When I was a kid, my mother tried to make me wear a toque on the coldest days and a sunhat on the hottest days, but I refused both. I would rather get frostbite or heat stroke than wear a hat. When I got the job as a line cook at Carnivores I thought maybe I could bend a little and wear a chef's hat. All that tall crisp whiteness and as many pleats as the number of ways a good chef knows how to prepare an egg. But all we got was a hairnet. There is nothing remotely attractive about a hairnet, but we didn't have a choice. To make myself feel better, I tried to think of it as a snood, those bejewelled affairs medieval princesses wore to keep back their hair.

Next in the pile of mail was a phone bill, with a long-distance call to my mother in Ingersoll, though June usually calls me. There was a letter from the Ryerson Alumni Association asking for money. Already. I had barely begun to look for a journalism job in Toronto. I might be able to handle work at a small-town newspaper where you covered things like Brownie Fly-Ups and ploughing competitions, where you wrote advertorials and reviews of local theatre. But after that morning I was beginning to think I might not be able to handle big-city journalism. Most news was bad news. Human tragedy, disaster, war. Someone had opened fire in the food court of the Eaton Centre, for God's sake, and people had died. Could I really look without blinking?

On the bottom of the pile of mail was an envelope which was addressed to me at the home I grew up in. My mother had crossed out the Ingersoll address and forwarded it to my Toronto apartment. The envelope held something heavier than paper, but even holding it up to the light, I couldn't tell what it might be. When I opened the envelope, a key fell out onto the table. A single silver-coloured key with the word WEISER on it.

One day, out of the blue, when I came home late from school, my father insisted that we get a deadbolt installed on the front door. "Even if this is only Ingersoll, you need to think about safety," he said. And the deadbolt had been a Weiser. I remember because my father told us that the company began in Hollywood in 1904 with a European craftsman who made locks for movie sets, eventually graduating to making real locks for real houses. My father was a compendium of this kind of trivial information. A week later he was dead. Albert McIlveen, his mended glasses over his closed eyes and his pale librarian hands folded across his chest, his wife and daughter safe behind their new deadbolt. I used to think about all the Alberts my father might have been—Einstein, Schweitzer, Camus—but I knew he was named for Queen Victoria's husband, the one known for a professorial manner and domestic calm.

There was nothing else with the key, just the blank piece of white paper it had been wrapped in. No letter, nothing. I held the envelope upside down and shook it, as if something else might suddenly appear, a rabbit or a dove. "Lift your feet," Es said, as she vacuumed under the table where I was sitting. She took a careful look at me and flicked the OFF switch. "What's up with you?"

"I just got a key in the mail."

"A key to what?"

"I don't know. Just a key."

"What do you mean, just a key?"

I looked at the key intently, turning it over and over as if there might be some inscription or clue.

"Maybe you won a new car," Es said, laughing.

"It doesn't look like a car key. It looks like a key to a door."

Es held out her hand for the key. As usual, her fingernails had spectacular designs on them, not the press-on kind you got out of a package, but designs she paints herself with different colours of polish. Lately, she has been working on Van Gogh motifs—sunflowers, swirling stars, black crows descending on golden wheat. When I complimented her once, she said, "Shhh, they'll be wanting to hang them in the ROM!"

"Who's it from?" Es asked, looking closely at the key.

"It doesn't say, and there's no message." Es began to hum the theme from the *Twilight Zone*. I picked up the empty envelope and read the return address out loud. No person. Just a place. "Honeysuckle Cottage, North Head, Gannet Island."

"Well, that doesn't sound too scary," Es said. "Where's Gannet Island?"

"I have no idea."

My building is supposed to have Wi-Fi, but it's notoriously unreliable, so that night when I got home, I looked for the *Canadian Oxford School Atlas: Third Edition* that I picked up at a thrift store. It had been published in 1972, long before I was born. All the facts and figures have changed, and even some of the names of the countries in places like Africa and the USSR, but the land has stayed in the same place. Changes like that take longer. The stamp on the envelope was Canadian, one of those celebrating Canadian highways, this time the Cabot Trail. So I knew to look up Gannet Island in "Canada" rather than "The World," which were the only two categories the atlas offered. I turned to the right page and found the island below the blue line indicating 45 degrees latitude just off the coast of New Brunswick and Maine. There it was, a jade pendant hanging on the cold wet throat of the Bay of Fundy.

"So?" Es asked when I got into work the next morning. I continued to put on my hairnet and apron, nonchalantly checking my reflection in the stainless steel of the refrigerator as if I hadn't heard the question. "So, where's Gannet Island?"

"Off the coast of New Brunswick."

"Oh," said Es, whose knowledge of the East got a little foggy after Montreal. "So when are you going?"

"What do you mean, when am I going?"

"Aren't you going to check it out?"

I reflected on what this might mean. Whatever "it" was, it could not be checked out like a book from the library which you could take home and peruse in the familiar light cast by the lamp beside your bed.

"Whoever sent you that key wants you to go and open something," Es said.

"Anybody could have sent that key." I couldn't help the impatience from creeping into my voice. I hadn't slept very well the night before wondering who that "anybody" might be. A key all by itself was just weird. "You don't think I'm going to travel a thousand miles on the off chance I can actually find the door it fits into."

"I would," Es said. I didn't doubt it. She cocked her head to one side and held out her hands with palms up, palms covered with intricate henna designs.

"There could be some wacko waiting on the other end," I said.

"Go on!" she said. This was one of the terms in Hemingway's bullfighting glossary. *Anda: go on! You will hear this frequently shouted at picadors who are reluctant to approach the bull.* Es continued to press. "Where's your sense of adventure?"

I didn't answer.

"Look," she said in an exasperated voice, "I will drive you there myself, if I have to. I'm off till Tuesday."

"What are we supposed to do when we get there? It's not like there's going to be a star over the spot."

"We'll ask around. If the place is as small as it sounds, someone's bound to know."

"It's a very loooong way," I said, beginning to tear apart a head of romaine lettuce.

"Well then, we'll have to start early. *L'oiseau tôt* and all that." Es was not backing down. "I could be at your place at six to pick you up."

I knew this was an exceptionally generous offer. Es is a nighthawk. She's allergic to early mornings. But all I could muster was, "I'll think about it." And I thought about it all day while I arranged the food of strangers in prescribed ways with prescribed garnishes. I thought about it while I chopped and sliced and fried.

Then Es brought back a steak for the third time. "Sorry, but he says he can still see a little pink."

"How can people describe 'burnt to a crisp' as 'well done'?" I hissed, grabbing the meat with some tongs and flinging it back on the grill yet again. People were willing, it seemed, to complain about almost everything except the salad dressings. No one complained about the salad dressings but, then again, the people who came to a place called Carnivores were not primarily interested in salads.

Other than this job, I had nothing holding me to Toronto. My studies were done and I had no idea what I was going to do next. Es had told me her grandmother was a bomb girl, a munitions worker in Montreal, and that they wore *résilles* to keep their hair out of the machinery, and to show they were committed to the war effort when fabric was in short supply. A bomb girl would be brave, hairnet and all. In the end it was a line from *The Sun Also Rises* that swayed me. *Road to hell paved with unbought stuffed dogs.* "Okay," I said when Es came back for the charred steak. "Okay, we'll go."

Es gave me the thumbs-up sign through the pass-through window. "*On y va!*"

That night, in my basement apartment with the orange fungus growing in the dampest corner, a bathtub the size of a teacup, and a single window through which I had a great view of people's ankles, I opened my closet. I got out the backpack I never used on the trip to Europe I never took. I looked at the maple leaf I had sewn on it, hoping to encourage strangers to be kind. I looked at the clothes in my closet, student clothes bought second-hand and worn within an inch of their lives, and thought about what I should take. What do you pack for a wild goose chase? I had no idea, wondering if it might be colder there than in Toronto because it was beside the sea. In the end, I packed nearly everything because there wasn't much and it seemed easier not to choose. I packed my clock radio/travel alarm and a few toiletries. I felt breathless and wild and a little crazy. When I was small my father would always say, "Simmer down," as if he were a chef struggling to cook at an unreliable stove where the actual temperature of the burners bore no relation to what was indicated on the dial. And I always did what he asked. I'd always "simmered down." But not this time. I didn't even call my mother to tell her I was leaving first thing in the morning. She would ask me for details, and I didn't have any. For once in my life, I didn't have any. Just before I finally fell asleep, I looked once more at the key that had come to me from the edge of the world. I ran my index finger over the irregular bumps along one side trying to imagine what foreign landscape would accommodate this unique and miniature mountain range.

True to her promise, Es arrived early and we set out eastward. Es got us safely out of Toronto, but pulled off the highway around Port Hope and told me I was going to learn how to drive a standard. I protested, as I always do when faced with something new and complicated that requires swift reactions and coordinated movements. We jumped and lurched around a parking lot for fifteen minutes before Es announced I was ready for the open road. "Will you relax!" Es said, more as an imperative than a question, looking at my hands white-knuckled on the wheel. "When my mother went to get her licence, the guy testing was such a bastard, he would get you to park on a hill, get out and place a wooden matchbox behind the rear tire, and tell you to start. If the matchbox was crushed, no licence."

I found that once you were out on the highway and in fifth gear, you could hardly tell the difference between automatic and standard. Like most things it was the starting and the stopping that were difficult. "I am not driving through Montreal, though," I said with finality. So Es drove while I watched for the little maple leaf of the Trans Canada to guide us through the labyrinth of city roads and tunnels and bridges.

We stopped for gas in a tiny Quebec village somewhere between Sherbrooke and the Maine border. I had just gotten back into the passenger side after filling the gas tank with *l'essence ordinaire*, thinking how much better things sounded in another language. Es, meanwhile, cleaned the bugs off the windshield with a squeegee. We both got back in the car, and I handed Es the coffee I had bought for her. "Naked. Naked," said Es, gesturing out the front and rear windows of the car.

"Pardon?" I was starting to get tired.

"He's naked…she's naked," Es said again.

I put my arm on the back of Es's seat and looked over her shoulder through the back windshield to where a large lighted sign advertised *DANSEUSES EXOTIQUES*, with a black silhouette of a naked woman like you sometimes see on the mud flaps of trucks. In front of us on the opposite side of the street was a Catholic church, grand in scale as they usually are even in the tiniest villages, with a stone cairn out front surmounted by a large crucifix. "He's not completely naked," I said.

"I don't know why they have to make him look so tortured and forlorn," Es said, struggling to open the sipping part of her coffee lid. "I bet he was a hottie."

I thought about this for a moment. "Really? A hottie?" Almost no one talked about Jesus anymore, and when they did they certainly didn't call him a hottie.

"Well, think about the things that make a man sexy." Es looked carefully at me. "My god, are you blushing? I didn't think anybody blushed anymore."

"Okay, okay," I said, suffering from that sudden singe I have never been able to escape. I am not a religious person but it seemed irreverent to put these two things into the same conversation, like discussing G-strings with your grandmother.

"Think about it. What intrigues you about a man? A good body, right?"

I don't always admit it but, yes, a slim strong man does catch my eye. "I guess."

"If he was a carpenter, he'd have those strong working muscles, all hard and lean, and working hands. You can always tell working hands…"

"Well, I doubt if Jesus was ripped." We both laughed.

"Is that really what attracts you?"

"Well, no, but it doesn't hurt."

"I don't know. I've dated gym rats who've invested a lot of time building big muscles, which means everything and everyone has to compete. Trust me, they're not worth it. But working man muscles, ripped for real, that's a whole different thing," Es said. "What else?"

"A good mind…?" I asked tentatively, not sure whether her list and mine would match up. For as long as I can remember, I've liked the smart boys, the ones who knew things but wore their knowledge lightly. If you didn't know how smart they were, you wouldn't know.

"No doubt the Messiah had a few good ideas rattling around up there," Es said gesturing out the window toward the crucifix across from the gas station. Because she had pointed with her thumb instead of her index finger, it looked like she was hitchhiking though she was already in a car.

She placed her coffee into the drink holder, fastened her seat belt and prepared to pull out of the gas station. The drink holder was one of the few things in the car that still worked, aside from the engine. Es would be the first to admit that her car was *un vrai bazou*, a piece of junk. She called it her *merde-mobile*. Hanging from the rear-view mirror was a medal, not of Christopher, patron saint of travellers, but of Jude Thaddeus, patron saint of lost causes. The body of the car was rusting away, and the odometer had close to 300,000 kilometres on it, which would take you around the world seven and a half times if you were driving in a straight line, and the windshield had a stone chip in it that seemed to be spreading like cracks in ice, and only the right windshield wiper worked properly so if it was raining hard the driver had to lean over and look out the passenger's side of the windshield. The air conditioning had died too. The heater still worked, but the knob to adjust it had fallen off and gotten lost, so at the end of each season you had to open the passenger door, lie on your back, reach up under the dash and pull the cord over manually. And besides all that, it was a standard.

"So what else makes a man sexy?" Es asked, after we were on our way again.

"A good heart."

"That's a tricky one," Es said, "because you can never know for sure what's on the inside. You can only judge by what makes it to the surface. A courting man is an editing man."

"An editing man?"

"Yeah, he's giving you his version of what he wants you to see."

"Apparently, you can tell a lot about a man by the way he treats kids."

"That's true, but even that might be part of the editing. You can tell most about a man by what he does when no one's watching."

"How are we supposed to know that?"

"I don't know."

As we were cresting a blind hill, a car suddenly appeared out of a hidden driveway. The signs say to slow down for those, but no one ever does. Es had just time enough to swerve and miss him. The guy pounded on his horn, as if it had been her fault. Seeing the Ontario plates the man yelled, "*Maudite Anglais!*" This was ironic because Es grew up near the Quebec border speaking mostly French. She fit right in with the Habitant style eaves of the houses we were passing. There might have been a practical reason to have the eaves curving like the roofs of exotic pagodas, but I suspect it was just an elegant touch, compared to the straight no-nonsense eaves of English Canada. Even now French words slipped into Es's vocabulary from time to time. Her favourite franglais phrase was something she'd heard one old guy ask another in the church parking lot after mass, "*Comment ça hang?*"

"Good mind, good body, good heart." I counted the list off on my fingers. "You think a man like this exists?"

"And that's not all; there's a secret ingredient..."

I laughed. "Now I *know* he doesn't exist!"

"He knows where he's going," Es said at last.

"So *that's* why they never ask for directions!" I rolled my eyes, reflecting that this had all started because Es had claimed Jesus was a hottie. We drove in silence for a few miles, then I asked, "So has Mr. Maybe got all that?" The name of Es's current boyfriend is actually Jesse, but I referred to him as Mr. May because Es first laid eyes on him in a calendar of Toronto firefighters for the month of May. And then after going out with him for a while, she added the "be" on the end. She had been with him longer than anyone she'd ever dated before. "Good body, good mind, good heart, and direction too?"

Es exhaled her breath out of rounded lips, with a whoo sound. "No question on number one," she said. It was true. I had seen the calendar. Mr. May's was one of the more tasteful photographs; some were just silly with suggestively held fire hoses or spraying hydrants. But Jesse was standing there, without props, looking directly at the camera. He was wearing his yellow fireman's pants without a shirt, the red suspender straps accentuating the muscles of his chest. He looked like he could fight whatever needed fighting. "The next three I'm still deciding."

Es had told me the story of how she found Mr. Maybe. In the calendar, he'd been identified only by his first name which, fortunately, wasn't a very common name. Es called every fire station in greater Toronto and asked if a Jesse worked there. When she finally tracked him down, she drove her *merde-mobile* to the fire station, and because it was a warm day and the trucks had just been washed, the doors were open. She walked right over to the lockers and found his black helmet with its yellow reflector strips and visor above and his boots beneath, all ready to jump into in case of fire, and she stood in them right where they were. She figured he would eventually come out and find her there, or someone would tell him, "There's a woman standing in your boots," and he would be intrigued.

This fire station was all on one floor so there was no pole to come sliding down like they do in movies, but when Jesse came out from the back room, he found Es standing in his boots. When he asked her what she thought she was doing, she didn't answer him. She just handed him her card and walked away. I've seen Es's business cards. Her work at Carnivores is just to pay the bills. What she really loves is painting people's nails, but she had to make sure that no one mistook her for a mere manicurist. She considered calling herself a "Nail Artist," but this evoked those pictures that were popular in the seventies and you still sometimes find at yard sales with string wound around nails to make pictures of sail boats or cityscapes. So Es called herself an *Ongle Spangler*, and beneath this title and her phone number was a line drawing of fingernails graced with some of her unique designs adapted from the masterpieces of the art world. And Mr. May had called her, because he wanted to know what the hell an Ongle Spangler was and because no woman had ever stood in his boots.

The closest I had come to a Mr. Maybe was *Des Oignons*, as Es called him. It happened during my fourth year at Ryerson. I came out from Carnivores one day to find someone had backed into my bicycle. I rarely took it to work because as far as I was concerned you had to have a death wish to cycle in Toronto, like those crazy bike couriers weaving in and out of traffic, but I got it to take over on the ferry to Centre Island when the city got too much for me. A man was standing by it, writing his phone number on a piece of paper, which he handed to me. He looked East Indian, but when he spoke his accent was Canadian. "I'm so sorry," he said, looking at the bike. Then he looked up at me. ""Your hair is wet."

"I was swimming." I have no idea why I lied, though somehow it felt true, like I had just broken the surface, breaching spectacularly like a whale. Actually a ketchup bottle had exploded on me and I had rinsed my hair under the sprayer we use for the lettuce.

"Do you swim often?" he asked. Now I'd done it. I could barely dog paddle. With my luck he was probably captain of the swim team in his youth. He had that kind of body.

"Sometimes," I said.

"I swim too," he said.

"Smells good," I said, pointing at the white box he had retrieved from where he had set it on the trunk of his green car. I guessed from the deep spicy smell that it must be from the Indian restaurant across the street.

"Onion *bhaji*. Anyway, call if you need to," he said, meaning if there was anything wrong with my bicycle other than a bent fender, anything that required serious repairs. I had no idea what *bhaji* was, but I went across to the Indian restaurant and ordered some as take-out. The onions were deliciously deep-fried in a spicy batter. "It had to be onions," I thought. With men, I had always used onions as a kind of barometer. If a man revealed that he didn't like onions, which usually happened the first time we ordered a pizza, or a sausage in the park, or I had him over for a meal, I knew instantly that the whole thing would fall apart. I could not imagine a lifetime of not putting onions in things or, even worse, putting them in and having him pick them out. I love onions. They make me cry, but I love them.

The next week I went to the local pool hoping I might catch a glimpse of him. I sat up in the gallery and watched a family playing with brightly coloured pool noodles. I had heard about a professor at U of T who had gotten into trouble for ogling, so the next time I went in a bathing suit. It was embarrassing to be splashing about when everyone else was swimming so efficiently, arms slicing the water like knives, so I signed up for swimming lessons and found I had a knack for it. I watched the movie on television about Marilyn Bell, who was the first to swim across Lake Ontario. Women seemed better at the longer colder distances. But all those times at the pool, I never once saw the dark-haired stranger. I never saw him, but I thought of him every time I sliced an onion. I know it's the sulphur in the oil that dissolves in our eyes to make us cry. I also know there are ways around the tears, slicing the onions under running water, chilling them, or leaving the root intact. But I never took such measures.

And then one day I saw him again. It was January, and a new supermarket was opening in the neighbourhood. I usually bought groceries just around the corner, but the flyers said there was going to be cake and giveaways and incredible bargains. When I walked in the door, stomping the snow from my boots as I passed the rows of empty shopping carts, I was suddenly confronted by his photograph on a big bulletin board that said: "We are here to help You." Capital Y. And under his picture was the title "Produce Manager." I felt relief. Of all the things one could do for a living, why not this? Bringing fruits and vegetables from all over the world so that it was always harvest, always summer, no matter the weather outside. I was impressed by the gorgeous carefully arranged stacks of red, yellow, orange, and aubergine. And what shades of green! Bunches of fresh herbs standing upright in water like fragrant bouquets, lettuce in several varieties, asparagus and zucchini, broccoli like small trees. I generally tried to eat local things in season, when they were freshest and best, but still, it was a kind of miracle to have the tropics brought near—mango, papaya, bananas—while outside the snowplough cleared the far reaches of the parking lot. And oh the onions! I gazed at the mounds of onions, cooking onions in orange mesh bags, Sweet Vidalia and Spanish onions in gold and burgundy mounds, pearl onions in jars, green onions in little sheaves. I leaned over to reach the green onions and suddenly a misty spray surrounded me as if I was strolling in a rain forest.

I caught sight of a man in a green apron unpacking bananas with his back to me, but his hair was blond. Maybe if I peeled back the husk of a cob of corn and found a grub curled among the yellow kernels, I could ask to see the produce manager, and then say, "Remember me, the swimmer?" And my hair would be damp from the sprayer over the green onions and it would seem plausible, maybe. But what if he didn't remember me? Maybe it was better that way. He would have a whole life. Men usually did or there was something wrong with them. The good ones went early.

I made the rounds of the store, had a piece of free cake, and paid for my groceries. Then as I was about to leave I did something I hadn't done since the seventh grade. In the display window of the department store there was a female mannequin lying in pieces awaiting assembly. No one was around, so I grabbed a hand, pulling down my sleeve so that it looked like my own hand, except with red fingernails. No one had noticed. I had gotten as far as the parking long before turning around and walking back into the store to put it back. What would I have done with a hand? But this time it was for keeps. I glanced around furtively, then swiped the eight-by-ten glossy of the Produce Manager off the bulletin board, slipped it between two boxes of raisin bran in my cart, and fled. Of course, after that I couldn't go back to the store, because maybe there was hidden surveillance, and I would be fingered as the person who kidnapped the Produce Manager in broad daylight. Who could explain such a thing?

I found the perfect frame — solid oak, simple yet shapely, well mitred, well joined. All the things I hoped of him. But I didn't dare put it on the shelf of my study carrel at Ryerson and invite questions I couldn't answer about a complete stranger, one I had stolen from a grocery store bulletin board. So I kept the photo at home on my only window sill. After looking at it for a week, I fished out the phone number he had given me which still smelled slightly spicy. I make my eights with two circles stacked on top of one another like the body of a snowman but he made his eights like a Möbius strip. I dialled the number, thinking maybe he has all he needs but, then again, maybe he doesn't. No stranger is complete.

We got together at the Indian restaurant and indulged in exotic dishes flavoured with spices that rolled off the tongue like poetry: cumin, cardamom, coriander, and always lots of onions. His name was Varsha but he went by Vern, for the sake of Canadians. I had just turned twenty-one and he was twenty-eight, but I could feel myself falling hard. I had seen pictures of the monsoon in *National Geographic*, women in saris walking in water as deep as their waists, carrying only what they most valued in the world. And that's how I felt, flooded. I bought a new recipe book called *660 Curries* that promised to demystify "the seemingly infinite art of curry making" and started to work my way through it. Sometimes I ate them myself, but Varsha joined me as often as he could. But before I was sixty curries in, Varsha said we had to talk. From the seriousness in his voice, I thought maybe he was going to propose taking our relationship to the next level. He took me out to the restaurant where we had our first date. After the meal was over and we were enjoying chai and sweets decorated with silver beaten thin as air, he nervously confessed that he was engaged to a girl named Keya in Delhi. "I fought it for a long time," he said. "Imagine, an arranged marriage in the twenty-first century! But then I started paying attention to what it was like for girls in India. Female infanticide, brutal gang rapes, and acid thrown on the faces of women who say no, and I began to think I owed it to Keya, to bring her to a country where she had a chance to be equal, to do what she wanted, to be herself without fear." When I went home, I took his picture down from the windowsill. I put it flat on the table and brought a fist down in the middle of it. It seemed impossible that he would leave a woman whose mind and body he had come to know to marry a woman he had seen only in pictures. Cracks radiating out from the point of impact looked like onionskin under a microscope.

As the miles slid from the back of the *merde-mobile* like a wake, I kept track for a while of the various licence plates on the cars we passed: "Land of Living Skies," or "Yours to Discover." I asked Es, "If you were a province, what would your licence plate say?"

Es had an answer right away. "Kaleidoscope Country," she said. She explained that one of her favourite gifts as a child had been a kaleidoscope made for her by her grandfather. It was carved of wood, and instead of the brightly coloured shards of glass or plastic that made the changing patterns in store-bought versions, he had used bits of mussel shell that shimmered in the subtle and shifting colours of sea and sky. The word, he said, meant to see the beautiful form. "What about you?"

I didn't have a ready answer. This is one of my challenges. If someone presses me for an immediate answer on an important issue, I'll panic and say something stupid. I can usually figure out the right thing to say on the way home, or lying in bed at night, or the next morning. "*L'esprit de l'escalier*," Es calls it. Staircase wit. I can never even think of kind or clever things to say in the birthday or farewell cards that sometimes get handed around at work, so I end up writing something lame like "Best Wishes" or just my name. To cover up for my lack of an answer I said "*J'oublie*," as a joke in reference to the Quebec "*Je me souviens*" licence plate on the station wagon travelling in front of us.

Before I could come up with a real answer, we arrived at the border of *États Unis* marked by a pair of towns that weren't much more than a gas station and a customs office. The last village on the Canadian side was called Woburn, and the first village on the American side was called Coburn Gore. Es found this funny, that these two places should rhyme. If they were mirror images of one another, which was the reality and which the reflection depended on the direction you were travelling. The American customs officer looked no-nonsense with his black shirt and shiny badge with an eagle on it. "Purpose of visit?" he asked crisply.

I would have hesitated because I wasn't sure of the true answer, but Es answered confidently, "We're on our way to New Brunswick. Can you tell us how to get there?"

"Perhaps you should purchase a map, Ma'am. They sell them at the service station."

"Thank you, we will," she said, and drove through the border marked by nothing more than a yellow line on the road, and the flags of both countries snapping and fluttering in the wind. "Perhaps we should purchase a map, Ma'am," she said to me in a mock deep voice.

"I knew we should have taken the Trans Canada," I said, unfolding the map of Maine and gazing at the maze of roads. At least in Canada, even though different stretches of the highway were called by different names, there was always that little maple leaf to guide you. Around Montreal there had been considerable discussion about which route we ought to take. It certainly looked shorter to go through the United States, instead of way up and around on the Trans Canada, so in Montreal we headed south on Highway 10 through Sherbrooke. "That way we could just get on the right road and keep going. This way we have to keep figuring out which turn to make."

"I trust you," Es said.

"Okay, here goes." For a while there was only the one road through the woods so there were no choices to be made. Since the border of the map was decorated with little painted images of the flora and fauna of the state of Maine, I suggested we test our wilderness IQ to pass the time. We did well recognizing the animals, though sometimes Es couldn't remember the English name, but not so well on the flowers. The birds we mostly knew because, except for the puffin and some seabirds, they were ones we had back home, but we completely fell apart on the eastern border of the map which pictured the creatures of the sea. All I could be sure of were the lobster and the starfish. But after that it was anyone's guess. I had always thought of Lake Erie, which was not far from Ingersoll, as a kind of a sea because you couldn't see the other side, but clearly the Great Lakes were no preparation for the ocean, a place glowing deep and various beyond the edge of the known.

The map of Maine had icons I had never seen, like pineapples for Bed and Breakfasts, a moose for Guides and Outfitters, little lobsters for lobster pounds and covered bridges that looked like detached garages with the door open. After a while, I had to stop looking at the map because the road became curvy as we passed by the Sugar Loaf ski resort, with the kind of dips in the road that as a kid had made you go "whee," but now as an adult made your stomach churn. The sun had long since moved around to our backs as the car licked up the liquorice of the highway headed east. At Skowhegan, we stopped at a McDonald's. Generally, I avoid fast food places like the plague, but Es wanted to try a McLobster. She claimed she might never have another chance, and it was less like chemicals and cardboard than we expected. When we left Skowhegan, I was behind the wheel. Soon we hooked up with Interstate 95 to save time, bypassing all the dinky little towns with names like Etna and Damascus. "Save time, eh?" I said, as the car in front of us started to slow down. I didn't expect to have to shift gears for a while, and it made me grumpy.

"Must be construction, or maybe an accident." It was an accident. Even though it wasn't even on our side of the highway, people still slowed down to gawk. "What is wrong with people that they have to get a look?" Es asked.

"So they can be glad it's not them, I guess."

"People are such *vautours*," Es said. "Vultures."

"Death is interesting, at least according to Hemingway."

"Ah!" Es yelled, jabbing at my watch. She didn't wear one because she looked at her cell phone instead. "I knew it was only a matter of time. We've been on the road, for what...fourteen hours, and you haven't mentioned Hemingway once. But I knew you couldn't hold out forever." She waited until we were well past the accident before she spoke again. "Why are you interested in such a macho misogynist anyway?"

I thought about how to answer honestly. It had started in grade nine when our teacher told us to do a report on *The Old Man and the Sea*. At first it seemed boring, an old guy going on and on about a fish, but then his words got inside my head. *Now is not the time to think of what you do not have. Think of what you can do with what there is.* My job was to find pictures of the author for the class presentation. I found two photos that made me fall in love, one of Hemingway at fourteen, and one when he was eighteen. In the first picture he's adjusting his fishing lure, standing in a river up to his thighs. He's wearing a slouchy felt hat, a long-sleeved white shirt, and twill pants. The one hand you can see looks large and capable. I liked the way the river pushes against him so he makes a wake even though he's standing still. In the other photo, he's lying on a bed in the American Red Cross Hospital in Milan when he was only eighteen. He volunteered for the Ambulance Corps and got hit by mortar fire while passing out chocolates to Italian soldiers. Though one leg is in a cast and the other in bandages he looks surprisingly radiant. He claimed there were 227 shrapnel wounds in his legs, so he must have been in pain, but he is looking straight at the camera and smiling, his hair dark against the white pillow, strong arms folded across his chest, an empty chair beside his bed like an invitation.

Even though he ended his life long before mine began, he had gotten under my skin. He had *gracia: grace and elegance of manner while undergoing danger.* He was brave in ways I couldn't even imagine. Like the bullfighters he so admired, he had *huevos,* or eggs, Spanish slang for balls. He could look at death without blinking. I thought all this, but what I said out loud was, "He gave us a way to talk about the remarkable violence of our time." This was a quotation from a *New York Times* book review, but I didn't identify it as such.

"Don't you think that's kind of gruesome? Always looking at people's suffering."

"I think he got away with it because he made himself a part of the suffering," I said, thinking of him on his hospital bed looking unbearably young and handsome.

"But to put it up for sale."

"You're one to talk," I said, wishing instantly I hadn't.

"What's that supposed to mean?"

"What about Eschart?" In her spare time Es makes art out of stuff she and Jesse find at burn sites. She calls it Eschart. Eschar, she explained, was the dead skin that kept a deep burn from forming a protective scab. You had to separate the eschar from the tissue underneath for healing to begin. It had started innocently enough, as most things do, with an old woman staring at the smoking ruins of her home and tugging at the sleeve of a fireman's yellow coat, saying "Bring me something to remember." After the old woman had been whisked away in an ambulance, Jesse had gone back in and found a partially melted spoon in what was left of the kitchen. He knew it was something he should not do. You could drench everything in sight or hack it to bits with axes but you could not take things. But the woman had sounded so desperate to regain a fragment of what she had lost. Es mounted the twisted spoon on a piece of navy velvet in a little gold frame for the woman as a souvenir, and they took it to the hospital where she was being held for observation. She was grateful. "*Je me souviens*," she said, over and over again. After that day, Jesse and Es did this with other little burnt bits of people's lives, fragments of crockery and utensils and knickknacks, and offered them to the people who suffered loss. Es and her firefighter were clandestine, half-imagining and half-certain of all the trouble that was in store, should anyone discover what they were up to.

"*Merde!*" Es said one careless day when another firefighter saw some of her creations and figured out what they were. She was surprised when he asked if he could buy the melted scissors. Es said "No, these are not for us," and the other fireman said, "But they're so beautiful." And they were, these little twisted, charred bits of people's lives that had been reshaped, not by any artist, but by tragedy and flame. Granted, Es, with her artistic eye, had the knack of selecting the perfect fragment and placing it against the perfect fabric in the perfect frame, so there was a kind of harsh poetry to it all. There was something so striking in the strangeness of an ordinary thing, away from its ordinary world, bent and casting new shadows.

In the end, Es refused to profit from misfortune, but she accepted donations to the fund that the firemen maintained for the people who had nothing, and she always asked permission from the people whose lives she was using, if there was anyone left to ask. But the ethics of it troubled her still, and she and I had talked about it at length — when it was all right to use other people's grief and when it wasn't. When you got right down to it, Es argued, much of life was using other people's grief for your own purposes, even if the motives were pure, if there even was such a thing as a pure motive. Lots of people counted on things going wrong to make their living, even people in the so-called "helping" professions, or maybe especially people in the "helping" professions. Doctors need sickness. Firefighters need fires.

"You ever been in a fire?" Es asked.

"Once, when I was ten." I had awoken to the sound of a screeching smoke detector and I was instantly filled with fear, although not because of the sound itself, which I was used to. My mother set off the smoke detector on a regular basis while cooking. She burned things all the time. She even kept an old cheese grater for the express purpose of grating the burnt bits off the cookies she made. She didn't believe in throwing anything out. "Waste not, want not." I was not afraid because of the sound, piercing and persistent though it was. I was afraid because of the film I had just seen at school. The voice in the film said that a whole room could be consumed by fire in only three minutes, that you had to crawl because the safest air was near the floor, and what was it you were supposed to do if your clothes caught fire? Stop, Look, and Listen? No, that wasn't it. Stop, Drop, and Roll. "Whatever you do, don't run," the man in the film said.

Then my father was there at my window in his striped pyjamas, dropping out the rope ladder he had purchased for just such an emergency and telling me to climb down. I felt like Rapunzel. We stood there on the lawn while the fire department came. In his haste, my father had knocked his glasses off his bedside table and stepped on them. I had never seen him without his glasses before. And my mother was standing beside him, her hand over her mouth. She was not good during a crisis. She was good after but not during. So I stood on the lawn between the man with no eyes and the woman with no mouth.

My father was holding my small hand in a tight, sweaty grip. The other was holding a framed picture, the back with the wire for hanging facing outward. But I was at eye level with it, and could see that it was not a picture of him on his wedding day, or a picture of me his only child, but his diploma that said *summa cum laude*, which he had explained to me was Latin for "with highest praise." There had been almost no damage, and my father said afterwards that he himself probably could have handled it with his new fire extinguisher that was qualified for A) wood, trash and paper fires B) flammable liquid fires C) electrical fires. He had explained all this to me when he took his new extinguisher out of the box. I imagined then that there must be a whole alphabet of disaster, getting worse and worse all the way to Z.

There in the *merde-mobile* hurtling through a foreign darkness, Es said something that took me by surprise. I had always thought of Es not exactly as a light person, but one filled with lightness, the lightness of texture and dazzle, exotic shades and shapes. "There's no such thing as unscathed," she said. "We're all so damned scathed, we can hardly stand it." She paused and then she said, "People think evil is interesting, "but it always ends up the same way. In death. It's only about taking advantage. The hunter takes advantage until the animal is dead. The soldier takes advantage until the enemy is dead. The murderer takes advantage until the victim is dead. Disease takes advantage until the body is dead. Always the same ending." She paused again and then continued, "But giving advantage…you never know where that will lead. That's where the real surprises are."

I was still thinking about this when Es launched into an energetic rendition of "Ninety-nine bottles of sauce on the wall…" It was a song we sometimes sang while filling up the condiments at Carnivores at the end of the day. "Take A-1 down, pass it around, ninety-eight bottles of sauce on the wall…" We tried to do it alphabetically to up the challenge. I picked up the refrain. "Take Béarnaise down, pass it around, ninety-seven bottles of sauce on the wall…." After we left Bangor, we headed, still singing, into a long stretch that was nothing but trees hovering at the edges of the road, a dense shield of green that the weak shafts of illumination from the headlights could not penetrate. Of course, the "brights" on the *merde-mobile* weren't working, but in a city you hardly noticed, sliding from one pool of artificial light to another without a gap. There were times when Es completely forgot to turn on her lights for night driving in the city, and didn't even notice the difference. But here, if it weren't for those feeble headlights illuminating just enough of the road to move ahead, the darkness would be complete. "Take salsa down and pass it around..." *Salsa torero* was an entry in Hemingway's glossary: *literally, salsa means sauce, but salsa is the indefinable quality which being lacking in a bullfighter makes his work dull no matter how perfect.*

"Getting tired?" I asked Es.

"I'm okay."

"Maybe we should stop."

"No, we'll take turns napping and driving." By the time we got to the Canadian border again, it was so late that it was early. Again there were two towns mirroring each other, though they were bigger and had the real border of the St. Croix River between them. On the bridge, we could feel the tremor of trucks crossing in the opposite direction. "Perhaps we should purchase a map, Ma'am," I said in the same mock deep voice Es had used earlier.

"Too dark to see it." The car's interior light didn't work either, of course. "I'll ask the guy."

"Simple," the Canadian customs officer said. "Take Highway One until you see signs for Deep Harbour and the boat." Es rewarded him with a charming smile. I don't know how she always manages that spark between herself and the men she encounters. Maybe men admire her because she admires them, the firm line of a freshly shaven jaw, the masculine confidence of voice and gesture that transforms the obscure into the straightforward.

When we arrived at Deep Harbour we followed the signs with a silhouette of a ferry shimmering out at us, a white boat carrying a single car afloat on stylized lines that waved like a woman's hair. These signs led us eventually to the ferry terminal that had a children's playground and a closed canteen to one side, a single street lamp illuminating both. A children's playground looks so ghostly at night. It was too dark to see anything else. "The dark here is really dark," Es said.

"I guess we're first in line," I said as she pulled the car into place. The terminal building with the washrooms was closed so we took a quick pee behind some bushes. Back in the *merde-mobile*, we both reclined our seats amidst a journey's worth of detritus: wrappers and fruit peelings and empty coffee cups, and a map folded back on its purpose. "What is that smell?" Es said, wrinkling her nose as she leaned back and drifted into sleep.

BOATER

When we awoke a few hours later the place looked completely different with the sun up and the tide out, trucks and cars lined up behind us, and the ferry boat docked and ready to load. Yesterday morning we were in Toronto and this morning we were here at the very edge of the continent. It made me feel kind of dizzy. "That's what you were smelling," I said as Es awoke. "The sea." It was a fresh and fishy, wet and windy kind of smell.

The metal ramp down to the ferry seemed at an impossibly steep angle. I couldn't figure out why until I realized it was low tide. You could tell by the dark seaweed and barnacles that clung to the dock and the fishing boats, some of which were practically out of the water lying on the sides of their rounded bellies. "Up the bay, the tides can be fifty feet high," the man in the terminal had said. That was a four-storey building. The same distance that the stranger in Toronto had fallen to his death.

"What a way to live!" Es said, meaning this hinged life that had to be built to accommodate the vast fluctuations of the sea. We drove down the steep ramp with Es at the wheel. Once on board we were directed by a man in an orange coverall to a parking spot that seemed unreasonably close to the side and the end of the ferry. This was the M.V. *Gannet* that carried twenty-six cars, thirty-two squeezed, it said in the brochure. This must have been one of the squeezed days. Even Es, who wasn't at all timid behind the wheel said, "You've got to be kidding," when the man kept waving her on. As it was, she had to scramble out the passenger door after me. This was the old ferry, known by the locals as the Black Boat, called out of retirement while the big new ferry, the White Boat, was undergoing maintenance. As we left the car behind to climb the steep steps up to the passenger deck, I noticed the tethering rings on the floor used, I assumed, for particularly stormy crossings, vehicles lashed to the green surface of a floating world.

Es and I went out on to the deck in the early August sunshine and watched the rocks slide past as we moved into the channel. Except for the signs of the tide, at first you could imagine you were in a lake, threading through the smaller offshore islands like a needle gathering beads, but soon the ferry headed for the shimmering horizon where there was no land at all. I had never seen the sea before, except in pictures. It was love at first sight. The sea gave you a sense of what eternity might look like, a thing that glistened with light and went on and on. The largeness of it seemed able to fill up the smallness in a person. Hemingway's old man said the sea is kind and very beautiful, but that she could also be cruel. I knew this blue sea in summer was only one side, but for now I was content with this gorgeous generosity. As we headed out into open water, a man with binoculars leaning against the railing beside us pointed out a whale. All we could see were plumes of spray at a great distance. He was excited because it was a right whale, and sightings are apparently quite rare. "They called them right whales," he said, "because the whalers considered them the 'right' ones to kill, slower and larger than their cousins." It seemed wherever you went here, there was someone willing to give you specialized information about strange things you were seeing for the first time. Often you did not even have to ask; they just gave it to you like a favour at a wedding, a piece of dark fruitcake you could put under your pillow and dream on.

"I'm still *fatiguée*," Es said. She had done most of the driving because of the standard thing. Rolling up her leather jacket like a pillow she stretched out on a bench on the deck underneath the smoke stack with the painted galleon, the symbol of the province of New Brunswick and its boat building past. With her sunglasses, dangly earrings, palazzo pants, and short black tank top that showed off her navel jewel, Es looked foreign to this place. She was so Toronto, wearing Punjabi outfits from Little India, super-short skirts or jeggings with bustiers, and wild vintage stuff she found on Queen St. West. Her hair at the moment was somewhere between purple and black, the shade of some uninvented berry that grew in the shadows. "Wake me up when we get there."

"Okay, I'm going to find something to eat," I said. It took me a moment to adjust to the swell, the rise and fall of the ferry floor. I soon found my sea legs but couldn't imagine what it must be like on a stormy day. In the cafeteria I tried not to be a snob about my options; my freezer back in Toronto had bags of coffee beans with names like Tanzania Peaberry and Mundo Novo, though I drew the line at civet poo. I ordered a regular coffee and a carrot muffin and sat down. The chairs were fastened with ropes to the floor, and there was a little lip around the edge of every table to prevent the condiments and plates from sliding over the edge in a swell. I looked around at the other passengers chatting or knitting or playing cards, realizing that, in contrast to Es, I did not look out of place. Es never blended, but I, in my blue jeans and green T-shirt, with my red hair pulled back in a ponytail and my skin freckled and fair, had already assumed the colours of the place.

On one wall was a map of Gannet Island hand-painted on wood, the island surrounded by chisel marks to simulate waves. Carrying my mug with me, I got up to take a closer look. A little painted ferry was arriving at North Head, the mysterious place marked on the envelope that had come with the key. There were other places as well with more fanciful names, Castalia, Seal Cove, Dark Harbour. In the gift shop on board the ferry, in addition to edible seaweed called dulse, postcards of puffins, and lobster trap key chains, you could purchase a poster which identified all the shipwrecks around the island. At the site of each wreck was the date, the name, and a little icon indicating the kind of vessel such as schooner, sloop, barque, or brigantine. The wrecks seemed mostly to bear the names of women, though there were other names like Turkish Empire, Neptune, Valkyrie, Good Intent, and Surprise.

I tried to read the island guide I had picked up at the tourism booth at the ferry terminal. It began by quoting one of the ferry captains, a Captain Shepherd: "There is more water coming into the Bay of Fundy in one day than flows from all of the rivers in the world combined," but I found I couldn't concentrate, so I went out on the deck again, feeling breathless and rash once more as we slid closer to the island with a low hum of engines. Es was where I had left her, still sleeping quite beautifully as people do in movies, her sunglasses reflecting little ovals of sky. I have never seen myself sleeping, but I suspect it is not this aesthetic, because the smudge of damp on the pillow means I have been drooling with my mouth open. And my dentist tells me I grind my teeth. I still sleep on the bed I slept on as a girl, though it was clearly designed for a boy. The fabric on the mattress is covered with sporting figures, little mustard-coloured men being vigorous with baseball bats and hockey sticks beneath my sheets. No wonder my dreams are restless.

I walked to the other side of the ferry, where I could now see Gannet Island rising from the waves like a huge breaching whale. I wondered whether this was starboard or port and thought this was something I ought to know, though it was not vital information for survival in Toronto. Soon the cliffs softened a little and on the promontory that jutted out towards us was a lighthouse, a classic lighthouse like you might draw if you were asked, glistening white and red in the sun. As the ferry wharf came in view, I began to feel nervous again. I put my hand to my chest where the key was hanging beneath my T-shirt on a piece of blue ribbon. The loudspeaker came on, announcing that people should return to their cars and prepare for unloading. I met Es at the top of the stairs to the lower deck. "Feel better?" I asked.

Es blew her bangs up out of her eyes and ran a hand with its colourful fingernails through her dark hair. She nodded. "Want a mint?" she said, reaching in her pocket and handing me a mint from

Carnivores. Soon we bumped against an unfamiliar shore and drove, our tires humming and clicking, up a ramp built like everything else on the island to adjust to the tides.

"Okay, bright eyes. What do we do now?" I asked Es, who was behind the wheel.

"Ask that guy."

"Excuse me," I called, rolling down the car window. The man in a navy coverall who was coiling rope turned to look at me, shading his eyes from the sun with one hand. "Is this North Head?"

"You got it."

"We're looking for Honeysuckle Cottage."

"Sorry, can't help you. I'm from the mainland." I looked back at Es. We were about to drive away as the man waved at us. "Try Charlotte at Aristotle's Lantern. If anybody knows, she will."

"Thanks," I said. We drove up the main road, and saw a sign directing us to Aristotle's Lantern Bed and Breakfast. We turned up the side lane and into the drive of a shingled Cape Cod with window boxes alive with colourful petunias. Driftwood and buoys marked the walkway.

"I'll wait in the car," Es said, fiddling with the radio dial though she knew it was more or less broken like everything else.

I rang the doorbell, and the screen door was opened by an older woman whose grey hair was pulled back in a bright Indian cotton scarf. She wore round Windsor-style glasses like Hemingway and Harry Potter, and her face was smudged with flour. "Sorry to interrupt you, but I'm looking for Honeysuckle Cottage."

A flicker of surprise passed over the woman's face when she saw the Ontario plates, but she did not say anything other than, "Sorry, don't think I can help."

I turned back toward the *merde-mobile*, with a thumb down for Es's benefit. I tried to think of some clever thing to say, but I felt like I was going to cry. Of course the whole thing had been too bizarre to be true. "Wait," said the woman coming after me. "Over on Cove Road, there's a sign for 'Stone Cottage.' The other cottages along there all have names. I think one might be Honeysuckle." As I got back in the car, I marvelled at a place where houses still had names, imagining the kind of chaos this would create in a big place like Toronto. In a city, there were too many houses and not enough difference between them, but even here on this island, the blue numbers used by emergency crews had begun to appear. In emergencies you need numbers, not names.

Stone Cottage was easy to find, both because of the sign and because it was so unusual to see a stone structure amidst all the shingled houses. The only other stone structure we had seen driving up from the ferry was a church. "Go on," Es said.

"No, I don't think I can."

Es sighed, and got out of the car. Walking toward Stone Cottage, she approached a very old man pushing a lawn mower, one of those old-fashioned ones without an engine, just blades that go round as it goes forward. This made sense to me. Why dig up the power in million-year-old ferns to do what your arms and legs could do perfectly well? A minute later Es was back in the car, beaming from earring to dangling earring.

"What did he say?"

"He said the woman who used to live at the end of the road challenged them all to come up with a name so essential and so obvious, no one would need numbers. Thus we have Stone Cottage, followed by Whale Cottage..." Es pointed out the car window to the bleached bones of a whale arched over the entryway of the next cottage we passed. The one that came next with almost more windows than wall was Glass Cottage. Driftwood Cottage had a fence of driftwood instead of pickets or rails, and voilà, the much-anticipated Honeysuckle Cottage. We pulled in the gravel drive of Honeysuckle Cottage and before I got out of the car I sat looking at it for a moment. There were houses along this shore that looked odd and out of place like erratics, the huge boulders deposited in unexpected places by glaciers, but this cottage, as grey as the pebbles on the beach, looked like it had grown here. The structure was simple but had a kind of wild charm, with unpainted shingles weathered grey, and window frames painted dark green. The walkway between the house and the drive was overarched by an arbour covered with pink and golden honeysuckle that also climbed gloriously up the fieldstone chimney at one end.

"Quaint enough for you?" Es asked.

I didn't answer. I got out of the car, took a deep breath, then walked toward the cottage and rang the bell. It was literally a brass bell that hung from a bracket beside the door. There was no answer. There was also a doorknocker shaped like a woman's hand.

"What are you waiting for?" Es asked, coming up behind me. "The key, the key!"

"Oh," I said, as if using the key was a novel idea that had just occurred to me, rather than being the purpose of our entire journey of nearly a thousand miles. I removed the ribbon from around my neck and looked sceptically at the key that had brought me all this way. There was no deadbolt, just a keyhole in the doorknob. The key slid in easily, like it belonged, but it wouldn't turn. "It doesn't work," I said, feeling panic set in. "Maybe we found the wrong door."

"Here, let me try. We didn't come all this way for nothing." Es held the knob firmly and wiggled the key, and it finally turned. "Sometimes there's a trick to it."

Es stood aside and let me enter first. The air was musty as if the cottage had been closed up for a long time. The interior was a simple space, sparsely furnished. On one side was the living room with a sofa upholstered in navy with wooden legs carved like claws, a Franklin wood stove, some easy chairs, and a large window facing the sea. Against the back wall was an open kitchen with a pine table surrounded by mismatched wooden chairs. "Glad you came?" Es asked, plopping down in one of the easy chairs slip covered in faded chintz.

"I don't know yet," I said, half-expecting a host to burst out of the back room like they used to on *Candid Camera* or *Just for Laughs*. On top of the table was a white envelope looking to me like a foreign and dangerous thing. There was my name, Pertice McIlveen, typed on a white envelope, on a kitchen table, in a house with a name, on an island on which I had never set foot before today, one thousand miles from home. "Here we go," I said sitting down in one of the chairs and tearing open the envelope, using my index finger as if it were a knife.

"Read it out loud," Es said.

The letter was from a law firm in Grand Harbour, according to the letterhead, and began in the formal legalese that one expects from such places. But the last paragraph got to the point. "My client, who prefers to remain anonymous, has willed the aforesaid property, Honeysuckle Cottage, North Head, Gannet Island, and all its contents to you, Pertice McIlveen, upon one condition…"

"Go on," Es said, when I paused.

"That you wear the hats."

"What hats?"

"I don't know what hats. This is so beyond weird." I had hoped and expected that all my questions would be answered by this letter when I saw it sitting on the table like the legend to a map of unfamiliar territory. Who had sent me the key? And more importantly, why? It was the kind of thing that happened in Dickens, long-lost uncles providing sudden and spectacular inheritances for impoverished nieces. The letter answered none of the questions I had, and even introduced some new ones.

"This one for starters," Es said, opening the door to the bedroom. On the bed was a straw boater with a black ribbon around the crown like the ones worn by barbershop quartets. I entered the room behind Es and sat down hard on the bed with the simple iron headboard and a quilt.

I picked up the hat and examined it. "I don't wear hats," I said like people say "I don't smoke," as if it were a distasteful and dangerous habit.

"You know," Es said, "I can't remember ever seeing you in a hat, unless you count a Carnivores' hairnet." It was true. Not even a toque. On the coldest days I wore earmuffs or wrapped a scarf around my head.

"I don't wear hats," I said again, this time in the kind of melancholy tone you might use to say "I don't play the violin," implying that you could have aspired to do such a thing had you been given the opportunity and the years to train yourself appropriately. I did wear a hat once. Typically Halloween at the McIlveen house was a low-key affair. I would tour the immediate neighbourhood in a makeshift costume like a tramp while my mother handed out Halloween kisses, those toffees in the orange and black wrappers that could take the fillings right out of your teeth. But one year June decided to do things up right and made a bonnet for me to wear along with a Laura Ingalls Wilder dress and pinafore. I looked good in the costume, but the brim, or whatever you call it on a bonnet, had been so large that I felt like a horse with blinders, prevented from seeing what was going on around me, just as I was prevented from having apples because they might have razor blades in them, and prevented from trotting across people's lawns because trespassing might make them grumpy. Earlier in the day, because of the terrible sharpness of knives, my father prevented me from cutting the eyeholes in the jack-o-lantern that would cast a vision of flame around the darkness, though I had been allowed to scoop out the stringy seedy mess that might be the pumpkin's mind. In the days that followed, because of the potential for cavities and stomach aches, I was prevented from eating the sweets people had dropped into my pillowcase all at once. An ounce of prevention is worth a pound of cure, my mother said. I hated that bonnet, which I always remembered as one prevention among many, even if Laura Ingalls Wilder was my pre-Hemingway hero. "I don't wear hats," I said.

Es started to laugh. It started low as a close-mouthed kind of giggle, then crescendoed into a loud belly laugh and stopped suddenly with a kind of snort. She sat down on the bed beside me. "You are pathetic. Someone has just offered you a house. And all you can say is, 'I don't wear hats.'"

Tucked in the band of the boater like a press card was a folded note. Es handed it to me. I opened it and started to read the slanting handwriting I recognized from the envelope containing the key.

Dear Pertice,

You don't know me from Adam, but that will change. To know my hats is to know me. This was my first hat, a straw boater, once all the rage among the sporting set because of the water resistant finish. Because it resembles the hats of Venetian gondoliers, it is thought to have been brought to North America by Italian immigrants. I am not sure why it shows up at political rallies, but I have seen a photograph of the Industrial Workers of the World gathered in New York's Union Square in 1914, all wearing boaters. It was so popular that it became known as "The Hat of the People" and was a favourite with Vaudeville entertainers, which may be why barbershop quartets still use it today.

I wore this hat all through my childhood without knowing the story behind it. For me it brings up images of boating regattas and striped blazers, early summer strawberries and homemade ice cream. When I got older I found out it belonged to my mother's sister who was one of the "persons of tender age," as the newspapers described them, who drowned in the Victoria pleasure steamer disaster in London, Ontario in 1881. My mother was supposed to go on the excursion, but she had a cold so stayed home with a mustard plaster on her chest.

The boat, a double-decked stern wheeler, was dangerously overcrowded and when the crowd shifted, it keeled over, bringing the boiler crashing through the bulwarks. Though the river was neither deep nor wide, nearly 200 people drowned that day, including my grandmother and my aunt, caught up in the wreckage or dragged under by the weight of their dresses. All they found of my mother's sister was this hat floating on the dark water. I think of it as my Phrygian cap where it all began, and where it begins for you. Go to the law office in Grand Harbour on the first of the month and there will be a new hat for you to wear.

Peace by the sea,
PM

"What's a Phrygian cap?" Es asked when I was finished reading.

"How should I know?" There was no way to look things up. Es had tried her Blackberry earlier, but couldn't get a signal. I overheard her saying to the guy directing cars on the ferry, "What is this place, the end of the world?" and his response, "No, but you can it see from here."

"More importantly," Es asked, "who is PM?"

"I haven't a clue."

Before I could protest, Es reached over and perched the hat on my head. "It suits you." I got up to look in the mirror over the dresser. If my hair had been in braids, I would have looked like Anne of Green Gables, an orphan newly arrived on a different island. Es was right. It did suit me, but it still felt like what Hemingway called *Adorno: any useless or flowery theatricality performed by the bullfighter to show his domination over the bull. They may be in good or bad taste varying from kneeling with the back toward the animal to hanging the straw hat of a spectator on the bull's horn.*

Still wearing the hat, I stepped into the bathroom, the only room I had not yet entered. It was a lovely sun-filled room with a white claw-foot tub and old-fashioned fixtures. There was no toilet paper but I had a tissue in my pocket. As I zipped up my jeans, I looked at the windowsill. Lined up there were little shells I did not know the names of, and I felt a sudden welling in my throat and eyes. Something about those unfamiliar shells gathered by a stranger's hand here on a windowsill in a house bequeathed to me for a reason I could not fathom, made me cry. This was strange. I am not a weepy person. In fact, except for the breakdown in the washroom at Carnivores, I couldn't remember the last time I cried, except for onions. I did not cry at my father's funeral. I did not shed a tear for the man who had fallen four Toronto storeys. I blinked but I did not weep. I thought about PM's mother and the sister she lost. I had no sister. My mother admitted once that I was a failure of contraception, so I guess any siblings I might have had were victories. "I must be tired," I thought, wiping tears away with my sleeve. When I turned on the tap, the pipe burped and let out only a rusty trickle.

"Well, I don't know about you," Es said, clapping her hands together when I emerged from the bathroom, "but I am not going to waste this gorgeous day. What about a picnic?"

The mention of food always makes me feel better. It's manageable and immediate. "We could walk out to the lighthouse we passed on the way in," I said, locking the door of the cottage with the Weiser key on the blue ribbon. I followed Es out to the *merde-mobile*. "There must be somewhere we can buy groceries. I'm starved."

What there was of a town was mostly strung along the main road that led to the rest of the island. We found a wonderful bakery across from the hospital, and picked up a few things at the general store. There was Wi-Fi at the bakery, and Es told me a Phrygian cap was given to slaves when they became free. Armed with the ingredients for a successful picnic, we drove to the lighthouse that was, we discovered, called Swallowtail Light. From the parking lot, the spit of land that jutted out into the sea did look a little like the forked tail of a swallow. On one point was the lighthouse, and on the other a concrete helicopter pad. The only way to get out to them was down a steep flight of concrete steps and across a narrow wooden footbridge high above a crevice in the rocks. A tourist with a dog got halfway down the steps and had to turn around. "Not good with heights. Haven't been since I was a kid," he said apologetically as he edged past us on his way back to the safety of the parking lot. As we hiked out the narrow ridge toward the lighthouse, rocks spilling away down both sides, we could smell the evergreen fragrance of small twisted spruce, the hay-like smell of dry bent grass, and over all the salt tang of the sea. The only sounds were the distant bell of a buoy and the clicking sound of the cicadas rubbing their legs together. A reddish-brown three-legged dog ran awkwardly past us, nose to the path.

"I bet a lot of people have been conceived here," Es said, gesturing toward the spruce-sheltered hollows in the grass and rocks. In some places, the roots travelled above ground because there was no soil, and the rocks were marked with lichens, grey and white, and brilliant orangey ochre. Es picked a wild rose from a bush that nudged up against the path and stuck it into the ribbon of my hat. Then I saw some daisies. Before long we had gathered twenty-one different wild flowers for the ribbon of my hat, one for each year of my life. Some we knew the names of—blue bell, beach pea, columbine, clover—and some we didn't. When we reached the lighthouse and I looked up, a whole garden tilted on my hair. Es took a picture of me with her phone. The lighthouse was clad in shingles painted white, topped with a cherry-red light casing. What you could not see from a distance was that it was tethered with eight iron cables against wind and storm. Es and I climbed out on to the far feathers of the swallow where the helicopter pad was on the highest elevation. In the centre of the concrete pad was a white triangle, paint peeling in the sun. "Wouldn't this be a great place for a dance?" Es said. I did not say that you need a partner to dance, but as if she had read my mind, Es said, "You'll find someone, or someone will find you."

"Yeah, what's the population of Greater Toronto, nearly six million? Say half of those are men. That's three million men. And what do you suppose the population of Gannet Island is, maybe 2000? That's 1000 men. If I stay here, what does that do to the odds of me ever finding someone?"

"I would say the odds of finding a good man in a place like this are greater than in a place like Toronto." Es had met her share of bottom feeders before Mr. Maybe.

I looked down the tumble of rocks that descended dizzyingly to the water. "You know what Donna told me? Donna was our bartender at Carnivores. She said she knew this couple who decided it would be romantic to be married in Acapulco, but at the reception the groom got drunk and walked off a cliff."

"What are you supposed to do with a story like that?" Es asked. Dating a fireman had taught her that impossible tales of grief were more common than people imagined, that life was an Ouroboros, the tail of happiness forever being swallowed by the serpent of sorrow.

I sat down on the edge of the concrete helicopter pad and started setting out the picnic ingredients, good crusty bread we had to tear because we had forgotten a knife, tiny Edam cheeses in their own red casings, and crisp apples. Nothing fancy, but delicious in the sunshine and sea breeze. After lunch we walked back to the parking lot, passing a father who was carrying his little girl on his shoulders. There was a house overlooking the lighthouse, tucked a little behind some trees. A sign out front said, "OPEN WHEN THE DOOR IS." Inside the garage was a table spread with sea urchins, sand dollars, and varnished lobster claws. I picked up the largest of the varnished claws, marvelling that it stretched from my wrist to my elbow. On some of the sand dollars, the petals of the flower design had been highlighted with red and blue and green. Taped on the side of a coffee can in the centre of the table was a sign that said, "Plain $1, Painted $2, Make your own change."

"You couldn't get away with that in the big city!" Es said. I assumed she meant the open can of coins, not the selling of sea treasures. She exchanged real dollars for ones of sand, and we drove back to Honeysuckle Cottage. I took off my hat and placed it on the table, the flowers in the brim now wilted. Es plopped herself down on the couch. "What are you going to do?" she asked. This was the question that had been gnawing at me since I opened the letter on the table and the one in the hat brim.

"I have to find out more," I said. "It's too creepy not knowing who's behind all this. He could change his mind. He could come back."

"What makes you think it's a he?"

"The boater is a man's hat, isn't it?" I asked, thinking of Dick Van Dyke dancing in *Mary Poppins*, a movie I had seen as a kid.

"I think it's a woman."

"Why?"

"The handwriting, I guess."

"Maybe the boating disaster is a clue. Maybe I can find a victim list online or something."

"But all you have is initials. And anyway, the mother's name would probably have changed through marriage."

"I'll call the lawyers and ask for more information."

"I think if they were going to tell you anything more, they would have by now. You read it, 'My client who prefers to remain anonymous...'"

"Things like this don't happen." I realized I was rephrasing one of my mother's maxims: "Nothing in life is free." Nothing large had ever been given to me that I could remember. I had worked like hell for it all. Marks at school, the tuition for the journalism degree, even to keep my dive of an apartment in Toronto. I couldn't remember a time when I had not worked as hard as I possibly could, paper routes and babysitting before I was sixteen, and then working summers, after school and weekends from then until now. And here was this sudden, generous surprise, unearned and unexpected.

"Things like this *do* happen," Es said. "Remember the time I bought that pair of pants for Jesse at the Salvation Army for two bucks and found 200 dollars in the pocket?"

"Yeah, but that was just random. This was intentional. Someone intended for me to come here."

"Well, all I know is that I have to be back to work on Tuesday and you have to get your shit together and decide what you're going to do."

"I can't stay here."

"Why not? It's not like you have anything holding you to Toronto." In the two months since graduating I had sent around a few resumes but it seemed no one was hiring journalists, and if they were, they wanted the really hungry ones. I had only gone into journalism because that was the path Hemingway had taken, and I wasn't sure what else to do. I had doubled my hours at the restaurant, but cooking at Carnivores was hardly a calling. "You want to rush right back so you can make more suicide wings and burn more steaks to a crisp? You want to rush back to sixteen lanes of traffic and air you can see?" She could see I wasn't being swayed, so she quoted Van Gogh. *The fishermen know that the sea is dangerous and the storm terrible, but they have never found these dangers sufficient reason for remaining ashore.*

"It's not like the place is bursting with journalism jobs. I doubt they even have a newspaper."

"I got the impression that you weren't even that keen on journalism, that it was the writing and not the reporting that interested you, and you can do that anywhere. Worst case scenario, you find you hate it here, you get on a bus and go back to Toronto, no harm done."

"What am I supposed to do here?"

"Same as you did there. You won't have to worry about rent. You already have a place to live. That's half the battle. All you have to do is find enough work to put food on the table, and that should be easy this time of year—tourist season."

I am used to having things very carefully planned. Spontaneous decisions make me dizzy. "You brought almost everything you own, Pertice," Es continued. "Give me the key to your apartment, and if there's anything you want, I'll pack it up and send it. If you decide you want to stay, I'll clean up and give notice to your landlord."

I tried to convince Es to stay overnight so she would be well-rested for the drive back to Ontario, but as the next day was a holiday, she was concerned that the ferry might not be running. She'd better start back, and she could catch the 5:30 pm ferry though she would have a nap first. She conked out in the bedroom while I sat on the couch trying to read the guide I had been too excited to read on the ferry. I thought about the only piece of advice my father ever gave me. "A bird in the hand is worth two in the bush." You would tell him something that had happened to you, and he would look up from his crossword puzzle and offer this platitude, the first half of it at least, that never really applied to anything. Who's to say that what you have is better than what you wish for? Maybe it was unfair to expect gifts from your parents, things that would arm you for the quest, things like shields and bucklers, whatever they were. My father gave gifts, but like the Magi, he gave them at my birth and then retreated to the obscure country from which he came. My existence, my name, my passion for bits of knowledge, these were his gifts to me. Growing up, things just sort of unfolded in a neutral way. I had always been grateful because nothing terribly bad had ever happened to me. I knew of people whose lives were nightmares, women raped by brutal strangers or their own brothers, men beaten so badly they could not walk, people who had been trapped or seduced into various dangers, but I had moved quietly through the tame space of my youth. Nothing particularly bad had happened, but nothing particularly good either. Maybe that's why I found Hemingway so intriguing. The way he took the bull by the horns. The way he plunged into all that was brutal and real and wrote about it afterward.

When Es woke up, I wanted to make her some toast from what was left of the picnic bread on an old-fashioned toaster I found in one of the kitchen cupboards, the kind where the sides flipped down like wings, but there was no power. "I'll be fine," Es said.

I reluctantly helped her gather her things. "I'll come down with you to the ferry, and walk back," I said. "It's not far."

As I locked the door, Es said, "Shouldn't you be wearing your hat?"

This made me all flustered again, thinking there might be spies watching me to ensure that I fulfilled my part of the bargain. I unlocked the door and went back into the cottage. I picked up the boater with its halo of wilted flowers, and placed it on my head. "Satisfied?" I said to Es as I relocked the door.

Es responded with a "Don't blame me" shrug. As we drove down the hill to the ferry, I could not believe what I was doing. I, who could stand for ten minutes agonizing over which bunch of broccoli to put in my cart, was now, without even batting an eyelash, as my mother would say, making the biggest decision of my life. There was still a chance to drive away from this small unpredictable place and go back to Toronto with Es. I could just not get out of the car as it drove down the ramp and passed from land to sea. At the dock Es bought a ticket and lined up for the 5:30 ferry. That was the way it worked. You didn't have to pay to get on to the island, only to leave.

As it turned out, I did get out of the car before the wharf stopped and the boat began. At first, I felt bereft, watching Es get smaller and smaller as she waved from the deck of the ferry disappearing around Swallowtail Light. Then I felt a little exhilarated. But as I watched, a fishing boat sliced across the sparkling wake of the ferry, and it was as if the thread tying me to that other life had been snapped in two. Feeling lost, I walked down to the water's edge, past the stacks of lobster traps on the wharf, not the picturesque wooden kind our neighbours in Ingersoll brought home one year from a Maritime vacation, but the more prosaic cubes of metal and nylon. The anchored boats bobbed serenely on their own reflections. Surrounded by the marine smells of fish and seaweed with a hint of diesel, I stood at the very edge of the sea, staring down. If you looked at the water one way, it seemed almost solid, reflecting the sky. If you looked harder, though, you could see through it to the broken bits of mussel shell, seaweed, and stones. Before I even realized what was happening, the sea rose over my toes. I jumped back, but not before my shoes got wet. The tide came up that quickly, that imperceptibly. You didn't even notice until it washed over you.

I began to make my way back to Honeysuckle Cottage, squelching past the booth where you bought tickets for the ferry and a short order place called Captain's that offered both burgers and fish. The smell of frying onions lured me in and I ordered some fish and chips and ate them there on the rocks with the gulls wheeling above. The fish was, according to the cook, caught that morning, and it did taste wonderfully fresh and firm. Feeling full and somewhat better, I walked over the hill past the Whale and Seabird Research Station, and a craft shop called Fathom That. Finally, I turned down the shore road with all the cottages with the whimsical names that matched their structures. When I got back to the cottage, I fumbled with the key in the lock, the key that had lured me away from the familiar life I knew, a key that was unclear in its origins and motivations. The honeysuckle over the doorway that earlier had looked and smelled so charming now looked kind of spidery. The sweet smell made me want to gag.

The cottage seemed hollow without Es. I took off my wet sneakers, loosened the laces and set them outside on the step to dry. The panic which had started when the ferry bearing Es had disappeared around Swallowtail Light now widened from my chest up into my throat and even seeped into that hard place behind my eyes. Hemingway called this *Perder el sitio: a bullfighter who through illness, lack of confidence, cowardice, or nervousness has lost his style and even his sense of where and how things should be done.* My mother's solution had always been cheer. She always looked on the bright side even if there wasn't one. My father's answer had been information. A bird in the hand. He believed the meagre known was better than the lavish mystery.

There must be a clue somewhere in the house, but the light was fading and the power wasn't turned on. In the vanishing light, I looked around for some candles but there didn't seem to be any. I did, however, find a present that Es had left behind. A pair of faux pearl earrings, with the old-fashioned backs that you screwed to tighten. Es knew my ears weren't pierced. My parents had discouraged me. "Why would you want to put holes in your head?" June asked. That was her description of someone who was crazy, someone with holes in her head. Es undoubtedly picked up these old-school earrings second-hand at some flea market and proceeded to transform them. They were painted in her latest ongle-spangling theme, the swirling moon and stars of Van Gogh's *Starry Night*. I put on the painted pearls, feeling almost like the Vermeer girl, and stood for a while looking out the window, though by now it was too dark to see anything. When the gift Es had given me started pinching my ears, there didn't seem to be anything to do but to take them off and go to bed. With the unfamiliar smells and sounds of the sea leaking through the open window, it took me a long time to fall asleep.

The next morning I arose hungry but refreshed. Standing by the kitchen counter, I ate what was left of the bread. If I was going to stay here there were practical things I would have to look after, getting the power turned on, the phone hooked up, food to put in the cupboards, as well as finding a job to pay for it all. But first, I wondered if I had overlooked anything, if maybe there was some clue about the individual who had brought me here, aside from the letters.

The house really was a cottage, as the name suggested, with a simple layout, with one half of it being the living/dining/kitchen room, and the other half occupied with the bathroom and bedroom which, like the living room, faced the sea. The best plan seemed to be to go through the rooms methodically, looking in drawers, under the bed, in the closet. This is what I found. The kitchen drawers and cupboards contained mismatched and tarnished cutlery, willow-patterned dishes, some of which were chipped, some old-fashioned appliances like the toaster, and a collection of dishtowels, some woven and some printed with images like the Royal Family or the Irish Blessing. *May the road rise before you*, etc. There was a kitchen trivet with a point by point comparison between the assassinations of Lincoln and Kennedy. I also found some pots and pans, mismatched like the cutlery, and some mouse turds. Other than these few odds and ends, the place had been picked clean.

In the bathroom, aside from the shell collection that had brought me to tears the day before, I found only a small stack of well-worn towels and washcloths in different colours sitting on a single chair. There was nothing in the medicine cabinet, or anywhere else in the room to indicate who had lived here. The dresser in the bedroom was also empty, and some of the silvering was scratched from the mirror. In the bedroom closet there was nothing except some wooden hangers, two of which had crocheted covers. The bed itself had a feather pillow in a pillowcase with a crocheted border, some threadbare sheets and the quilt. Other than this, the room was empty, though one wall was filled with shelving that might be the right size for hats. Five shelves right up to the ceiling with space for six hats each, one for every day of the month. Empty, the cubby holes had the appearance of blank spaces in a crossword puzzle that had no clues. If anything held the clues to the mystery it must be the hat, because there was nothing else personal in the whole cottage, nothing that gave any indication of who had once lived here. Not even the walls betrayed a trace of personality. They were painted white throughout and the pine floorboards were bare of rugs or mats. I could find absolutely nothing that clarified who wanted the cottage to belong to me or why.

It was well past two o'clock, and I was hungry. I ate the last of the cheese, which smelled much more strongly than it did yesterday from not having been refrigerated, but that was the best way to eat cheese anyway, at room temperature, like red wine. And I ate the last apple, looking out the window at the sea and wondering why the cottage felt so strange other than because it was so strange. I was so distracted that I almost ate the little sticker on the apple, the little sticker that said Golden Delicious. And it suddenly struck me. This was what was missing. Words. I was used to being surrounded by words. My apartment in Toronto was cluttered with them, novels and textbooks and newspapers and magazines spilling everywhere; even my fridge had one of those magnetic poetry kits stuck all over it. And everywhere I went in the city, words found their way into my eyes from billboards and newspapers and mail, from blackboards and libraries and menus and screens of all sizes. Here there seemed to be no words but the two that I had almost eaten.

Except of course, the words in the letter from PM I had found in the hatband, and the letter from the lawyers that still lay on the table. I picked it up and looked at the letterhead again. JAMES & FLAGG, FULL-SERVICE LAW FIRM, GRAND HARBOUR, GANNET ISLAND. I would go ask this James and this Flagg what the meaning of their words could possibly be. And on the way home I would take care of the necessities. I looked at my watch. It was almost three. I remembered Grand Harbour from the map I had seen on the ferry. It was about halfway down the island. There probably wasn't a bus or a taxi service, and even if there was, I had no phone. Es always mocked me for being the only person on the planet my age without a cell phone, but I couldn't be bothered because it reminded me that next to no one was trying to get in touch and I didn't want to get caught up in one of those sneaky plans with all kinds of hidden fees you had to pay off forever. I looked at the tourist brochure. The whole damn island was only fifteen miles long. I figured I could walk if I had to. I pulled the dead flowers from the day before out of its brim and put on the straw boater.

I hadn't gone very far on the main road when a car pulled up alongside me. "Need a lift?" a man hollered through the open window in a deep and scratchy voice that carried the trace of an English accent.

I hesitated. "Better safe than sorry," June was fond of saying. If you got into a car with a stranger in the big city, you could be dead. You heard about it from time to time on the news. Even good Samaritans sometimes paid a price. "I'm fine," I said, even though my feet were starting to hurt, and I wasn't sure how long it would take me to get where I needed to go.

The man in the car didn't appear to hear my refusal, and kept driving alongside. "Wherever you're going, it's a long walk," he said.

This time I looked directly at him through the open passenger window. His beard was almost white, but there was something youthful about his eyes. "No, really, I'm okay," I said.

"Suit yourself," he said, touching his right hand to the brim of an imaginary hat. He began to drive away, though not very fast.

Whether it was the old-fashioned gesture of tipping a hat that wasn't there, or the way he had not pressed me, or the light-headed way I was feeling from being hungry, I felt reassured. I ran to catch up with the car, and the driver pulled over on the shoulder and came to a stop. "Well, actually, I could use a lift to Grand Harbour," I said through the window.

"Grand Harbour it is." The car smelled of cigarette smoke and something else, maybe turpentine. His hands on the steering wheel had paint on them. Other than to offer me some of the dulse that lay beside him in a bag, he didn't say another word until we arrived in Grand Harbour, where he dropped me off with a goodbye wave. I had never eaten dulse before, the seaweed dried to a purple so deep it looked almost brown. I found that it was the salty taste of the salty smell Es and I experienced when we first arrived at the coast, the very taste of the sea.

2 MERRY WIDOW

There wasn't much to Grand Harbour aside from the houses and harbour, the bank, the school, the museum, a Home Hardware and grocery store all in one, a gas station with a lunch counter, and the law office. The sign said "James & Flagg" with one of those especially elaborate ampersands in gold paint on a navy background. "A Full-Service Law Firm." It looked official and promising. I felt more hopeful than I had since Es had gotten on the ferry and disappeared. But first things first. I got a bite to eat at the lunch counter. Despite the fact that I didn't look much different from anyone else, with the exception of the hat, the waitress pegged me for the newcomer I was. "Ah, The Big Smoke" she said, when I told her I was from Toronto. "What brought you all the way down here?"

"I'm still trying to figure that out," I said. Before she could ask me any more questions I asked her where I should go to get my power turned on and my phone hooked up.

"Nothing will be open because of the holiday." When she saw me looking at her blankly, she added, "New Brunswick Day."

"Oh," I said, realizing how inconvenient this was going to be. In honour of Es and all waitresses, I left a large tip and crossed the street to the law office, just in case. The door was open, but no one was sitting at the reception desk. I waited for a few minutes, then knocked on the door behind the desk.

A balding middle-aged man in a wrinkled navy suit and a loosened tie with a cartoon Tasmanian devil on it came out and ushered me into his office. It wasn't a very big office, but there were official-looking diplomas over the desk. "We're not really open because of the holiday. I just happened to come by to pick up some files. But since I'm here, how can I help? The name's Flagg," he said, extending his hand.

I shook his hand and placed his letter on the desk between us, the trifold waiting to burst into meaning. He looked surprised. "You're Pertice McIlveen."

"Yes, and I'm here for my hat." I paused. "And more information."

"I'm sorry. I can't give you any more than what's in the letter."

"Look, Mr. Flagg," I said, surprising myself with my aggressive tone. It must have been the hat, like the boaters worn by all those United Workers of the World demanding their rights in Union Square. "This is my life we're talking about. No one gives houses away."

"Would you like to sit down?"

I sat down. Mr. Flagg nodded at me across the desk in what I took to be a sympathetic way. This gave me courage to proceed. "No one forces a complete stranger to wear hats."

"The hats are an unusual circumstance," he agreed, chewing on the end of a pencil in a way that made him seem younger than he was.

"Is someone watching to make sure I wear the hats?"

"I can assure you that no arrangements have been made for surveillance."

"That would be creepy."

"I agree."

"What makes your client think I'll wear the hats if no one's checking up on me?"

"That I don't know. It's always a risk, letting someone have a choice."

"What if I choose not to?"

"That's up to you, of course, but most people are curious when presented with an intriguing option. And you will find that in small places, people notice what you're up to." He paused to let that sink in. "Can I get you a coffee or something?"

I ignored his offer. "If I am going to know how to proceed, I need information."

"I'm sorry, but I can't give you any more information."

"You said that already."

"Well, it's true."

"Look, Mr. Flagg. I would like to talk to the other lawyer," I said, pointing at the "James" in the letterhead at the top of the paper that lay between us on the desk.

He put his hand up to his forehead and rubbed his eyebrows. "That could be arranged."

"Well, let's arrange it then."

He put his hands together like children do to make the church and held the steeple of his index fingers against his lips for a moment while he looked at me. "You're talking to him now."

I gave him my best I'm-from-the-big-city-and-I don't-have-time-for-this-nonsense! look of exasperation, but he continued. "It's me. I'm James and I'm Flagg." This was unexpected. I had assumed that James was a last name, like the author who said, *Live all you can; it's a mistake not to.* The lawyer folded his hands in his lap beneath his Tasmanian devil tie and shrugged. "When I went to get the sign made up, it looked so unimpressive. "Flagg: Full-Service Law Firm." It didn't have the right ring. Who ever heard of a law firm with only one name?" Because I had never had dealings with a lawyer before, I didn't answer. "It doesn't sound very convincing, does it?" he continued. "So in the end we decided to put both my first and last name. Arnie over at the Boat Shop who made up the sign for me suggested the "and." He said all the law firms on TV had an "and" in them. I said it would be misleading, but he said, 'Everybody on the island knows it's you, Jim, and that you're just one person, but it'll look good on the sign.' People take the complicated stuff to the mainland, anyway, like when babies are born."

"Just how 'full-service' is this law firm?"

James laughed. "I mean, babies used to be born on the island first with midwifes, then at the hospital in North Head, but now anyone who's due goes to the mainland, just in case anything goes wrong.

They're too scared of being far away from the necessary equipment if things don't go the way they're supposed to."

This new information was distracting. I meant to be firm, even angry, and now I found that the person I had counted on for revelation needed an ampersand to be convincing. "Oh," was all I could think of to say.

"Things rarely do, go wrong I mean, but you wouldn't want to take any chances."

"Maybe I will have that coffee," I said.

"It's only instant," the lawyer said apologetically, stirring a spoonful of dark crystals into hot water he got out of the red tap of the water cooler. The water jug part had a padded fabric cover with cows on it pulled over the top like a tea cozy. "Want some white death?" he said, gesturing toward a jar of powdered creamer.

"I take it black." I took the offered mug, noticing that the handle had been broken and mended with glue. The coffee tasted vile, but it was hot. The picture of the Gannet Island ferry on the mug reminded me of my purpose. I brought the mug down heavily on the desk so it made a bang that was louder than I expected. "You have to help me."

"Since August has begun, I will give you your new hat, but that's all I can do." He disappeared into a back room and emerged with a huge pink hatbox with *Beau Chapeau* written in fancy gold cursive on the lid. He set it down on his desk between us. "Miss McIlveen, I'm sorry. I have to go to pick up my daughter and then I'm headed home for supper."

"I'm not leaving until you tell me more." I stood up as I said this, putting my hands down on the desk in what I hoped was an intimidating way.

Mr. James Flagg of "James & Flagg: Full-Service Law Firm" shrugged his shoulders. "Well, I'm heading out then. I'll leave the light on for you. If you could just pull the door to when you go, that would be grand." He took his trench coat from the hall tree in the corner, and said as an afterthought, "There's a washroom at the back, if you need it."

After the lawyer was gone, the hat on my head suddenly felt like the one that stayed afloat while the girl that wore it was drowning. I sat down in the lawyer's chair, which was bigger and softer than the one I had been sitting in. Plus it swivelled. I eyed the hatbox the way a security guard might watch an unattended suitcase at the airport. I might as well find out the worst. I lifted the lid and found a truly ridiculous hat in black velvet, as huge as those ones in the Gainsborough paintings, piled high with multi-coloured feather ornaments and huge ostrich plumes billowing out the back like a tall ship under sail. And here I'd been complaining about the plain little straw boater with the simple black band. I couldn't imagine wearing this hat to a fancy dress ball or a royal wedding. Forget about around town. But Es had been right about one thing. PM was clearly a woman, which made everything so much more difficult. Women are very hard to find if they disappear into the men they love, if they marry into names other than the ones they were born with. Damn.

I looked at the things on the lawyer's desk. There was a photo of him with his wife and his very pretty blonde daughter, all of them wearing matching Christmas sweaters. The parents were smiling, but the teenager looked pained. There was also one of those office toys with the hanging silver balls. When you hit the closest one the farthest one swung outward, leaving all the others in between motionless. Some papers were held down by a wave-smoothed beach stone with the white silhouette of a seagull on it. And of course, there was a phone. I looked at the phone for a while. And I looked at the hat. This hat was nothing like Hemingway's unfashionable felt hat that he claimed had lost *a little something in every country it had shed rain and wind and sun in*, the green burned out as if by the Thracian desert, the felt weathered by sailing down into the sun-baked sand of the bullring.

What the hell. I put on the hat. This I had to see. There would be a mirror in the washroom the lawyer had mentioned. Along with a framed cross-stitch of teddy bears on the wall, and a basket of potpourri that smelled like vanilla on the toilet tank, there was a mirror lit by one of those curly fluorescent energy-saver bulbs. The hat was so huge I had to stand with my back against the opposite wall to even see the whole thing in the mirror. My first impulse was to take it off, it looked so theatrical and foreign. So unlike me. But I adjusted the angle a little and looked again. I had to admit, for all its excess, the hat looked surprisingly elegant, as did the woman wearing it. The play of shadow over my face prompted a shy little smile and the downturned chin and uplifted eyes Princess Diana was so famous for. I found myself straightening my shoulders. No slouching in a hat like this. Of course it looked ridiculous with the jeans and T-shirt I was wearing. If I had to wear a hat like this I would have to do something about my wardrobe. So be it. I looked at my unfamiliar but fabulous reflection. Game on, I said to PM, whoever she was.

Still wearing the hat, I walked (or, more accurately, sailed) back into the front office and looked in the hatbox, hoping for another letter like the one with the boater. There was one.

Dear Pertice,

Why hats, you might ask? The famous New York milliner, Lilly Daché, once wrote: "A woman's hat is close to her heart, though she wears it on her head. It is her way of saying to the world: 'This is what I am like' —or 'This is what I would like to be.'" Christian Dior went so far as to say "Without hats ...we would have no civilization." Certainly, our country as we know it might not exist but for the beaver hat, and the quest for furs that pushed the frontier ever westward. And though almost no one wears one anymore, hats have entered the way we speak; keep it under your hat, at the drop of a hat, hat in hand, pass the hat around, hat trick.

This hat, the first I purchased for myself, is a Merry Widow, named for an operetta by Franz Lehár, first performed in English in London, 1907, in which the leading lady wore a large hat lavishly decorated with feathers. The style was much copied in the years leading up to the war, getting ever bigger until it attained truly astounding dimensions, sometimes up to three feet wide. I have in my possession a witty little series of postcards poking fun at these huge hats with captions like, "When the elevator's crowded, what's the use to wait for that? Just make a parachute of your Merry Widow Hat."

For me, this hat was an act of rebellion. My father was an ornithologist. He was always more interested in the male birds since they are the ones with the spectacular plumage. One needs only to compare a peacock with a peahen to see that this is so. He did not keep secret the fact that he would have much preferred a son to a daughter or, at the very least, a daughter who was interested in enduring science instead of ephemeral art. One summer, when I was in my teens, I travelled to Chicago and visited the Art Institute there. Among the many amazing paintings I saw was an oil by Edgar Degas entitled *The Millinery Shop*. Perhaps you know it. The young woman in the painting is making a hat that resembles the exquisite shape and colour of a conch shell. She is wearing a plain brown dress and has pins in her mouth. But on the table beside her are the glorious hats one assumes are her own creations, a lovely flounced affair with a gorgeous bow the colour of apricots, another bearing a small garden of flowers and trailing loosely tied ribbons of pale green, and another all the colours of the sky. If the young woman in the plain brown dress donned any one of her own creations, people could not help but notice her.

And I thought that perhaps if I adorned myself with bright plumage like the birds my father loved, he would at last take notice of me, and indeed he did. He lectured me endlessly on how the vanity and arrogance of young women like me had driven some bird species to near extinction. He was right, of course. The Plume Boom in the early part of the twentieth century involved the death of hundreds of millions of birds the world over, but Virginia Woolf argued that while it might be women wearing birds, it was men who were killing them and reaping the profits. Breeding plumage is often the most elegant, so hunters killed adult birds, leaving chicks to starve, and feathers and entire wings were cut from living birds left to die. Egrets, herons, terns, entire songbirds on women's hats. Eventually laws were passed, but a letter supposedly "written" by 37 songbirds to the *Ladies' Home Journal* asks, "Will you make another, so that no one shall wear our feathers, so that no one will kill us to get them? We want them ourselves. Your pretty girls are pretty enough without them." And that's to say nothing of exotic birds from faraway places. I once saw a whole bird of paradise on a woman's hat.

I considered abandoning the wearing of hats, but decided ranting and raving were better than nothing, and by then I was hooked on millinery. The word itself came from Milan, known for its exquisite trimmings and accessories. A woman in a good hat possessed a certain panache even then, when walking down the street without one meant you were wretchedly poor, wildly eccentric or faintly obscene. Elegant hats are wearable artworks that draw the eye, as they do in that exquisite painting. Degas himself said, "Art is not what you see, but what you make others see." I desire for you this experience of elegance. When a woman wears a hat she makes a statement. This is who I am and who I want to be. People smile at her on the street. Complete strangers come up to her and strike up a conversation. Men take notice. I wanted you to discover the magic of transformation, as I did so many years ago. Yes, beauty has its price, but if it's any consolation, by the time this hat was made, the feathers on it would have been harvested humanely.

Peace by the sea,
PM

Hemingway had written in the *Toronto Star* about millinery driving some birds to extinction. But then milliners in Paris discovered the sparrow. The world would never run short of sparrows, he said. There were those who learned how to live with humans and those who didn't. Milan, the birthplace of millinery. Milan, the city where the young American lay hatless on his hospital bed, dreaming away his wounds. I thought about all the flying creatures that had been pierced by a hat pin like a butterfly. There was a bullfighting manoeuvre called a *Mariposa*, Spanish for butterfly: *a series of passes with the cape over the man's shoulders and the man facing the bull, zigzagging slowly backwards, drawing the bull on with a wave of first one side of the cape, then the other, supposedly imitating the flight of a butterfly.*

I walked over to the file cabinets on the back wall. They were locked, but the keys for them were hanging beside the cabinets on the wall with a tag that said "File Cabinets." I felt nervous about snooping, but the conviction that I had a right to know and the boldness of the magnificent hat I was wearing made me feel intrepid. I had always wanted to be intrepid. In a file labelled "McIlveen" there was one item, a copy of the letter that had been waiting for me at Honeysuckle Cottage. Nothing more. I went back to the lawyer's desk and pulled open the top drawer to find a wooden letter opener with a handle carved like a puffin, a box of chocolate-covered digestive biscuits and some mouthwash, as well as the expected office paraphernalia, paper clips, a stapler, pens, and pencils. I helped myself to some biscuits, and looked at my watch. Es would be home by now. That is if the *merde-mobile* hadn't broken down somewhere. First I called her cell, but no response. Then I called her landline. I got the answering machine. "Es, it's me. I'm in the lawyer's office. I told him I wouldn't leave until he gave me more information. Passive resistance. Like Gandhi, for God's sake. He refused, so I'm still here. Anyway, I'll call back in a bit. Hope you've made it home safe."

I thought about looking through all the drawers and the file cabinets, but since I had no idea what I was looking for, I didn't expect to find it. Also, I was beginning to feel vaguely guilty. "Maybe June knows something," I thought. I doubted it, but I had time to kill and it was worth a try. And I should really have let her know I was taking off, in case something happened.

"Hi, Mom, it's me. How are things?"

"Things are perking along." This was what my mother always said every time we spoke on the phone.

"You'll never guess where I'm calling from."

"You're not calling from Toronto?" She sounded surprised.

"No, Mom, I'm calling from Gannet Island."

"Gannet what?"

"Gannet Island in the Bay of Fundy."

"Oh, what are you doing there, dear?"

"I got a key in the mail that you forwarded to me. Es and I drove down yesterday and found the door it fits into. It was the door of a cottage. Anyway, there was a letter on the table saying I could have the cottage." I was aware as I said this in my most matter-of-fact voice how very bizarre it all sounded.

"My goodness."

"But there are strings attached. I have to wear hats."

There was a brief pause. "Well, that doesn't sound too bad. Don't look a gift horse in the mouth, I say."

"Mom, do you even know what that means?"

"Yes, I do know." June sounded a little hurt. "It means if someone gives you a horse as a present, you shouldn't check its teeth for cavities or something like that."

"So you don't have a clue about any of this? The key, the cottage, the hats."

"Not an inkling, dear. None of us have ever been east of Ottawa."

"Well, is there anyone who might know anything?"

"I'm afraid not." It was true. Relatives on both sides of the family were gone, my father was gone, and my mother had been an only child, like me.

"When are you coming back?"

"I'll let you know as things evolve," I said, more conviction in my voice than I felt. I hung up and swivelled the chair completely around. I played with the pendulum of silver balls, and ate some more digestive biscuits. Then I tried Es again on the phone. It was getting dark outside. The answering machine started to play the message, but halfway through, Es picked up the phone.

"Hello, Es. Is that you?"

"Pertice! *Comment ça hang?*"

"No one will tell me anything. I came to see the lawyer but he wouldn't give me any more information. I told him I wasn't going to leave unless he told me something. Eventually *he* left. I'm still in his office, using his phone."

"Wow, what are you going to do?"

"Wait, I guess. Maybe he'll see the error of his ways and come back. And you should see the new hat. It's crazy huge with feathers." I took it off and set it on the desk, the plumes glowing in the dim light. "How weird is that?"

"Well, something weird also happened to me on the way home." I braced myself. When Es was involved, "weird" encompassed quite a spectrum of possibility. "I was in a run-down diner off the Trans Canada in Quebec somewhere, drinking shitty coffee and feeling bad. Wishing I didn't have a bazillion more miles to drive. Wishing you were with me. Then suddenly, I smelled this smell...What can I say, Pertice, all the *misère* just seeped away. At first I didn't know what it was, it had been so long. Then I realized it was *tourtière*. Real *tourtière* smells so good because of the cinnamon and *noix de muscade*, how do you say it in English...nutmeg."

"*Noix de muscade*," I repeated, loving the way things sounded when Es said them in her own language. They sounded like poetry. Seat belt became *ceinture de sécurité*. Good bye became *au revoir*.

"You know, Pertice, when I was very small in Belle Vallée, back when the family was still together, my mother used to make *tourtière* on *la veille de Noël*, Christmas Eve. And we would eat after coming home from midnight mass. It was my favourite time of the year, everybody there happy and together, and Christmas morning still to look forward to. That was what that smell brought back." Es paused. "Pertice, are you still there?"

"I'm here."

"Anyway, I thought maybe I could make this happen for other people. You know, for a while people used to get their 'colours' done. My mom talked about it. If you didn't look absolutely amazing it was because you were a 'winter' dressing like a 'fall,' and you were wearing green and rust when you should have been wearing black and royal blue. And I thought I could maybe help people get their scents done, you know, what smells they feel good in. I could interview them to find out their scent history. People could even try on smell swatches, like cinnamon, or vanilla, or magnolia, or baby powder, or whatever it was that banished the *misère*. I could find out what smells made them happy, and find a way to package them up to send home with them. What do you think?"

Es was always coming up with schemes, artistic responses to people's needs, first Ongle Spangling, then Eschart, now this. It sounded hokey, and yet…when I was a child, there was a tree outside my bedroom window, a tree that was deeply fragrant for a few days in the spring just when the leaves were unfolding. It wasn't a floral smell, but it was still somehow sweet, insinuating its green and spicy self through the just opened window and between the tightly tucked white sheets that I slipped into each night. And outside of Ingersoll, there were still pockets of country scents you never came across in the city. Apple blossoms and wood smoke. All the delicious cooking smells you could replicate anywhere with the right ingredients, frying onions and spices. And now there was this dark new smell of the sea that had been in the twisted deep brown dulse offered to me by the stranger who had given me a lift to Grand Harbour. "Maybe you're on to something."

"And I even have a name. It came to me somewhere between Montreal and the border. Heaven Scent. You know, scent with a 'c.' Do you think that's too corny?"

"Maybe. But Es, I'm using the lawyer's phone. He's going to freak when he gets the long distance bill."

"Sorry."

"Wait. Someone's at the door. It's probably him. Maybe he's changed his mind." I set the receiver down and went into the reception

area. It wasn't Mr. James Flagg. It was an RCMP officer with a big
black flashlight. He motioned for me to open the door. I gestured a
"just a second" sign with an upheld finger and retreated back into the
office. "Es, I gotta go." I quickly hung up the phone and went to open
the door.

The officer wasn't any taller than me, but there was something
about the crispness of his haircut and uniform that was intimidating.
He looked at me while he banged his flashlight in his hand like it was
a billy club. "I'm afraid I'm going to have to ask you to leave," he said.
I could tell he wanted to comment on the hat sitting on the lawyer's
desk, but he restrained himself. He spoke with a French accent
though it was different than Es's accent. "Staying here is trespassing."
The yellow stripes on his black pants looked like the solid lines in the
center of the highway, the ones that mean no passing.

"I told Mr. Flagg I would leave if he gave me some information." I
didn't feel quite as brave now.

The officer's face was not unkind, but the brim of his hat cast a
shadow over his eyes. "So he told me."

"I just need some information."

"I understand that, Miss." By now he had gone into Mr. Flagg's
office and I followed.

"See, this key was sent to me out of the blue, and I don't know
anything about who sent it or why, and it's making me crazy, and then
there's these hats. He's the only one who can tell me anything, and he
won't."

"*Can't*, Miss. I talked to him and he said you know everything
he knows. He was instructed to type up that letter and leave it in the
house and wait for you to show up. And you did, eventually."

"Who instructed him?"

"The last person who rented the house. The papers were all in
order, and the fees were paid. But no forwarding address was left. Jim
tried to track down the person who made the arrangements but had
no luck."

"Well, who owned the house? Someone must know."

"I'm from the mainland, posted here only two years ago, and it's been empty all that time." He looked at his watch, one of those chronograph ones with the extra dials. "It's late. Can I give you a lift home?"

I looked around at the office of James & Flagg. There now seemed no point in lingering. There appeared to be nothing more to learn. I looked toward the officer, at the bison head on his insignia and the motto: *Maintiens le Droit*, Maintain the Law. "I used his phone."

"I'm sure he won't mind."

"I called long-distance, and I ate his biscuits." I pulled a twenty-dollar bill from my wallet, not one of the new see-through polymer ones, but an old paper one that featured *The Spirit of Haida Gwaii* with a quotation from Gabrielle Roy, *Could we ever know each other in the slightest without the arts?* I placed it on the lawyer's desk under the beach stone he used as a paper weight. I wanted desperately to put the Merry Widow back in its pink *Beau Chapeau* hatbox, and carry it, but I remembered what the lawyer said about people noticing what you do, so I put it on my head and placed the boater in the box. I looked at the officer with a helpless little shrug. He smiled, and I couldn't help smiling back.

The officer waited for me in his squad car while I picked up a few things at the convenience store. Again, I wanted desperately to leave the ridiculous hat behind me on the seat rather than wear it into the store, but I squared my shoulders and faced the inevitable. Surprisingly, the looks I received were more admiring than scornful. I overheard someone say, "It's the hat girl." When I came back out, he drove me back to Honeysuckle Cottage. This was what it meant to be in a small place. To depend on others. The officer was clearly doing more than his job of dealing with the trespasser. Above and beyond.

He took off his cap and set it on the seat between us. Without it, he looked very young. "The name's Belliveau," he said. "Thomas." He pronounced it Toe-ma, in the French way. He asked if I had power.

"No, everything was closed today because of the holiday. And someone told me I'd have to get an electrician to check things out before they could hook me up, anyway."

"Candles?"

"I forgot."

"You should take my flashlight then."

"Are you sure?"

"I've got another one back at the station."

Whether or not he was telling the truth, I needed his flashlight to fend off the darkness that was waiting for me inside. "Thank you," I said.

Officer Belliveau helped me carry my few groceries into the cottage, then he left. As I watched him drive away, fireworks lit up the horizon. Not wanting to drain the flashlight batteries, I crawled immediately into bed. Before falling asleep I thought about what Thomas the officer had told me about James the lawyer. Despite the ampersand, he had been telling the truth after all. But surely there were other things I could do: visit the real estate people on the island, put up posters, ask around. Check with the land registry. Maybe there was an ornithologists' union or society I could look up; although without a name, I couldn't imagine how that would help. There must be some kind of archives where obscure information was filed away. The hunt was on. Hemingway had loved to hunt birds as well as big game: *When you have shot one bird flying you have shot all birds flying. They are all different and they fly in different ways but the sensation is the same and the last one is as good as the first.* If you shot a bird on the wing, but did not see where it fell, things got difficult. A dog might find it, but even then there were so many factors that affected the chances, wind, terrain, even the amount of moisture in the air. Any hunt is risky business. Maybe there would be someone on the island who knew something about the elusive owner of the feathered hat, but for now the scent had grown cold, as if the pheasant had wandered into the sea.

Early the next morning a truck outside my window woke me. I opened the door to find a man whose eyebrows were so frizzy he looked like he'd stuck his finger in one too many sockets. "I'm Stanley, the electrician."

"How did you know…?" I began. The office to see about power had been closed because of the holiday. Stanley walked past me carrying a large toolbox. "The girl who served you at the lunch counter is my niece. She called me up and said you'd need looking after."

"Oh," I said. And he was off, looking at the fuse box, and checking for junction boxes and behind switch plates. "If the power has been off for more than a year, you have to have someone look things over before they'll hook you up," he explained. A half hour later he was done. "Everything is old-fashioned but in good shape. Knob and tube is a good system, despite what the insurance companies say. Works great as long as you don't mess with it." He would give the power company the go-ahead, he said, and they would be out to connect things at the meter, but he couldn't promise when. "Fellers might have to come over from the mainland."

The amount on the bill startled me. Stanley didn't even fix anything and still it came to a lot. I would have to make some decisions soon, since the journalism degree had eaten up almost all my savings. My parents always drilled into me to "save for a rainy day." I wasn't even sure what that meant, or whether relocating to an island in the middle of nowhere would qualify.

At the convenience store in Grand Harbour, I had purchased markers and construction paper to make posters. Maybe it would have made more sense to make one poster and photocopy it, but there wasn't much to write. WANTED: INFORMATION ABOUT THE ORIGINAL OWNER OF HONEYSUCKLE COTTAGE, COVE ROAD, NORTH HEAD. Beneath this I drew a quick silhouette of a head with a question mark in it. Then, on second thought, I got a new sheet and drew a silhouette with a head with a hat on it. The drawing was crude, but you had to have something to catch people's eye. What about contact information? The place to arrange getting the phone hooked up had been closed yesterday, along with almost everything else. There was an old-fashioned telephone on the wall with a dial like the kind secretaries in old movies used to turn with pencils to save their elegant fingernails. On a whim, I picked up the receiver, like you press the elevator button even though you know it has already been pressed. I was expecting it to be dead, but there was a dial tone. Just a little creepy. Maybe that was also the work of the waitress, Stanley's niece, or perhaps the RCMP officer, worried in case I had some kind of emergency. This would take some getting used to. Yesterday, I had been told there was no such a thing as long distance on the island. It was all local.

There was a typed phone number on the centre of the dial and I put this number on the posters I was making. "I have to stay until I get to the bottom of this," I said to myself, knowing this meant, among other things, trying to find work. "No time like the present," my mother always said. Since I was heading out to look for work, I would use the opportunity to put up my posters. "Kill two birds with one stone," my mother would say. I always hated that phrase. It seemed unlikely and vicious. Armed with my posters, a box of thumbtacks, and wearing my ridiculous feathered hat, I set out, tacking a poster to every fifth telephone pole. Maybe it had been a mistake to wear the only skirt I brought with me because the wind kept filling it like a sail. But it made sense to dress up a little because I was hunting for a job and because the hat looked kind of insane with casual clothes like jeans. I couldn't afford to look insane.

I walked right by Captain's fish and burger place. That would be a last resort for job hunting. I couldn't imagine going back to sweating over a deep fryer and a grill as I had at Carnivores. Looking at raw meat all day had been a chore. At Carnivores they brought in the ground beef by the garbage bag, and if things weren't too busy, it was part of my job to make giant patties. But that much meat, dark pink and marbled with fat, always made me feel a little nauseous. On those days I would go home and eat only salad while reading a book about edible flowers that I picked up in a used book shop around the corner from my apartment. Angelica, Bee Balm, Chive…. Yes, Captain's was definitely a last resort.

Instead, my first stop on the job hunt was The Compass Rose Restaurant, a picturesque Cape Cod, painted mariner's blue with a roof of weathered cedar shingles. "I'm looking for work," I said to the waitress who greeted me as I took off my hat and hung it on one of the hooks by the door. I would have to check into the etiquette of this sort of thing. When you remove your hat and when you don't. And do women doff? I had read somewhere that raising your hat came from the medieval custom of lifting the visor of your armour to be recognized by friends. I wanted to be recognized by friends.

"I'll get the manager. Please have a seat." The windows were open to the sea and the tables had bouquets of white flowers tinged with pink and a multitude of pale feathery leaves, flowers I had never seen before, flowers we had not picked for the brim of my boater. "She'll be a moment," the waitress said, reappearing from behind doors that swung both ways and had windows like portholes. I asked about the flowers, but she didn't know the name of them.

While I waited, I looked at the artistic renderings of the restaurant hanging on all four sides of the central pillar that supported the ceiling. There were artistic interpretations in oil, watercolour, pen and ink, pastel, even crayon. Some were very detailed and realistic, and some were much more abstract, even cubist, and one was quite Chagall-like with a lobster floating in the sky next to the sun. Odd that artists go to a place to paint it, while writers go to a place to write the place they have left behind. I thought of Hemingway sitting in a good café on the Place St. Michel writing about Michigan and because it was a wild, cold, blowing day in Paris, it became that kind of day in the story.

"Those are musk mallow," the manager said, gesturing toward the flowers. "But I'm sorry; all our positions are already filled for the summer."

"Okay, thank you," I said, moving toward the door. "Would you have a place to hang this?" I asked, offering the manager a poster.

"No, I'm afraid not," she said. It was going to be a long day. I retrieved my hat and looked at the framed definition of a Compass Rose in tilting calligraphy that hung near the cash register and the bowl of mints. *The circular dial resting on the pivot of a mariner's compass on which the 32 points and 360 degrees are marked.* In the city, when you thought about directions at all, you made do with four, which meant that all the rest were wasted. On the ocean, traversing an invisible topography, you must make use of all the petals of the rose.

"You could try at Aristotle's Lantern," the manager suggested. I thanked her and left.

It had started to rain lightly and already the posters I put up were bleeding in the wet. Last night I had intended to purchase permanent markers, but conscious that there was an RCMP officer waiting for me in his squad car, I hurried. Consequently my message was already washing away. Across the road, a woman was trying madly to get the laundry in from the clothesline before it got wet all over again. All the items of the same colour were grouped together, giving the effect of a moving rainbow. Coming up from the ferry, we had seen clothes flapping from almost every yard. I knew of Toronto neighbourhoods where you had to sign a covenant promising you wouldn't put up a clothesline because they were considered unsightly, but here everyone used one. Why not, when wind and sun are free?

I walked up away from the shore, worrying about what would happen to my hat if it started to rain in earnest. I knocked on the door of Aristotle's Lantern as I had done two days previously when Es had been with me. Had it only been two days? "I'm sorry, there's no vacancy," the woman said, obviously not remembering me. It was the hat. People remember the hat, not the face. They had proved this with bank robbers.

"No, actually, I'm looking for work."

"Ah well, do come in. My name is Charlotte. Can I get you something? Coffee maybe? Cappuccino?"

"Yes, that would be good."

"Sit, sit," Charlotte said, pointing at a wicker chair in the sunroom that had windows on three sides and plants everywhere. She disappeared and I could hear the whir of fresh beans being ground, and then she reappeared. "It'll be just a minute. So, what did you have in mind?"

"I can cook," I said, thinking of Es recommending the house dressing at Carnivores.

"Really? How did you learn to cook?"

I felt I ought to be able to say I had apprenticed at a posh Toronto restaurant, or taken a course at a community college, or learned at my grandmother's knee, but what came out of my mouth was "Persimmons."

"I beg your pardon?"

"One day when I was grocery shopping, a tray of persimmons ended up in my cart. I didn't remember putting them there; they just appeared. Maybe someone else put them there by accident, thinking it was their cart. You know how that happens sometimes. Anyway, I was going to put them back in the produce area, when I decided to buy them after all. They were a very beautiful shade of orange."

"Yes, cadmium orange, I know that shade," Charlotte said, nodding.

"When I got them home, I didn't know what to do with them, so I dug out the two-volume *Joy of Cooking* my mother had given me when I was going away to university. It says on the cover, *The Cookbook You Will Use Forever*. I think that's what appealed to her. She's very thrifty. Anyway, up to that point, I had never cracked the cover, but there was, amazingly, a recipe for persimmons, Japanese Persimmon Salad. I tried it, and it was delicious. I might not have tried persimmons, you know, but I'm a Hemingway aficionado and he would eat anything: sea slugs, bird's nests, one-hundred-year-old eggs, mule meat, which he said was somewhere between boiled moccasin and tallow candles, even poison ivy once on a bet. And after that I started being more adventurous and trying all those odd things from faraway places you can buy now in grocery stores. Especially in Toronto, where I live, you can get any kind of cuisine in the world. And then I got a job as a cook in a restaurant, where I was especially known for my salad dressings." This was more than I intended to say, but something about Charlotte and the informality of a job interview without paperwork of any kind pushed me to let my guard down.

"I see," said Charlotte, rising to check on the coffee.

I looked down at my hands. I had talked too much, but I hadn't even got into what an epiphany this had been. Not that Japanese Persimmon Salad had changed my life, but well, yes, Japanese Persimmon Salad *had* changed my life. It had opened a door. Like in that Isak Dinesen story about how Babette's feast made people raised on gruel believe that the stars had come nearer and grace was infinite.

Charlotte came back with painted pottery mugs sitting on a tray beside a little white pitcher filled with extra cream. Except for the overalls, she looked like the little woman with a tray that appears on each square of Baker's Chocolate. Her long grey hair was in braids like a girl's. Taking a sip of the aromatic coffee that was worlds away from what I had been served by the ampersand lawyer, I felt I was in good hands. Charlotte had even taken the time to make a lovely leaf shape in the froth. "Sorry to go on like that. It's just that in my house, when I was growing up, food was so functional, you know. You ate so you didn't starve, and that was about it. Food was prepared as quickly and cheaply as possible, and you didn't even realize there was a better way. Alcohol, too, was frowned on, because my father always maintained that it made you weak, that it made you do things you would never do sober. With my mother I suspect it was part of the thrift thing." I was nervous and still talking too much, but I couldn't seem to stop. Charlotte had that listening way about her. "The first time I had crêpes Suzette at a restaurant," I continued, "I was so torn. I was longing to try them but I didn't realize the flames burned away the alcohol. I had been pumped so full of fear that I felt sure it was the first step down the slippery slope, and that I might end up destitute on the street drinking aftershave. They were so good and I couldn't even enjoy them." Charlotte laughed. "Later I heard that recipe was invented by a nervous Parisian chef lighting Prince Edward's crêpes on fire by mistake." There it was. All the delicious things that happen by accident. Someone else's persimmons in my shopping cart. Someone else's hat on my head."

"Well," Charlotte said, "we're into the busy time of year, so perhaps I could use a hand in the kitchen. My daughter used to help me in summer but she's moved to Fort McMurray where her husband got work. We really only serve breakfasts and afternoon tea, but we need sweets."

"I can do sweets," I said, thinking of how grateful I would be to leave behind the Carnivores' instructions for Death by Chocolate.

"Let me show you the kitchen." The pine kitchen cupboards were painted with brightly hued birds which looked like they were flying when the doors were opened quickly. "My husband's an artist," said Charlotte. "I'm sorry; I didn't catch your name."

"Pertice."

"Ah, well, this is it. Not very fancy, I'm afraid."

"It's lovely." It would be wonderful to cook here, surrounded by the painted birds and all the flourishing green plants and the well-used but shining surfaces. The flour was stored in an old-fashioned bin that pulled out like a drawer. And when Charlotte pushed open the screen door from the kitchen into the backyard, there was a herb garden laid out like a compass rose.

"Could you start tomorrow?"

"Yes, I could."

"I'm afraid I can only pay minimum wage and, if things work out, a percentage of the tips."

"That would be fine." I hadn't been getting much more than that in Toronto, and there the cost of living had been crazy. Seeing things were drawing to a close, I asked the question that had been on my mind since I had first heard the name of the bed and breakfast. "I've been dying to ask. Where did the name Aristotle's Lantern come from?"

"Of course. Shall I show you one?" Charlotte reached to her throat where a tiny ivory carving hung on a black cord. "My daughter Fay carved this one. Can you guess what it is?" I looked carefully at the carving that was about the size of a thimble and looked like those old-fashioned lanterns that hung from poles on the decks of ships with metal ribs holding panes of glass. "Let me show you one *in situ*." Charlotte walked over to a bookshelf by the door that held a collection of little found objects. She hadn't been wearing the glasses she was wearing the first time I saw her, but she put them on now. "My Gandhi glasses," she said as she picked up the shell of a sea urchin with one side broken away, and there was the little bone lantern upside down in the very centre. "It's actually the jaws of the sea urchin, fifty little bones that work together to scrape the algae from the rocks."

I turned over the tiny sea urchin to examine the star-shaped aperture that I could see would work something like the claws that pick up crushed cars in a scrap yard. "But what about the name?"

"Aristotle didn't just write the *Poetics*," Charlotte said, showing me other specimens. "He also wrote about natural history. Apparently, he was the first to describe the mouth of a sea urchin as a lantern, and the name stuck, I guess. And when it came to naming this place, we thought it was appropriate. We wanted something nautical but not too cliché."

"It's perfect," I said, thinking about the fifty bones gathering the green like the fifty little towns we had driven through to get here.

"My daughter also carved these." There in the glass case were exquisite little carvings of a panther stooping to drink, a horse, a laughing Buddha. "It's illegal to use elephant ivory now, so these are carved from fossil ivory. Mastodon tusks from Siberia, if you can believe it." Charlotte laughed. "That doesn't exactly make them affordable, needless to say. But she recently hit on a brilliant idea. She recycles the ivory veneer off old piano keys to make these." Charlotte handed me a smooth black stone with the flat outlines of two ivory whales cavorting. "They make great paper weights." I remembered the one I had seen on the lawyer's desk. Looking at this transformation, I suddenly missed Es. How like her, this ability to turn what was discarded or ruined into art. "I think she has the gift, don't you?" Charlotte didn't say, "a gift," she said "*the* gift."

"Yes," I answered, not entirely certain of the distinction.

"And she can talk to horses. If anyone on the island lost a horse, they called on her. She knew how to find them and bring them home." This was unusual information. Even if you had one of those old-fashioned roll-top desks with all the little pigeonholes and tiny drawers and secret places it would be hard to decide where to put such information. I didn't know what to say, so I didn't say anything at all. I wondered if my own parents had ever talked about me this way, with such pride and awe.

"That's a portrait of her when she was small. I miss her terribly." Charlotte gathered herself. "If you'd like, you could make something for this afternoon's tea, just to get your feet wet." This is what happened while I watched Es disappear around the point, the tide rising over my toes. I had gotten my feet wet. I glanced at my watch. It was nearly noon.

"I can whip us up something for lunch while you decide on what you want to bake," Charlotte said, handing me a well-used recipe book. "That's the one I usually use; maybe you'll find something that tickles your fancy. You can look it over while I make the sandwiches."

The book contained "Island-tested recipes," and was, as it said on the cover, "compiled by the cooks of Gannet Island" who had unfamiliar old-fashioned names like Beulah, Hattie, Eunice, Hazel and Eudervilla. And I thought the name Pertice was hard to live with! I began to leaf through the cookbook, beginning with the opening page which featured an ode to the herring by Alfred Percival Graves.

> Let all the fish that swim the sea,
> Salmon and turbot, cod and ling,
> Bow down the head, and bend the knee,
> To herring, their King!

I had never heard of Alfred Percival Graves but expected he was a Maritime equivalent of James McIntyre of my own home town in Ontario who was famous for his "Ode on the Mammoth Cheese." The real-life cheese he had been celebrating measured three feet high and seven feet in diameter and weighed over 7000 pounds. After it was made in 1866, it travelled to Toronto, New York, and England. I still remembered the first few lines of the poem.

We have seen thee, queen of cheese,
Lying quietly at your ease,
Gently fanned by evening breeze,
Thy fair form no flies dare seize.

The pages that followed the ode to the herring in the cookbook were filled with lots of recipes for things that I had never heard of like Finnan Haddie and Shrimp Wiggle, Pork Cake and Whoopy Pies. There were special sections entitled "Sauces for Fish," and "Cordials and Jams." There was even a section entitled "Helpful Household Hints" including tips like: "When putting curtain rods in freshly ironed curtains, place thimble or finger from an old glove over the rod and the curtain will slip on easily without tearing," or "When cooking cauliflower place it head first and it will keep white."

Charlotte came back with the sandwiches on a tray. "Find anything interesting?"

"A few things," I said truthfully. I was about to close the book when a title in the "Cordials and Jams" section caught my eye. "Honeysuckle Syrup." It was a simple recipe with only two ingredients, three if you counted the water: "Four pounds of fresh honeysuckle petals* infused in eight pints of boiling water and twice the weight of sugar." The asterisk directed you to an ominous warning that appeared at the bottom of the recipe. "Use only the flowers. Green foliage and berries are poisonous." It was submitted by a PM. I had noticed that some of the other recipes in the book were submitted by initials rather than names, and I assumed that it could be men submitting recipes to what might be considered a woman's endeavour. But then again, I had seen a fisherman knitting on the deck of his boat, so maybe a man wouldn't need to hide behind initials. Some things were more traditional here, but some things were less. It would make sense if people did what they were good at. But there was still something about the title of this recipe that sounded so much like the home I had inherited. This and the fact that the initials were my own made me wonder if this was my PM.

"Who's PM?" I asked.

"Actually, I don't know what the initials stand for. People just called her Miss M. That was how she introduced herself to people. I guess her name was foreign and hard to pronounce. She came here first as a rusticator. That's what islanders used to call the ones from away who summered here. You know, people from big cities who find the island quaint and inspiring. They come to write or paint or enjoy the sea and then they go away again. At first they love the silence and then they hate it." Charlotte paused. "Anyway, Miss M bought a cottage over on Cove Road to live in when she retired.

"Honeysuckle Cottage?"

"It does have honeysuckle growing all over the place."

"What happened to her?"

"I'm not sure. Apparently she couldn't stand the winters, so she rented it out after that. Small faraway places take a little more courage in winter. As far as I know, she never came back, not even in summer. That was soon after we got here, and we've been here for two decades. Come to think of it, someone stopped by a few days ago asking about the cottages with the names over that way."

"That was me," I said.

"I'm sorry, I was distracted."

I looked down at my sandwich of homemade molasses brown bread with sliced turkey, tomatoes, and fresh mesclun greens picked no doubt from the compass rose out back. It looked delicious but my appetite had slipped away. My head felt like the inside of a pumpkin, that jumble of seeds and stringy orange tangles so complex they make cat's cradle look like child's play. "PM." Could this be the clue I had been waiting for, appearing after "Green foliage and berries are poisonous" like a postscript that promised everything and said nothing? How to place Miss M *in situ*, that phrase Charlotte had used about the mouth that was also a lantern? How to put Miss M in a context that had meaning? "Do you know anything else?" I asked. "I would be grateful for any details."

"That's about all I know," Charlotte said. "I once tried to make an overture." That's what Charlotte called it, as if it was the opening of an opera. "But she wouldn't answer the door. She kept entirely to herself. She even submitted that recipe for Honeysuckle Syrup to the book by mail rather than in person, so I never actually met her, even though I was on the committee. I did see her out walking once or twice." Charlotte paused and looked at me carefully. "Come to think of it, she was a little like you. She wore hats."

Even though I was not really any nearer to my destination, I felt I was at least on my way after what Charlotte told me. Miss M had been as much a stranger to the people of the island as she was to me, but her cottage began to feel more like home when words were added. Es boxed up and sent the things I had left behind in Toronto, the magnetic poetry kit from my fridge, my books (Hemingway mostly, some cookbooks, and other favourites), and what I call my toolkit, in which I keep the special little utensils that I use when cooking, like a zester for making citrus shavings, an olive spoon, a pastry crimper, a melon baller like a kayak paddle with a scoop on either end so one could cover a range of melons from cantaloupe to water, my mezzaluna, and my mandoline. Charlotte helped me find the rest of what I needed. When she first asked if I wanted to go sailing, I eagerly said yes, with visions of white canvas snapping in the wind or a colourful spinnaker swelling like the bosom of an opera singer. It turned out Charlotte meant yard sales, not the kind of sails that take you out to sea, but she made it fun, questing for a kitchen gadget or an outfit like knights for a grail.

Since that first day talking with Charlotte, I had not made any progress on the mystery of Miss M. The words on the posters washed away and I retraced my steps, taking them all down. No one had responded, not even to the ones that had been posted indoors, safe from weather. Maybe I should have offered a reward, but what reward could I offer? All that I knew, Charlotte told me that first day I was hired. No one except Charlotte remembered Miss M. Twenty years was a long time. People said Serena, a woman who lived in the old folks' home in Castalia, might remember more, but when I went to see her, it turned out she had Alzheimer's and couldn't really put any

significant details together except that there was a woman who would
yell at trespassers, even at anyone who rowed by, as if even the water
belonged to her. "No one owns the ocean," said the old woman. She
would not answer any of the questions that I put to her. She only
wanted to talk about the hats. "I remember the most glorious hats,"
she would say. Then she held her veined and wrinkled hand closer to
her mouth and said in a conspiratorial whisper, "I coveted those hats."

I had been intending to get to the museum in Grand Harbour to
see if there was anything in the archives that might shed light, but I was
still without transportation, except a bicycle I picked up second-hand,
one of the old-fashioned ones that didn't even have handbrakes so
you had to pedal in reverse to stop. I did call the museum and explain
my situation, but no one could find anything useful. The archives had
mostly to do with islanders born and bred, said the woman on the other
end of the line, with little about rusticators, unless they happened to
be famous. Also, two letters, a P and an M, weren't very much to go
on. I got in touch with the land registry office on the mainland to see
about the ownership deed, but it was held in the name of a numbered
company so I was no farther ahead. I tried to remember everything I
had learned about investigative journalism, researching, interviewing,
and gathering facts. I kept notes of everything I tried, but it was always
a dead end, or *cul-de-sac*, as Es would say. I had reached the "back of
the bag" and it contained nothing.

Meanwhile, life had a way of filling up the spaces. I found myself
busy with work at Aristotle's Lantern, rising while it was still dark to
bake croissants, brioches, and other breads for breakfast, and island
goodies. I put in eight-hour days, leaving only after everything was set
up for afternoon tea. Working with Charlotte did not feel like work
at all. She was a wonderful kitchen companion, chatting about her
daughter Fay, about the books she was reading, about art and ideas.
She was a wonderful listener and seemed genuinely interested in the
stories I had to tell. We talked and laughed while we cooked. I had
learned a lot on my own about making food delicious, but Charlotte
taught me a great deal about making it beautiful. She would not let a

plate alone until it was a work of art with garnishes, and I don't just
mean a sprig of mint or an artful drizzle of raspberry coulis. I learned
how to make chocolate filigree, and tuiles, and marzipan. I learned
how to candy flowers: pansies, violets, begonias, Johnny-jump-
ups, rose petals, and scented geraniums. People say "presentation is
everything" but Charlotte preferred Einstein's version: "Imagination
is everything." She had two elegant sets of china dishes and one of
clear green glass. She had a silver tea service, a three-tiered tray for
displaying both savoury and sweet, and a seemingly infinite number
of pretty teacups. She had lace tablecloths and linen napkins. She
had hand-painted pottery bowls and trays of wood and hammered
pewter and brass. In Toronto I had a few bits of mismatched Corelle
in discontinued patterns and one ugly mug with a mended handle that
I used for coffee to get me through late nights, so this kind of elegance
was a revelation.

Charlotte's husband was away on the mainland, teaching courses.
I asked her what it was like to be the wife of an artist. I had been
thinking of Hadley Hemingway, and all the other women who built
the nests their husbands came home to. "There's lots of ways to be
an artist," Charlotte said. And I understood then that she meant
gardens and garnishes, kids and kindness, listening and love. "He's my
eyes," Charlotte said, with a sweeping gesture toward the paintings all
around us, "but I'm his ears."

My days with Charlotte were long, but they started early and
ended early. After work there was time to walk. I explored much of
my end of the island, wearing the merry widow if the weather was
good. I found, though, that I couldn't just pull my hair back in a
ponytail as I had always done, because the hat didn't sit right then,
so I experimented with different ways of putting my hair up, buns,
braids, and chignons, sometimes even leaving it down altogether. I
also found I had to make adjustments in what I wore for the rest of
my outfit to suit the hat; I found myself wearing things other than
jeans — flowing skirts I picked up at yard sales, a graceful dress with a
scooped neck and lots of buttons and tailored, slim-fitting pants with

zippers at the side or back, which I ordered by phone from the Sears catalogue. When I was younger the catalogue had awful fashions from what I could remember, flowered dresses built like tents, and pages and pages of girdles in white and beige, but now there were things that were quite stylish, things Es might even approve of, in a pinch. Shoes were an issue still. At work I still wore the *cauchemars*, the nightmares, as Es used to call the black shoes I wore at Carnivores, but I purchased a good pair of walking sandals for tromping around. They weren't elegant exactly but they weren't horrendous either. For the first time I began to feel my body was a walking canvas rather than just a satchel of skin my mind had to lug around. For the first time I felt sensual rather than sensible.

After it got dark, I would read one of the books from Charlotte's overflowing bookshelves, since there was no television, and apparently reception was not great anyway, unless you had a dish. Cable didn't come this far. Just as well. Who needs crime news from Detroit and smog reports from Toronto, anyway? There was always CBC radio for what was going on across the nation and around the world. At the end of the day, I would fall into bed, bone tired but in a good way. If I couldn't sleep, I'd stare at my clock radio until the red dot moved from PM to AM. On these nights I'd think long and hard about what the letters PM might stand for. *Post Meridiem. Prime Minister. Post Master. Police Magistrate. Post Mortem. Pertice McIlveen.* I'd ponder sweet flowers and poison berries. I'd wonder what I was doing here at the edge of the world, wearing hats. Some evenings, I made notes about the things I had seen and done, and imagined articles I might write and where I might send them. Maybe there was even a book on Hemingway that had not yet been written. For the most part, I tried to foster the habit of happiness, which Hemingway said was rare in intelligent people.

Sometimes, on warm nights, with the scent of the sea heavy in the air and a cool breeze off the water, I'd go outside and lie on my back in the grass and look at the stars. In Toronto, with all the light pollution and the other kind of pollution, you could barely see the stars, but here they seemed to jump towards you out of the crisp black sky. I never really learned how to find the constellations, except the obvious ones like Orion and the Big Dipper, but thought it was something I might look into. This was the way to look at stars, lying on your back with the sky spread over you like a bowl, like the planetarium at the Royal Ontario Museum, except real. There were, I was discovering, many things the island did better than Toronto, the foremost being seafood and stars. I went to bed reluctantly and gazed up at the bare white ceiling, cracked from the settling over the years. It would be good to lie in bed and star gaze. What I needed was a skylight.

3
DEERSTALKER

When I finally make a decision, I have to act quickly, before I get cold feet. I had no idea what a skylight would cost, but it was bound to be expensive. Ordinarily, the only thing I spend money on willingly is food and related paraphernalia. Even books I mostly get from the library, but I was determined to look at the stars inside and out. Es had been reading Van Gogh's letters, and every time we talked on the phone, she'd quote him. Yesterday it was: *Be clearly aware of the stars and infinity on high. Then life seems almost enchanted after all.*

I asked Charlotte if she could recommend someone to do the work for me. "Here's the number you asked for, Persimmon," Charlotte said, handing me a piece of paper. The first day I showed up for work, Charlotte accidentally called me Persimmon because of the story I'd told her about the Japanese Persimmon Salad and it stuck. I didn't think I would like having a nickname, but I didn't mind it from Charlotte.

"Thanks," I said, folding the paper and putting it in my pocket.

"I'm afraid there isn't much choice," Charlotte said. "That's the trouble with a small place; there's usually only one of everything. One doctor, one lawyer, one plumber, one electrician, like it or lump it. Except mechanics, that is. We have loads of them to keep the boat engines in order. With the rest you take your chances."

That night I called the number Charlotte had given me. The man on the other end of the line said he would have to order the skylight from the mainland.

"Hinged or fixed?"

"What's the difference?"

"One opens and one doesn't."

"It would be nice to be able to open it, I guess." He said that if he got right on it, he might be able to have it sent over on the first ferry.

"Don't you have to measure or something?"

"These things are pretty standard, and if there's a problem, we'll cross that bridge when we come to it."

"It's for the bedroom, right over the bed." It felt weird saying this to a stranger, but if he thought it odd, I didn't hear it in his voice. I couldn't tell from his voice how old he was.

"Okay then, I'll get on it. I can install it on Thursday morning."

"I'll be at work then," I said.

"Just leave the door open." This would be a ludicrous request in the city, but here it seemed to make perfect sense. You could just leave the door unlocked and trust that only the right person would make his way in. "All right then," he said, after I gave him instructions to Honeysuckle Cottage.

When I got home from work on Thursday, there was a truck in the driveway. I could hear the hammering as I entered the cottage. I threw my bag on the table and opened the door to the bedroom. A drop cloth had been draped over the dresser and the bed to prevent them from becoming covered in plaster dust. It gave the room a kind of theatrical look, as if a play were about to take place. The bed was pushed up against the wall, and there was a ladder in the middle of the room.

I looked up through the new window in my ceiling and saw a man's torso. It was a hot day and the man was not wearing a shirt, just jeans, and his torso was muscled and tanned. Vertical, this image might have seemed like a cliché, but horizontal, it was quite a bit like art. Suddenly Honeysuckle Cottage became the Sistine Chapel, and I was looking up at the formidable chest of the first man. I knew the Sistine ceiling had once been painted blue flecked with gold stars, but when the foundation settled, a deep crack opened the length of the vault. When it came time to repair the broken place and cover up the repairs with a new coat of paint, Michelangelo was called in. This was the kind of useless information that lodged in my brain. I did not collect it intentionally. It just seemed to build up like the flotsam and jetsam that gather around a branch fallen in a stream. Maybe I inherited this from my archivist father, or maybe it was just something that happened to people who read a lot.

I walked outside and looked up, putting my hand on my Merry Widow to keep it from falling off. I was afraid of heights, so I admired his agility in working on the steep pitch. After watching the stranger on my roof for a few minutes, I called up to him, softly so as not to startle him. "How's it going?"

"Just got to seal the edge with caulking," he said, "and I'm done for now." After watching for a few more minutes, I went inside to make some lemonade, the way I like it best, freshly squeezed with lots of sugar and ice, and the lemon half put right in the glass. There was a farmer's market on the island where you could buy local produce and dulse, but anything exotic has to be brought over by ferry, so it was a bit of a luxury to use lemons in this extravagant way. But I just can't do without lemons and garlic. I keep a whole garland of garlic hanging from a nail on the wall and a bowl of lemons on the kitchen table like a bouquet.

By the time the stranger came into the house, he had put his shirt back on but had not buttoned it. I got the sense that he knew his chest might have interested Michelangelo, but I did not begrudge him this. It surprised me though. I was never really drawn to the good-looking ones, preferring the smart ones and the funny ones. But here was a man who was good-looking in an artistic sort of way standing with his shirt open in my kitchen. He ran a hand through his dark curls. Behind one ear he had a pencil that had been sharpened with a knife. He looked Greek, or maybe he was just tanned from working out of doors. "Luke," he said.

"Pertice," I said, extending my hand.

"Nice hat."

"Thanks. Would you like some lemonade?"

"Sure, unless you got beer. That's thirsty work."

"Sorry. Wine?"

He shook his head. "Lemonade, I guess." As he reached out his hand to take the lemonade, I noticed he wore a silver ring with a black X on it, like the X on a map that marks a treasure, a pirate treasure. He looked at the glass I handed him with the half lemon still in it, and took a tentative sip. "My mom always gets the pink stuff." He paused and then said, "You're not from here."

It was a statement not a question, though I responded to it as if it were. "No, I'm from a small town in Ontario called Ingersoll." I thought if I said I was from the big city, the price might go up. I took off my hat and put it on the table.

"That anywhere near Toronto?"

"Not too far."

"That's where I'm headed. I figure there'd be a lot of work for a renovation specialist like me." This seemed a step up from a roofer, which is what Charlotte had called him. "Then I wouldn't have to run my life by the bloody tides."

"I lived in Toronto before moving down here," I said, thinking he would do well in the big city where everyone got weary of things quickly, changing the look of their houses almost as often as they changed their clothes. You couldn't blame them really, when so much money and effort was invested in convincing people that what they already had was not good enough.

Luke walked back to the bedroom to get his ladder and tidy up. He tossed me one end of the drop sheet so I could help fold it. Most of the men I had met on the island seemed so weathered and shy, and here was someone ambitious and aware of his own good looks. He moved with ease and suppleness. Lissom. That was the word. "I'll come back and fix up the ceiling for you. I got another job lined up, so I should get going. See you around."

"How much do I owe you?" I asked, fishing in my bag for my chequebook.

"I'll catch you next time," he said.

On the first day of September I was back at the lawyer's office in Grand Harbour awaiting my new hat. He handed me a striped hatbox that was half the size of the box for the Merry Widow I had left at home in anticipation of something new. "Aren't you going to open it?" he asked.

"Here?" I looked at him and realized he was as curious as I was about what was inside. I lifted the lid to find a double-visored Sherlock Holmes hat. The fabric was Harris tweed in a houndstooth check of beige and forest green, with a touch of rust. The earflaps were tied up with matching beige grosgrain ribbon, and the label on the lining said "Dunn & Co, Great Britain" under the crest and motto of London, *Domine Dirige Nos.*

"Oh…" Mr. Flagg said, sounding a little disappointed, as I released the clip that held my hair up in a chignon, and put the man's hat on my head. "Does it come with a magnifying glass and pipe?"

I laughed, but I too felt a little disappointed. After a month of wearing a spectacular plumed Merry Widow, I was getting used to being noticed when I walked into a room, to being referred to as the Hat Girl. "See you next month," I said. I would save the letter for later. Clearly the lawyer hadn't realized there was one included with each hat.

As I cycled home, the cold wind found its way through my thin jacket. I stopped and undid the ribbon on my new hat, appreciating the warmth of the earflaps. That was the thing about men's hats. They were so functional. Women's hats and bodies were appreciated as ornaments, but men's hats and bodies were instruments. This was something new.

Dear Pertice,

My father wore this hat while birding, which he considered detective work of the highest order. It is called a deerstalker because it was used in rural areas for hunting, the checked pattern serving as camouflage, with the dual brims providing protection from the sun. We now think of birding as an innocent activity with binoculars or a camera, but once birders were hunters. Take a look at portraits of John James Audubon if you don't believe me. He is almost always pictured with a gun. Before binoculars and the zoom lens became commonplace, the only way to look at a bird close up was to shoot it. Audubon became famous for painting the birds he shot as if they were still alive. He visited White Head Island, one of Gannet's small outlying islands, in 1833. He was hosted by William Frankland, father of fifteen, who was a ship's carpenter and Bay of Fundy pilot. Audubon's glowing descriptions of the rich bird life around the island inspired many other naturalists to follow in his footsteps, including my father. I was told that 363 species of birds have been identified on the Gannet Island archipelago. That's just two shy of a bird for every day of the year.

You will, no doubt, associate this hat with Sherlock Holmes, though Arthur Conan Doyle never actually made specific reference to a deerstalker in any of his stories, referring only to his "ear-flapped travelling cap." I noticed that the latest movie portrayal of Sherlock Holmes set in London doesn't include his deerstalker, which is appropriate since Holmes never would have worn a rural hat in an urban setting. My father, who was as fastidious as Holmes, wouldn't have either. But I must admit I miss the deerstalker. Who is Holmes without the hat? In her poem "The Man-Moth" Elizabeth Bishop says, "The whole shadow of Man is only as big as his hat." Hats still carry powerful associations, but this was even more true in the past. "Chapeaugraphy" was the name they gave early vaudeville acts based on these associations. The performer had only a large felt hat brim with a hole in the middle instead of a crown, and he would twist this brim into different styles of hat, and make the expression to match. A good chapeaugraphy performer like Felicien Trewey of France, who packed theatres on two continents, could create as many as thirty-five different characters. My father created only two.

Peace by the Sea,
PM

A few days later, Luke showed up again. This time his shirt was buttoned up and he was wearing a baseball cap. After he finished mudding the ceiling, I offered him a beer. By this time I had stocked up. "Let's go sit outside," he said. I pushed open the screen door to the front of the cottage that faced the sea, but he did not follow me.

I hesitated, gesturing in the direction of the ocean. "I'm sick of the view," Luke said. "I've been looking at it my whole life." He went out the back door and sat down on the steps. I sat down on the concrete ledge of the flowerbed, which looked empty because I had pulled out all the weeds and had only planted bulbs which wouldn't be seen until the spring. Someone had tried to decorate the concrete with seashells, and I fiddled with a couple of scallop shells while we talked. I thought Luke might want to know what brought me to Gannet Island but he did not ask. His questions were all about Toronto. "Hey!" he said, suddenly noticing the way I had stacked the scallop shells together. "That looks like the Sky Dome. My buddy Jack texted me photos."

The curving white shells did look quite a lot like the Sky Dome.

"You like the Jays?" Luke continued. For a moment I thought he meant the birds, but rescued myself in time, by taking my cue from his hat. I nodded. I went to a ball game once with Jesse and Es and liked it. It was a lot more peaceful than basketball, which was the sport my father liked to watch on TV. Dribble, dribble, shoot. Pass, dribble, shoot. In baseball there was lots of room for the mind to wander and it wasn't over until it was over, however long that took. During the warm-up it started to rain, and they closed the Dome. With a great grinding of gears they had shut out the sky. Just like that. "The Jays are my team," Luke said, "though I'm beginning to think they're getting paid too much for their own good." He stood up and used a stick to draw in the soil of the flowerbed. "Let's say you put the Sky Dome here, this is the water, right?"

He said, "the water" as if it was all the same, whatever cup it was in, as if it could even begin to compare with the water that unrolled from the other side of the cottage like hammered pewter. "Yes, Lake Ontario," I said, arranging the shells where he indicated.

"Where's the CN Tower?" He broke off the end of the stick he had been using to draw with and handed it to me.

"Right here, beside the Sky Dome." I stuck it upright in the soil. "And this would be the Gardiner Expressway," I said, making a furrow with my hand. I never understood why people would place a highway between themselves and the water but without a car I didn't have to admit to the convenience of the highways that encircled the city like a noose.

"Where's Yonge Street? That's the one you always hear about."

"It runs up here away from the water," I said, indicating the wall of the cottage. "And there on the other side of the flower bed, running parallel, that's Spadina."

The next time Luke came over to work on the ceiling where he had installed the skylight, he brought a tiny sea urchin, which he poked on to the stick that was the CN tower, and two razor clams and a sand dollar for City Hall. A big barnacle became Roy Thomson Hall and we constructed the Art Gallery of Ontario with beach glass. I found a wedge-shaped bit of driftwood that had been eaten by shipworms and looked remarkably like the Flatiron Building. Luke also brought a bunch of old weir twine that had been tarred, and asked me to lay out the streets between Spadina and Yonge. I was trusting to memory but I got the major ones, and we filled in the flower bed with the other landmarks built of periwinkles and pebbles, mussel shells and sea glass. When it started to get dark we went back inside to gather up his painting gear and rollers.

"Well, I guess that's it for this job," Luke said, looking up at the skylight he had installed. "Need help moving the bed back?"

"I guess," I said, cursing myself for blushing. Es always said women were suckers for men who were good with their hands. Male strippers never dress up as accountants, she said. They wear tool belts. The new "it" guy was the handyman.

Luke's toolbox, like my own, was filled with a variety of intriguing gadgets. There were fewer kinds of tools, but more of each kind. He had a screwdriver for every task, and he knew their names and functions. There was the slot, and the Robertson, invented in Canada apparently, the Philips. This was hard for me, remembering useful information like the names of screwdrivers and the rules to card games. I had to devise elaborate memory schemes that ran something like this: Philips was the one shaped like a star, which made me think of the Lone Star state, which reminded me of the Lone Ranger, and I knew that the name Philip meant "lover of horses," and it was through this convoluted path, this awkward and tangled web of association, that I kept these two disparate pieces of information together, kept them from flying apart into space where they would be no good to anyone. And then there were the saws he kept in the big aluminium storage box in the back of his pick-up. Some you could figure out, because their names were related to their shape or function, like mitre or circular, but there was also jig, hack, band, scroll, reciprocating, keyhole, and coping. Maybe I could benefit from someone who could keep all this straight, someone whose vocabulary included words like soffit and fascia, gutter and flashing. Someone who thought in nails and screws. Luke's particular skills had their appeal. I could tell he was perfectly at home in the world. Except for cooking, I had always found the physical world to be a challenge, moving through it awkwardly, like someone in the wrong element. Just at the moment when a gem-like fish disappears into the coral with a flutter of tailfin, I have to rush for the surface, lungs burning for air.

What I said next was as much of a surprise to me as it was to him. "Would you like to come to supper?" Reflecting on this afterward, I thought I would not have extended such an invitation had I not been standing next to my deerstalker which I had tossed on the bed. I had deduced that if his work here was done, I might not see him again unless I specifically asked him to come back.

"Sure," he said.

"How about Saturday at six?"

"Good enough." He picked up what he could carry of his gear and headed out the door. I followed him out with the rest.

I agonized over what to cook, poring over the *Joy of Cooking*, which was a favourite as far as cookbooks went because it dared to have opinions, to say things like, "The meat is ready to cook when it looks like Dali's limp watches." I almost decided on Bay Scallops Fondue Bourguignonne, because of what the recipe book said: "We love this dish inordinately." What a word to use in a cookbook. Inordinately. Extravagantly and without restraint. But in the end I decided on a recipe I came across for *Bacalao a la Vizcaina* (Bay of Biscay Salt Cod with onion and red chili peppers) which Hemingway's last wife Mary considered one of her specialities and made for Ernest's sixtieth birthday party along with fireworks, flamenco, funny toasts, and a firing range.

Now that the tourist season was over, Charlotte couldn't afford to keep me on, so I found other work cooking at the Island Inn, one of the few places open year round. I did the breakfast shift, mostly cooking classic bacon and eggs and sometimes pancakes which I jazzed up with blueberries. I worked with two girls, Jennifer and Jasmine, who had the same last name but were not sisters, which was common on the island. Everyone seemed distantly related to everyone else. They were friendly at first but became a little stand-offish after I suggested we try offering crepes with fresh fruit salsa or yogurt with home-made muesli. Maybe they thought I was putting on big-city airs. "What's the point of garnishes?" Jasmine said, scraping a citrus rose into the compost. "Just more work for everybody." The atmosphere in the kitchen was more like that of Carnivores. The priority was getting food on the table and coffee in the bottomless cup with none of the intimacy or imagination of cooking with Charlotte. Even alone in her kitchen with the painted birds I felt less lonely than I did surrounded by the scurrying staff at the Inn. When I thought about quitting I remembered the Indian proverb Varsha used to quote: "The money you dream about will not pay your bills."

On one of those last warm September days that trail after summer like a silk scarf, Luke arrived right on time wearing jeans and a white shirt with the sleeves rolled up to the elbow. You could tell the jeans had been ironed because of the crease down the front, which could only mean he still lived at home. I was glad I had dressed up a little but not too much. The Merry Widow had forced me into tripling the number of dresses in my closet. Luke was carrying a hostess gift in a shoe box. "Should I open it now?" I asked when he handed it to me.

"It can wait," he said, so we sat down to dinner. I had prepared the cod well, in a way he had never experienced, but you could tell he was a little disappointed. He'd had cod baked and barbecued, in chowder and Dutch Mess, he said, but never before in *Bacalao a la Vizcaina*. I love the seafood here, crisp and real, like the stars which I could now see through my bedroom ceiling, but had I been thinking clearly, I would have realized that this might not be the best meal for an island boy. He probably would have preferred a steak, something from the land for a change. Maybe, given the choice between "surf" and "turf" on a menu, he would not make the same choice as I would. After all, he was sick of the view. He was more enthusiastic about dessert, which was puffed pastry with whipped cream, chocolate, and brandied apricots.

"You can open that box now," he said, after the meal. It was certainly not a typical hostess gift like a bottle of wine or flowers. Inside was a pair of black high heels, not something I would have chosen for myself, but elegant in a slinky kind of way with narrow black straps that crossed in the front, and a heel that tapered to the size of a thumb tack. Something that small could hardly be called a sole. "I thought they would look good with your fancy hat." He paused to gauge my reaction. "If you want I can saw off a bit of one heel for you," he said. "That's what Marilyn did to get that sexy walk." Apparently he had his own store of arcane information. "She was a redhead like you before she became a blonde."

"I'll break my neck," I said. High heels were something you had to get used to, work up to slowly, like wearing hats.

"At least try them on," Luke said. I don't know how he knew my shoe size, but he got it right. I was surprised at how good they looked, that is, compared to the black shoes Es called my *cauchemars*. I knew the pumps with the tiny soles plus the comment about Marilyn Monroe meant things were headed in a certain direction. In my mind I had managed to turn down the heat like you would turn down the dial on a gas stove, so the little purple bumps could never join into a ring of flame, but maybe it was only a matter of time. The oil was starting to ripple and smoke in its hotness, so that you knew whatever you placed in it, even something as tiny as mustard seeds, would instantly begin to singe and pop. I thought of the list Es and I had talked about on the long drive down from Toronto and how it might apply to Luke. He was certainly easy on the eyes, *splendide*, as Es would say. I was not used to attention from men and found it flattering. Here he was, clearly attractive, clearly attracted. A bird in the hand. "Got any music?" Luke asked.

"Just the radio."

"I got a new CD player in the truck. The truck's a piece of shit, but I put in great speakers. Let's go." With one hand he grabbed his beer and with his other he grabbed my hand, pushing the screen door open with his back. "I like the old stuff," he said. By "old" he might have meant Mozart, but he meant Elvis Presley and Jerry Lee Lewis. He put on "Great Balls of Fire," and left the truck windows open, so the music spilled out into the evening. This music got my toes tapping and made me wonder why there hadn't been more music when I was growing up. At my house, no one played an instrument. June had taken piano lessons as a child but hated it. No one played vinyl or CDs. The same old quiet raked this way and that, over and over again, like the sand in one of those tiny Zen gardens you put on your desk.

After a while Luke went inside to get himself another beer, and I walked around the side of the cottage so I could look at the sea. When he returned, he came up behind me. The wind off the water was cool, but I could feel the heat of him against my back. I felt wobbly in the new high heels. He did not put his arms around me or touch me but he spoke into my ear. "You want me," he said. I suddenly remembered a conversation I had overheard during one of those many Toronto subway rides, hurtling underground toward Carnivores. Rush hour forced me to stand holding a pole to steady myself against the sway and rattle, and my hand on the pole was jammed up against a stranger's hand like in the child's choosing game, "one potato, two potato." The stranger was telling the man beside him that he was trying for a record in sleeping with the most women. One of his strategies for success was, "Come up behind them and talk in their ear." If he said why this was effective, I couldn't recall, just that it was, and I wondered why at the time. Maybe hearing someone you couldn't see caught you off guard. With him behind you, you wouldn't be able to see his eyes, gauge their candour and intensity; all you would have would be his words in your ear as warm as breath.

Luke had used the word "want" instead of need or love or any of the other verbs that might fill the gap between "you" and "me." He made it my business, not his own, which was arrogant but compelling. I knew there would be immense pleasure in bringing our bodies together. All that was lissom in him would lighten all that was awkward in me. He followed me inside and swung a kitchen chair around so he could sit on it backward as men do when they are at ease. He watched while I began unfastening the buttons on the front of my dress, both of us hungry for whatever came next, but then Luke said, "Take off everything but the heels, and put your hat back on." I'm not sure whether it was what he said or how he said it, but something made me pause. Confidence in a man was appealing, but Luke was cocky. He was clearly used to getting his own way, especially with women, and I did not want to be just another performer under his direction, another notch in his tool belt.

I stopped unbuttoning and said the first thing that popped into my head. "We should put on a dance." I was not a good dancer. My father had never allowed any kind of dance lessons for me as a child because his assistant librarian had a daughter who had taken ballet and gymnastics and ended up as a table dancer at a strip club. "That was not what I had in mind," she told Albert, "when I bought the first pair of pink satin toe shoes." But Es had suggested a dance that very first day on the island, and I now reached for the idea like a knight in peril unsheathes his sword. I knew there were square dances from time to time at the Hall in North Head, and the Sand Dollar had step dancing every Friday night, and there was usually a dance at island weddings, unless it was at the Baptist church, where there was always lots of eating and talking, but no drinking or dancing. "And you know where it should be?" I paused for effect. "Swallowtail Light." Luke looked at me and laughed, and it was this laugh that broke the electricity of the moment as surely as a blown fuse.

That night Es called me to say she had moved in with Mr. Maybe who she was now calling Mr. Yes. I thanked her for sending what was left of my stuff and dealing with the landlord. Apartments were always at a premium in Toronto, even ones as tiny and disadvantaged as mine, what we fondly called a 3-D apartment: dark, dank, and defective, so there had been no problem finding a new tenant. She was delighted by the news that I was holding a dance at Swallowtail Light like she had suggested that first day.

It was Luke's idea to make it a costume party. "I know it's only September, but if you wait for Halloween to dress up you freeze your ass off," he said. Hemingway had talked about masquerade or *Mojiganga: in the old days bulls would be let into the ring at novilladas while a procession was in progress or a play being acted… a young bull is released into the ring while the band is playing and is fought and killed by some of the musicians while the rest continue to play their instruments.* I had never been good at transforming myself for costume parties, but this time I was determined to be spectacular. At first, I thought my costume would involve one of the hats, but realized I had come to consider them as part of my everyday wear, not part of masquerade. Walking the island shore, I always picked up amazing objects I had never seen before and found out their names, like whelks or moon snails or a skate's empty egg case that was called a Mermaid's Purse. Luke had no use for sea stuff unless it could be made to resemble a part of the city he yearned for. He was a real stickler for accuracy. It wasn't just about knowing where things were. There was Google for that. It was about building it in three dimensions. Maybe it seemed to him that if he completed the city with sufficient precision, he could step into it and disappear, lose himself inside this urban scape built from island ingredients. Now when I walked along the beach, my eyes were toward the ground seeking sea treasures with which to build the Big Smoke.

One day, walking along the beach searching for bits of Toronto, I found some antlers, tines draped with seaweed. The deer, I discovered, hadn't arrived on the island by themselves. The waters would prevent that, and the salt and the tides meant those waters would never become a solid way. Someone told me they'd been introduced by a merchant from the mainland in 1845. I liked the word "introduced" as if they were two friends meeting for the first time, though I knew that the world over species had been "introduced" to places they didn't belong with disastrous results. I took the antlers home and scrubbed them up, loving the feel of the horn under my fingers, sometimes bumpy, sometimes smooth. And then I knew what I would be. I asked Luke if he knew where I could get a union suit, and once I explained it was one of those sets of long underwear with the top and bottom attached, he said he could get an old one off his dad. When he dropped it by I asked if he had time for a beer. While I was getting the drinks he disappeared into the bedroom to take a photo of the skylight for his "renovation portfolio." He only stayed long enough to finish his drink and that was the only time I saw him between the night he came to dinner and the dance at Swallowtail a week later.

I dyed the union suit brown, and with face make-up, leather boots and gloves and a white tail, the costume was quite effective. The crowning glory was, of course, the antlers wired to my bicycle helmet, which I had acquired for safety's sake, though helmets were only mandatory for those under eighteen in New Brunswick. "Better safe than sorry," June always said. I didn't tell Luke what I was going to be. I wanted to surprise him. And he wouldn't tell me what he was going to be either. I was curious, thinking I would learn something important about him by the costume he chose. I hoped there might be parts of himself he had not revealed.

Charlotte agreed to help me with the food and the decorating, which consisted mostly of patio lanterns strung from makeshift poles and Christmas tree lights on the wind-stunted spruce trees. We ran a cord from the lighthouse so there would be power. It turned out that Jim of "James & Flagg: Full-Service Law Firm" was the one people called on to DJ at weddings, and he agreed to help out, though he was nervous about getting his equipment safely across the footbridge. Only the coast guard used the helicopter pad at Swallowtail Light, and only rarely, or I would not have been allowed to hold a dance there. Thomas Belliveau, the RCMP officer who brought me home after my night of trespassing, would come to *maintenir le droit*. Officer Belliveau felt strongly that we should rope off the helicopter pad to prevent people from dancing off the edge into the darkness. He said we could use the yellow tape that said, POLICE LINE DO NOT CROSS, but it was generally agreed that this would produce the wrong effect. No one wanted the dance floor looking like a crime scene, so we got rope instead and, in the end, it looked a little like a boxing ring.

The night of the dance, Charlotte and I went over early to set up a piece of plywood on saw horses for the refreshments. We kept things simple because everything had to be carried down the stairs and across the footbridge over the Sawpit, the chasm in the rocks. At one time there had been tracks up the side of the cliff to carry supplies to the lighthouse keepers, but now it was all gone, including the huge fog bell at the very end. Now everything was automated and the windows in the lighthouse had been removed to reduce maintenance. Next to the base of the lighthouse was our beer tent, which was literally a tent, one of the old orange canvas ones with a card table set up in the centre. This was the greatest cause for nervousness on my part. It seemed like sheer folly to put beer and cliffs together. I thought of getting people to sign a waiver before they could get a drink, but with Thomas around, people were more likely to behave themselves.

I was arranging broccoli and cauliflower florets and various hues of sweet pepper on a tray when I looked up to see Luke arriving. He was dressed as Sherlock Holmes. I was shocked to see he had taken my deerstalker without asking. He must have swiped it the night he brought over the union suit. I knew the hat was missing but thought I must have misplaced it somewhere. Until it turned up, I was wearing the boater as backup. But here was Luke wearing my hat, and one of those Australian outback raincoats with a cape at the shoulders over a white shirt and dress pants. And to complete the look, he was carrying a magnifying glass and a liquorice pipe which got eaten over the course of the evening. He actually looked quite dashing and I suddenly became self-conscious about my brown union suit, blotchy brown face, and antlers. "Oh, dear!" he said when he caught sight of me, trying to be funny but not succeeding.

Charlotte was dressed like a gypsy, with a colourful scarf, spangles tied around her waist over her skirt, and giant hoop earrings, and her husband Will wore denim work clothes and a battered straw hat. "He's Van Gogh," Charlotte said. He leaned against one of the speakers eating sunflower seeds and spitting the hulls into the grass. Working at Aristotle's Lantern, I had, of course, run into Will a few times, recognizing him as the man who had given me the lift to Grand Harbour and offered me dulse way back in the beginning, but I had never really talked to him because he travelled often, and when he was home he disappeared for most of the day into the studio shed behind the house which he called his *atelier*. The door was always shut. But Charlotte, who loved dancing, had prevailed upon him not only to come to the dance but to judge the costumes, when the time came.

As it turned out, the dance was a disaster. There was no other word for it, except maybe catastrophe, debacle, fiasco, utter failure. Besides the few people I had personally invited to look after specific things — music, refreshments, judging, security — no one came. Well, almost no one. There was one guy I had never seen before dressed like a hunter in an orange vest and cap with ear flaps. I was sitting on the edge of the concrete helicopter pad wondering if anyone was going to come when he sat down beside me. I was able to get the permit for the dance at Swallowtail on the condition that liquor intake would be strictly monitored, but this fellow clearly had his own private stash. He reeked of it. "Hunting season ain't begun yet, but maybe I could get a head start. Whaddya think, Bambi?" he said in a thick voice, clumsily placing his arm around me.

"Oh, puh-lease..." I said, and stood to greet Jim Flagg. Jim the lawyer/DJ was dressed as a pirate, with purple satin pantaloons, a billowy white shirt, a patch over one eye, and a dead parrot rigged to his shoulder. He brought his daughter Tiffany. I recognized her from the picture I'd seen on his desk that first night at James & Flagg, Full-Service Law Firm. She was dressed as a flamenco dancer with a red rose in her hair and a black lace fan. She looked a lot better in in her tight red dress with the ruffles than she had in the Christmas sweater. She danced while her father was testing the sound system. Because she was lovely and slender and had benefited from years of lessons, her dancing was a thing of beauty. Luke ditched his coat and my hat, and stood in one corner of the dancing ring stamping one foot and clapping to keep time.

When it became clear that no one else was coming, I said we should all pack up and go home, but Will said he had been asked to judge the costumes and he wasn't about to shirk his duty. He was just about to hand me first prize for my deer costume when a latecomer strode up the path looking like a badly executed ghost. Instead of having the white sheet over his head with eyeholes, he had cut a neck hole so he wore it like a poncho. Realizing that the judging was already underway, he pulled his red toque down over his ears and put the pocket flashlight he was carrying in his mouth. Then, as we all watched, he turned slowly round and round, like Swallowtail behind him. He got second prize, and Luke and Tiffany got honourable mention.

Tiffany didn't want to stay until her father got his gear packed up, so Luke offered to drive her home. He tossed my deerstalker to me and disappeared into the darkness. He had said he would come back to clean up, but he never did. The deer, the gypsy, and Van Gogh gathered up the lights and the uneaten refreshments and lugged them back over the footbridge. The RCMP officer took down the ropes. The drunken hunter offered to help the pirate carry the sound system and the speakers back to the parking lot, but the pirate declined, asking the lighthouse and me to help instead. Jim had been spinning vinyl. To a lot of people our age, a record player was already as foreign and ancient as a Victrola, but the lighthouse man used the magnifying glass Luke had left behind to show me a record up close, pointing out the intricate grooved valleys that made the music. "It reminds me of tree rings," he said. After we were done, I looked back at the windswept point from the top of the stairs, the beam from Swallowtail light sweeping in a wide arc over the stunted spruce and out over the waves. It was as if we had never been there.

Charlotte and Will gave me a ride home. When I stepped into the cottage, I felt suddenly very tired, almost to the point of nausea. I placed my antlers on the table, and sat down heavily in a chair. What was I thinking? A come-from-away snap organizing a dance. Of course no one came. And a costume party too, even though it wasn't even Halloween. Adults almost never dress up and pretend. Dressing up was for children. I got out the brandy I had used to make the apricot dessert for Luke and took a swig straight from the bottle. Then another and another. I picked up the phone and dialled Es's number. First I tried her cell, which was turned off, then her home phone. Even though it was late, no one was home. I listened to it ring until the answering machine came on. "Es and Jesse, leave a message…" then a few bars from Beethoven's Fifth. After the beep I began to talk. "Es, the dance was a complete disaster. Besides the people I asked to be there, only three people came. Only three!" I practically shouted this into the receiver and then said more quietly, "How come everything I touch turns to shit?" The allotted time to leave a message came to an end. "Okay then, love ya, Bye…" I said, even though I knew this part would never be heard. I went into the bedroom, pulled off my boots and fell into bed, not even bothering to take off the rest of my costume

It was still dark when I awoke, feeling disoriented, stiff, and very sad. I also felt hung-over, and thought of what Hemingway had said: *I have been drunk one thousand five hundred and forty seven times in my life, but never in the morning.* I went into the bathroom for some cold cream to remove the brown make-up from my face. There with my hand on the door of the medicine cabinet, I suddenly decided to go out and find the sunrise. There was glory in first light climbing out of a dark sea. Leaving the mirrored door ajar, I picked up my helmet from the kitchen table and walked out of the house. I grabbed my bicycle that was leaning against the side of the cottage and, still hung-over and half asleep, strapped on my helmet, antlers and all. There was no time to lose. If I didn't hurry, the sunrise would come and go, and I would miss it all. I followed a trail I had never tried before, thinking it might get me to the eastern shore more quickly, but soon the path became too rough to cycle on, so I leaned the bicycle against a tree and continued on foot.

The despair of last night had not gone away. The *misère* as Es called it. It wasn't Luke, or the girl with the black lace fan. Not really. It was humiliating to hold a dance and have no one come. I knew Es would have succeeded where I had failed. Es had the energy and the enthusiasm to make a thing sing, no matter how unlikely or outrageous. I, on the other hand, felt all my inadequate efforts to function effectively in the world come back at me. Sadness was like this, never solitary and singular. Always cumulative. All the other moments rose up in the present one, filling it with sorrow to the point of bursting. I missed Varsha and the delicious curries and conversation we shared. I missed Es, who was always surprising me with her latest scheme. I missed Charlotte, too. I saw her occasionally, of course, but it was not the same as seeing her every day, working side by side in the kitchen full of painted birds, expanding on those early discussions of poetics, natural history, and the gift.

Stumbling alone through the half-dark over uneven ground, I felt singularly inept at holding people to me. All the people I cared for most seemed to slip away, like in "Hurt," that Nine Inch Nails song Johnny Cash sings. *Everyone I know goes away in the end.* Sometimes it was my fault, my own carelessness or misstep, but often it wasn't. Circumstances just intervened, like the provinces between me and Es, all that highway, a black elastic band stretched to breaking. The yawn of death and difference between me and my father. The tumble of triteness that fell between me and June like a rock slide, making passage impossible or unsafe. I had discovered that it's not what you get but the fact of not being able to choose that causes the greatest grief. Varsha had gone to his bride in Delhi and Luke had disappeared in the night with flamenco girl. With men, it seemed, I either wanted too much or too little. I never minded being alone before, but now it loomed before me like a desert without sustenance or pity.

Whether the trail had petered out or I had left it without realizing, I was soon walking through the woods. It was hard going through the tangle of windfall and rock. The branches of the evergreens kept out much of the thin early morning light and a touch of fog reached through the trees like tentative fingers. I hunched my shoulders against the chill and scrambled forward. I had been half-walking, half-climbing for almost an hour when the silence was broken by rifle shots. For all I knew, hunting season had begun. I froze, realizing I was still wearing my antlers. This might have seemed comical, if I had not been feeling such despair. I could not tell how close the shots were or in what direction, but suddenly I was afraid, deeply and purely afraid. Still moving as quickly as I could through the underbrush, I yanked at the strap of my helmet and flung it off. I turned and began to run in what I hoped was the direction from which I had come, head and heart pounding. Hemingway would call this *tomar el olivo: to take to the olive tree, a phrase used to describe the action of the matador when seized by panic or through having let the bull put him in an impossible terrain…*

As I clambered over a fallen log I heard a crackle of twigs to my left. Without stopping, I glanced in that direction. It was not a man, as I had expected, but a deer, a real deer. All I caught was a glimpse of wary black eyes, a flicker of white tail, and it was gone. A branch caught at Luke's father's union suit and I tore it off too, shedding it there in the forest with a shower of buttons, leaving me in leggings and a tank top. To get it off completely I had to pull off my boots. When I got them back on I kept running, hoping that I was going in the right direction. I knew that even if I wasn't I would eventually come to a place where the edge of the island met the edge of the sea. There was a terrible ache in my side now, and my breath was coming ragged and uneven. Ahead, the trees seemed to be thinning and I ran towards the light. I kept on until I came out of the woods, running across a grassy stretch and at last my feet struck pavement. It took me a minute to realize where I was. It was not the road I had left behind. The unlit lights lining what I had assumed was a road meant that it was not a road at all, but an airstrip. I caught sight now of the windsock, striped like the hat of the *Cat in the Hat*, the hat with room for a whole alphabet of diminishing disasters. Scratched and bruised, I sat down on the runway and wept, my breath coming in great sobs, my face and shaking hands smeared with brown.

When I first arrived on the east coast after driving through more trees than I had seen in my whole life, I had been amazed at how much land there was that was not being tilled and harvested, bought or sold, built on or excavated, land that was not earning money for anyone, that was just there being itself, providing haven for wild things. I was determined never to take it for granted, all this glory unexploited, but now my eyes were down. There was a road from the airstrip back to town, and I took it, stumbling slowly home toward Cove Road and Honeysuckle Cottage. Afterward, I could barely remember that walk, putting one foot in front of another, head down, seeing only the hard black road. Walking on asphalt was the same wherever in the world you did it, though the edges were always different. But I was feeling too weary and wretched to notice the edges, autumn leaves as scarlet gashes against the green, bulrushes erupting in fluff like smoke from extinguished candles.

After scrubbing away the last signs of masquerade, and taking something for my headache, I lay on my bed with my back turned to the window and slept for hours. When I got up I left the cottage and went to retrieve my bicycle, but I had no idea where the rest of my costume had ended up, shed on the run. As I cycled slowly home, the sayings of my mother circled in my head, no use crying over spilt milk, you can't unscramble eggs, what can't be cured must be endured, but found no comfort there. Cycling into the driveway of Honeysuckle Cottage, I suddenly remembered something Es said while teaching me to drive a standard in the parking lot in Port Hope. It was probably meant as mere driving advice, but it seemed now to be wisdom of a wider kind. "If you want to keep from hitting things, never back up farther than you have to."

BERGÈRE

4

Weeks later when I picked up my mail at the North Head post office and found Luke's present, it took me by surprise. Not his present to me, but my present to him. I had ordered it online back when I thought something might evolve between us. I had been worried it would not arrive in time for his birthday. But now here it was, and I didn't even know if I would have an occasion to give it to him. It had been gift-wrapped in gold foil by the company at no extra charge. All that remained was to add a bow. I did not feel happy as I tied Luke's present with red ribbon, curling the trailing ends with the sharp edge of scissors. He had not dropped by. He had not called. I could call him, of course, but I did not want to appear sad or afraid, though I had been both since he had put his tanned hands on flamenco girl's small waist. Maybe I had misunderstood the situation. Maybe he was not interested in me after all, except as a novelty from Toronto, the city into which he wanted to disappear.

Just as I finished curling the red ribbons, the phone rang. I felt curious about what he was going to say, how he was going to explain his disappearance. But it was not Luke on the other end of the line. It was his mother. That was how she introduced herself. "This is Luke's mother." Luke had mentioned that his family would like to meet "the girl from away." "We were wondering if you could join us tomorrow for Luke's birthday party," the mother said. "Birthday party" sounded so young for someone who was turning twenty-two.

"I would like that," I said.

"Fivish for supper then."

"Is there anything I can bring?"

"No, just bring yourself. We'll be having pork cake. Do you like pork cake?"

"I've never had pork cake," I said truthfully, thinking how vile it sounded. I had seen the recipe in Charlotte's *Island Cookbook*, so I knew it was a lot more benign than the name suggested, being essentially a fruitcake with strawberries, dates and currants, but still the name was unfortunate.

"Folk don't generally make it except at Christmas time, but it's always been Luke's favourite. Do you need a lift or anything?"

"No, it's all right. I have my bicycle." Luke's mother proceeded to give me the exceptionally thorough kind of instructions that seem to account for every blade of grass and pebble between the place you are leaving and the place you are headed.

The next afternoon as I got ready for the party, I poured myself a glass of Chardonnay to fortify myself, reinforce my defences against the unknown. According to Hemingway, white wine was appropriate for any meal of the day, including breakfast with brioche and the knowledge that your wife was dying trying to bring a life into the world. I wasn't anxious to face Luke, but it would be best with other people around, in case the awkwardness was too much to bear. I poured a second glass and could feel the wine moving through my limbs, into my fingertips, emerging as pale pennants flapping on the ramparts. Next for the armour. I didn't want to look too formal or too casual. In the end, I chose a navy skirt with a white blouse with little pink flowers embroidered on the placket. All the darts made the blouse fit rather tightly, and the neckline was maybe more scooped than appropriate for meeting "the mother," but as Charlotte was fond of saying, what the H-E-double-hockey-sticks. I felt I ought to wear the high heels Luke had given me, but knew I could never cycle in them, so I put on my *cauchemars* and carried the shoes and a jacket, because it was October and chilly even though the sun was shining. I didn't want to be late. I wanted to make a good impression.

As I wheeled my bicycle around to the front of the cottage, I realized with a jolt that my bicycle helmet, the antlers still wired to it, was lying somewhere in the woods, so I went back inside and grabbed the new hat I had received on the first of October with the usual letter.

Dear Pertice,

When I was young, my mother always said, "Idle hands are the Devil's workshop," and so she insisted on busy work to keep me out of mischief. I was given a needlepoint pattern for Thomas Lawrence's *Pinkie*, a portrait of a girl in a white muslin dress with a pink hat and sash. Most people are familiar with her, especially when paired with Thomas Gainsborough's *Blue Boy*, though the two were painted a quarter century apart by different artists. The dress and background was all needlepoint in that familiar continental stitch on the diagonal which took forever, but not as long as the face, which was in petit-point, impossibly small stitches in silk rather than wool, though the end result was quite life-like. That girl in the pink hat who looked down upon our dining room table for years always reminded me of Little Bo Peep, but when I was older I found out the real girl, Sarah Moulton Brown, was eleven when the portrait was painted. She went from Jamaica, where her family owned sugar plantations and 2000 slaves, to England to be educated, and within a year she was dead. The portrait eventually passed to her brother whose niece Elizabeth Barrett Browning wrote in *Aurora Leigh* that the works of women are symbolical.

> We sew, sew, prick our fingers, dull our sight,
> Producing what? A pair of slippers, sir,
> To put on when you're weary — or a stool
> To stumble over and vex you. . . "curse that stool!"
> Or else at best, a cushion, where you lean
> And sleep, and dream of something we are not,
> But would be for your sake.

When I came upon this hat, trimmed in pink silk roses, I thought of Sarah. It is a bergère, from the French for shepherdess, modified for use as a motoring hat. Pinkie's windblown pink ribbons were replaced by long wide tails of chiffon that could be wrapped around the neck and brought down over the face like a veil to shield it from the dust on the road, though no amount of chiffon could shield Sarah from dust and ash. I always felt particularly beautiful in this hat, remembering the tiny stitches that make a face look alive.

> Peace by the Sea,
> PM

I put on the hat that reminded me of the ones Truly Scrumptious wore in *Chitty Chitty Bang Bang* with its shallow crown and broad brim laden with roses, and voluminous chiffon tails that could be wrapped and tied, just in case your car started to fly. Because I was in a hurry, I didn't tie the tails in a bow but just looped them loosely like a scarf. I put the high heels and Luke's gift in the wicker basket attached to the front of the bicycle, and went back for the dill pickles I had made with cucumbers from Charlotte's garden. People were so generous here. The joke was that if you had a car you should lock it, not because things would be stolen, but if you didn't, people would fill it with garden produce, especially zucchini. As I placed the jar in the wicker basket it slipped out of my hands and shattered, sending the small pickled cucumbers rolling down the drive. So much for impressing the mother. As I carefully picked up the shards of glass I thought that on this occasion one of my mother's hollow little sayings might actually apply. "Haste makes waste." I placed the glass bits in a little pile on the front step. Once upon a time Luke and I might have found a use for them in building Toronto, maybe for those tall glass towers in the financial district. I waved my dill-smelling hands in the air to dry them. The cottage was already locked. I would wash up when I got there.

The pedalling on this side of the island was easy. These were the lowlands that sloped gently into the sea. Here people lived and gardens grew. It was the other side of the Island that had the huge cliffs of dark stone rising out of the waves. I passed an abandoned garage with a sign that read: "Andrew J. Peter & Sons Salvage: Redemption Centre," and spotted the house as I came over the rise. Luke's mother's instructions had been very explicit. "It's the only house with lightning rods... If you get to the ball diamond you've gone too far." It was a beige clapboard with an empty clothesline out back, and a lilac bush out front, though at this time of year it was not in bloom. As I gathered speed coming down the slope toward the house and the cars of guests parked on the shoulder of the road, I saw a red helium balloon float around the corner of the house, and a moment later a small girl in a green party dress came running after it, arms reaching upward, but by then it was already headed skyward. I looked up, watching as the red balloon became smaller and smaller in the blue, blue sky.

And that was the last thing I remembered. Others had to do the rest of the remembering for me. One guest at the party who had been looking out the window just as I hit the opening door of a parked car saw me soaring over the handlebars and later said I looked for a moment like a maiden carved at the prow of an old-fashioned ship, a figurehead fresh from the chisel. Later I learned that Thomas Belliveau, the RCMP officer, stayed with me during the triage at the Gannet Island Hospital. He was trained for crisis, he said, but could never get used to mortality among the young. "When we were kids, before a film at school, some clown would always make shadow shapes. Interfering with the light shouldn't be that easy," he said. "When I see blood, I know it's the light leaking out."

After my condition was stabilized at the hospital on the island, it was decided I should be airlifted to the hospital in Saint John. As James of "James & Flagg: Full-Service Law Firm" had pointed out, not even babies were delivered on the Island any more, except for the time that tourist unexpectedly went into labour on the ferry, and had twins at the hospital, much to everyone's surprise and delight. There was a charter plane right on the island, which was used when time was of the essence.

My mother later told me that when she first saw her daughter unconscious and bandaged and tethered by various tubes to the bed in the intensive care unit of the Saint John Regional Hospital, she wept. "The loss of a husband makes you a widow, and the loss of parents makes you an orphan," she said, "But what word is there for the loss of a daughter?" The nurses told her to hold my hand, to speak to me of places and people I once knew, to sing to me. Familiar sounds and smells may bring her back, they said. So in the midst of the hum of medical machines, my mother, who could not, as she herself was prepared to admit, "carry a tune in a bucket," sang to her daughter all the songs she could remember. She did not remember many songs, mostly children's songs like "Twinkle, Twinkle, Little Star," and various Christmas carols. So while the last leaves fell from the hospital maple trees, and the keys spun down like the blades of helicopters, June sang, "Hark the Herald Angels Sing" and "Silent Night" and "What Child is This?"

One afternoon, the nurses encouraged her to take a break and she slipped out to the department store around the corner from the hospital and went to the fragrance counter. On one of her few visits to my tiny 3-D apartment in Toronto, she had noticed a small bottle of Mystère on my dresser. Deciding this must be my favourite perfume, June was determined to buy some now. Had she known me better, she would have realized that I never wore scents that had been manufactured in a lab because they gave me headaches, but this had been a gift from a Secret Santa at work and I kept it because I liked the unusual shape of the bottle and the amber shadow it cast when the last light slanted through my small window.

"That will be $67 plus tax," said the woman with the perfect make-up and the perfect hair. June could not keep herself from calculating swiftly that that came to about $27 a tablespoon and she wondered for one appalling moment if spraying the free tester on her wrist might be enough to do the trick. Then she gathered herself as she had done at the ticket counter at the airport in Toronto and paid for the wildly expensive perfume. "I have done all I can do," she said to the nurses and to herself, "to bring her back from wherever she is." With her husband Albert there had been no time for a vigil. There had been no time for anything. His departure had been sudden, with no intention of return.

One of the nurses who was often there in the evenings was named Gudrun. She was originally from Germany and spoke with a hint of an accent. Even in these ugly circumstances performing ugly tasks, she somehow seemed filled with radiance. One night as she was changing a catheter, she said to June, "I told the people in my church about you. We're praying for Pertice." June later told me this didn't impress her. Talk is cheap, but the next day, small casseroles started arriving, homemade comfort food that June could heat up in the microwave in the nurses' lounge. And sometimes there were muffins and other sweet things. As the days passed, June wondered if there was anyone she should tell, anyone important to me who might want to know. She expected that anyone I knew on Gannet Island would already be fully informed. The only other person she could think of back in Ontario was Es. "She's alive, but she's in a coma," June told her, feeding quarters into the payphone in the hospital lobby.

"I should be there," Es said immediately.

"Until she wakes up, there's really nothing we can do." June was always careful to say "until" not "if," though the doctors had said there was no way of knowing.

"My car is in the shop, but I could take the bus or something," Es said, suddenly envious of Jesse, who could get to the scene of any emergency at top speed with lights flashing and sirens wailing.

"Really Esther, I don't think that would do any good at this point. I'll keep you posted if there's any change."

"What happened?"

"I was told she was on her way to a birthday party on her bicycle. She hit a car door and went over the handlebars."

"Is that Luke there with her?" I hadn't told Es much about Luke, but enough to make her refer to him as "*that* Luke."

"No," June said. "He's not."

June was given a box of the things I had with me the day of the accident. For the first few days, she couldn't even look at it. But eventually she sat down in the visitors' lounge on the vinyl couch which she had been using as a kind of camp cot since her arrival, and set the box on the coffee table. Then she began to take out the items and set them on the table like exhibits in a trial. First a hat. This made her think that they had given her the wrong box. June had never seen me wear a hat, not since the bonnet she had made for my Halloween costume so long ago. But here was a hat that was clearly more elegance than function, adorned with clouds of chiffon and pink silk roses. It was surprisingly undamaged. The force of the impact must have sent it sailing out of harm's way. A hat. A pink hat with roses. It seemed to June as odd as if she had found her daughter wearing a dog collar or a huge tattoo, and yet it must be her daughter's hat — there were the initials PM chain stitched in pink embroidery floss on the inside of the crown. And yet, though it seemed totally unlikely, there was something about that hat that seemed familiar, something about it that rang a bell.

The next item in the box was a navy skirt that was torn and dusty. June noticed that the button at the waist was hanging loose. If she had a needle, June thought, and the right colour of thread she could secure it before it was lost forever. A stitch in time... but she did not have what she needed for mending, not here. Then a white blouse, also torn and dusty, with a large bloodstain on the front dried almost black, a stain in the shape of Australia. June was surprised that one could have such a thought at such a time, but there it was. Also, curiously, two pairs of black shoes, ugly but sensible walking shoes and slinky high heels. If shoes were a means to an end, two different trajectories had somehow gotten tangled in this moment.

At the bottom of the box was a present wrapped in gold foil and tied with curls of red ribbon. The tag read "To Luke, who could use another set of hands." I had mentioned Luke to June in a casual way during our last telephone conversation. Always hopeful, June had immediately begun to ask questions. She might have asked what kind of man he was, but instead she asked what he did for a living, and I said, "Renovation specialist." Of course, most of what he had to do on the island was roofing, but fortunately for him, shingles didn't last as long as they used to. "They were forced to take out the asbestos," Luke explained. "And now they're not much more than felt and tar." So he was doing okay as a roofer, but it was a nasty job, and everyone knew he had his eye on bigger things.

June had been told it was his birthday party I had been going to when I came to harm. She remembered all the birthday parties she had sent me to as a child. Maybe all the tragedies we come to as grownups are only magnifications of the troubles we encounter as children. That we will come bearing the wrong gift, or be too dressed up or not dressed up enough, or we will have to sit next to the boy we like or the boy we do not like, or we will spill grape Kool-Aid all down the front of our new dress, or our tail will be nowhere near the donkey, or, and this was almost unimaginable, that we will leave for the party, present in hand, and never come home. All the brave paraphernalia of parties, loot bags, balloons, party blowers unfurled like the tongues of toads, all suddenly foolish and forlorn.

June was not able to identify what it was she felt for this boy who had invited her daughter to a birthday party at which she had never arrived. Not anger, because she had never met him, but a kind of trepidation. And no doubt, he was a man and not a boy, though she thought of him this way. One of those impossible boys with eighteen speeds on their bicycles that her daughter had tried to keep up with when she was younger. June had never learned to ride a bicycle; it seemed that the wheels were dangerously narrow and the speeds dangerously swift. How could anyone enjoy a sport where going forward fast was the only way to keep from falling down? It was difficult to be the parent of a daughter. There were a lot of ways a girl could be hurt. It all seemed so risky and fraught. And now this. Children were supposed to outlast their parents. That was the assumption everybody lived by. Piling her daughter's belongings back into the box, the golden present with the mysterious tag, the glorious pink hat, the navy skirt with the loose button, the practical black shoes and the impractical black high heels, and the stained white blouse, June felt a resentment that lingered like a stitch in the side from running too far too fast. She took the blouse to the ladies' washroom, and scrubbed it vigorously under very cold water, fearing that a stain that was set like this one would probably never come out.

I was told what happened, but I could not remember any of it. Everything after the red balloon was gone. How I flew over the handlebars looking for an instant like the figurehead of a ship, how the doctor wiped away the blood in order to assess the damage underneath. How I lay for three days as if I were dead or asleep as my mother watched from the chair beside my bed. How one afternoon my eyelids finally fluttered open tentatively, like the wings of a butterfly. These details were supplied by others, slowly and in pieces. My brain felt like a jammed cassette tape; my parents had a cassette player in their car that they used for talking books, long after everyone else had switched to CDs, and when the fragile tape escaped from its casing and looped dangerously through the machine, I had to work very hard to yank it out without breaking anything. And if I managed this, there was the tedious process of rewinding the tangled mess of spilled bits, sticking a pen in the hole and turning and turning until it was all safely back where it belonged.

"Your eyes..." June said. "It was like no one lived there." I had heard this cliché about the eyes as the windows of the soul, but maybe there was something to it. I recalled the houses of people away on vacation, with the windows remaining unlit, or perhaps only lit by a lamp that came on mechanically by a timer, always at the same time, but never out of spontaneous activity and movement and need. "Even after you awoke, it was like you were away," my mother said. June no longer resorted to proverbs as often as she used to. It was as if she was really looking at things now. But still it surprised me that two people who had so little in common could once have been so intimately connected, the daughter actually carried inside of the mother, using her blood, as close as a heartbeat. Occasionally and in flashes, I could see how at one time I might have fit into the outline of my mother, as South America once nestled against Africa, though the two had long since sailed away from one another. I knew plate tectonics affected human geography as surely as they reshaped the earth, so one could find seashells on top of a mountain, or a fern in a glacier.

I could also see how happy my mother was, caring for me again. She had never had any other job but caring for others, her daughter and her husband, and had been at loose ends since Albert's death. No one to do for. Now that I was "out of the woods," as she described it, June seemed almost content that this tragedy had brought the daughter she had not really seen in years suddenly back into her sphere of influence. I was now dependent on her. Willing to listen and be helped. Needing her for the simplest things.

Luke had suggested coming soon after my arrival in Saint John, perhaps more out of guilt than affection, but June had discouraged him. She had wanted to spare him, she told me later. But I suspect it was something else. True, I was a mess. I was ravaged from my forehead down to my ankles, and there was nothing he could do. But maybe my mother sensed that Luke was part of my life that had nothing to do with her, and would perhaps accelerate my recovery back into that distant place. That birthday party I had almost arrived at before things went wrong.

By the time Luke finally came to visit me, two weeks after my arrival at the hospital, I had been moved from intensive care into a ward bed. He strode through the river of injury and illness wearing the hip-waders of health, completely dry and untouched. Amongst all these broken people he looked so perfectly strong and whole. All the same, it seemed to me, as he walked through the door of my hospital room, that he wavered. I didn't know what to think about Luke's gift, white carnations with frilly edges died an impossible shade of blue, stems stiff and wiry. I remembered that some carnations had a spicy smell, like nutmeg, but doubted these fake-looking flowers had any fragrance. I certainly couldn't smell them. "Carnation petals are

one of the secret ingredients used in making chartreuse," I said to fill
the silence as I arranged them as best I could in a water pitcher that
Gudrun had scrounged from the hospital cafeteria. Luke looked at me
blankly. "You know, the French liqueur," I added, trying hard to sound
casual and not condescending. I never liked cut flowers unless they
were still bright and dewy from a garden or meadow, spontaneously
wild like the flowers Es and I had picked for the brim of my boater
that first day at Swallowtail. Even then, they were a little depressing,
already wilting their way into death. Cut flowers were a cliché, and
these in particular reminded me of Mother's Day, or funerals, or maybe
boutonnières appropriate for those hideous baby-blue tuxedos I had
seen in old photographs of high school proms. There was nothing
here that reminded me of the world outside the ward or the island
I missed. He could have done so much better than this. But I was
glad to see him, nonetheless. One of the first things I remembered
clearly after waking from the coma was the feel of strong male arms
around me, but it was only the arms of an orderly lifting my body so
the sheets could be changed, an embrace of function and not love.
"Thank you," I said to Luke.

"I wanted to come earlier, but your mother said you weren't up to
it." Maybe he was only here because he felt guilty. I had been on my
way to his birthday party, after all. He did not sit down on the edge of
the bed, though I patted the sheets, gesturing for him to do so. Instead
he paced around the room. The curtain that slid between the beds was
pulled halfway shut, but we were aware of the roommate's presence on
the other side. June had already made herself scarce to accommodate
the arrival of "the gentleman caller," as she referred to Luke. After a few
minutes the roommate popped her head around the end of the curtain,
wearing, as she always did, what looked like the balaclava of a bank
robber or a tight-fitting beige ski mask that covered her face completely
except for holes for the eyes, mouth, and ears. "I'm off for treatment,"
she said, waving goodbye. It was impossible to tell her expression.

"What was that thing she was wearing?" Luke asked me after she
was gone.

"A Jobst garment," I said, "and her name is Alice." When I first received an answer to that same question, I thought Alice said, "Job's garment." There was a Gideon Bible in the drawer of every bedside table in the hospital, and out of boredom I occasionally read a page or two wherever it fell open. Eliphaz saying to Job, "Man is born to trouble as sparks fly upward" and Job trying to survive every bad thing that could possibly happen to a human being. As Alice and I lay in the darkness night after night, haunted and unable to sleep, we told each other our stories, and I, for reasons that I did not fully understand, pressed for all the details. Alice was reluctant at first because it had been a nightmare for her, but she found herself telling me all about her treatment, explaining horrific processes like escharotomy, debridement, and grafting. I knew about eschar because of what Es had told me about burns when she showed me the melted mementoes she had made, but the rest was new to me. "You know, before the doctors grafted my own skin permanently in place," Alice said, "they used the skin of dead people." When I didn't say anything, she continued. "I know it sounds creepy, but it's no different than an organ transplant. Skin is our largest organ."

"Does it hurt?" I asked.

"Ironically, the deeper the burn, the less pain there is," she said. If you're burned to a crisp, all the nerve endings are gone." Her burns were the deep kind. "It's the edges that kill."

Listening to Alice tell her tale, I felt the cast on my arm, and the splint on my nose, and the stitches on my face slipping into insignificance. A few more days in a coma and I would have had to have a tracheotomy, but I was spared that by waking up in time. I knew these things would go away eventually and that I would be "as good as new," as my mother put it, at least on the outside, but Alice in her Jobst garment that pressed against her burns, containing the rawness like skin, would never take up the old life that had been peeled away. Her face would always keep a cubist quality as if it had been assembled rather than arrived at. Alice pulled out her purse, where she kept a photograph of her two daughters, the eldest about the age of the girl in the green dress reaching for the red balloon the day of the birthday party back on the island, and the other just a toddler. "I don't want them to be afraid of me," she said. Alice herself was also in the photograph, looking young and vibrant and beautiful, her hair curling around her face like dark flame. "That was me," she said, using the past tense and starting to cry, although the action did not look the way it usually did, because her tear ducts had been damaged by the burns. When the physiotherapist came to help Alice with her "range of motion" exercises, I watched with admiration, knowing how painful it was for her. They were called ROM exercises, but I thought of them as Royal Ontario Museum exercises, imagining Alice in the Ancient Egypt exhibit surrounded by hieroglyphs, standing strangely swathed beside Djedmaatesankh, a temple musician from 850 BC, who also was once beautiful.

"What happened to her?" Luke asked.

"Her nightgown caught fire while she was making a cup of tea."

And this was how it was; simple ordinary acts swallowed you in tragedy: making tea, crossing a street, watching the escape of a red balloon. Luke had not said anything to me about how I looked. There were no mirrors in the hospital rooms, but June had given me her pocket compact, and I had seen a face I did not recognize. My hair partially shaved to accommodate the stitches, one eye swollen almost shut, a splint on my nose, bruising. But I tried to reassure him, just as the doctors had tried to reassure me. "All this," I said, waving at my face as if I was fanning it, "is going to go away eventually. Pretty much without a trace." I reached over to touch his arm, but he pulled away.

"Do you honestly think I'm that shallow?" He was angry.

"I don't know what to think." Luke did not say anything, so I continued. "Did you know that bones start to heal the moment they're broken?" I added. "The trick is to align them properly." He gave me a hard look that suggested he knew more about this than I did.

According to the doctors, the only thing that might not go away, though it might also resolve itself if the olfactory nerve was only damaged and not severed, was the anosmia. I didn't tell Luke about this loss of smell and the accompanying loss of taste, though for me it was the most devastating of my injuries—the most invisible and yet the most fundamental. I would have been grateful even for those unpleasant hospital smells of antiseptic and anxiety, but now there was nothing at all. Now Es would never be able to do my scents to discover what glorious smells could drive the *misère* away. Hemingway had said that death smelled *a little like the brass handle of a screwed tight porthole on a rolling ship, a little like the kiss of an old woman who has whiskers sprouting from her chin and has come from drinking blood in the slaughter house, and a little like wet earth, dead flowers, and semen.* But for me death would always smell of dill. I used to love the look of fresh dill growing like loose green Queen Anne's lace, and the sharp smell and sour taste of it. But I remembered the way the jar slipped through my hands and exploded against the pavement, sending gherkins skittering down the driveway, and the smell spilling over my hands and through the air. As I was rushing to get to the birthday party, this is what I smelled last of all. This and the sea. "I'll be back to the Island in no time," I said to Luke to reassure him.

"I thought you would go back to Toronto."

"What made you think that?"

"The Island hasn't been good to you." He did not say what he meant by that.

"There's nothing for me in Toronto." Luke did not respond, so I continued. "On the Island there's the cottage and my job." Luke shifted uncomfortably. Since he had arrived he had seemed nervous and uneasy, refusing to sit down but instead moving around the room. Hospitals had this effect on some people, but I suspected there was more to it. I did not know whether it was because of how I looked, or because we had not seen each other since the dance when he had gone home with someone else. "I've been saving this for you," I said to bridge the awkwardness, and from the drawer in my bedside table where the Gideon Bible was, I retrieved his gift.

"You shouldn't have," he said, holding it gingerly between his fingers the way you hold a crab to prevent it from pinching you.

"Aren't you going to open it?"

"Okay." The gift that had never arrived at the birthday party was a wrist watch with hands that were little tools, a hammer, a saw, and a ruler. The face was simulated wood grain, and the cardinal directions of the hours of three, six, nine, and twelve were marked by the heads of tiny screws. I realize that most people our age don't wear watches anymore, preferring to look at their smart phones or laptops instead for the time, but it had seemed so perfect. Luke strapped it on his strong slender wrist and set the time to the little watch that hung upside down from the uniform of the nurse who came in at that moment. "Thank you," he said into the air. He read the words on the tag out loud, "To Luke, who could use another set of hands," but did not comment on them. When I wrote those words, they had seemed like the right ones, but now they seemed inappropriate and vaguely sexual, not warm and witty as I had intended. In fact, what had seemed the perfect gift when I ordered it now worried me. A watch was not like a neck tie or a belt that a man might choose to wear on a particular day if it matched whatever else he had on. A watch was intended to be worn every day, to be looked at often, to convey significant messages about time and eternity.

As Luke was leaving, June came into the room, taking note of his carnations next to my bed, and the discarded gift wrap and red ribbons. "Obviously that went well," she said, with a smile.

"No, it didn't, Mom."

"Well, he seems like a nice young man."

"Shut up. Just shut up, shut the hell up!" June stepped back as if I had struck her. I immediately apologized and June, after considerable encouragement, went to a matinee at the movie theatre around the corner from the hospital.

That afternoon, I saw Alice without her Jobst garment for the first time. She wore it twenty-four hours a day except for bathing, so I had never seen her without it. A cosmetologist had come in to help her put on corrective make-up, camouflaging scars, straightening crooked lips, and drawing on eyebrows where there were none. "How do I look?" she asked.

"You look lovely," I said. I did not say beautiful, but worthy of love, because I wanted to mean it, "but you know what would complete the look?" I went to my closet, and got the hat I had been wearing the day of my accident, the bergère, that meant shepherdess. I placed it on her head and tied the voluminous chiffon tails in an elaborate bow under her chin. Somehow that flattering hat forgave her face for all it had been through, as if the chiffon had really kept out the grit as intended. That night I read from the Gideon Bible what I would later discover was the only reference to hats in the entire Book. It was in the story of Daniel and his friends, a few chapters before the familiar Lions' Den part: *Then these men were bound in their coats, their hosen, and their hats, and their other garments, and were cast into the midst of the burning fiery furnace.* But miraculously *the fire had no power* and they emerged unscorched, unsinged, and unscathed.

Two days later, I called Gannet Island to find out if Luke might be able to come and get me. The risk of infection was gone, and I was ready to go home. June wanted to rent a car and drive me to the Island, get me settled back in at Honeysuckle Cottage, but I insisted that I would be fine. Back when I needed help with everything, going to the bathroom, brushing my hair, cutting my food, my mother's presence had been a kind of miracle, but now she was driving me slowly insane, wanting to do for me what I could do for myself, constantly worrying that I was taking on too much too soon, reverting to the path of aphorisms and advice. "Ingersoll needs you," I finally said, meaning that I did not. Gudrun, the nurse who had been so kind throughout my stay in the hospital, offered to drive June to the Saint John Airport, for the return trip to Toronto. The other end was taken care of too. Under normal circumstances June would have left her own car at a Park and Fly at the Toronto airport, but she had been too shaken to drive after the news of the accident, and a friend had taken her to the airport. Es was going to borrow Jesse's car to pick her up at Pearson and drive her home.

When I called Luke's number, his mother answered the phone. I tried to imagine a face for this woman I had never met, this woman who had invited me to a birthday party at which I never arrived. "Hello. May I speak with Luke please?"

"I'm sorry, he's not here."

"Well, can you tell me when he'll be back? I'm calling long distance from Saint John."

"Is this Pertice?"

"Yes."

"He's gone to Toronto."

I was totally unprepared for this. I grasped at the only explanation I could muster. What was the name of that buddy of his who sent him photos of the Sky Dome? "To visit Jack?" I asked, trying to sound less shaky than I felt.

"No, he's moving there."

"Well, is there somewhere I can reach him?"

"No, we haven't heard from him yet. He said he'd get in touch when he found a place."

"Oh."

"I'm sorry, dear." She sounded as if she really was.

I once took an art history course in university in the hopes of gaining insight into the painters Hemingway had loved and loathed. I can't remember the professor's name, but his dog came to all the classes. The dog, who slept in the aisle near my feet, wore a red kerchief around his neck and was named Picasso because he was from Spain. In that class, we were shown a bronze door picturing God holding out an accusing finger at Adam, and Adam pointing at Eve and Eve pointing at the serpent. I don't remember the name of this work of art on the door of some European cathedral, but the image of bronze blaming always stayed with me. Up to this point, I had refrained from blaming anyone but myself for what had happened the afternoon of the birthday party. I had been drinking. I had been hurrying. I had looked up when I should have been looking straight ahead. I had not worn the helmet that was designed to protect me, because it was lost in the woods after a masquerade dance no one had attended. But now I thought that if flamenco girl had not waved her black lace fan, Luke might not have gone home with her, and if Luke had not gone home with her, I might not have been sad enough to fly through the woods in search of a sunrise, shedding my horns on the forest floor, and I would have worn my helmet to the birthday party instead of a pink hat with roses which could not be expected to protect anybody from anything. Then maybe Luke would not have slipped away to Toronto. I wasn't even sure if I wanted anything to happen between us, but at least the possibility had been there and now it was gone. He might even have been the one who handed the red helium balloon to the little girl in the green dress, saying, "Are you sure you don't want me to tie it on your wrist?"

Alice generally ate her meals in our room because she felt self-conscious about the Jobst garment, but I made a practice of going down to the cafeteria. Many of the young men in rehab were there because of motorcycle or ATV accidents, but there was one young man, Kip, who sometimes ate lunch with me, who had been in a car accident. He told me that he'd been severely injured because his seat belt had broken. It was difficult to watch him struggling to eat, spilling soup on his bib, talking with a slur as if he was very drunk, laughing like a donkey braying, and, all the while, the puckered scar from the tracheotomy moving on his throat like an extra mouth. He said watching someone carrying a full cup of coffee across a room without spilling a drop was enough to make him weep with envy. He had wanted to sue because he had done everything right; he had been wearing the belt designed to keep him safe, but the lawyer pointed out that it was right there in the owner's manual that you were supposed to regularly check the belts for wear. If they were frayed, you were supposed to replace them, as if anyone ever did such a thing. Alice in her Jobst garment said, "You can't dwell in these things." I thought at first I had misheard, but Alice had said "in" and not "on" because, as we both discovered in those hard days of recovery, there was no true shelter there, nothing in the way of "what if" that could keep out the rain.

A month after I arrived, on the last day of October, I said farewell to Alice and Kip and all those who had yet to heal on the outside, and found my own way back to the island I could not remember leaving. I left by plane but came back by boat, crossing over on the ferry as a foot passenger. This was not the Black Boat, the old ferry which had taken Es and me to the island the first time, complete with the map of Gannet Island chiselled on the wall, the tethering rings, and the life preservers, but rather the big new White Boat called *The Adventure*. Charlotte knew Captain Shepherd (as long as she could remember there had been a Shepherd piloting the ferry), and she and other islanders who had kept me constantly in their thoughts and prayers made arrangements to come aboard and decorate the cafeteria with balloons and streamers, and a large banner that said "Welcome Home, Pertice." The ferry staff were in Halloween costumes which made things even more festive. Charlotte herself made the crossing as a foot passenger to greet me at Deep Harbour. We spent the passage catching up on island news. She had just learned that her daughter Fay was expecting. She and Will were thrilled. A number of people were there to meet me when the ferry came to shore. If anyone thought that I still looked shattered, they were gracious enough not to say so. I was alive, and that was a place to begin.

Thomas, the RCMP officer who sat with me that first night amidst all the blood and grief and could not quite believe that I would survive, was there to give me a ride in his cruiser back to Honeysuckle Cottage, as he had done that first night from the lawyer's office. "Someone must have been looking out for you," he said. Motorists opening their doors into oncoming cyclists was one of the most common kinds of cycling accidents, he explained, and it was often fatal because the cyclist was thrown into oncoming traffic. But on Gannet Island there had been nothing oncoming but the asphalt.

By the time I arrived back at Honeysuckle Cottage, it was snowing, a rare thing for the last day of October. There was not much snow, but because of the way it drifted against the back of the house, the Toronto I built with Luke was completely buried from view.

5
PILLBOX

In the week since I had been back from the hospital on the mainland, I was having trouble sleeping, and the clocks falling back didn't help. I slept in till nearly noon, but when I awoke, I already felt exhausted. There is nothing like sustained weariness to fill the world with woe. I rolled over and turned on the clock radio. Though Remembrance Day was still a week away, they were leading up to it by interviewing people who had lived through the wars, their numbers diminishing year by year. This morning the voices were talking about an abbey somewhere in France. When the inhabitants returned after the war, they noticed that the snowdrops in the courtyard were growing in different places. They thought that maybe the Nazis had hidden something, and they had—the bodies of young Canadian prisoners of war who had been shot in cold blood while standing in a circle, their hands joined.

Hemingway thought that writers who dismissed war as an unimportant or abnormal or diseased subject were just jealous because they had missed out on something irreplaceable. He himself had been just the right age to get a crack at all the major wars of the century. It wasn't that he thought it was all guts and glamour. In *A Farewell to Arms*, he wrote: *Now for a long time, I had seen nothing sacred, and the things that were glorious had no glory and the sacrifices were like the stockyards at Chicago if nothing was done with the meat except to bury it.* Nonetheless, he believed war gave a writer a great advantage. Where else could you observe this kind of desperation and wounding on a daily basis? Where else could you see courage and fear and violence stripped clean of domestic complications and rituals? Where else could you learn to look at death without shutting your eyes?

I looked up through the skylight, remembering my first glimpse of Luke's torso through that gap. Luke was gone, taking his lissom body with him, taking the large tools in his red metal box, and the tiny tools on the timepiece I had given him. He had vanished to the life-sized version of Toronto, away from the miniature version the two of us had built in my backyard. And now I found myself thinking about Hemingway again. Ernest came seeping back, the way seawater will eventually fill up the hole you make in the sand, if you dig it deep enough.

The Sovereign Remedy was one of Hemingway's many names for death. *There would be only the moment of taking the jump and it is very easy for me to take almost any sort of jump*, Hemingway had written, explaining that going off an ocean liner at night would be best, next to dying while asleep. But there were only cruise ships now, and people would notice if you jumped off the Gannet Island ferry. They would throw out life preservers, or dive into the cold water after you. I felt sure I would start to fight for life the moment I struck the chilly surface. The American dream was a gun. Hemingway demonstrated to his third wife exactly how it was possible to shoot yourself with a shotgun, springing the trigger with your toe. And after finding him "a crumpled heap of bathrobe and blood" his fourth wife had had the gun cut to pieces and buried in different secret places so it would not fall into the hands of souvenir collectors.

Hemingway's first published story ended in suicide and for him it was a theme that never went away. After Hemingway went down in a plane crash over Africa, the world thought he was dead, and the obituaries said he had been trying to kill himself for years. If death to him was that old whore, he repeatedly tried to crawl in bed with her. After that first serious injury at eighteen, shrapnel to the leg in Italy, he seemed forever to be putting his body at risk, always pushing the edge of the possible. He boasted about how many scars he had. The thought of *Selbstmord*, self-murder as the Germans called it, did indeed provide calm passage across many a bad night, before his first wedding and after his first divorce, and later in those last dark days when he felt his powers receding.

"How old was he when he killed himself?" Alice had asked during one of our late-night conversations when neither of us could sleep.

"Sixty-one," I said, thinking how once that had sounded very old but with each year that passed, it sounded less old. "His son thought he would make a good old man, if he had allowed himself to become one." I told Alice about all the people in his circle who had brought their own lives to an end. His father, and his first wife's father, his sister Ursula, his brother Leicester, his muse Adriana Ivancich, his granddaughter Margaux. "Hemingway asked his mother to send him the gun his father used to shoot himself," I said.

"Did she?"

"Yes, she sent it to him in a parcel along with a chocolate cake. By the time the parcel arrived the cake was mouldy, but the gun was fine."

The interview on the radio about the snowdrops and the dead young Canadians was followed by the news. Wars and terror everywhere, pollution and poverty everywhere, disease and despair everywhere. The destruction of the earth and its inhabitants in full swing. I looked at the clock radio. It was unlike me to sleep in. It had become P. M. and I was still in bed. PM, the initials embroidered in chain stitch on the inside band of the pink hat I had worn the day of the accident, the pink hat like the one Sarah Moulton had worn in the last year of her life, the pink hat I had given to Alice to soften the cruelty of flame. I looked at the three hats that remained — the boater, the merry widow, the deerstalker. I hadn't yet dragged myself into the lawyer's office to pick up my November hat. The whole enterprise was losing its charm. I had worn all the hats as instructed, but they had achieved nothing. They seemed anachronistic and false. They seemed as fake as props in a play. And I was still no closer to finding out anything more about the woman who had lured me down here. And for what?

I dragged myself to an upright position. The floor was icy under my feet. The cottage felt cold and bare and somehow sinister. The physical pain resulting from the accident was nearly gone, and my face had more or less returned to normal, but the anosmia remained. I still could not smell the salt tang of the sea sharpened by the coming of winter, or the herbs in the window box I kept in the kitchen. Basil and sage, rosemary and thyme. These *arômes bien-aimés*, as Es called them, would they ever return?

Maybe I could make myself feel better with a good meal, a Valencian paella of rice, tomato, sweet peppers, and seafood the way Hemingway loved it best. I didn't have any saffron hand-picked from the hearts of the purple crocus (100 crocuses for a single gram!) so I had to substitute turmeric. With anticipation I looked over the recipe, but found myself reduced to tears by the phrase "season to taste." What was the point? Eating that had been such a pleasure and an art from the time of the persimmons had been reduced to methodically ensuring I did not starve to death. Though my sense of smell was stolen by the accident, my actual taste buds had not been damaged. I could still distinguish the extremes of sweet and salt, sour and bitter, but because one sense was so intimately connected with the other, the subtleties were gone. And anyone who valued the art of cooking knew it was all about subtleties. Since the accident I had been burning things because I couldn't smell the scorching until it was too late. I had taken to making a big pot of some kind of stew or soup filled with things I knew were good for me, it didn't really matter what, and heating it up a bowl at a time, day after day. And I would read while I ate, shovelling the food into my mouth without setting down my fork or spoon, without relish or pause.

I had only ever splurged with food, and only since the experience with the persimmons. Always buying the best, the most exotic, the freshest and the most flavourful. But after the accident, I had returned to buying the cheapest cuts of meat, if I bought it at all, day-old rolls, bruised fruit, and wilted vegetables. I didn't go as far as wizened, but definitely wilted. What did it matter when I couldn't smell or taste anything anyway? I could feel my mother's cheapness creeping back. Some people inherit a talent for music or sport, but I had inherited a talent for thrift from my mother, who truly believed that a penny saved was a penny earned. Because she had never worked outside the home, she was forever cutting coupons and cutting corners. You could put a positive spin on it and call it a virtue: frugality, prudence, economy, or good management. Or you could call it a vice: parsimony, stinginess, penny-pinching. Before the accident, I had seen what June considered a virtue as a cold bony hand holding me back from the good things in life. But it was not easy to shake off, to leave behind. It was like an addiction that caught you off guard. Even though you had been sober for a while, a chance to save a few dollars sucked you in again.

Now everything tasted like food under fire, like the *Pasta asciutta* Hemingway described in *A Farewell to Arms: cold cooked macaroni in a metal basin, a quarter of white cheese, dropped during a shell burst and covered with brick dust, sliced with a pocket knife and laid across the macaroni, served with wine in a canteen that tastes of rusty metal.* Like everything else these days, food was a disappointment. I thought of Alice, who was so good and brave in her Jobst garment, or out of it with her eyebrows drawn on with a cosmetic pencil. In the hospital I had felt inspired by Alice and by Kip with his lurching gait and tracheotomy scar, and all the others who were battling such enormous loss, barely held together by stitches and staples. Now I just felt guilty and bad. It seemed so petty to be grieving the loss of one sense when the other four remained. If you asked people which of their five senses they would least mind losing, they would probably say smell. Who would want to be blind or deaf or immune to embrace? But how many symphonies had been composed for the nose, how many masterpieces for olfactory enjoyment? And yet, as Es had discovered in that diner off the Trans Canada, scents beloved in the past and brought back to the present, had the power to drive away the *misère*. There weren't that many things I was good at, and this was integral to one of them. Once when a grade two teacher had blindfolded her students and asked us to sniff various bottles and identify the contents, I was the only one in the class with a perfect score. Remembering this made me feel even worse.

I was just sitting down to a bowl of paella when there was a knock on the door. It was Jim Flagg. "You didn't come in for your November hat, so I thought I'd drop it by." He took a quick look at me and then at the state of the cottage. I had always been a flurry cleaner, letting things pile up for a while, then sweeping through like a tornado and putting everything away. I knew that if you kept things quietly and steadily in order, you wouldn't ever have to do this, but even though the theory was attractive, it took a long time to reform the practice. I would leave the key to Honeysuckle Cottage in the pocket of the jacket I had been wearing the previous day, or on the dresser, or in the jumble in the bottom of my purse. You just never knew. When I finished cooking a meal, almost every pot and pan was used, and every spice jar had the lid off. When I'd lived with my parents, I had no choice but to be tidy, because my father had been painfully organized. On his desk were two mugs, one for pencils and one for pens. The pens you put in tip down to keep the ink flowing, but the pencils you put in tip up, so you could tell at a glance which ones were sharpened. Living alone, I felt free to be as messy as I liked, though I regretted the time I spent looking for things, but as Jim could tell at a glance, things had gotten out of hand. "Are you okay?" he said with genuine concern.

I shrugged. "My skills have slipped a bit, but do you want some paella?"

He looked again at the cluttered and spattered kitchen. "No thanks, I have to run." He let himself out without even waiting to see what kind of hat was in the box. After he was gone, I opened the box and pulled out a beige pillbox hat with a veil and, as usual, there was a letter.

Dear Pertice,

I bought this hat in 1963 to be married in, but that year turned out to be an *annus horribilis*, as Queen Elizabeth would say. In February, Sylvia Plath committed suicide, then in June, a monk in Saigon set himself on fire. In July, I was to be married to a draft dodger who had come to Toronto. Perhaps he saw it merely as a marriage of convenience for the sake of citizenship, but I was in love. Years later, as the Vietnam war dragged on, there was a lot of encouragement for women to support peace in this way. I remember seeing a poster of three women (two in bare feet and all wearing hats) on a sofa beneath musical instruments hanging on the wall. The caption read "Girls Say Yes to Boys Who Say No." But even in the early days of the war, it was considered by some to be a heroic gesture.

I was in Toronto on my way to see a friend when I met him. We met on the streetcar and, as often happened, it was my hat that started the conversation. One of the styles in fashion in the late fifties was the Asian-inspired pagodine, or "coolie hat," as we called them in those days before political correctness. Because mine perfectly matched a suit I loved, I was still wearing it. A bearded man across from me said, "You shouldn't be wearing that hat."

"Why not?" I asked, trying not to sound defensive. I was used to people admiring my hats, so his tone took me by surprise.

"Because, as we speak, women wearing hats like that are bending down in rice paddies for the last time before napalm turns them into human torches." One thing led to another and before long, we had decided to marry quietly at Toronto city hall (the old one). I purchased this nuptial pillbox to wear with a cream-coloured suit. White somehow seemed too innocent for a bride of thirty-three at such a time in history, so I chose one that the saleslady called ecru, which I found out later means "unbleached" or "raw." As it turned out, my groom never showed up, though he did send me a note. He said he loved me, but to stay would make him a coward. He owed it to his parents and to his country and to his buddies who were already there to go and fight after all. By August, he was dead, like 58,000 other young Americans were by the time it was all over.

And in November of that year, John F. Kennedy was assassinated. As I'm sure you know, Jackie Kennedy was famous for her pillbox hats. She disliked wearing hats, but the pillbox at least was off the face, allowing her perfect hairdo to be the star. She got her hats from Halston, then milliner at Bergdorf Goodman in New York, because his head was the same size as hers, so she could be sure of a good fit. Halston took inspiration from Greta Garbo's hat in the film *As You Desire Me* for the larger and softer version he made for the First Lady. No longer the little military cap worn by cigarette girls and organ grinder monkeys, the pillbox became her signature hat, and the one she was wearing that day in Dallas. The blood-stained pink Chanel suit is in a Maryland vault, not to be seen by the public for a hundred years, but no one knows the whereabouts of the pillbox hat. Because we were watching black and white television we did not know until after that her pillbox was pink. But the hat with the veil she wore to the funeral, we all knew that was black. The world looks different through a veil. Brides know this. Women in purdah know this. Widows know this.

A pillbox also refers, of course, to those small concrete fortifications for machine guns or other weaponry. There are still many from World War II overlooking the beaches of Normandy where so many Canadians were slaughtered. The pillbox was also used, though less frequently, in Vietnam. One became my beloved's grave.

Peace by the Sea,
PM

I put on my November hat, the ecru pillbox with the veil that all but disguised the few scars the stitches had left behind. I took a deep breath. Sometimes a walk helped a black mood, or "black ass," as Hemingway called it, the despair that made him repeatedly want to bring his life to an end, though there were things that kept him from it. His father had taken his own life, and he thought his father was a coward. It would be a bad example to his children. Life always got better and it was one's task to endure. *The real reason for not committing suicide,* he wrote thirty-five years before he pulled the final trigger, *is because you always know how swell life gets again after the hell is over.*

After a hike through the woods, it was like coming to the edge of the world to arrive at the cliff top, the light and the wind exploding upon you. I arrived at the cliff the islanders called "Seven Days' Work." From the water you could see the seven distinct layers of lava flow that gave the cliff its name. Island people were used to cliffs, took the necessary precautions, but those from away didn't always understand. The night of the fiasco at Swallowtail Light when Thomas, the RCMP officer, was insisting upon ropes around the dance floor, he told me about one couple who were lost in a fog and trying to find the shoreline to orient themselves. When the woman went suddenly over the cliff edge, the husband had her by the hand and the force of her fall pulled him down too. A family passing in a boat below saw them at the base of the cliff and called for help on a cell phone. She died but, miraculously, he survived.

Darkness was coming sooner and sooner these nights. Though this was not the sunset end of the island, the redness of the sky was reflected in the pools left by the receding tide far below on the rocky ribbon of beach. The radio program about the dead Canadians I had awoken to had continued with soldiers who were at Normandy speaking of the sea turning to blood, the beaches slick with it. How could a world where humans slaughtered their own be a good one to live in? No sailor's delight here. Even on this island in the sea, where everything was so harshly beautiful it brought a lump to my throat, where ringed-neck pheasants burst beautifully from hedges of wild rose, the mouths of sea urchins looked like tiny lanterns, and the first snow fell on the shoulders of Swallowtail like an exquisite lace shawl, the human was still so shambolic. I came across that word in a book once, and it seemed perfect to describe the state of the world. Chaotic, disorderly, undisciplined. You didn't need any special equipment to see that the world was a mess; it was visible to the naked eye, and I felt lately that my eyes were naked, painfully pinned open so I could not help but look. If you were in a wheelchair, people knew you were suffering. They gave you special parking spots and ramps and washroom stalls. It had been easier when people could see that I was hurt, when the cast and the stitches explained my pain. But now, once again, I was like most people, with the injuries on the inside, involved but invisible.

I stood at the very edge of Seven Days' Work, the cold wind making my eyes water, stunted shrubs pushing against my legs, my head spinning with vertigo and desire. The wind suddenly lifted my pillbox and sent it sailing over the cliff. Watching the hat descend, I could feel it in my gut—the intrigue of the brink. The bottom was so far down I could barely make out where the pillbox finally came to rest, nothing more than a pale smudge against the dark rocks at the water's edge. I had seen gannets, the seabirds that gave the island its name, waddling and hopping towards the cliff's edge, awkward and ungainly, moaning strangely. But airborne, they became suddenly full of grace and power, perfectly equipped for the plunge. Gannets, I had learned, could see forward with both eyes, which was rare in birds. They could clearly see the deep dark water rushing towards them. The splash they sent up on impact was taller than a human being. The sweetness of descent. Effortless when everything else seemed so hard.

At that liminal and shambolic moment, the three-legged dog I had seen that first day at Swallowtail Light, a dog that seemed to belong to no one and was the colour of a fox or a flame, suddenly appeared from the underbrush. He ran with his strange hopping gait along the path at the edge of the cliff, sniffing all the while with his nose to the ground as if he were sniffing at a crack of light under a closed door. Beside a twisted spruce he paused and looked back at me. Because of this strange gesture of invitation, seemingly directed at me, I turned away from the edge and followed him. Before I was halfway home, he disappeared again into the bush.

When I got to the cottage, the *misère* had not gone away. The home that had once seemed a haven now seemed filled with menace.

Suddenly everything became a weapon I could use against myself. The medicine cabinet, the kitchen drawers, the vanity, all filled with hazards. Even my shoelaces. I looked at the kitchen knives that I always kept razor sharp because Julia Child insisted that you must not bruise or mash whatever it was you were slicing. I pulled the largest and deadliest of these knives from the block and held it in my hands. I decided to put a notion to the test. From the back of my closet I retrieved the black high heels that Luke had given me, and I took the knife and sawed the tip off one of the heels. There was a full-length mirror on the back of the bedroom door, and if I craned my neck to look back over my shoulder I could see myself walking away. It did not seem to have the effect that Luke said it would. I did not feel sexier. I did not feel like Marilyn Monroe. Or maybe I did, the way she looked in that photo Luke had taped on the inside of the lid of his toolbox with a mesh scarf over her face like chicken wire, her eyes as shadows only, her mouth an open red gash.

In the bathroom, on a shelf over the sink, were the pills the doctor had given me against the nightmares. I had been careless. I had let myself look up at a red balloon soaring into a blue sky, but surely lapses of this kind were permissible. The number of moments of grace people were granted in the course of a day was staggering. Time after time people were allowed to escape from the consequences of their carelessness. When they tumbled into the soft snow instead of into the tree that sheared off the front of the toboggan. When they arrived safely at their destination, though they could not recollect the drive. When they walked away from the tornado-ravaged house that had been smashed by the fist of fate. Maybe it was something larger, more intrinsic, maybe hubris or desire. Or maybe it was nothing at all.

I took the pill bottle to the kitchen table, struggling with the cap because it was childproof, pressing down and turning, pressing down and turning with a futile click, like an empty chamber in Russian roulette. But I got it open at last and the pills spilled out on the table. This was neither original nor brave, but it was all I could manage. I considered how they could be taken. Slowly, with sips of water, as you took medicine to make you well one after another until they were gone, or greedily, stuffed in your mouth all at once like candy. I watched the pills for a while until they looked like purple beetles crawling towards me.

There alone in the cottage, with darkness pressing in and winter coming on, I felt completely defeated by absence, completely tempted by annihilation. Who would mourn? June, of course, but she would bounce back with her cheer and determination to be useful. She would buck up and move on as she had done when her husband had quietly succumbed to death. She would mend her way out of sorrow as if it were a loose button or a fallen hem. My father was dead, beyond the reach of any sorrow. There was Charlotte, but she had her own family to worry about. There was Es, but she had Mr. Maybe, who had turned into Mr. Yes.

I looked at the purple pills and heard a ringing in my ears. I thought maybe it was the purple beetles making the noise that cicadas make as they call to their mates or when they are captured or disturbed into flight. But then I realized it was not the pills on the table but the phone that was ringing. Identified, it was still a harsh and foreign sound like curses in another language. It did not make any sense to me and I believed if I ignored it long enough, the sound would go away. But it did not stop as I expected. It kept on ringing, until it began to sound familiar and urgent, like the particular cry of one's own child which, Charlotte had told me, mothers distinguish even in a room crowded with fussing children. I picked up the receiver to stop the ringing but I did not answer.

"Hello, Persimmon. It's Charlotte." I did not say anything but Charlotte could hear me breathing. "Could you come over? There's someone who wants to talk to you." As I hung up the phone, I suddenly felt certain it must be the hat lady, the mysterious Miss M, the stranger who had intervened in my life in a dramatic and irrevocable way by sending me a key to a door that I had not known existed. Maybe she had come back to the island, ancient and near death, to gauge the success of her experiment. Maybe she was ready for what they called on home renovation shows "the reveal," when the results of all the hours of renovation and redesign would at last be unveiled, and everyone would gasp and hug and use all kinds of superlatives whether they meant them or not. I wanted to meet the hat lady, to ask her why she had bequeathed the house and the hats to me, why she had insisted that I draw attention to myself with feathers and finery. I wanted finally to put a face to the stranger I had so often imagined and dreamed. It was this desire, as muddled and uncertain as it was, that compelled me to brush the pills like breadcrumbs from the table into a cupped hand and to flush them away.

I blew my nose hard and got ready to go. I put on my *cauchemars* and tied the laces like someone who was following instructions, rather than someone who knew how to do this simple task. The pillbox was at the bottom of the cliff or already dragged out to sea by the tide. The beautiful *bergère* was being worn by Alice. The merry widow reminded me of dead birds, and the boater of drowned girls. I didn't really want to wear the deerstalker, because it reminded me of the black fan and the red balloon. If there had been a black *montera*, the bullfighter's hat with its knobs like blunted horns, I would have worn it, but there wasn't, so for the first time since I had arrived on the island over four months ago, I headed out hatless. I walked out the door and down the shore toward Aristotle's Lantern. I felt eager and anxious and on fire. My breath came in pale little clouds. It was beginning to snow again, flakes gathering like dandruff on the dark shoulders of the road. The key on its blue ribbon was cold against my chest. It was the key that reminded me of the deal I had agreed to, and I went dutifully back and fetched the deerstalker since it was the latest before the two hats that were now gone. Perhaps at last the mystery would be solved.

It was not the hat lady after all. Of course it was not the hat lady. Things rarely happen that way. Wishing does not make it so. Charlotte met me at the door. I would not look at her directly, and wondered if my face beneath the deerstalker looked as pale and haunted as I felt. "Would you like a cup of something warm?" Charlotte asked.

I knew if I said yes, she would return in a moment carrying a tray. Charlotte always brought everything on a tray, even if it was only a cup of coffee. But what normally would have been construed as a cozy invitation struck me in my current state of mind as an insult, like offering a thimble of water to a man dying of thirst. There was no salve for the pain of distances. "No," I said, more abruptly than I had intended to.

"Will wants to talk to you."

I had not seen Charlotte's husband since the night of the dance, when he had awarded me first prize for my deer costume. Even when I'd been working every day with Charlotte over the summer, I had rarely seen him. From time to time he would breeze in to get a coffee or check the mail, but he spent most of his time in his studio or travelling to the mainland to do watercolour workshops. I could count the words we had exchanged on one hand. And now, suddenly, he wanted to talk to me, had called me from urgent tasks to speak? "Why?" I asked, feeling disgruntled and shaky.

"I was telling him you were feeling blue." This is the way Charlotte described it. I knew she meant melancholy, but perhaps to an artist like Will it meant turquoise, or cerulean, or cobalt. I envisioned myself as an elongated man from Picasso's blue period, wistfully playing a guitar. And I thought at the moment it was not blue I was feeling but red—magenta, vermilion, incarnadine—the harsh shade of rage. "He wants to talk to you."

I was on the verge of saying I did not want to talk to him, of turning and walking away, but then Charlotte said, "Please." And it seemed rude suddenly to walk away from Charlotte's kindness, from her effort, from her goodwill, from the tray that would arrive laden with a steaming cup and sweet things. And this is what kept me there against my will, not any philosophical triumph over despair, but rather a tradition of gratitude I had long attempted to cultivate. "He's in his *atelier*," Charlotte said.

Calling a converted garage an *atelier* had always seemed pretentious to me. I was still feeling ungenerous. On one side of the door was a brass carriage lamp, and on the other a little bird house, built to look like a Swiss chalet, and over the door was a horseshoe, pointing up like a U so the luck would not fall out. I knocked on the door, but there was no response. I wanted to leave, but did not because Charlotte was standing in the kitchen doorway watching me. So I turned the handle and walked in. The room was awash with paintings and empty canvases stacked on the floor, on the tables, against the walls. Everywhere paintings leaning against one another like dominoes in the process of falling. It seemed very cold, though there was a Franklin stove in the middle of the room. Will was at work, sitting on a chair with his back to me, wearing a sweater like the one Hemingway wore in that Karsh photo that was so famous. Apparently, just before that photo was taken, Hemingway had been weeping in pain because of the injuries from the airplane accident in Africa, and that was what gave him that sad, inscrutable expression that people said foreshadowed what was to come.

Because his back was to me, I could not see Will's expression. I cleared my throat but he did not turn. He was not making this easy. Beside him a range of brushes lay on a tray, as neatly as if they were a surgeon's tools, the camel hairs pointing all one way. There were several empty coffee mugs and an overflowing ashtray. He must be so focused on his work he does not hear me at all, I thought. I did not know what to do, so I walked over to him and touched his shoulder. He turned instantly, his paintbrush in the air like a baton. "Ah, Persimmon. Sit, please." He rinsed his brush and pulled up another chair to face his own. "I want to tell you a story." His English accent was stronger than I remembered it, his voice scratchy from cigarettes but also kind of sing-song and loud.

I took off my deerstalker and put it in my lap. I did not say anything, so he proceeded. "Once upon a time, there was an English boy who wanted to be an artist. But his father, who was a businessman and good with figures, thought this was foolishness. He got him a job in a shipping office instead. And then one day the boy woke up feeling terrible and thinking he had lost his voice, because he could not hear himself shouting. His mother came tearing up the stairs, but all he could see was her mouth opening and shutting. Overnight he had gone stone deaf. He was seventeen years old. People thought he would die and he was in a lot of pain, so much so that they had to strap him to a bed so he would not throw himself about. They discovered that it was spinal meningitis, which is usually fatal. But he did not die. Eventually, he got well, though he had to learn to walk all over again. But he could no longer work in the shipping office, because he was deaf and could not talk on the telephone. He eventually learned to lip-read, but he could not talk to people he could not see. His cousin, who was an artist in London, persuaded his father to support him while he went to art college, where he learned to draw. Then he went to Paris, where he learned to paint. Then he went to Canada, where he learned to make a living at these things." Will paused and looked at me while he lit a cigarette, cupping his hand around the flame as if there was an indoor wind.

I looked at him very carefully, realizing this was a parable directed at me, a tale meant to cut through the blue like a palette knife. I marvelled that I had not known. When someone is deaf you expect them to speak in that bubbling underwater way, but here was someone who was not native born, but only an immigrant to that harsh country. This explained why he had not carried on a conversation that very first day when he had given me a lift to Grand Harbour. He could not watch my lips and the road at the same time. "I didn't know," I said, chastened and still.

"I guess you could say hearing is one less thing I have to put up with," he said, laughing. "If anything, being deaf has made me visual in terms of being an artist. Deafness adds to the way I look at things." He paused to allow what he was saying to sink in. "There's more." He stood up and started to unbuckle his belt.

Nervously, I got up and began to back toward the door. "Please," I said, not in the two syllables I had used to the drunk who had called me Bambi at Swallowtail, but in one whisper of a plea, as I turned my back to him. I knew whatever he wanted to show me would be intimate and painful.

"Look at me," Will said, as he unzipped his blue jeans and let them fall to the floor. I was afraid to look. I had one hand on the doorknob. But I did look. The first thing I saw was a pair of silk boxer shorts with golden sunflowers against a deep blue background, but I knew it was not these he wanted me to see. There, where his right leg should have been, was a leg made of metal and plastic instead of flesh and bone. Amazingly, I hadn't known about this either.

Will pulled up his pants and sat down, patting the empty chair facing him for me to return to it. "This happened in a parking lot in Saint John. It was winter. I'd just come back from paying the parking fee, and I stopped for a moment to put my wallet away. Then I saw a big car come off the road. Heading right for me. And I thought it was a friend fooling, you know, playing a joke on me. But it was an old man I didn't recognize. He suddenly ducked down behind the wheel and kept on coming at me. So I turned around and tried to jump on his car, but I missed. He just came in WHAM! He had his foot on the throttle, not the brake." Will slammed his fist on the drawing table as he said this, to show how the car had lurched against him again and again as he was trapped between the bumper and the wall. "So he went WHAM! WHAM! WHAM!" The brushes jumped each time his fist fell. "He was seventy-three, the old man. He didn't know what he was doing. So he just panicked." Will picked up a burning cigarette from the ashtray, and inhaled. "The doctors were good. They came and got me quickly. I damn near died because I lost so much blood. One of my legs had turned back, twisted right around. And the other one was broken in fourteen places just below the knee. But as I said, the doctors did such a good job. They still kept the broken leg on for about a month. And then it developed gangrene. So off it came. They had to insert a metal rod down the twisted leg which stayed there for about a year."

He paused as he stubbed out his cigarette. "An actress friend from England sent me a telegram: 'Beethoven was deaf and Sarah Bernhardt had one leg, and if they can make it so can you.'" He laughed, remembering. "If it weren't for the deafness I might have gone into

theatre." He paused for a bit before continuing. "There's still more." I
wondered what else there could possibly be. "Since the accident I've
developed Crohn's disease. And believe me, a disease of the digestive
tract is a disaster for someone who loves food and Scotch as much as
I do!" He laughed again. With his white beard and his sparkling eyes
he looked just a little like a mischievous St. Nick.

"Is there a cure?" I asked, gripping my deerstalker very tightly.

"It can be controlled but not cured." Will leaned forward so
that his bearded face was very close to mine. "I don't tell you these
things because I want your sympathy. I don't. And I don't tell you this
because I am trying to diminish what has happened to you. But I am
trying to tell you what I've learned." He put his hands behind his head
and leaned back in his chair. "I think everything you go through gives
you something. You learn something from it. And then, you…well,
you just have to get over it. Get over deafness. Get over the artificial
leg. You have to do it for your own sake… When you wake up and see
one leg is gone, you get a shock, and you go through a depression. But
it passes. It passes. You just get on with things."

He lit another cigarette. I noticed that the fingers of one hand
were stained yellow, and knew it wasn't from pigment, or varnish, or
anything painterly. "My doctor tells me I should quit smoking," he said,
shaking the flame out of the match. "I told him that Jeanne Calment
didn't quit until she was 117, and then only because she couldn't light
her own cigarettes anymore."

The oldest woman in the world. I had read about her. She had lived
another five years after she quit smoking. "She met Van Gogh," I said.

"Yeah, and she thought he was ugly as sin and probably loco."

I laughed.

"Now, I don't mean this to be taken the wrong way," Will
continued. "But anyone who has been lucky enough to never suffer
anything very much, they don't know what things are about. I think
you have to suffer either physically or mentally to know what it's
all about. Just look at history. Most of the great people suffered in
one way or the other. And some of the not-so-great people, too. But

they didn't let that stop them. They kept right on with their lives." I remained silent so he continued. "Affliction is a treasure, and scarce any man hath enough of it. If I hadn't gone deaf, I'd still be in the shipping office. Wouldn't that be awful?"

"Yes," I said.

"Instead I'm here painting, and I have Charlotte, and a daughter who can carve things and talk to horses. I can honestly say that I've got 95 per cent of what I've always wanted."

When Will stopped talking, I rose and began to look at the paintings. There were portraits early on, but from the more recent watercolours, the human figure had entirely disappeared. "All artists are thieves," Will said. I did not know what he meant by this, and he did not explain.

"Are you famous?" I asked.

"You have to look at me when you're talking," he said, catching only the last word.

I had already forgotten about the deafness, he was so adept. I turned my face toward him and repeated the question, "Are you famous?"

"Not very. Before my accident I worked on more public paintings. Statement paintings. Huge things in oil and acrylic. But I haven't got the stamina for that anymore." I hadn't thought about him being old as well as injured. He did not seem old at all. "For years I had been preoccupied with abstract expressionism—crucifixions, fragmented torsos, renderings of the Othello tragedy. The work wasn't satisfying me as much as it had in the past, so on one snowy December morning, I destroyed many of the tormented torsos, re-crucified all the crucifixions, and allowed Othello and Desdemona to reach their own tragic end. Then I sat down and executed an unaffected realistic painting of a little white church that marked the beginning of my work as an Atlantic artist."

My hand was up to my mouth. I didn't even really hear the bit about the church and the new beginning. I was shocked that someone would invest all that effort in making something only to destroy it. "You destroyed them all?"

"Not all. The museum at Grand Harbour showed interest in a series I painted when I first came here called the *Human Compass*, four paintings named for the cardinal directions that expressed the things I've been trying to tell you. I could have been over there with all those bloody birds. But a man from Dark Harbour offered me more cash, and at that time I really needed the money. They weren't paintings you'd exactly want to hang over your couch. So the guy's probably got them stashed in his attic or something. I thought they were good paintings."

"Do you think I could see them?"

"I don't know. The last person who tried didn't have any luck. But who knows, the man, Mr. Harmon, I think his name was, must be getting very old now, if he's not already dead."

"I'm going to try," I said, picking up my Holmes hat and turning toward the door.

"Persimmon, wait," Will said, leaning empty canvases of three. different sizes against the wall. "Pick one and paint your anger."

Looking at the three blank rectangles, I knew that something had changed. Before my conversation with Will, I would have chosen the largest of the three, but now the smallest seemed enough. "This one," I said, pointing.

"Good," he said, placing it on the easel. He gave me a painter's palette and let me choose colours. I chose mostly reds. He handed me a brush.

"I can't paint," I said.

"We can all paint as children. Then we forget." And so I painted. Not anything you could recognize, just slashes and swirls that looked like blood and bruises.

"Now," said Will, when I was more or less done, "we'll burn it." He helped me tear the canvas from the frame, ball it up and put it in the Franklin stove. The stove had no window to watch it burn, but I imagined it withering to ash. We stood in front of the stove together for a few moments. I turned to Will and hugged him hard. I pulled back and whispered, "Thank you."

Will nodded with a smile.

Then I went back to the house, where Charlotte was waiting for me with a mug of hot cider with a curl of cinnamon bark floating in it, served on a tray as always. "Stay here for a few days, Persimmon," she said. "The beds upstairs are all made up, and we have no guests this time of year." When the cider was gone, Charlotte led me by the hand, as if I were a child, up the stairs to the room I had always thought was the prettiest, with its view of the sea and Battenberg lace bed linens so white they seemed dazzling. Charlotte was a great believer in the power of sleep, and the power of linens to take you there. The higher the thread count, the happier she was. She scoffed at anything under 400, and claimed once to have slept on Egyptian cotton of 1000 threads per inch, which could be purchased for a king's ransom. "Like sleeping on cream," she said.

I stayed at Aristotle's Lantern for three days, sleeping and eating and relaxing. Will wasn't around most of the time, gone on some painting excursion, I assumed, but Charlotte and I hung out watching black and white movies and looking at old photo albums and laughing. "Res age tutus eris," she said. Be busy and you will be safe.

When I'd come back from the hospital, the Island Inn assumed I would just go back to short order cooking as if nothing was wrong, but everything was wrong. Yes, I was more or less mended except for the anosmia, but Charlotte understood that it would take a while for my spirit to catch up to my body. She encouraged me to call in sick. When I said I wasn't sick, she said I was "sick with desire and fastened to a dying animal," quoting Yeats. She prepared wonderful big breakfasts for me like we always did for the guests at the B & B. It didn't matter that I could barely taste the cloudberry preserves I spooned on my crumpets. I could taste the good will. She cut my hair in such a way that the bangs fell flatteringly across the area that had been shaved for stitches. She pushed the furniture to the edges of the sunroom and taught me dance steps from back in the day. She encouraged me to read a Jane Austen novel and take long leisurely baths in the lovely claw-foot tub.

When I thanked Charlotte and Will for their kindness and hospitality and finally went back to Honeysuckle Cottage, refreshed and renewed, I was amazed to see Will had transformed my kitchen by painting birds on the cupboard doors, but instead of the bright little songbirds on the cupboards at Aristotle's Lantern, he had painted seabirds that spent their life over water, terns and kittiwakes, gulls and gannets. On the door of the cupboard I used the most, Will painted two northern gannets engaged in a fancy courtship ritual, their graceful saffron-tinged necks entwined like sculpture.

I realized in that moment that Will and Charlotte had performed a *quite*. A *quite*, according to Hemingway, *from* quitar—*to take away*—*is the taking away of the bull from anyone who has been placed in immediate danger by him… Quites made to take the bull away from a man he is goring or who is on the ground with the bull over him are participated in by all the bullfighters and it is at this time that you can judge their valor, knowledge of bulls and degree of abnegation since a* quite *in these circumstances is highly dangerous and very difficult to make as the men must get so close to the bull in order to make him leave the object he is trying to gore that their retreat, taking him out with the cape when he charges, is very compromised.*

That first day home after my stay at Aristotle's Lantern, surrounded by Will's painted birds, I found I couldn't stop thinking about the large paintings Will had told me about and the old man who had prevented them from hanging in the museum for all to see. I wanted to know why. This was another mystery worth exploring. It wasn't the bird in the hand, after all, as my father had always maintained, it was the ones rustling among the leaves or on the wing. Those were the ones to watch for. Mysteries kept things bearable. That and thread counts. I decided I would spend the next day trying to find Mr. Harmon. After a series of phone calls, I discovered that he used to work out of Dark Harbour, the only community on the forbidding side of the island, but no one really lived there anymore, except seasonally. He had moved back to his home in Castalia to live near his daughter. I considered calling ahead, but forewarned was forearmed, and I thought it might be more effective if I just arrived and caught him off guard.

I looked out the window. The little bit of snow from the previous night had not resulted in any accumulation, but now freezing rain was coming down. I had not ridden a bicycle since the day of the accident. Like me, my bicycle had been bent and broken, and I had not had the courage to have it repaired. It had somehow lost its innocence, like the knives in my kitchen or the contents of my medicine cabinet that I now knew had the capacity to put me in harm's way. Charlotte had offered me the use of their car for errands as long as neither she nor Will needed it on a given day. I was afraid of imposing and it was a stick shift, so I almost never took them up on their offer, but today was different. As I dressed warmly to go out, I looked at the hats in my bedroom, and opted again for the deerstalker. I set out to fetch the car that would take me to Mr. Harmon. Charlotte was worried about the roads being slippery, but Will had been out earlier and said they were well salted, and I should be fine.

"Is Mr. Harmon at home?" I asked the woman who answered the door. She was probably in her fifties. Her short hair was dyed brown but you could see the grey roots. She was wearing a grey T-shirt and what my mother used to call pedal pushers, though now they call them Capri pants again as they did in the fifties, after the island in the Bay of Naples. She was carrying a bottle of Windex and a roll of paper towel.

"I'm sorry," she said. "My father's not accepting visitors. He's been quite ill."

"Well, actually, I came about some paintings. I understand he has some of Will Murdoch's paintings which I'm very anxious to see."

"I don't think so," the woman said, nervously looking over her shoulder.

"Please, this is very important to me."

"All right, if you don't take too long. They're in the back room." The woman led me down the hallway to a room filled with broken and discarded things, including a treadle sewing machine and a chair with a fist-sized hole in the caning. She put the roll of paper towel under one arm and pulled on the chain of the naked light bulb overhead. "I've got work to do," she said, holding up her cleaning supplies. "Those home care girls look after him all right, but not the house." Then she left me alone. She rushed immediately away, possibly to clean but possibly to distract the man who didn't want these paintings seen, the man who had taken great pains to prevent such an eventuality.

Four huge canvases leaned against the wall with their backs to me. I walked over to the room's one window and tugged on the blind. It rolled up with a kind of slithering snap. The unframed canvases were about the size of very wide doors. With some effort I could just manage to turn them around by myself. I turned the first one and sat down in the chair with the broken seat to look at it, as I had often done at the Art Gallery of Ontario in Toronto. It was a crucifixion. This surprised me because Will said he had destroyed the crucifixions he had been working on. Also, I did not get the sense that he was a religious man, though I knew Charlotte went to church. In *Death in the Afternoon*, Hemingway spoke of the crucifixions of Goya, Velasquez and El Greco: *You can only judge a painter by the way he paints the things he believes in or cares for and the things he hates.*

The paintings I had seen in Will's studio were watercolour landscapes almost entirely devoid of human figures, but here was a painting crowded with faces. The composition was clearly influenced by El Greco's *El Espolio*; there were the three Marys in the left-hand corner, the soldier, the thieves, the carpenter, and the crowd all as spokes turning around the still hub that was Christ. But Will had not chosen the moment of despoiling, just as Christ's scarlet robe was to be taken from him, but a later moment when he was being nailed to the wood of a cross not yet hoisted into place. The crown of thorns was in place and the figure was foreshortened like Mantegna's *Dead Christ*, but this was not as surprising as the fact that he was naked, completely naked. There was no artistically draped loincloth like you see in all the paintings or the sculptured crucifix across from the gas station and strip club in Quebec. I wondered whether this was historically accurate but it seemed likely if the goal was to shame the criminal as well as kill him slowly and painfully in public view. But still it was surprisingly shocking. You saw nude after nude of women, but men were not often exposed in this way, even in contemporary art. You could look at a lot of religious paintings and never think about the fact that the Son of God had a penis.

But in Will's painting, unlike El Greco's, there was no anachronism, no centurion dressed in the Spanish armour of the artist's era. The armour, the clothing, all the details were consistent with the point in history two thousand years ago when this life was taken. The carpenter with his tanned and muscular arms was working with the tools of his day, his back turned to the action. Like El Greco, Will had signed his name on a rumpled and torn piece of paper painted into one corner. I could just make out the signature, the date and the letter "E" for East. The Easterliness of the painting leapt toward me now, especially the richness of the Middle Eastern fabrics and the dark faces of the crowd, and glimpses of olive and palm in the background.

I turned over the second canvas and set it beside the first. This painting, which was identified with the letter "W," was a portrait of the same man, though this time he was clothed and bending before a guillotine. He wore no crown but his own dark shorn hair contrasted with the powdered wigs of the men around him. The costume of the three Marys (or three Maries) who looked away from the scaffold and the blade shining in the sun was that of the French Revolution, though I knew the guillotine was still in use in France as late as 1978. The executioners, like the carpenter of the other painting, were intent on their tasks, only cogs in the terror. And almost to the very top of the painting, gilded architecture squeezed out the sky.

The third painting was marked "S." It was difficult to see what the man at the centre looked like since he was tarred and feathered and hanging from a tree, so that he almost resembled a bird more than a human being. But the three women in the foreground were out of Africa, the bright colours of their headscarves shining like gems.

There were no soldiers here, just a mob of ordinary people hungry for death. Through the legs of the crowd you could see cotton growing like bits of cloud tethered to the earth.

There was only North left, and this was a painting of the same man in a chair that looked at first like a crude throne. His head was crowned with electrodes, and his strong brown arms were strapped down. Everything about the room was meticulously reproduced right down to the nausea bags supplied for those in the crowd who couldn't take the smell of burning flesh. The man with his hand on the switch looked like the carpenter of the first painting intent on completing his task. The women in the foreground, though all dressed in modern clothes, appeared to be the ones from each of the three previous paintings. Olive skin, white skin, black skin. Someone in the crowd was pointing a television camera at the spectacle. It took me a few moments to realize what made this picture different from the others; in all of them the execution was a public spectacle, but this one alone was indoors without the sun as witness. The only thing that was reaching the man from outside was the current, beginning first in the northern snow and rushing south past the inukshuk, the thing that looks like a man, past caribou grazing, rushing downward to the dam, and through the great churning turbines, and into the wires, singing from hydro tower to hydro tower, things that also look like men though made from steel instead of stone, and down and down finally into the mind of the man who sat there waiting to die.

I looked at these paintings for a long time—East, West, South, North—thinking about the man who had painted them and the man they portrayed. There was Will, who had hovered around the fringes of my island life for months without making himself felt, but now, with his words and these images, he had suddenly thrown off his camouflage. And there was that other man that I hadn't really thought about since Es had called him a hottie on the trip down from Ontario in the *merde-mobile*. That other man facing his death from every direction. I was so absorbed in the images that I didn't hear the woman re-enter the room. "I think you better go now," she said in a low nervous voice. I moved to put the paintings back as I had found them. "I'll do that," she said.

As I came out into the hallway, a voice tumbled down from the top of the stairs, a raspy, bitter voice. "Why do you defy me? I thought I told you not to show anyone those pictures. Not ever! They're profane. They're obscene is what they are!" The woman ushered me out quickly. As the door shut, I could still hear the man's feeble voice trying to shout.

ᏕOU'WESTER

Those who went to sea harvested scallops, ground fish, herring, and finally, lobster until Christmas, while those who stayed on land picked strawberries, raspberries, cloudberries and blueberries. Traditionally the groups that made the most of these cycles of bounty were divided by gender but now there were a few women who went to sea and a few men who made jam, though many of the old divisions remained. "Thank goodness they don't come to ripeness all at once," Charlotte said, struggling to get the ripened berries preserved under glass like paintings. There was something so beautiful about jars of homemade jam. Without the commercial labels listing all the ingredients and chemical additives, one could admire the dark rich swirl of fruit shining through the glass. I watched Charlotte pack jars of cloudberry preserves in an old cardboard box. Charlotte was famous for her cloudberry preserves. I had never eaten cloudberries before coming to Gannet Island. They grew in the sphagnum bogs on White Head Island. The locals called them "baked apple" but Charlotte preferred their other name.

"These are for the Helping Hands Club," she said. "They always have a table." Charlotte had invited me to go with her to the Christmas bazaar in Grand Harbour. The thought of looking at other people's cooking and craft projects did not exactly appeal, but then Charlotte added, "You could go to the museum. It's just across the street." As we set out, I would have liked to feel attractive and festive, but no, my December hat was a black sou'wester like those in Van Gogh's drawings of fishermen, one of those oilskin hats waterproofed to protect from foul weather at sea.

Dear Pertice,

This hat was given to me the first time I was on Gannet Island when I was fifteen. My father came here because of Audubon's high praise of the bird population, but also to see Allen Moses, who spent his life collecting specimens for museums, including the one on Gannet Island. They called Moses the Island Bird Man. In the last days of Easter Island, leadership was given to the Birdman, the first to scale down the steep slopes, swim through shark-infested waters to one of three outlying islands, and bring back an unbroken egg of the nesting tern. Moses wasn't this kind of Birdman, but he must have gone through a lot to gather birds from all the difficult and dangerous places around Gannet Island.

My father was very busy all that summer, so I was mostly left to my own devices. The son of the fisherman that my father hired to take him out to Seal Island where there were puffins and petrels, a boy about my own age, saw that I was from away and lonely because of it. He took pity on me and when he wasn't out to sea or otherwise occupied, he befriended me and showed me around his island. He took me dulse picking at Dark Harbour and hand-line fishing over the rocky seafloor of the Devil's Half Acre. Watching him catch two fish on a hand line he was holding in his mouth while he gutted a third was one of the most impressive things I had ever seen. I accompanied him to feel in the weirs, those offshore nets you see around the island with a submerged fence to drive the herring into the heart-shaped enclosure that holds them captive. Feeling in the weir, he explained, is how they estimate how many herring there are, rowing around the weir towing a weighted copper wire. Amazingly, by feeling the number of times herring bump into the wire, an experienced fisherman can get a good idea of how many fish he has to sell. He asked me about my world and taught me about his own. Always he talked about the tide, which is more important to a fisherman than daylight and dark.

The day I left the island, he gave me his sou'wester, named after the worst kind of storm on the North Atlantic. Fishermen would soak sailcloth with linseed oil to make it waterproof even in a squall, and the low back brim kept the rain off the neck. You see them still these days in yellow, but traditionally fishermen preferred black because the dark shade drew the heat of the sun, and out there on the ocean, God knows they needed whatever warmth they could find. The black came from the soot from oil lamps they added to the oil they soaked them in. What was I going to do with a sou'wester in Ontario? I asked.

Wherever you are there's bound to be rough weather, he said. He was right of course. I have never forgotten his kindness.

Peace by the Sea,
PM

Feeling ridiculous in my sou'wester, I set out with Charlotte. My heart sank even farther as we arrived at the bazaar that was being held in the gymnasium of the Gannet Island Community School. There were some half-hearted attempts at Christmas decorations, red and green balloons filling up the basketball nets at either end, a few strings of Christmas lights strung here and there, some tinny Christmas tunes being piped through the speakers. "I'll be occupied for about half an hour," Charlotte said.

"Doing what?"

"I agreed to help with some judging."

The fact that Charlotte was being evasive made me curious. "Judging what?"

"Pies…" Charlotte's apologetic tone implied that she knew this was a sensitive issue for me. From the outside, I appeared to be healed. The cast, the splint, and the stitches were all gone. There was hardly even a trace of what had happened, but Charlotte knew about the anosmia, and how this invisible injury had all but broken my heart, though I was getting better at covering for it, following recipes meticulously, carefully watching the clock so things wouldn't burn. I had asked for shorter shifts at the Island Inn. In my absence Jasmine had taken over as the main cook, but I was happy as sous-chef, since it meant they were less likely to find out about my affliction. A few months ago, Charlotte and I might have judged the pies together, evaluating the pastry for flakiness, the filling for originality, taste, and consistency, as well as the overall aroma and aesthetic appeal. But now, I, who could barely tell the difference between sugar and salt, was useless. It would be like suggesting a blind man judge a painting contest.

The folding chairs had been put away on the racks that slid under the stage, and there were tables set up all around the perimeter of the gymnasium. I drifted from table to table, looking at cookies, squares, and loaves on Styrofoam trays, and various home-made crafts like toilet paper dolls where the crocheted skirt went down over the roll, and a variety of wreaths and sprays made with silk flowers, crosses of burned matches artfully arranged, baskets of potpourri, and ceramic Christmas trees with little plastic lights which glowed in different colours when you plugged the tree in.

There were a few booths that captured my interest, like the one with the man selling glass fishing floats, but I kept finding myself back at the table of pies, as someone who has been stricken deaf might look at instruments, admiring the curve and beauty of them, but longing for the sweet, sweet sound. There were pies with meringue and lattice and crumble toppings. The little card beside each indicated the contestant by number rather than name to preserve anonymity, as well as the title of the pie; there were traditional fruit pies, apple, cherry, even cloudberry, but also ones with more whimsical names like "Sunny Silver Pie," "Flapper Pie," "Rhubarb Cream Custard," and "Heavenly Pie." One said "Mystery Pecan Pie," and instead of fluting around the edge it was bordered with tiny pastry leaves winding their way around the pie as if it was a trellis in a garden. "If that one tastes half as good as it looks," I thought, "it's the winner."

Sure enough, a moment later Charlotte emerged from the wings of the stage with a clipboard. Behind her, corn stalks from the recent high school production of *The Wizard of Oz* loomed in the shadows. "Can people hear me?" she said. There was no microphone.

"No," someone at the back yelled.

"Could someone turn down the carols for a minute...Thanks. I'm pleased to announce the results of the third annual Island Pie Contest. The winner is Number Three, Mystery Pecan Pie. Could the winner please step forward to accept the prize?"

People looked around waiting for the winner to emerge. I was surprised to see a young man wearing worn Levis and a green plaid shirt come forward. From my vantage point right next to the pie table and the stage, I got a good look at him. He seemed vaguely familiar and had the look of someone who spent a lot of time out of doors. His brown hair was cut very short and he was wearing work boots, one of which had a gash in the leather, exposing the steel toe beneath. He didn't bother with the stairs, but hopped directly onto the stage, using his hands for leverage. He said something to Charlotte that I couldn't hear. Then she said, "Congratulations to Mr. Clive Ferguson."

As he went by me, he held up his prize, which was a tiny watercolour of fishing boats, painted, I assumed, by Will Murdoch. "Last year the prize was a ceramic Christmas tree," he said, flashing me a grin. I wasn't sure whether this implied that he had also won last year or if he was just expressing a preference for this year's prize. Up close I could see a pale scar on his upper lip, and one slicing through his eyebrow like lightning forking through a dark sky. His nose was slightly crooked, as if it had been broken, and his eyes were somewhere between blue and grey like the sea. He paused and looked at me closely. "I know you," he said, shaking a finger in my direction. It sounded like a pick-up line, but I had the same feeling. "You're the deer," he said after a moment.

"You're the lighthouse," I said, remembering how he had stuck his pocket flashlight in his mouth and turned slowly before the judge as behind him Swallowtail Light sent her revolving beam far out to sea, and how he had used Luke's magnifying glass to show me the vinyl valleys where the music lives. He nodded. "Congratulations," I said. "Your pie looked great."

"Want to try it?"

"Why not," I said, unwilling to explain that all I would get was a vague sensation of sweetness. Using one of the fancy silver servers that were there on the table for the judges to use, Clive cut a small sliver for me and for himself. There didn't appear to be any plates or forks so we ate it from napkins like pizza.

"It's good," I said truthfully, but as I finished the last mouthful I almost choked with surprise. "I know what the mystery ingredient is," I said. "I could taste it…" Clive looked at me closely. "It's cream cheese, isn't it?"

"Yes," he said.

"I could taste it…" I said again, my voice trailing off. At last, the first sign that subtleties were returning. The doctors had said the anosmia might cure itself if the brain was able to reconfigure its wiring, but there was no way of knowing if or when.

A woman with a camera tugged at Clive's sleeve. "My public wants me," he said with a wink, waving over his shoulder.

I asked Charlotte what Clive had said to her before she announced the results. "He was concerned about eligibility," she said.

"What do you mean?"

"He lives on the mainland." That explained why I hadn't run into him before, other than the night of the dance at Swallowtail Light.

"Doing what?"

"Something to do with silviculture. He occasionally comes back to help his dad with fishing, but not often." I knew the second Tuesday of November was the most important day in the Gannet Island fisherman's calendar, the day the lobster traps went in the water, and that the days leading up to Christmas were especially busy ones for island fishermen. "I'm going to be a few minutes here," Charlotte said. "I haven't had a chance to look at the other displays. Why don't you go check out the museum?"

The museum building across the street from the school was relatively modern, having been completed, said the plaque, for Canada's centenary, but the painted dory by the wheelchair ramp and the huge old millstone leaning against the front were older than that. The guide at the desk said, "They built it for the birds," gesturing toward the display cases by a sign that said "Moses Memorial Bird Collection." There were eighteen in all, each filled with stuffed birds of all kinds, from eagles to puffins. One of the most impressive was the northern gannet, not so much for the plumage, which was white with black-tipped wing feathers and a smudge of saffron at the throat, but for the size. The wing span was two metres, the height of a man. I had occasionally glimpsed the bird that gave the island its name at a distance, but I had also read about them. Half a century ago, there were more here, but now they went to Newfoundland and islands off Gaspé, less populated places. But even there the pollution had found them. DDT and other pesticides had thinned the eggshells and hindered the hatching. The museum display card read: *Gannets dive with half-closed wings into the sea at speeds up to 100 kms per hour in order to catch fish and squid. They waddle on land but are expert fliers, alternating rapid wing beats with gliding. They spend most of their lives over water.*

In the Marine Gallery, I admired the huge lens from the Gannet Rock Light. The original museum building was too small to accommodate the huge light with all its lenses and hardware, so they just set the light up in the open air and built an addition around it. The lighthouse keeper had kept journals that carefully recorded all events including the smoke and ash from the Great Chicago Fire of 1871 that somehow found its way to this remote place. No island, it seems, is an island.

There were also rock samples illustrating the geological history of the island, frightening-looking medical tools that belonged to one of the island's early doctors, and the island's first permanent wave machine brought over in 1935, which looked like something out of Doctor Frankenstein's lab. According to the card, the hairdresser claimed she wasn't afraid to use it except in a lightning storm. Hanging on the wall was a Bicentennial quilt with squares depicting various facets of island life, buoys, boats, ferries, and weirs. I was not surprised to find that, according to the caption, Charlotte had worked some of the squares, but I was a little taken aback to see that some had been worked by Tiffany Flagg, flamenco girl, daughter of James of the Ampersand.

I was preparing to leave when I caught sight of a modest little display case tucked in beside the birds. The title read "Artist Opens Atelier," and it was about Will Murdoch. There was a wooden palette wonderfully smudged with paints in the many colours of sea and sky, and a field easel, one of those wooden ones that cleverly fold up into a carrying case. On it was a painting of "The Flock of Sheep," the local name for the glacial erratics, odd white boulders left behind by a glacier on the black rocky beach near Southern Head. There were a few drawings in pencil, including one of a fisherman wearing a ball cap and a suit jacket over a plaid shirt, his large wrinkled hands on the oars. There was also an excerpt from a book, explaining, of all things, Will's acquaintance with the Beatles in his early days back in Liverpool, where he was from. This also I did not know. Apparently, Will painted the murals in one of the bars the Beatles sang in, and he had even opened a jazz club of his own called the Kinkajou, though he himself could not hear a thing. The display also included several newspaper clippings. One of them dated from twenty years before and had a picture of Will with his hand on the door of his then brand new *atelier*. The horseshoe was there over the door but the bird house shaped like a Swiss chalet must have been a later addition. Will had a beard even then, though it had very little grey in it. On his head he was wearing a canvas hat with one side snapped up. At the front desk, I purchased one of the signed copies of Will's book *The Little Boats*, featuring his watercolours of various fishing craft of Atlantic Canada, dories and scows, shallops and skiffs, lobster boats, and even a whaler. That night I read Will's description of what coming to this ruggedly beautiful part of the world had meant to him and his art. *The quietness sharpened my perceptions. I became more responsive to the remarkable fluctuations of the seasonal weather and I found a blessed retreat from the ever-changing* avant garde *of metropolitan art…*

When the winner of the third annual Island Pie Contest showed up at the door of Honeysuckle Cottage early the next morning, I was caught off guard. "Charlotte told me where to find you," Clive said, in response to my surprised look. "I was wondering if you would like to go fishing."

I had never been fishing before, unless you count those early efforts with the red and white bobber like a little world pulled under by the tug of hunger. "Yes," I said, not caring if I sounded eager. "Yes, I would."

"I thought so. Charlotte mentioned that you were keen to go out on a boat and yesterday you looked so prepared in your sou'wester that it seemed wrong not to invite you. That's a great one, by the way, very old-school."

And so within the hour, I found myself climbing aboard a "Cape Island" lobster boat called *Hazel*. "After my mother," Clive said.

Clive's father was a wiry, taciturn man dressed, like Clive, in yellow rubber overalls. His face under his ball cap looked as leathery and worn as an old catcher's mitt and the way he squinted made him look grouchy. He did not seem happy to have me on board. "Don't get in the way," he said brusquely.

"He's never had a woman on board," Clive said to me by way of explanation. And I wondered what kind of negotiation had taken place to allow me this gift of experience, what it had taken for Clive to ask his father for this. I saw from the moment I stepped on the boat that the dynamic between the two men was anything but smooth. They seemed to get in each other's way, and his father seemed irritated by the smallest things, but clearly not enough to pass up the free labour.

As we moved away from the shore, Clive pointed out the floating cages for salmon aquaculture. "Lots of people think that will save us, but the stuff they feed the salmon and their excrement fouls the lobster grounds." Clive was almost shouting to be heard over the noise of the boat's motor. "People don't seem to realize it's all connected. Like the seaweed they're planning to chop down and sell for sushi. That's where the young of many species shelter until they're strong enough for open ocean." The *Hazel* motored past the herring weir that had belonged to the Fergusons for generations. Clive pronounced it "where." All the weirs on the island had names, names like "Struggler," "Ruin," and "Jubilee." Theirs was called Grit. The one by Swallowtail Light that always showed up in the postcards and photographs was called the Cora Belle. "The names," Clive said, "are passed down from generation to generation, like the weirs themselves." Some were abandoned, the nets gone but the black poles still standing like trees after a forest fire.

"Not as much call for herring as there used to be," Clive's father said, addressing me for the first time since he had told me not to get in the way, "except to make women sparkle."

Clive explained that the "pearl essence," the iridescent coating on the fish scales, was sold to add shine to lip gloss and eye shadow, as well as metallic paint. The December wind off the open water slashed at us like knives. I hugged my arms around myself. The coat I was wearing seemed impossibly thin and I was glad I had worn the sou'wester, which looked far less ridiculous on the lobster boat than it had at the Christmas bazaar. "Are you okay?" Clive asked.

"I'm fine."

"You're cold," he said. Before I could resist, he took off his slicker, dropped his suspenders and pulled his sweater over his head. The snug thermal shirt he wore underneath revealed he was definitely well-built, *bien-bâti*, as Es would say. He put his slicker back on and handed me his sweater. It was not at all like the rugged sweater Hemingway wore in the Karsh photo. It was one of those knit on circular needles in the Icelandic Lopi style that hadn't been fashionable since forever, but that Clive still wore because his mother had made it for him and because it was warm.

"Don't you need it?" I asked.

"I'll warm up when we start hauling traps." And so I put on Clive's sweater, realizing it was not an insignificant gesture. Offering someone your coat might be considered chivalry, but to give someone your sweater still warm from your body, that was more personal.

"I've never met a Clive before," I said.

"Well, I've never met a Pertice."

"Apparently, my father had a school teacher by that name. I was named for her but I have no idea what Pertice means, and not for lack of trying to find out. You?"

"My first name is actually Matthew, after my grandfather, but my parents always called me by my middle name, Clive, which means from the cliff. My mother says I was named after Clive Brook, a British movie star from the 1930s. He was in *Shanghai Express* with Marlene Dietrich, and he played Sherlock Holmes." He turned his head to profile and struck a pose. "Put that in your pipe and smoke it."

"I'm sure my school marm can't compete with that," I said, laughing.

"I haven't got that chin divot thing going on, but we do what we can…"

"I guess I should be grateful," I said. "I almost got Mabel, after both my grandmothers, but they gave me that as my middle name. And if I'd been a boy it would have been Melvil."

"Melville as in Moby Dick?"

"No, Melvil as in Dewey. My dad's hero. The man who invented the Dewey Decimal System. Apparently, he wasn't a very nice guy."

"Matthew, my father's father, *was* a nice guy. I think they named me for him in hopes there'd be more in the will." Clive's voice left behind the playful tone when he said, "Those are ours." He pointed at the buoys with a single green stripe floating on the choppy water. "Each fisherman has a different mark so they'll know where their traps are set."

The first few traps had no lobster in them. Mr. Ferguson looked at me as if it was my fault. As if I had jinxed the whole endeavour. But soon there were lobster big enough to keep, three and 3/16th inches from eye socket to the start of the tail. Each trap was re-baited with herring and salt and returned to the sea. "I wish there was something I could do," I said watching the two men hard at work.

"You can put on the bands," Clive said, showing me how to use a tool that looked a little like a pair of pliers to slip the elastics over the claws of the lobsters, so they would not harm one another in the holding tank.

"How come you don't do this full-time?" I asked. "You seem to love it." I had been watching him. He moved with such ease on the rising and falling deck, and seemed so at home on the water. On the way out to the lobster grounds, he had explained everything that was going to happen, so his head clearly contained all the necessary knowledge. He was "cut out for it," as my mother would say.

"It's a long story," Clive said. "There are things that force you ashore."

Mr. Ferguson became a little more relaxed as things improved. "In my grandfather's time," he said, "lobsters were so plentiful, you could wade into the water and scoop them up. They used to haul cartloads into the fields for fertilizer after storms had driven them onto the beach."

"People are greedy," Clive said. "The only reason we still have a lobster fishery is because a trap only takes one at a time. Each licence is only allowed a limited number of traps, and the number of licences is frozen." When we took a break for sandwiches and tea from a thermos, I noticed that Clive paused to scratch his eyebrows. The neighbours who had taken me to Sunday school as a child had been eyebrow-scratchers, so I recognized this clandestine action of grace in a public place. The closed eyes, the bowed head, the silent words of thanksgiving flying out to space. When he opened his eyes I could tell he knew I had been looking at him. He answered the question I had not asked aloud. "Yes, I believe." Then he said, " "Stick your hand in there," pointing toward the lobster box where the lobsters we had caught were crawling over one another in the shallow water. I took off a glove and stuck my hand in the water. The water was so cold it stung my hand as if it had been very, very hot. "That's what the water was like when the *Titanic* sank," Clive said. "Colder maybe. And the way I see it, we're in the water. In my opinion," he continued, "it's more of a risk to stay in the water than to get on the boat."

"What if the whole thing's a figment of your imagination?

"What if it's not?"

After that, the days flew by until Christmas. Alice, my roommate from the hospital, sent a postcard from Antarctica, of all places. She had told me in the hospital that since the fire, she had dreamed of visiting the continent on the bottom of the world, the last unscathed place. She signed it, "Alice in Wonderland." Since Christmas was one of the busiest times of year in the restaurant business, it was out of the question for Es to get away. June and I debated back and forth about visiting. She had an invitation to spend Christmas with neighbours in Ingersoll, but felt she should be here with me after all I'd gone through. I didn't like the way she hovered over me as if I was still an invalid or a child, so I made up a lame excuse about the risky business of travelling in winter. As it turned out, there was no snow after all, though I was longing for a white Christmas. Other than a string of twinkly lights I had looped from my seabird kitchen cupboards, there was no sign of the season. I was feeling lonely and sorry for myself Christmas Eve, when there came a knock at the door.

It was Clive, holding a little evergreen in a pot with a few foil ornaments tucked in the branches. "We can't live without trees," he had told me as we were making our way back from the lobster grounds and he told me more about his work on the mainland. When he first signed up for forestry, his father used to boast about him, calling him Paul Bunyan, but after participating in a few forestry competitions, chopping and sawing and lighting fires, Clive moved into silviculture, preferring conservation to consumption. It was a change his father couldn't stand. Now he called him a pansy tree hugger. Aside from a passion for fishing, Hemingway and Clive had this in common—a love of trees. In 1923, Hemingway had mourned for the oak trees in Toronto, dying of dust and pollution. *They are dying because they cannot stand the city. And the city comes nearer and nearer all the time.* When a huge ceiba tree threatened to tear apart the foundation of Hemingway's house in Cuba, his wife Mary hired someone to destroy it. Hemingway arrived with a shotgun before too much damage was done but he made her bow before the tree and pray for forgiveness.

"Merry Christmas," Clive said.

"Merry Christmas," I responded, feeling bad I had nothing to give him.

"If you don't have plans for tomorrow, would you like to join me and my family for Christmas dinner? I think Charlotte's going to the Christmas service at the Church of the Straits and Narrows. You could catch a lift with her. I'll meet you there and we can walk over to my house."

Before going to bed I looked more closely at the tree Clive had brought me. Nestled in the branches were three tiny origami ships beautifully folded from gold foil. They reminded me of the *Nina*, the *Pinta*, and the *Santa Maria* glistening as they sailed across the green. As a child in Ontario, I'd gone every year with my father to an asphalt lot to pick out a tree. The trees were stacked behind ropes and closed up like umbrellas so you couldn't really tell whether the one you chose would be a good tree or not, even after the man took a knife to the strings to free the branches. Christmas at our house had always been a tame affair and, I realized now, a somewhat hollow one. Just an excuse, it seemed, to get people to spend more money, or in June's case, to save it. Every year, after Christmas, she set up the ironing board beside the tree, ironing the used gift wrap for next year, while I was given the task of taking the tinsel down strand by strand and packing it away.

When I went to bed, I found I couldn't sleep so I got back up and went to look for scissors. The only scissors I had were the big kitchen shears and the little ones in the sewing kit that June had given me, saying "A stitch in time saves nine." Next to thread wound round a piece of cardboard like a truncated rainbow and needles in descending sizes was a tiny pair of scissors with blades no bigger than a humming bird's beak. I found some writing paper and began to create snowflakes by folding and snipping as we used to do in grade school. After I had a whole stack, I taped the snowflakes all over the cold glass of the living room window. This was the second time I brought my hands together and wished weather into being. I drew the curtains against the darkness and went to bed knowing it would be a white Christmas after all.

The next morning, I called Charlotte and we made arrangements for her to pick me up. "We should go early," she said. "All sorts of people who wouldn't normally darken the door of a church go at Christmas and Easter." I had planned ahead for my Christmas gift for Charlotte and Will, a beautiful coffee table book on the art of El Greco. But Clive had caught me by surprise with his invitation to his house, and I didn't want to go empty-handed. With everything closed I couldn't even pick up a bottle of wine. Feeling a little like crazy Aunt Bethany in *Christmas Vacation*, the one who wrapped up her cat and jelly salad as presents, I put the sou'wester that Clive had admired in its box along with Will's book on fishing boats, and wrapped it up for him.

Charlotte arrived, bearing a bouquet of holly from her garden. Since the black sou'wester was wrapped up to give to Clive, I put a sprig of holly in the black band of the boater, and headed out, feeling festive. At church there were some familiar faces aside from Charlotte. Jim Flagg and his wife, although not their daughter Tiffany. The electrician with the frizzy eyebrows. Even Jasmine and Jennifer from the Island Inn. A few others that I recognized from North Head, and lots I didn't. I didn't see Clive, but there was a balcony which I couldn't see from where I was, and I thought he might have been sitting up there. Inside the sanctuary there were no pews, only folding chairs in rows, and the lamps that hung on long chains looked remarkably like Aristotle's lanterns. There was only one stained glass window on the wall that faced the sea. It pictured the scene of Jesus walking on the water, saying to his frightened fishermen, "Courage. It's me." I had not been at a church service in ages, and I felt awkward, not knowing when to stand and when to sit, and when and where to look for the information I needed, like which hymn was being sung and so on, but I followed what the others did, and at least the carols were familiar.

After the service, Clive met me at the church steps. "Merry Christmas," I said, presenting him with the hatbox which he opened then and there. He was thrilled by Will's book *The Little Boats*, and equally excited about the sou'wester. "You said you admired it, so I thought you should have it."

"There's a photograph of my grandfather as a boy, wearing one just like it," he said. We walked together on the edge of the road, over the hill to his house. It looked different in winter, but I realized with a start that I had been here before. No sooner had I recognized the beige house with the lightning rods than Luke was striding toward us across the frozen lawn. I had not seen him since that day in the hospital when he had given me the dyed carnations and I had given him the watch. I noticed he was not wearing it now.

"Pertice, this is my brother Luke," Clive said, by way of introduction. Luke held out his hand as if we had never met, as if he had never offered to saw off my sole to make me sexy and get me into bed. But I couldn't keep the flicker out of my eyes. Clive seemed to pick up on this, though he said nothing. I had wondered the day I first heard Clive's last name announced at the pie contest if there was any connection, but the island was full of people with the same last names, Flaggs and Spragues and Shepherds. Luke and Clive were so different, it had never occurred to me that they might be from the same family. Luke had only ever talked about Toronto and said next to nothing about home.

As it turned out, everyone's kindness made lunch at the Fergusons' far less awkward than it might have been. There was another moment of shock for both me and Clive's mother when we realized we had also met before. She was the woman who had nervously allowed me to view Will Murdoch's paintings in Mr. Harmon's back room. And Mr. Harmon himself was there for Christmas dinner. He was too feeble to sit at the table, but remained in the living room on an easy chair in the fully reclined position, his portable oxygen by his side. If I couldn't even put two and two together for people who lived with me on the same island because of maiden and married names, it was no wonder I was having trouble figuring out the identity of Miss M. I desperately wanted to know more about Mr. Harmon and the paintings, but Mrs. Ferguson seemed anxious to avoid any discussion with her father there, so I didn't press the issue.

The Christmas turkey looked like something out of a Norman Rockwell painting and was as delicious as it looked. Over lunch, Luke related how he had been determined to make it home for Christmas. "My buddy Jack's working for Allied now, and he was driving a load of furniture down to Saint John. I hitched to the ferry, but I've got to be back tonight because he's due to pick up a load in Fredericton tomorrow." He did much of the talking, entertaining us with stories of Maritimers making their way in the big city. Clive was relatively quiet. I could tell he was watching me, seeing how I behaved around Luke, around his family.

"Your island is so beautiful, Mrs. Ferguson," I said after a pause in the conversation. I wanted to say "our" but didn't wish to sound presumptuous.

"Yes, it is, and please call me Hazel." The lobster boat under her husband's booted feet. The daughter under her father's thumb. She was silent for a moment before continuing. "And yet we have our problems. The young people have so much money from the fishing and nothing to spend it on but drugs."

"Time was, the Coast Guard helicopters looked in the water for people to rescue," Mr. Ferguson said, "but now they're looking on land for marijuana."

"And it's not just the small stuff," said Hazel. "We have cocaine and heroin coming across on the ferry. They've tried but there seems to be no way to keep it out."

"You've heard about the Island Five?" Luke said. I hadn't. A few years back, five island men had turned on the owner of a suspected crack house in Castalia and succeeding in burning it to the ground. Some called them heroes, but they were convicted as vigilantes. It was complicated. I had once thought of the island as a kind of isolated paradise but, of course, the world always finds a way in. No island is an island.

"And accidents. The Sinclair family here in Castalia has four teenage boys, and the oldest two have both been killed in separate accidents, one a hit and run. Naturally, they're worried to death about the younger two." She looked across the table at her sons. "My boys are safe so far, knock on wood."

"Now Luke's hauling down the big bucks in Toronto," Mr. Ferguson said proudly. "Unlike you, Clive, nothing to show for all the money you're making. You giving it away? How do you think you're ever gonna get ahead?"

"You don't get it, do you, Frank?" Clive said. I had noticed on the fishing boat that he almost never addressed his father and when he did it was by his first name. "I don't care about your big fancy truck and hundreds of channels, all your toys and trips to Florida." His voice rose in frustration. It was clear he'd said it all before. "How many times do I have to tell you? I don't want or need any of that, old man."

"Now Clive...we have company," Hazel said, sounding a little surprised. Clearly, Clive was usually the well-behaved one.

Between courses, we went into the den to watch the Queen's Christmas speech on TV. "Clive has the gift of salvage," Hazel said, when she saw me admiring the entertainment unit the TV was sitting on. Clive explained how he picked up the piano for next to nothing at a yard sale because the musical parts were shot. He gutted it, restored all the beautiful carved wood, and made an entertainment unit for the TV and stereo with space to store CDs and DVDs. The leftover wood from the project became an aquarium stand for his apartment on the mainland. "I have to surround myself with fish however I can," he said to me.

"If Clive sees something abandoned on the side of the road, he'll stop and rescue it," Hazel said. She told me about the metal frames from ruined awnings that became the roof of a new pergola for the backyard, and the broken handles of rakes and hoes that became a

tepee for the runner beans. "My father says Clive's the only one he
can really count on to fix things. Luke'll only do it if he's getting paid."

After the Queen's speech about finding strength from our families
was over, Mr. Ferguson changed the channel to watch the football
game. We left him alone with Mr. Harmon, who was now dozing,
and returned to the dining room, but Mrs. Ferguson. suddenly said,
"Oh, the cake!" and hurried off to get the pork cake, the same kind
of cake I was to have tasted the day of the birthday party at which I
never arrived. Clive followed her into the kitchen, leaving me alone
with Luke.

"*Dulcius ex asperis...* What does that mean?" I asked, pointing
at the clan crest hanging on the dining room wall behind Luke. The
motto was beneath a carving of a bee resting on a thistle.

"Sweetness something something..." Luke said. "I forget. You'll
have to ask Clive. He's interested in all that heritage stuff."

"Sweetness from Difficulty," Clive said, emerging from the
kitchen, holding a plate of dessert in each hand. The McIlveen motto,
as far as I could determine, was "Touch not a Cat without a Glove,"
which was somewhat less inspiring. And Ingersoll's crest was the wavy
blue Thames with a wheel of cheese on one side and a cog on the
other. Hemingway had invented his own crest, with three mountains
symbolizing the three *monts* of Paris as well as the three hills of Finca
Vigia, his Cuban farmhouse. Beneath them was an arrowhead of the
Ojibway tribe of northern Michigan, the wilderness of Hemingway's
youth, and two bars indicating the rank of captain he'd held in World
War II, his last, most glamorous war. You had that kind of power if
you were famous, to build a heritage out of the things you wanted, and
discard the rest. Ordinary people had to live with what was handed
down.

On the hutch under the clan crest was a lamp in the shape of a
lighthouse. "My first shop project." Clive smiled. "Luke's not the only
handyman in the family."

"Renovation specialist," Luke said, rolling his eyes. "I've even
got cards." He pulled a business card out of his wallet and slapped

it down in front of Clive. Luke rose to take a piece of cake in to Mr. Ferguson, who was still watching the game, and he never came back. Clive volunteered to do dishes while Hazel put the food away and I offered to help. When Clive put an extra squirt of dish detergent in the sink, tiny iridescent bubbles squeezed upward. He leaned forward and blew them toward me, and two or three floated across the air between us and landed on my arm, where they rested for just a second before winking out like stars. While Hazel was down in the basement dealing with Luke's duffel bag of dirty laundry, Clive said the first mean thing I ever heard him say. "He didn't earn the ring, you know."

"Who?"

"Luke." I knew Luke's ring, the ring worn by graduates of St. Francis Xavier University with the black X on a gold field that I had once thought of as X for treasure, but after Luke vanished to Toronto leaving no forwarding address, like a crude signatory X placed by someone who does not know how to write.

"He only went to St. FX for a year before dropping out to go to community college. He found the ring on the floor of a bar and, instead of trying to find the owner, he had it resized for himself."

"Why are you telling me this?"

"Because I don't want you to get the wrong impression." I didn't say anything but silently continued to pick up plates from the dish rack and dry them with a towel almost too damp to use anymore. "Sorry," Clive said. "But with that face he gets away with a lot." I knew this was more than the sting of the unchosen child in the schoolyard, the one not picked for the team until the end. Clive was also good-looking, though not in the eye-catching classical way Luke was. With his close-cropped hair and strong scarred features, Clive's looks were more rugged, more lived-in than Luke's. And his eyes looked straight at you, and sometimes through you.

"We had a sister," Clive said suddenly, pausing to allow the past tense to register. This explained the family portraits in the hall, the girl who was there and then not there. "We had visitors from England, people who heard about the Island from my grandmother, and Mom said we should take their daughter on a hike. I was in grade eleven at the time. I suggested we hike along the beach from Whale Cove past Seven Days' Work toward Ashburton Head, you know, the cliff named after the ship that went down there. The English girl, her name was Joan, wasn't that pretty, but she was well developed. So Luke suggested we go swimming because he wanted to see her in a swimsuit. My little sister Nina wanted to come along. She'd just gotten a snorkel for her twelfth birthday, and wanted to try it out. We didn't want to take her, but Mom insisted." Clive ran more hot water into the sink. "I don't know what came over me, but I set out to swim towards the rocks. I guess I wanted to impress the English girl. Luke didn't have to do anything spectacular with his body but stand in it to impress girls. As I was swimming back I could see Nina's pink snorkel sliding through the water and then it vanished. I expected her to appear again in a moment, but she didn't come up. She was gone."

"Oh, Clive," I said, carefully putting down the plate I had been drying on the counter, afraid I might drop it. Hazel had brought out the good china for Christmas.

"Luke and the English girl were splashing farther down the shore and didn't even notice. I yelled at them but they couldn't hear me because they were laughing and horsing around. I swam as hard as I could toward the spot where I had last seen Nina. I could touch bottom there and as I walked toward the shore I bumped into her with my legs. When I pulled her up out of the water she was limp in my arms, and already turning blue." I reached out and touched Clive on the arm for a brief moment. "I don't know whether she blacked out or struck her head on a rock. There are lots of them just below the surface, ballast rocks from the shipwreck, even after a century. I laid her on the beach, trying to remember what to do. She wasn't breathing, so I tilted her head back and gave her mouth-to-mouth while Luke ran for help. I don't even know if I was doing it right. It's hard not to panic. You know how in movies they always cough up water and everything is okay? That didn't happen." Clive reached up and rubbed his eyes with his hand. It was a gesture reminiscent of his prayer over the sandwiches on the lobster boat. There was a catch in his voice. "Her body was empty. As if she had moulted and moved on."

I put my hands on the kitchen counter to steady myself. All the time I had been with Luke, I had never heard about Nina or even about Clive. There was no way for Clive to reel back the reality he had cast in my direction, even if he wanted to. He reached into the soapy water and pulled the plug. "What did you think of church?" he asked, changing the subject to smooth over the rawness of the moment.

"It felt warm. Welcoming," I said. Then I asked something I had been wondering since I realized that Luke and Clive were related, "How come you believe and your brother doesn't?"

"It's not like it's hereditary," Clive said. "My grandfather Matthew was a believing man, but look at my father. You have to choose it." He paused. "For me, it began the day we buried Nina. I felt I didn't deserve to be in the world if she wasn't. Hanging seemed the simplest way out, but the bootlace snapped under my weight. I wore a turtleneck for weeks to hide the scab that circled my neck like a snake. Simon was the minister who conducted Nina's funeral, not because my parents went to the Church of the Straits and Narrows, but because it was the closest. He called me that week and asked to see me. I thought he was going to try and 'save' me, you know, but he asked me to try out the new sea kayak he had built in his garage. Things look different from the water, he said."

Since coming to live beside the ocean, I had learned that this was true.

When it came time to leave, Clive said, "I have something for you."

"But you already gave me the tree," I protested.

"One tree deserves another," he said, laughing. "It's in the back seat of the car. C'mon, I'll drive you home." When we got to Honeysuckle Cottage he presented me with a hat tree made of three old hockey sticks ingeniously fastened together. He said he still played hockey occasionally with the lads at the old outdoor rink, though last year a new indoor rink had been opened in Grand Harbour. He had been a goalie when he was a boy, he said, his small limbs weighed down with equipment, tending his little patch of ice as if it was a garden, roughing it up with his skates at the beginning of each period, stretching across its length to make save after save. He set up the hall tree for me just inside the front door, and I went to fetch my hats to hang on it. "There," he said. "Your very own Hat Trick."

ENDURABLE

The last day of the year, I made *tourtière* in the French Canadian way with that incredible mix of aromas that could drive away the *misère*, cinnamon and cloves and *noix de muscade*. I had missed the chance to have it on Christmas Eve like Es and her family, so I thought New Year's Eve would do. I hadn't made any resolutions, except to make the most of all my senses, now that all five of them were back. I would look hard at whatever the island brought my way. I would use the most fragrant spices to create the most delicious dishes. I would take the time to touch and be touched. I thought about Es's latest Van Gogh quotation: *In the end we shall have had enough of cynicism and skepticism and humbug and we shall want to live more musically.* I would make sure that there was more music than silence.

To that end, I was listening to a countdown of the year's best songs on the radio while I was doing the supper dishes, when I heard a car honk in the driveway. There was no mistaking that wonky honk. It had to be the *merde-mobile*. I could hardly believe it was Es. I could never decide whether it was because you were thinking of someone that he or she appeared, or whether people came to mind because they were already on their way. She and Jesse had had a fight and so she had jumped in the *merde-mobile* and driven all night. "I wanted to make it for Christmas but there was family shit I couldn't get out of and things were busy at the restaurant. I just made the last ferry."

A huge flat package almost filled the back seat. "Give me a hand with your present." Between the two of us we wrestled it into the house. "What are you waiting for?" she said, impatient for me to open it. It was the photo she had taken of me in my first hat on my first day on the island enlarged and multiplied into a brilliantly coloured Warhol-like silkscreen. The black frame was ornamented with an assortment of old stray keys glued on like a mosaic. On the back she had written in both official languages. "Art heals. Absolute art heals absolutely."

"I love it," I said, giving her a hug. "You got my present, I hope." I had sent her a carved Aristotle's Lantern, with a note, "It is the mouth that lights our way." "You don't know how happy I am to see you, Es."

"Me too."

"What happened with Jesse? I thought he was Mr. Yes."

"I thought so too, but I brought up marriage, and that freaked him out. He asked if I'd heard the one about sex in marriage. The first year you have 'Everywhere Sex,' meaning on the dining room table, in the shower, hanging from the chandelier, then the next ten years you have 'Bedroom Sex,' then after that you have 'Hallway Sex.' You pass each other in the hall and say 'Fuck You.'"

"I was convinced he was the one."

"We'll see when we've both had a chance to cool off. Oh well, c'est la guerre. I brought champagne!" Es pulled a bottle out of her big orange handbag and sat it on the table. "Just what the doctor ordered."

"I'm supposed to be going over to Charlotte's for New Year's Eve. I'll just call her and let her know you'll be coming with me. I know she'll say the more the merrier."

"Well, we should definitely dress up then. I brought just the thing."

We changed together in the bedroom of Honeysuckle Cottage, like we used to do in the washroom of Carnivores, though into dresses far more elegant than our uniforms for cooking and waiting tables. Her dress was of patterned green silk that shaped to her curves in such a way she looked almost like a mermaid. Mine was a strapless black bubble dress, with a grey sash at the waist. "I must say, I'm impressed," Es said, when she saw me in my new dress, my Merry Widow hat, and Luke's high heels which I had repaired. "And here I was, thinking you'd wear your *cauchemars*. You have changed!" she said. Not to be outdone, she pulled the smallest hatbox I'd ever seen out of her suitcase. "You inspired me," she said. "I found this great hat shop on the corner of College and Bathurst called Lilliput Hats. You would love it. Check it out." With the help of the mirror in the bathroom, she put on a charming fascinator with black and green feathers that swept down dramatically, framing her lovely face. "Eat your heart out, PM," she said.

We bundled into winter coats, which diminished the elegance of our outfits considerably, and piled into the *merde-mobile* with two *tourtières* and Es' champagne, but no amount of coaxing or cursing on Es's part could get the car to start. "Must be exhausted from the long journey," Es said, only half-joking. Finally, she released the hood and got out to look under it. Then she got back in the car and put her head down on the steering wheel.

"Need a boost?" It was Clive in Will's car. He had this way of appearing just when he was needed. Charlotte had sent him out for some last-minute stuff for the party before everything closed. Soon the two hoods were open, the car that was working lending its power to the one that wasn't. When the *merde-mobile*'s engine finally coughed into life, Clive looked in through the driver-side window where Es was sitting wearing her fascinator and a radiant smile. I introduced her as my friend from Toronto. "Try and keep that one out of trouble," he said, nodding at me and giving the *merde-mobile* a friendly pat.

Will and Charlotte's New Year's Eve party was held in the *atelier*. Large speakers had been put on the floor and cranked up so Will could feel the music. Charlotte had gotten a book of retro cocktail recipes for Christmas with Carmen Miranda on the cover wearing a hat like a fruit bowl. So along with lobsters and tourtière and Clive's prize-winning Mystery Pecan Pie, there were lots of fancy drinks garnished with parasols and cherries and orange slices pierced by tiny plastic swords. Clive had offered to be the designated driver so he had stopped after one beer, but he took over from Charlotte making drinks for the rest of us. He seemed more comfortable with me in a sou'wester, but he was clearly not immune to high heels and a little black dress. When a slow dance came on, it was his arms that encircled me. Everyone moved happily to the music, but Charlotte in particular was a wonderful dancer, loving every swirl around the centre of the studio in her pale blue fifties-style cocktail dress. Her elegance came as a surprise; I was used to seeing her in overalls.

Es in her fascinator fit in beautifully with these artistic people. I found her in an animated discussion with Will. "I like your friend," he said to me as I came over to where they were looking at a watercolour painting of a bleached and weathered old boat on a winter shore. He had lined up all his tubes of watercolour paint and was challenging her to choose the only three you need to paint a winter scene. He was impressed because she got two out of three right. Payne's Gray and Raw Umber. She only missed Raw Sienna.

We counted down at midnight Atlantic time and cracked the champagne and took a cup of kindness as we sang "Auld Lang Syne." After that Es taught us the words of a French New Year's song, "Choral des Adieux." My favourite of the lines she translated for us was, "For the ideal that brings us together will know how to reunite us." Then we got into telling island ghost stories. I had heard the one about the half-man half-horse that was said to wander the back woods, but not the one about the sailors who set fire to a Native girl and left her to burn. "Some of the old-timers say they've seen her ghost wandering on Indian beach in flames," Clive said. Will told us stories about his life back in England and about going cod fishing in Newfoundland, where he had lived when he first came to Canada. As the evening progressed, it came out that Will loved limericks, so we got into telling any we could recall or make up on the spot. Some were pretty good and some were pretty bad. I only remember Charlotte's contribution:

> There was an old man of the isles
> Who suffered severely from piles
> He couldn't sit down
> Without a deep frown
> So he had to row standing for miles.

At half past midnight, Clive got a phone call and said he had to go. His grandfather, Mr. Harmon, had taken a turn for the worse. The home care worker had called the Ferguson house but everyone there was pissed to the gills, so she called Clive hoping he would be sober enough to deal with things. The rest of us weren't ready to go home yet, so we hung around until 1 a.m. which was midnight Eastern, so we could watch the ball drop in New York on TV. Will went out on the porch for a smoke, and Es and I joined him. Es was smoking her pipe again, now that she was far away from her fireman. It was quite an incongruous picture, Es bundled up in a winter coat, wearing a fascinator and smoking a pipe, and me in my Merry Widow sipping one of the outrageously garnished cocktails Charlotte had created. Will did most of the talking, because it was hard for him to lip-read in the dim light. I learned that while he worked as a curator at a museum on the mainland, a lot of people never even figured out that he was deaf because he talked to them on the phone. A flashing light on his phone signalled him to answer, and his assistant would pick up the other extension, mouthing the words of the person on the other end of the line, so he could lip-read and respond. When he was young, he'd been told by a British Board of Education that he couldn't teach art because of his deafness, but he had ignored them and taught hundreds of art students over the years.

"What does it take to be an artist?" Es asked, as Will finished up his cigarette and stubbed it underfoot.

"No one can paint unless they first learn to draw," Will said as we went back inside. "Michelangelo knew that. Rembrandt knew that. Picasso knew that… Realism has lasted for centuries. And it won't go away. You can play with it. You can distort it. You can experiment with it. But you can't ignore it."

As we were getting ready to go, Es took the keys to the *merdemobile* out of her coat pocket and put them on the table. "I don't think I should drive, even if the car does start this time."

I looked at her and giggled. "Me either."

"I wouldn't mind meeting that nice RCMP officer you told me about, but not under these circumstances," Es said, holding on to the stair rail to steady herself.

"It's not that far. We can walk."

"In these?" Es said, gesturing down to her shoes, which were even more stiletto than mine.

"I'm sure Charlotte can lend us some boots." While we were getting organized, Will was rummaging through the bookshelf in the hall. "These are for you," he said, handing each of us a copy of a book he had written on Japanese printmaking called *Ukiyo-e: Art for the People*. I gave him a thank-you hug. When Es and I finally tumbled out the door in the wee hours to walk home along the shore he yelled out after us, "Ukiyo-e means pictures of a floating world."

New Year's Day we slept in. Es had always loved the beginning of a fresh new year with no mistakes in it yet, and this year I felt the same. We had no choice but to lounge around because everything was closed, though in the afternoon I challenged Es to join me in a polar bear swim in Whale Cove. Not surprisingly at this time of year, Es hadn't brought a swimsuit, but she didn't let that stop her. Emerging from the pewter grey waves she looked just like a selkie. "That was crazy!" Es said shivering, as we raced back to the cottage wrapped in blankets.

"I know, but I've always wanted to do it," I said, preparing Irish coffees with extra whiskey while Es got first crack at a hot bath. For the rest of the day we sat around in our pyjamas catching up on all the news. I showed her the deerstalker, and described the two hats I had given away to Alice and Clive, and the one that had flown over the cliff.

"Did you take photos of them?"

"A nurse took a picture of Alice in her hat, but no, it never occurred to me to get photos of the rest."

"You should keep a record. Look, I'm going to leave you my phone. I'm about to upgrade anyway. And as soon as you get a new hat, you send me a picture. And we can text." She explained that unlike a landline, it cost her long-distance charges, even when I was doing the calling.

I gave her all of the letters that came with the hats to read. "So have you found it?" she asked.

"Found what?"

"Peace by the sea?"

"I'm working on it."

The next day, Es drove me to Grand Harbour to pick up my January hat. "How long do you suppose this is going to go on?" she asked.

"No idea," I said. "This is number seven."

I opened the box in the reception area of the law office and put on the new hat, as had become my custom once I realized Jim was as curious as I was. The new hat was one of those Tilley Endurables, an off-white canvas hat with a wide brim that could be snapped up, brass ventilation grommets and a wind-cord. When I picked up the hat to put it on, I could not believe what was there hidden from view. The entire underside of the canvas brim had been painted with a continuous landscape, cliffs, meadows, villages, but it was the familiar lighthouses that made me realize I was looking at the perimeter of Gannet Island, painted as if the crown filled with a human head was the centre of the island and the 360 degrees of brim the shore. At the front was Seven Days' Work with the stripes of lava clearly visible and Swallowtail Light casting its beam out to sea and at the back the Southwest Head Light with Castalia, Grand Harbour, and Seal Cove on one side, and nothing but cliffs on the other with the one exception of Dark Harbour, where the dulse was harvested at low tide. There was no artist's signature that I could find, but on the inside band someone had written in black fabric pen: "NO MAN IS AN ISLAND." I recognized this as the part of the passage where Hemingway had found his title *For Whom the Bell Tolls*, but I had never actually read the line in context, *in situ*, as Charlotte would say.

"That's amazing," I said, standing in front of the mirror in the lawyer's bathroom. Tip your head down and you would never know such dazzling scenes were circling your hair like a halo. It looked for all the world like an ordinary canvas hat. Tip your head up and there you were in the centre of all that intricately tinted glory held by the tough hands of the sea. It was the difference between the peacock's green tail trailing in the dust, or fanned out like a spectacular psychedelic sunrise.

"Read the letter out loud," Es said. I looked in the box but this time there didn't appear to be one. "There's got to be," Es said, taking a look in the empty box. She looked at me, and took the hat from my head. As always, she was not prepared to give up. She found the secret pocket in the crown, and sure enough it contained the letter, but because Jim still didn't know about the letters, we waited until he went back to work, and we walked over to the lunch counter at the gas station for a coffee. "Happy New Year, Hat Girl!" the waitress, Stanley's niece Rita called as we came in. After we'd given her our order, I read the letter out loud.

Dear Pertice,

I stole this hat. There, I said it. When you are in your eighties, there's no time for lies. It is not the first thing I have stolen, and it may not be the last. All the other hats in my collection I came by honestly. I either bought them or they were bequeathed to me. But not this one. What can I say? It was lying out in the open like forbidden fruit, and I acted on my desire. Veni, vidi, vici.

When I retired from teaching in 1992, I thought I would come back to Gannet Island where people had been so kind to me twice before. And so I returned for what I thought was just a visit, but I fell in love with a cottage by the shore with weathered grey shingles clinging with honeysuckle. It was everything that Toronto was not. I had all my things shipped from Toronto, including my extensive hat collection, and moved into Honeysuckle Cottage. It seemed like it would be a good place to live out my days, but that's not how things unfolded. I found that first winter very hard. The severity of the weather, the isolation from the mainland, and the great silences combined against me.

Admittedly, I did not try very hard to fit into the community, keeping to myself and my memories. I have never been a joiner. And everybody belonged to someone else. There was a woman who tried to be friendly, but I did not let her in. No matter how much I had come to love the island, I knew that I would not stay. I was too old and weary to be healed by its beauty and grace. When I knew I was moving back to Ontario, I considered selling, but I couldn't bear to part with the cottage, so I made arrangements to keep it rented. By then, hats were all but out of fashion for women, so I selected only my very favourites to take with me. The rest I put into a huge bag which I slung over my shoulder like Santa Claus and carried out to the car I had hired to take me as far as Saint John. Once the ferry had pulled away from the shore and everybody else was occupied getting a snack or playing cards or watching for whales, I snuck back down to the vehicle deck. I pulled out the big bag of hats and began to distribute them among the vehicles. You could tell who was an Islander and who was a tourist by whether the car doors were locked or not. If the door was unlocked and there was room to open it, I placed a hat on the seat or on the dash. If the door was locked, or if there was a grumpy dog in the car, I sat the hat on the roof or hood or hung it from the side mirror.

When all the hats were distributed, I surveyed my work. I knew some hats would get thrown away, and some would get exchanged, and some would get worn for real life and some for masquerade. Some would stay on the island, and some would go out into the big wide world. Some would end up in tickle trunks for the pleasure of children. One or two might even be thrown into the ocean like some exotic bird driven off course in a storm, to float for a moment before sinking beneath the waves or being hauled to safety by a strong brown arm. It struck me as an elegant and worthy solution.

One of the hats I kept with me was this one. It struck me as the perfect island souvenir. I wanted it for what it was in and of itself and for the objet d'art it had become. The man who makes these hats is now famous, but back then he was just getting started. He worked in a bank until he was told he "was too full of piss and vinegar to survive in banking," so he failed at various jobs including selling printing presses until he became an art dealer in Toronto, operating artmobiles that sold and rented Canadian art. When he bought a boat for sailing on Lake Ontario, he couldn't find a decent hat that would float and keep out the rain without shrinking, so he designed his own, and before long others wanted one too, including such celebrities as Sir Edmund Hillary, Pierre Trudeau, Paul Newman and Prince Andrew.

And as you can see, this worthy hat has become a work of art. No wonder I wanted it. I had learned that the man who took a good hat and made it better was also in a job he couldn't stand until he was rescued by affliction and art. The passage from Donne that says we are all part of the same continent, also says we are chapters in the same book, being translated one by one into a better language.

Passion by the sea,
PM

"That's new," I said, looking at Es. PM had signed all her previous letters with "peace by the sea." "Come on." I grabbed Es by the hand, and we walked over to the museum across the street. I dragged her past the Bicentennial Quilt and the Moses Memorial Bird Collection, to the little display in honour of the Island Artist. I put my face as close as I could to the clipping that began "Artist opens Atelier." It was hard to tell because the photograph was old and grainy, but it definitely looked like the underside of the brim was painted. "Will Murdoch is wearing my hat!" I said out loud, stepping back from the display.

"Pardon?" said the man at the desk.

"Nothing," I said, slowly realizing that it was probably the other way around. I was the one wearing his hat. What was Will Murdoch's hat doing on my head? No man is an island. Perhaps Will had known Miss M, after all. Charlotte had said that they had all arrived on the island around the same time, twenty years ago. Charlotte said it was hard at first for those who were not island born. Even after sixty years, one war bride was still referred to as a come-from-away, and Charlotte and Will had suffered for their English accents in the beginning. Will might have given this one-of-a-kind creation to another stranger from away as a token of welcome, a token of solidarity. But no, she admitted to stealing it. She must have believed a hat like this, carrying the whole exquisite weight of the island on its brim, would be worth the risk.

Miss M had stolen this hat. It would be easy to do. People often set down gloves or mittens when they came indoors, and then forgot them. Perhaps in another time it was the same with hats. Except for those people who wore hats for work, people like firemen and miners, a hat was an accessory, not an essential. Maybe she saw Will Murdoch's hat on a coat rack somewhere, unguarded and irresistible, and she slipped it under her coat and walked away. And who would ever suspect, because hats are easy to lose. It's not like your shoes or your coat, which you are not likely to leave behind without noticing. You might easily set a hat down on a big rock while examining starfish in a tide pool, or set it with your luggage on the ferry when you stepped inside to get a bite to eat, only to come back a moment later and find it gone.

Soon I was at Will's *atelier*. There was no answer when I knocked, so I let myself in. He was at his easel, painting, and I touched him on the shoulder to get his attention. "I have your hat," I said.

"Well, I'll be damned!"

"Miss M stole it. Did you know her?"

"No, only saw her from a distance, walking the shore. Charlotte can tell you she kept to herself."

"How did she get this hat, do you think?"

"I don't know. The last time I saw that hat, it was hanging from my field easel I had set up in the front yard. I went back to the studio to fetch some colours I needed, and when I got back it was gone."

"Well, it's back. Here," I said, holding it out toward him.

"I've done without it for twenty years. I say, finders keepers."

"I couldn't possibly keep it," I said. Even as the words escaped my mouth, I remembered rejecting the rings of Saturn so many years before. I wondered why I had said such a thing to Will, thrusting away the miracle he held out to me.

"Well, find someone who can."

That night I got out of bed, quietly so as not to wake Es, and looked carefully at the hats that had come to me from the unknown, hanging from the hockey stick hat tree. Suddenly they did not seem so innocent, these random bits of elegant plumage and shaped fabric. PM had claimed all her hats but Will's had come to her honestly, but who knew. Suddenly there was something sinister and strange about these hats from heads I did not know.

The week that Es was with me went way too fast. Clive offered to drive Es and me to the other end of the island. He drove us all the way from the Bishop, a rock pinnacle at the north end of the island, to the south end of the island where no one lives anymore to show us the rock formation called "The Southern Cross." "It used to be really famous," he said. "A doctor from Boston bought a bunch of land and was going to build a hotel here."

For Hemingway, the cross was the *Cruz: Where the line of the top of the bull's shoulder blades would cross the spine. The place the sword should go in if the matador kills perfectly.* "I don't see a cross," I said, feeling defensive because I never could "magic eye."

"That's because there isn't one anymore," Clive said. "Erosion got to it. The arms fell off, the last one in 1972, but I've seen photos." We stood there together, leaning into the wind, watching the waves wash over the rocks. Even stone succumbs.

After we'd dropped Clive at his parents' house we returned to Honeysuckle Cottage. Es helped me hang her picture of me in my boater on the one wall that wasn't either cupboards or windows to the sea. "Art changes a room, doesn't it?" she said. The picture of me and my hat in colours that would have made Warhol proud did make everything look more modern and vibrant. Es insisted we pick up some felt squares in nautical colours and borrow Charlotte's sewing machine to make cushions for the navy sofa. We took the faded slipcovers off the easy chairs, to find red leather underneath. And there were the gorgeous hats hanging from Clive's Hat Trick.

At the end of the week, I reluctantly prepared to say goodbye to Es. "Don't forget to use that smart phone," she said. "I checked around and Rogers won't work but Bell Aliant should." Later, as she drove onto the ferry to go back to Ontario, I didn't feel as bereft as the first time she had left me alone on the island, because I had her phone in my pocket, happy that it was called a Bold.

As the *merde-mobile* was driving onto the ferry, Clive was coming down off the ferry on foot. He approached me where I was standing on the wharf to wave goodbye.

"How's your grandfather?"

"He pulled through, tough old bugger. They're looking after him in the hospital in Saint John."

"Good people there," I said, thinking of how well they had looked after me.

He nodded and then asked, "Would you do something for me?" Clive never wasted time with small talk.

"Yes," I said, not even waiting to hear his request, already certain I would do whatever he asked.

After the ferry disappeared from view, Clive walked me back to the cottage and asked his question on the way: "Would you bake me a cake?" I'm not sure what request I had been expecting, but it certainly wasn't one that sounded so chauvinist. I didn't know whether to laugh or be offended. "A birthday cake," he added.

"Whose birthday?"

"Our church is turning twenty-five." He talked about it as if it wasn't just a building.

"Why don't *you* bake it, blue-ribbon-pie guy?"

"This has to be really special." He had not seen my toolbox but knew from Charlotte that cooking was one of my passions. She had recommended me for the job. And so I was charged with the task of creating the cake for the twenty-fifth anniversary of the Church of the Straits and Narrows. By this time, we had reached Honeysuckle Cottage and I invited Clive in. This was the first time Clive had actually been inside. When he had come bearing the evergreen tree with the three ships he had stayed on the front stoop.

"Wow, he sure liked to kill things," Clive said when he saw the list of the animals Hemingway had killed during his last African safari posted on my fridge like a grocery list.

"When he was young, Hemingway shot a porcupine for fun. His father made him eat it. 'If you kill a thing you must eat it,' he told him."

"That advice obviously went by the wayside," Clive said, reading the list out loud.

> *2 lions*
> *2 oryx besia*
> *1 leopard*
> *1 buffalo*
> *2 Grant's Gazelle*
> *1 lesser Kudu*
> *6 Wildebeest*
> *8 common zebra*
> *11 Thomson's gazelle*
> *7 impala*
> *3 Coke's Hartebeest*

"And the weird thing was, he found women who wanted to kill things with him." I had seen picture after picture of his various wives holding dead pheasants or crouching beside lions they had slain. I first posted the list on the fridge to prompt me to eat what I bought, a reminder I needed after the accident when I lost my sense of taste, but it stayed there because I had been thinking lately of how I might use my spare time to write a book about Hemingway.

"Hasn't he been written to death?" Clive asked, after I had explained this to him. It was true. Even in the little library in Grand Harbour, there were nearly a dozen books on Hemingway. Hemingway's women, Hemingway's youth, Hemingway's quarrel with androgyny, Hemingway and Spain, Hemingway and Cuba, Hemingway and Toronto, Hemingway and every other place he had spent more than five minutes.

"Mine is going to be a book about death, and this list will appear in the first section about humans killing animals, culminating, of course, with the bull. Or maybe the bull will have a separate chapter of his own." Clive rolled his eyes. "To Hemingway, killing other animals was sport, but killing the bull was art." I gave the red jacket I had just taken off a flourish like a matador's cape. "Nothing between you and the wild animal but a bit of scarlet cloth and a sword." Clive didn't say anything, so I continued. "And then there will be a section on humans killing other humans. That will be a long section. And the last section will be on humans killing themselves."

Clive didn't even try to hide his scepticism. "What would you call it?"

"*The Sovereign Remedy*. One of Hemingway's names for death." I tried to lighten the moment. "He also called it 'that old whore,' but that's a little less elegant, don't you think?"

"There's nothing elegant about death," Clive said. It was my turn to be silent. "What is it with you and Hemingway, anyway?" he asked.

This was the question Es had asked on the trip down from Ontario. It was a question I often asked myself. It didn't make a lot of sense. Hemingway was anti-Semitic, racist, macho, unfaithful, and obsessed with killing. Es didn't get it. Clive didn't get it. I wasn't even sure I got it anymore, and yet there was something about him that still drew me in. Here was a man who, despite his many failings, found a way to say some things about as perfectly as they could be said. Here was a man who knew how to take life by the horns. "There was nothing timid about him," I said after a long pause. I looked at Clive's face and the scars there. I had asked him about them coming back from the lobster grounds, but all he had said was "Long story," and he had never offered to make it short. "Hemingway used to boast that he had two hundred scars and could tell the story of every one of them."

"And you think that's something to be proud of?" Clive asked. "All the times you've placed yourself in danger? What about the people who loved him?"

"I don't know. I just wish I was more daring."

"You don't need to be more daring, Pertice. You need to be more joyous." I couldn't remember ever hearing that last word in casual conversation, but somehow it didn't sound old-fashioned coming from Clive.

When making the cake, I tried to be both daring and joyous. I took my task seriously, working with every skill in my repertoire, ordering what I couldn't buy on the island from the mainland, and labouring late into the night. I felt just like Dinesen's Babette. *Righteousness and bliss shall kiss one another.* When it was done, I surveyed my work. June would be proud. Every year at Christmas throughout my childhood, my mother would assemble an elaborate gingerbread creation which I secretly believed was penance for the terrible cooking she did during the rest of the year. She had long since left behind the humble house, experimenting with gingerbread castles, cathedrals, and Parthenons. The year we went to Ottawa for our family vacation it was the Parliament Buildings. Mind you, her gingerbread was like concrete, and the white frosting she used to keep it all together was as hard as mortar. With my cake, everything, including the ornamentation, was exquisitely edible.

When the big day arrived, Charlotte came to give me a lift with the cake. When we arrived, I placed the cake under wraps in the annex for after the service, and made my way into the sanctuary, which was transformed with balloons and streamers everywhere. Instead of a service there was a celebration, with people sharing their memories of the old days. Afterward, everybody spilled into the annex, but I lingered, looking at the stained glass of Peter stepping out of the boat and onto the waves. This was not an unfamiliar scene to most people, but what was surprising was Peter saying, "If it's really you, tell me to walk on water toward you," and being able to do it. An ordinary guy walking on water. Whoever made the stained glass knew, of course, like I knew from having read about it in the Gideon Bible in the hospital, that in about five seconds Peter would notice the wind and the waves, lose his nerve and start to sink, and that Jesus would have to reach out his hand and grab him. But the stained glass artist chose to depict the miraculous moment before that happened. The miraculous moment when a humdrum human being was able to defy reality with belief.

"No one can take that away from him," said a voice behind me. It was Julia in her wheelchair. Clive had pointed her out earlier as the founder of the Church of the Straits and Narrows. "What were you expecting, some old guy in a long beard and funny hat?" he had asked, responding to my surprised look. He explained that it was multiple sclerosis that put her in the chair and made her voice a little slurred. Her blonde hair was pulled back in a ponytail and she wore a black turtleneck that showed off a Celtic triquetra etched like scrimshaw on a piano key, no doubt by Charlotte's daughter. She smiled. "Imagine Peter's kids saying, Dad, tell us again about the night you walked on water."

"I'm Pertice," I said, holding out my hand. Hers were gloved, to ease the turning of the wheels.

"I'm Julia. My grandmother, Gammy Green," she said, pointing out the dedication under the stained glass, "was the midwife on White Island. Once when my grandpa was sick she walked to the drugstore in Castalia, picking her way across the tidal passages between the islands at low tide. By the time the next low tide arrived it was night. She knew she had to get back to him with the medicine, so she felt around the highest rocks for the rockweed, and she could tell the direction of the true ebb by the way it lay. Feeling the seaweed from rock to rock she made it home in the darkness, when most people wouldn't have even set out for fear of getting lost or drowned." I looked up at the window dedicated to Gammy Green, who died on this day, the eleventh of January, at ninety-four. The ordinary human being walking on water. "She always said it's in the straits and narrows we find out who we really are and what we're capable of." Julia began to wheel herself toward the annex, but paused. "We think we're islands, but at low tide, we discover we're not."

In the annex, tables had been set up to hold salads and rolls, but the main attraction was roast beef. A young woman with short hair dyed a shade of aubergine, who turned out to be the minister's wife, had brought vegetarian chili for the non-meat eaters in the crowd. She worked at the Whale and Seabird Research Station, she said, and refused to eat anything she would not be able to kill with her own hands, anything with eyes. She mentioned a book she was reading about the fast food industry, with truly horrifying descriptions of abattoirs and food flavouring laboratories. And yet, she believed that fine food, like other art forms, brought people together. When Jesus met up with his friends for the last time, she said, it was for supper. As I ate, balancing a plate on my knees, I thought about what Hemingway had written in the *Toronto Star*: *I have discovered that there is romance in food when romance has disappeared from everywhere else. And as long as my digestion holds out, I will follow romance.*

After the meal, a piñata was set up for the kids. Clive helped hang it from the rafters. It was in the traditional shape of a seven-pointed star with streamers coming from the points. "All the way from Mexico," the minister's wife, whose name was Bronwen, said to me. "We honeymooned there, and I've been hanging on to it ever since, waiting for the right occasion. This seemed like it." We watched as the blindfolded children used a baseball bat to take whacks at the colourful star, with Clive and Simon, the minister, making sure no one got injured in all the excitement and confusion. "The man who made it told me that traditionally the piñata stood for the devil," Bronwen said. "You have to hit him hard to make him let go of all of the good things he has stolen." Then she began to cry.

"What's wrong?" I asked, a little disconcerted.

"I'll be okay," she said, wiping the corners of her eyes with her sleeve. I didn't understand her tears, but Es was right. We're all so damned scathed, we can hardly stand it. And Julia was right. We're all connected, even if the connections are submerged. I reached down and gave Bronwen's hand a squeeze. "If there aren't lots of kids around, it's just creepy," she said, "like the kingdom in *Chitty Chitty Bang Bang*."

Just as the candies showered out on the floor, Simon yelled, "Time for cake!"

Suddenly I began to feel nervous. Clive had said the cake should be special, so I had agonized about what to do. Often at big functions they have those large white cakes with frosting roses referred to as slab cakes, and I knew that just wouldn't do. In the end, I translated the stained glass window at the front of the church which I had first seen at Christmas into three dimensions. The frosting was ruffled to look like waves and glazed with mint jelly to give it the glass green colour of the sea. Off to one side was the yellow dory, but at the very centre were two marzipan figures walking on the waves. They were clearly masculine, with arms muscled from swinging hammers and casting nets, but the way they were reaching toward one another made them look just a little like a bride and groom. The cake was a huge success. Julia even started to cry. She had been the one who had commissioned the stained glass window in honour of her grandmother the midwife.

"Give me a hand," Clive said, as people began pushing the tables toward the perimeter to clear the floor. Before long the church annex was transformed into a ceilidh, with the minister's wife playing the fiddle and Stanley, the electrician with the bushy eyebrows, on the accordion. Simon, the minister, was calling the steps of the reels and Scottish dances, but most people already knew what to do. Clive took me through the steps, his hand on my waist, until we were both breathless with exertion and laughter. Young and old, hale and frail were dancing, and those who weren't were tapping their toes and clapping to the music.

"I'm going to give Simon a break, so he can get some dancing in," Clive said to me. "No one's dancing with Julia," he added. I took the cue and grabbed the handles of Julia's wheelchair and swung her out onto the dance floor, twirling her around and popping up the front wheels. Julia was laughing and I was winded and laughing too. Looking around at all the people having a good time, alive with music and movement, and at the cake that was all but eaten except for the tiny island of green water that held up the two figures, I felt joy. There was that old-fashioned word, but no other word would do. This, I realized, was what I had been hoping for the night of the disastrous dance at Swallowtail Light, when all I found was masquerade and *misère*.

During a break between dances, I went back to get another sliver of cake. "You guys know how to party," I said to Clive, licking the frosting off my fingers.

"So did he," Clive said. It took me a while to realize he was talking about Jesus.

As the evening wound down, Simon came over and thanked me. "The cake was a real work of art," he said. "I love seeing people do what they're good at."

"You seem good at this," I said, gesturing in the general direction of the church members, who were variously occupied packing up the party.

"It's simple really," he said. "It all boils down to love and choice."

CLOCHE
8

The next day I caught a lift to Grand Harbour with Will, bringing with me the list from my fridge of animals Hemingway had killed. With the help of the new colour photocopier at the Grand Harbour Library, I made pictures of the living animals to replace the list of dead ones, knowing that gathered there on the smooth white Serengeti of my refrigerator, the living would be lovely and various. And they were lovely, especially the antelope and gazelles with their horns, the perfectly straight horns of the oryx besia, the curling horns of the lesser kudu, the tapered horns of Grant's gazelle curving like callipers.

With one thing and another, I hadn't thought about Ontario or the mystery of Miss M for a while now. It didn't really seem to matter anymore. So it took me by surprise to hear from my mother, of all people. From time to time she would send a brief cheery note with bits of Ingersoll town news that I mostly found irrelevant, since I hadn't lived there for ages. In her last note, June explained that she had finally decided it was time to sell the house I had grown up in, and move to a condominium overlooking the Thames, the one in Ontario, that is, not the English one. It would be less to look after, she said, but it meant sorting through a lifetime of accumulated junk.

This time what I found in my mailbox from June wasn't even a letter. Just a photocopy of a page from a high school yearbook with a yellow Post-it note stuck on it. On the small yellow square over an arrow pointing toward the photo, June had scribbled, "I knew that hat rang a bell." I sat down heavily in the easy chair that Es had flopped into that first day at Honeysuckle Cottage, though now the chintz had been removed to reveal red leather. I looked at the photograph of the class, rows of young men and women in sober clothing. Behind the students was a banner with the school crest and motto. *Emitte lucem...* "Send forth your light..." There was my father in the back row, looking thin and earnest behind his spectacles. And there at the opposite end of the same row was a teacher wearing the hat June had looked at for several days in the hospital while she waited for me to wake up from the coma. Instead of tying the lengths of chiffon under her chin as you might for motoring, the teacher had looped them loosely in a way that framed and flattered her face. In the black and white photograph, made fainter by reproduction, the pink looked grey, but it appeared to be the same bergère crowned with roses that had "PM" chain-stitched on the inside of the crown, the hat that sailed clear of the bicycle accident that day in Castalia, the hat that I passed on to Alice to remind her of her own beauty before and after.

I scanned the caption for a name. There was my father's name, listed as Bert McIlveen. This seemed odd to me because I had always heard him referred to as the adult Albert, never the boy Bert. And the last name in the caption, at the very end of a long row of names, was my father's grade twelve teacher, the woman after whom I had been named. Pertice Malczewski.

The key slowly turned, allowing the tumblers to fall into place and the lock to open at last. The PM of many sleepless nights, the mysterious Miss M of the hats and Honeysuckle Cottage and Pertice Malczewski of Ingersoll District Collegiate Institute were one and the same. I felt dizzy. I looked at the hats hanging from the hockey stick hat tree. There were gaps like those in the teeth of a hockey player who has been in too many fights. Alice's bergère, the one in the yearbook photo, was gone, as was the ecru pillbox, and the black sou'wester, but there was still the boater, the Merry Widow, the deerstalker, and the painted Tilley Endurable. Now I knew that the woman who had sent me the key to Honeysuckle Cottage, or arranged to have someone send me the key, was the woman after whom I was named. According to June, Albert had asked if they could give their only daughter the name Pertice, and when June asked why, he said that he had once had a teacher by that name who had inspired him greatly. The alternative for a girl would have been Mabel, which happened to be the name of both my grandmothers, but they could not bring themselves to give a baby that name, at least not as a first name, so Pertice it became. Pertice had sent a key to Pertice.

Charlotte had referred to the stranger who walked by the shore as Miss M, so she was likely a spinster, and maybe in the absence of an heir, she considered the child that was named for her a suitable person to inherit her Gannet Island home. It seemed far-fetched but possible. Maybe there was something more to it. Maybe my father, the shy conservative man who spent his life in a library sorting books and papers, had been wildly in love with his teacher. I myself had had crushes on school teachers, men who seemed infinitely smarter and more interesting than the pimply awkward boys my own age. I tried to sort out the math. I had been told that Miss M had intended to retire to Gannet Island in 1992. That would mean she was in her mid-sixties then, which would make her around forty at the time she was teaching Albert. Forty was not so very old. When you were in elementary school, it seemed impossible to like a boy even a few grades ahead or behind, but as adults it all sort of evened out and you found yourself tangled in attractions you couldn't imagine. There had been seven years between me and Varsha. Hemingway's first wife had been eight years older, and his last two nine years younger.

AM loved PM. It seemed unlikely, not so much because of the timing but because of the man. AM: *artium magister, amplitude modulation, ante meridiem*. AM loved PM. Or maybe it was the other way around. Maybe PM loved AM and gave his only daughter this inheritance because he himself was gone. Since my father's death, I realized that the things I knew about his youth I could count on one hand. There was the strange fact that he had worked the summer after high school in a gold mine in northern Ontario, although maybe it was not such a leap from the mines to the archives in the library basement out of reach of the sun. I had seen his black rubber mining boots. The huge treaded bumps on the toes, he explained, were made of steel that prevented falling rocks from crushing your feet. "Did you know that a quarter of the bones in the human body are in the feet?" he asked. "Twenty-eight in each."

And then there was the time I visited my grandmother Mabel's house as a child and found a wallet-like pocketbook about the size of a spectacle case with paper pages pierced with fishing flies. They were very beautiful, with intricate combinations of coloured feathers that would tempt even the most timid of fish. I was told that my grandfather had tied them but my father had used them. I could hardly imagine my father outdoors, the current of a river tugging at his legs, like in that photograph of Hemingway as a boy. Except for that one canoe trip that had almost ended in disaster, I had only ever seen my father indoors, bent over a desk or a crossword puzzle. It was surprising to come across these strange glimpses of people you did not know in people you thought you knew, like a paper fan that opened for a second to reveal a spectacular and unimagined scene, but most of the time remained closed, showing the plain edges of folds held shut with a little metal hook.

I looked again at the photograph of my father's teacher standing next to her students and suddenly remembered the first and last sweater I ever knit, the sweater that would surely fit no anatomy I knew. I had unravelled all my hours of labour and it seemed impossible that the huge confusing snarl of wool that resulted had once been contained in tidy skeins wrapped in paper labels or in a plausible garment made from a pattern. The mystery of PM had been unravelled, but now seemed even more tangled and obscure than before. I texted Es: "PM is revealed."

When she finally moved to her condo, June sent down a box of my father's papers that she thought might interest me. As an archivist he had never thrown anything out. They were mostly what my mother called compositions, though that term wasn't used anymore. Now they called the things that people wrote in school "essays," as if the students were trying. But I preferred the term "composition," as if writing was akin to music. My father's essays on Herodutus and Hamlet and Hardy were all given grades of A+ with favourable comments in the distinctive handwriting I recognized from the envelope in which the key to Honeysuckle Cottage had been sent, and all the hat letters that followed. Also in the box were drafts of letters Albert had sent over the years. One in particular captured my attention. The first line read, "I have never been in a war, but I imagine it would be something like this with the explosions, the darkness, the dripping, and men's faces tainted with earth." The rest of the letter had a hard time living up to that first sentence, but it was nonetheless a vivid description of what it was like to go down a mine shaft into a world of immense peril and possibility.

Now that I had a name, I could step up my search. I googled her but nothing came up. I looked in online white pages. I went back to all the places I had first looked without success and tried again. Still nothing. It was amazing how people could disappear, even in this information age. Maybe she was dead, but then there would likely be an obituary. Maybe she was buried in an old folks' home somewhere with no ties to the outside world except for the letters she sent out with the monthly hat. Now that I knew that the connection was much closer than I originally thought, I was more curious about my February hat than I had been about any of the others. It was one of those close-fitting bell-shaped hats popular in the twenties, a moss-green felt cloche with arrow-shaped ribbons in forest green.

Dear Pertice,

This is the hat my mother was wearing the first time she saw my father. It was a daring hat back then because it looked best with a short hairstyle like the Eton crop and it was still considered scandalous for a woman to cut her hair. Even into the forties books with titles like *Bobbed Hair, Bossy Wives, and Women Preachers* were being published to discourage such outrageous behaviour. In the twenties, cloche hats were very popular with flappers, referring to young birds flapping their wings while learning to fly, though it was also a term for young prostitutes. After all, such women smoked and drove automobiles and listened to jazz! They would trim their hats in code, firm knots meant married, arrow-like ribbons meant in love, and bows meant single.

The cloche is sometimes credited to Coco Chanel, though hats that draw inspiration from history and nature and current events can hardly be "invented" by a single individual. Paris milliner Caroline Reboux created cloches by placing a length of felt on a lady's head, then cutting and folding until she was satisfied with the fit. Felt is said to be a gift to milliners everywhere from the patron saint of hat makers, Ireland's Saint Clement, whose sweat and pressure compressed the wool padding of his sandals while he was on pilgrimage. The close-fitting cloche, along with the long, lean, low-waisted dresses of the twenties, gave a lady a streamlined appearance like Brancusi's bird. Some objected to the style, saying it made the young look old and the old look ancient, but it lasted well into the thirties, and, I have noticed, is now enjoying a renaissance among the young.

One wonders what brings men and women together, especially one's parents. My father was part of the second wave of Polish immigration that came to Canada after the Great War, as it was then called. He was distantly related to the symbolist artist Jacek Malczewski, who painted strange mythical creatures and angels encountering children in fields, but my father was more embarrassed than proud of the connection. He was a scientist, after all. He found work banding geese at the Jack Miner Bird Sanctuary in Kingsville, Ontario. More than a century after his hero Audubon first tied yarn around the leg of an Eastern Phoebe to learn that it always returned to the same nesting spot, my father became part of the great enterprise to

keep track of where the winged ones go. Not being keen on the
bible verses Miner stamped on his bands, he eventually ended
up at a university with the motto: Veritas et Utilitas.

As the trimming on this hat suggests, my mother was in
love with another at the time, one who had gone away to war
and never came back, as happened with so many young men
of her generation. My father knew that it would be more of
challenge to battle a ghost than a man of flesh and blood. He
could not, like the birds he studied, rely on extravagant courting
rituals, like the red heart-shaped balloon the frigate bird makes
of his throat, or the elaborate dancing of the bird of paradise.
But he could take his cue from the bowerbird and build for my
mother an elaborate bower in the Ontario countryside, not of
twigs and orchid stems, but of stone and gingerbread. He could
fill it with the treasures he collected, organized by colour and
shape, like the leaves and flowers and acorns and beetle shells
gathered by the bowerbird. Huge monochromatic mounds of
effort. Despite the plainness of his plumage he could just keep
on gathering until she at last wanted to be his.

Passion by the Sea,
PM

On Valentine's Day I worked late because it's always a popular
night for dining out. It was dark by the time I walked home from the
Island Inn in the snow. Oncoming headlights flashed at me and I was
surprised to see Luke's pickup, and even more surprised to see him
driving it. I hadn't seen him since Christmas dinner at the Fergusons.
"Hey, stranger, want a lift?" he called from his open window. I got in
because I was cold and tired from a long evening on my feet. "Nice
hat." I took off the cloche and put it in my lap. Sparkling flakes clung
to the felt like snow to the branches of an evergreen before melting in
the heat of the truck's interior.

"What are you doing here?" I asked bluntly.

"Toronto didn't pan out after all. So I'm back."

Just like that. When we arrived at Honeysuckle Cottage, I did not invite Luke in, but he followed me anyway. He was carrying a long black case about the right size for a machine gun. He laid it on the table and unzipped it, pulling out a stringed instrument that looked like a medieval lute. "A Martin Backpacker," he explained, "a guitar for travellers." He sat down on a kitchen chair and began to strum. "I want you to hear something I've been working on," he said. He pushed up his sleeves, maybe to play better, but maybe so I could see that this time he was wearing the watch I had given him. He proceeded to sing a song about a girl in an ostrich feather hat.

Well, you must tell me, baby
How your head feels under somethin' like that
Under your brand new ostrich feather hat

There was definitely something mesmerizing about a man playing a guitar, the subtle movements of the muscles in his forearms as his supple fingers moved swiftly across the frets. I should have recognized the song as an adaptation of "Leopard Skin Pillbox Hat," but I didn't. "You write that?"

"No, Bob Dylan, but I tinkered with it a little." Clearly he had understood that the direct approach he had tried last time had scared me off. He was not going to be able to count on physical attraction, as he usually did with women. If he was going to woo me, it was going to have to be in a more traditional way.

"That was nice," I said. At least it wasn't a heart-shaped box of chocolates or dyed carnations. I had not known he could play an instrument, one of the things Rita said she was looking for in a man in the movie *Groundhog Day*, which I had watched every February 2 for years. "Can I offer you something?" I asked wearily, winding my hair into a messy bun, and sticking a pencil in it to hold it together. I could cook, but I didn't have Charlotte's gift of hospitality. Like a magician she could conjure a tray laden with sweet things out of thin air.

"I'm sure you can," Luke said with a grin, laying his odd-looking guitar on the table, and I realized I had committed the faux pas all waitresses learn to avoid. "Never take an order with a phrase that sounds like an invitation," Es said. "Especially if the customer is male."

"I can make tea," I said, reaching for the kettle. "Or there might be something stronger in the fridge."

"Tea's fine." He stood up and took the kettle from my hands. "You relax. I'll make it." I remembered how his bare torso glimpsed through the gap in my bedroom ceiling had once taken my breath away. He placed the kettle on the counter and put his hands on my face and slid them down around my neck like a sculptor wishing the stone would turn to flesh. "I've missed you," he said.

I knew that if I softened even a little, he would take advantage, so I kept my arms at my sides. "The tea bags are in the canister," I said. "I'll have decaf. If I don't, I'll be up all night."

"That would be nice," Luke said.

I realized that this was just going to go on and on. "You know what? I'm exhausted. Maybe we could catch up some other time." Luke took his hands from my face and held them up for a second in a gesture of surrender. "Thanks for the song, though," I said, not wanting to be rude.

"You're very welcome," he said, realizing that he was being dismissed. He zipped the backpacker guitar back into its black case and left, but not before taking a long look at the Hat Trick by the door where I hung my cloche. Maybe he even recognized the hockey sticks. I wondered if he knew that his brother and I were friends though Clive had not yet made any kind of move. Maybe that brought out the competitor in him. I could tell he was used to getting what he wanted and this time he wasn't messing around, showing up with the food of love.

That weekend Clive came home from the mainland and called me. I hadn't seen him for weeks, not since the party at the Church of the Straits and Narrows back in January. He explained that he was timber cruising, measuring the density and size of trees on a plot with tools like a Biltmore stick and a relascope. This kind of forest inventory was easier to do in winter, he said, when access was improved. Then he got to the reason he was calling. The movie channel was showing

For Whom the Bell Tolls with Gary Cooper and Ingrid Bergman. Clive had never seen it and I had not seen it in a long time. Would I like to join him?

I hadn't been at the Fergusons' house since Christmas dinner. Hazel had been meaning to get stateside since the cross border shopping limits had been changed, so Luke had driven her to Maine and Frank was out somewhere. Clive pressed the power button on the remote control. The TV was set to a porn channel and for a moment there was a glimpse of writhing flesh and the sound of moaning. "I'm pretty sure that's why Frank has the dish," Clive said as he flipped over to the movie channel. "He always had that crap around when we were kids, except then it was in magazines. And now he's looking into getting the Internet, for 'e-mail.'" Clive put air quotations around the last word.

While the opening credits of the movie were rolling, Clive went into the kitchen to make popcorn and get some drinks. There he ran into his father, who had just come in and was unloading a case of Moosehead beer onto the kitchen table and then into the fridge. I could hear them talking over the soundtrack. "Isn't she a tall drink of water," Frank said. When Clive didn't answer, Frank kept going. "Luke knows what to do with a woman, but I bet you haven't even fucked her yet."

"Stop, Frank."

"What's your problem? That's all women are good for, making meals and making men. Don't you forget it!"

Clive came back into the living room empty-handed and said, "I think we better leave."

Frank was not finished yet. He followed Clive into the living room. "Seems your pecker's shrivelled up since you've been going to that church of the straight-laced and narrow-minded. You make me sick."

Clive turned to face his father. Though they were the same height, Clive looked taller. His voice was so low it sounded more like a growl. "I said stop."

"You telling me what to do? In my own house, Goddamn it!" Frank was yelling now and he pushed Clive on the shoulder. "You fucking telling me what to do?"

Clive didn't answer, but instead walked back into the kitchen and overturned the table, sending all the beer bottles smashing and splashing to the floor. I was on my feet now, wondering what to do. I had never seen rage that raw. This was what Hemingway called *Rabioso: raging—a matador is said to be rabioso when he has lashed himself, mentally, into a rage of bravery as contrasted with the cold, consistent valor of a truly brave man; a bullfighter who is coldly brave will only be rabioso when he has been made furious either by the taunts of the crowd or by the bull bumping and tossing him.* "Don't *fuck* with me, Frank," Clive said with real menace in his voice. Then he turned and walked out of the house with me behind him.

Clive didn't say a word as we got in the Forestry Department truck he had borrowed for the weekend, and we drove through the darkness past the spot on the highway where my flesh had been torn, past the Castalia Marsh where the tide pools reflected the moon and a lone heron wandered in the shallows, past the white steeple of the Church of the Straits and Narrows piercing upward through the dark trees. When we were almost to Honeysuckle Cottage, he looked over at me. "Sorry about that."

"It's okay, really," I said, still feeling a little shaky. In my family, my father had set the tone, so it was all very quiet and subdued. If he could have, Albert would have arranged for us to argue in writing. If there had to be confrontation it would be better on paper than in the flesh. As it was, we actually had a family suggestion box, like the ones in libraries, and we were advised to count to ten and other tactics designed to assuage and allay. So it was a shock to see Clive this way, looking as if he could actually kill the man who had raised him.

Clive slowed and pulled the truck over onto the shoulder of the road. Then he crossed his arms over the top of the steering wheel and leaned into them. After a moment he rubbed his hand over his eyes and looked at me. "Welcome to my childhood," he said. Now I wondered if the scars on Clive's face and on his body did not just come from the ordinary wear and tear of boyhood. Those were there as well, the stray hockey puck, falling from a tree, scraped-knee kinds of scars, but the rest must have been caused by a man against a boy, a father against a son.

I looked around the truck Clive used for work. There was no need for a tree-shaped air freshener because every day he brought the smell of evergreen home on his clothes. There between us on the seat were the tools of the trade he had taken up when the trade he really wanted was taken away. Tools he had described that day on the phone, a Biltmore stick, relascope, callipers. Tools for measuring the slow growth of the outer layers that protected the heartwood. I had read once that injury made for the most interesting grains. Wounding triggers sprouting, which, when the wood is cut and polished, shows up as the eyes of birds. Everything shows up in the tree rings, seasons of rain and drought, scars of forest fires, the lean years and the good.

"That's a hobby of mine," Clive said, when I picked up an almost perfectly spherical pebble from the drink holder. I held it up to look more closely. It was not a geode that was naturally globe-like, but a pebble that had been brought to roundness by the constant tumble of wind and water. "They're hard to come by, but I try to find one every time I come home."

"Do you want to come in?" I asked as he walked me to the door.

Clive didn't seem to hear me. "You know, one time when I was about seven, there was a terrible storm and he was out in his boat. And everybody thought that he might not make it back. It sounds terrible, but I felt this tremendous relief. In the end, he did come back. Over and over again he came back. But that feeling that things would be better without him never went away."

"It must've been bad."

"It was…" Clive paused and in the silence I could hear the surf pounding on the rocks. "Just before Nina died, I came home from school late one day. My mom was out shopping, and Nina was on the phone crying. She had called the RCMP, because she thought my dad was going to kill Luke, beating on him. When he was too lazy to take off his belt he used the dog leash or his fists. Usually, he kept his hands off Luke and Nina, because he took it out on me. But that time, I wasn't there."

I didn't know what to say, so I reached over and hugged him. It was an awkward hug because Clive's arms were rigid at his sides and his fists were clenched, but it somehow seemed a familiar gesture, my arms the elastic band around claws poised for harm. "Now you know why I'm not here fishing," Clive said. "He forced me ashore."

"Do you want to come in?" I asked again, thinking he hadn't heard me before. It was bitterly cold.

Clive shook his head. "If it's harder to get to, it's harder to leave," he said without explaining what he meant. As I turned to go, Clive held me back by the arm, "Did you sleep with him?" Even though we had just been talking about his father, I knew Clive was referring to Luke. I was getting used to his candour that came at you from every angle, like rain in a wind.

"No," I said. "No, I didn't."

After that night, I never went back to the Ferguson house in Castalia, but I did invite Clive's mother Hazel out for coffee. "Actually, I don't drink coffee anymore," Hazel said. "I ended up in hospital with heart palpitations and they couldn't figure out what was wrong until someone asked me how much coffee I drank. I was up to more than a dozen cups a day. Sometimes I would wake in the middle of the night unable to sleep and I would make myself a cup of coffee. Can you imagine? Anyway, I'll have some tea."

The waitress brought the hot drinks and set them on the table with cream and sugar. "Do you need anything else?" she asked.

"Not at the moment, thanks." I poured cream into my coffee and thought about how to begin. "Hazel, I want to talk to you about Will Murdoch's paintings." Since I had first seen them in the back room of Mr. Harmon's house, those paintings had haunted me. The cross, the guillotine, the noose, the electric chair. And the unquenchable light at the core of each, grace under pressure. *The odour of courage,* Hemingway wrote, *was the smell of smoked leather or the smell of a frozen road or the smell of the sea when the wind rips the top from a wave.* "Those paintings should be in the museum," I said, trying to hold Hazel's eyes with my gaze the way Clive could.

"But it's not what my father wants. And until he's dead, I don't feel I can go against his wishes."

"We've got to get them where people can see them." Hazel fished around in the little stainless steel teapot with a spoon. She lifted out the tea bag and set it on the saucer. She didn't appear to want to discuss it any further. Seeing I wasn't getting anywhere, I suddenly asked something I hadn't planned to ask. "Why Frank?"

This question could have been interpreted in a variety of ways, but Hazel answered it the way it had been asked. "You heard my father," Hazel said. "And he was much worse when he was younger and stronger. He was always No, No, No, and Frank was always Yes, Yes, Yes. Frank was loads of fun and mischief early on." She paused as she took a sip of her tea. She looked at me and continued, as if she had decided to take a chance at the truth. "I was supposed to go to college on the mainland. Not many girls did that then. My father scrimped and saved to send me, but I got pregnant. He was a church warden and desperate to save face. 'Either you give that baby up for adoption or you find a man who will marry you.' My mother died that year of cancer, but he blamed me. Said I broke her heart. When he got sick he thought I'd take him in, a daughter's duty, he said. But I didn't. He used my college money to buy those paintings." She narrowed her eyes, and looked at me as if she was done talking even if there was more to say. "Frank has always been a good provider."

I was determined not to let her get away that easily. "But what about the way he treated the children?"

"I know I didn't think about them as much as I should have."

"Is Frank even Clive's father?"

"Yes, though I think both of them had their doubts over the years."

As the waitress cleared away the cups and saucers, I thought about love and choice, the two great forces that keep the world from spinning off into space. As I handed Hazel's little stainless steel teapot to the waitress, I caught a reflected glimpse of myself in my green felt cloche. I decided to make one last effort on behalf of Will's works of art. "The paintings, Hazel. Do the right thing."

When I walked in my door, the phone was ringing. "Persimmon?"

"Yes, Charlotte," I said into the phone. No one else called me that.

"It's Will. I would have called sooner but everything happened so quickly. His Crohn's flared up and we got him to the hospital in Saint John, but then necrotizing fasciitis set in, and before we knew it he was gone."

I stood, the telephone pressed against my ear, stunned. After all Will had survived, after all he had conquered, now this, flesh-eating disease consuming him in the end. Hemingway would call this a *Cornada: a horn wound; a real wound as distinct from a varetazo or bruising scratch. A cornada de caballo is a huge cornada, the same sort of wound in a man that the bull usually makes in the chest of a horse.*

"I've arranged to have the funeral on Thursday. Would you be willing to say a few words?"

"Of course, Charlotte. Of course." Suddenly I broke down with all the tears I had not shed for my father and the rest. How could Will be gone? Charlotte let me cry. Then I sniffed hard and said the only thing I could think of to say. "I can help with the refreshments."

"That would be a relief. Thank you, Persimmon."

The next thing I knew, I was on the phone yelling at Clive's mother. "You had a chance to stand up to your father, Hazel, to get those paintings to the museum while Will was still alive. But now he's gone."

"These things take time."

"Well, it took too much bloody time. Your father didn't even want them, and still he kept them away from everyone else." Hazel didn't say anything. A pause on the phone sounds longer than a pause in person. "You screwed up, Hazel. Show some spine for once in your life, and fix it!" As I said this, a flood of images washed over me of what it must have been like for Hazel, living first with a father who was full of anger that he disguised as religion, and then with a husband who was full of anger that he didn't even bother to disguise as anything but what it was.

"Frank thought if we waited we could get more money. He said paintings are worth more after the artist is dead."

I wanted to say, "You make me sick" but I didn't. I knew most anger was suppressed sadness or fear. If you pushed it down in one place, it popped out in another. "You have until Thursday to fix it, Hazel," I said. "I've spoken to the people at the museum, and they'll stand by their original offer. So it's up to you."

"I can't promise anything," Hazel said.

"That's not good enough," I said, as forcefully as I could. "People from all over will be coming to Gannet Island to celebrate Will's life and I want them to be able to see his work in the museum." The cardinal directions of suffering made visible through time. "You owe us all," I said, before hanging up.

What happened at Swallowtail Light that Thursday was too festive to be called a funeral. It was fitting really. Will preferred the subtle umbers, ochres, and greys of landscapes in winter. He always said the bright greens, blues, and yellows of summer were "too lush and gaudy." He had been drawn to the sombre black and whites of German artist Käthe Kollwitz, who said, *I do not want to die… until I have faithfully made the most of my talent and cultivated the seed that was placed in me until the last small twig has grown.* The dead of winter seemed the right time for his passing, if it had to come.

Though the sun was shining, it was still too cold to linger for long. I was glad I was wearing my cloche. Charlotte's winter coat was black, but underneath she was wearing a blue dress dotted all over with tiny blue flowers, forget-me-nots. "He always loved me in this," she said to me. She had asked Simon for a brief blessing for those who remained behind. At two o'clock exactly, Charlotte had arranged for

all the island churches that had bells to ring them while Simon read
from the John Donne passage Will had quoted on the inner band of
his painted Endurable:

*Who bends not his ear to any bell which upon any occasion rings? but
who can remove it from that bell which is passing a piece of himself out
of this world? No man is an island, entire of itself; every man is a piece
of the continent, a part of the main. If a clod be washed away by the sea,
Europe is the less, as well as if a promontory were, as well as if a manor of
thy friend's or of thine own were: any man's death diminishes me, because
I am involved in mankind, and therefore never send to know for whom the
bell tolls; it tolls for thee.*

    Then Charlotte stood in the shadow of the lighthouse at the very
edge of the cliff and cast Will's ashes out over the sea, saying softly,
"Hear again." I was standing near enough to catch what she said, but
I wasn't sure whether she meant "hear" or "here." Either way, I thought
it was a good thing to say.

    At that moment there were fishing boats headed out in different
directions from the point, and their wakes seemed to make the rays
of a star in the calm water. Then Charlotte brought out an old-school
ghetto blaster and switched it on. "Will chose the music," she said,
explaining how this was the one tune he remembered from the time
when he could still hear, the one tune that had played for years in
his head, when all other music was silenced. And so it was that the
Andrews Sisters sang at Will Murdoch's funeral.

*Mr. What-ya-call-em all you needed was fun
You can see the wonders that this evenin' has done
Your feet were so heavy 'til they hardly could move.
Now they're light as feathers and you're right in the groove
You were only hungry for some musical food
You're positively, absolutely in the mood.*

    Instead of a gravestone, Charlotte had a bench placed at the end
of the Swallowtail, anchored with bolts to the concrete where the
fog bell had once been. It would be a place to rest for anyone who
ventured out this far, a place to look out to sea and listen to the wind
and the bell-buoy that rang with the rocking of the waves. On the

back of the bench was a small ivory plaque made from a piano key that read simply "Will Murdoch, Artist" with his dates. Anything else he had been—husband, father, teacher, friend—was encompassed in that word.

In the mood — that's it 'cause I got it and I'm
In the mood your ear will spot it when you're
In the mood bobbity bop a diddly-bop-a-bop-a
Be alive and get the jive
You've got to learn how.

Afterward, Charlotte welcomed us all back to Aristotle's Lantern for a bite. I told her I was going to walk back by myself to clear my head. For a while, because it was low tide, I walked along the shore, a beach where the waves had smoothed the pebbles to roundness. Now that Clive had brought them to my attention, I had started looking for them too, the perfect spheres. You would think you were finding a globe as perfect as a marble or a Christmas tree ornament, only to pick it up and find that one side, the side you couldn't see at first, was dented after all. But much to my surprise I found one that was as symmetrical as the one in Clive's truck, though tending ever so slightly to the oval. I put the pebble in my pocket and walked on, looking for a place to cut through the woods and hook up with the road.

At last I found a narrow path, but what started out as a trail soon opened out to a graveyard at the shore's edge. A white picket fence held back the winter-dead bushes and alder saplings that threatened to take over. Most of the gravestones were old and leaning. What writing there might once have been was completely effaced by time and weather and the same orange lichen that grew over the rocks at Swallowtail Light. Other gravestones were more recent and bore island surnames that I recognized. In one corner was a lovely rounded stone that bore the name of Gammy Green. A wave design was laid into the stone with a mosaic of beach glass, the green and blue twinkling in the light that slanted through the trees. Beside it was a gravestone like none I had ever seen. It was a roughly hewn pillar of rock, no taller than my knee, surmounted by a small crudely carved bird. The only inscription was the word BIRD and the year 1968. Looking at these unique tombstones made me think about my father's gravestone back in Ontario, a thousand miles from here. The stone with my father's name beside my mother's, though hers still had a blank after the dash between dates.

There in the graveyard by the sea, I thought again about AM and PM and my father's belief that everything could be explained and archived, his belief that there were no mysteries, at least none worth going after. A bird in the hand. I realized now that I had always held this against him. Could someone be faulted for believing the world was flat or that the wind always died down this time of evening? He was, after all, working with the information he had at the time. But why not turn your caravel to the far horizon? I felt a stinging sensation spreading in my chest, and thought it might just be a wave of forgiveness breaking over the stubborn rock of my heart. I reached in my pocket and pulled out the rounded stone I had found on the beach. I rolled it between my palms, remembering the Jewish tradition of placing pebbles on graves as a sign that the dead were not forgotten. Albert McIlveen's grave was in Ingersoll, not here on Gannet Island, but who knew when I would get back to Ontario? So I improvised, placing the pebble carefully beneath the wings of the small rough-hewn bird where it looked just like a little egg, delicately speckled and curving into the future. I would find other pebbles as round or rounder. What good is a stone in the hand?

Back at Aristotle's Lantern, the mood was as festive as it had been at Swallowtail Light, with people eating and drinking, listening to more of the Andrews Sisters and reminiscing about Will. His art was all around us on the walls. His art was in his wife and in his daughter, and in all the people whose lives he had touched over the years. People who knew Will spoke of his influence in their lives, and it was surprising how many people were there. Family, friends, acquaintances, students, people who had never met him but admired his work. The very old and the very young. His daughter Fay, the one who made carvings and talked to horses, spoke eloquently of her father's example: "Despite everything, he just kept keeping on."

One of his students spoke of how fifteen years after she had studied with him, he still remembered her work. I spoke briefly of the night he had showed me the truth about blue, and how, in so doing, he had rescued me from red. I quoted from his book about fishing boats of the Atlantic shore.

There is something sorrowful about a boat abandoned in a remote field or on a lonely beach...one cannot help but gaze upon it and speculate on the trials it has been through, the calms and the storms, and wonder if it has served a useful life worthy of its designer's dreams and builder's skills.

With Will, I said, there was no need to wonder. I spoke of the power in his paintings represented in over a thousand collections, including the Queen of England's, and how that power made some people afraid. I closed by announcing that anyone who wished could now go and see *The Human Compass*, Will's four great paintings of great suffering at the Grand Harbour museum. There had been no time to arrange a place on the walls next to the little display on his work. The four huge paintings were just leaning against the glass cases full of stuffed birds, so people could see them. Hazel had acted at long last. And next to them was Will's painted Endurable, which, after discussing it with Charlotte, I had donated to the museum for everyone to enjoy. After what I had asked of Hazel, it only seemed fair.

I had suggested we put out a Book of Remembrance and by the end of the day almost all the pages were filled with anecdotes and observations and notes of gratitude, along with an occasional little sketch or doodle. "Be sure they put their names and addresses," Charlotte had insisted, "so I can send thank you notes." Charlotte is a great believer in thank you notes. She was managing very bravely, carrying trays of delicious things from one room to the next, making sure everyone had what they needed. It meant a lot to her that Fay had been able to make the trip from Alberta. I was standing next to Fay when Charlotte put her hand on her daughter's growing belly and whispered, "Someone goes and someone comes."

It wasn't until most people had gone home that the hairline cracks began to appear in her composure. She showed me a brochure that had arrived that day in the mail advertising a watercolour workshop that Will was supposed to give the following week on the mainland. "They could not have known, of course, that he would be gone," she said. "But it bothers me to see his smiling face there where he cannot be...where he can never be again." I looked at the brochure describing Will's workshop that would never happen now, as well as workshops in pottery and intaglio. I couldn't bear the grief in her eyes.

"You should do something different for yourself," I said. "Why don't you take one of those courses?" I didn't even know what intaglio was, but it sounded interesting.

Charlotte said she would think about it.

BOWLER 9

I awoke one night from a dead sleep because it was raining on my head. "That's never a good thing," Es said later when I texted her. It should have been snowing at the end of February but there had been a thaw and instead a bitter cold rain was driving down, and the wind was howling furiously. I was completely disoriented, and the power was off because of the storm. I hunted around for Thomas's flashlight, which I still kept in the drawer of my bedside table, and shone it around the bedroom. Water was pouring through the overhead light fixture as if it was a bathtub faucet and it was also trickling down around the skylight and down through the windows and door frames. I stumbled into the living room, but it still seemed dry in that half of the house. The hats hanging from the Hat Trick were out of harm's way as was the silkscreen of me in my boater that Es had created. I went back into the bedroom, realizing the amount of water coming down through the ceiling made the strategic placing of pots a lost cause. I dragged out the two large Rubbermaid containers holding summer clothes from the bottom of my closet and dumped them out on the couch. I placed them under the worst of the gushing leaks, and repeatedly carried them to the tub to dump before they got too heavy to lift. I considered whether there was something I could do on the outside to keep out the rain, but I wasn't about to get up on the roof in the dark, though I did have the presence of mind to turn off the main power breaker.

By the time the storm finally subsided, daylight was coming on. I looked around at the damage. The plaster around the skylight was bulging in some places and in others had actually fallen in huge chunks onto the floor beside the bed. I lit a fire in the stove to warm things up since the electric baseboards weren't working without power. I filled the kettle and set it on top of the Franklin stove. You can face anything after a cup of tea, Charlotte always said.

It was too early to call anyone, and still too blustery to go out and check what was going on with the roof. Probably shingles had blown off or the flashing around the skylight was wrecked. There was access to the attic crawl space through the bedroom closet, a little square in the ceiling that lifted up like a trapdoor you could hoist yourself through. I had never had cause to look up into what I imagined to be the domain of spiders and bats, but now I fetched the stepladder I had purchased last fall to put on the storm windows and climbed up. I poked my head through to see a cold dim space lit only by a tiny window at one end that was largely covered with a tangle of dead honeysuckle. There wasn't enough headroom to stand and there was no floor, just exposed joists. The space was empty except for piles of old newspapers and magazines sitting on some planks within reach of the access. Because the stacks of magazines and papers were waterlogged from the leak around the skylight, I figured they should be removed, or the whole ceiling might cave in because of the weight. I decided I could put all the wet pages in the tub till they dried out, then burn them in the stove. It took me about an hour and several trips before I had removed all that I could safely reach.

No wonder there had been no words in the cottage when Es and I first arrived. They had all been hidden in the attic. I had the tub half-full of soggy pages when one of the magazines caught my eye, not so much for the title, which was *The Phoenix*, but because there were several identical copies. I picked up one of the copies and tried to open the wet pages carefully so they would not disintegrate. The first item in the Table of Contents was the annual *Phoenix* short story contest. First Prize had gone to Pertice Malczewski. The story was called simply "Mine" but the opening line was familiar to me. "I have never been in a war, but I imagine it would be something like this with the explosions, the darkness, the dripping, and men's faces tainted with earth." The story was illustrated with a woodcut of a miner's cap, the lamp aglow.

Clearly my father had sent Pertice Malczewski the letter he had written from the mines that summer after his graduation from high school and she had submitted it as a story of her own that had won a prize of one hundred dollars and a year's subscription to *The Phoenix*. A bird in the hand. She had stolen from the boy who had admired her enough to name his only child after her. Anger came at me like a wave gathering strength and height till at last it curled over and crashed toward my shore. "All artists are thieves," Will had said. But this was surely not what he meant, though maybe it explained why this stranger, this Pertice that I had never met, had given her hats and house to me. Will also said, "Nothing is ever really stolen, only circulated."

I felt I should call Luke because maybe it was his shabby workmanship and not just the storm that had created this chaos. My house was a wreck. I was a wreck. Even the bond I had felt with the giver of the hats was wrecked, now that I knew she was a thief, not just of Will's hat, but of my father's words. But my first instinct was to call Clive, and fortunately, he was home from the mainland.

It had been a long night and a long morning and I felt exhausted and overwhelmed. When Clive showed up at the door, I burst into tears. I showed him the mess in the bedroom, still sobbing. He put his arm around me. "There's nothing here that can't be fixed," he said, pushing the hair out of my eyes. He put his hand under my chin, and lifted my downcast face so I had to look at him. "It's going to take a while," he said, "but we got this." Maybe he was right. If the Sistine ceiling could be gloriously repaired, so could mine. I leaned into him with weariness and relief.

Clive said he had logged enough overtime to take several days off work, so for the next week he came every day. He took down all the wet plaster, carted it to the landfill and replaced it with new drywall. He replaced the shingles on the roof and repaired the skylight and flashing. He replaced the light fixtures and the trim that had been damaged by the water. "It's going to be okay," he said, in a way that made me believe him. Sometimes I poured a glass of wine and watched him do his thing. Occasionally he asked for my help holding one end of the ceiling drywall up with a T-bar so he could screw it in place, but mostly he had the tools to handle the job by himself. As Hazel said, he had the gift of salvage.

It was a big job and Clive only took breaks to eat. We lingered over meals laughing and talking about everything and anything, and one night when the moon was full, Clive dug up a pair of his old hockey skates and took me skating on the outdoor rink he used to play hockey on as a kid. I had never skated under the stars. It was enchanting. When the week was done, Clive took me by the hand and showed me what he had accomplished. Everything looked better than new. He raised my hand and put it on his chest so I could feel the beating of his heart through the flannel of his shirt. "I told you there was nothing here that couldn't be fixed."

"Maybe I can get some insurance money to pay you for all your work."

"Forget it. They'll just crank up your rates if you put in a claim. It was my pleasure, really."

"I don't know how to thank you," I said, giving him a kiss, not a chaste little peck on the cheek, but on the lips like I had been wanting to for a while.

"That works," he said, grinning, "but I really do have to get back to the mainland if I want to keep my job!"

While I was in Grand Harbour to pick up my March hat at the lawyer's office I ran into Luke. When I asked him how he was, he said he had been really busy. My house wasn't the only one that had been damaged in the storm. It looked like he might be home to stay. Other than saying that one time that Toronto had "not panned out," he hadn't provided any details, but clearly he had been disabused of any romantic notions about the Big Smoke. Now seemed to be the time to ask him straight out, "Why did you come home?"

"DUI." Seeing my blank look he went on. "New Year's Eve, I wrapped my truck around a lamp post. The truck I used for work was totalled, plus my insurance premiums went through the roof because I'd been drinking, so I was doubly screwed. I tried for a while to get to work by public transit, but carrying my tools on the subway or the streetcar was a nightmare. I was always forgetting something I needed, and the foreman had no patience for that shit. And it took longer than you'd think to get anywhere. Those little TTC transfer slips they give you say: 'Thanks for Riding the Rocket!' Rocket, my ass!"

Here I had thought just maybe his return had something to do with me, but in fact he had created his own mess, and didn't know how to get out of it other than by leaving it behind. I looked over at his handsome clean-shaven face, and thought about all the scars that didn't show. It almost made me wonder if there wasn't a portrait hidden somewhere where all the darkness was showing up, because it sure wasn't there in his face. All the things that had happened to him and all the things he had done, things you would never know because he would never say. Unlike Clive, he never spoke about his family, about his father or Nina or about his childhood. He did take off suddenly for Toronto, but he had never hidden the fact that he was dying to leave the island the first chance he got. And to be fair, he had come to see me in the hospital after the accident, and he would have come sooner, he said, but my mother had prevented him. Despite his faults, there was a kind of clarity about him, but then again I knew of a lake in Ontario so clear you could see right to the bottom. It looked pristine, but it was years of invisible acid dripping from thunderclouds that had made it that way. Nothing lived there anymore.

For some reason, I was a little nervous about my March hat, thinking about the Alice illustrations of the March Hare and the Mad Hatter, both said to be insane, the first because it was breeding season, and the latter because of the mercury fumes from the felt making. As it turned out, my March hat was a black bowler hat adorned with a single white dove. As always there was an accompanying letter. It was the longest yet.

Dear Pertice,

This is the hat I wore the last time I saw your father, named a bowler after the family of felt makers who made it, and called a derby in America after the Earl of Derby who wore it at the horse race of the same name. Some people say the bowler and not the Stetson was the hat that won the West. All the outlaws and gunslingers favoured it because it would not blow off in the wind, or get knocked off by branches, which was why it was invented in the first place for the gamekeepers of a man named William Coke. Top hats were too easily knocked off or damaged, and soft hats wore out too easily, so this was the solution, a hat so hard, when Coke stood on the crown, it bore his weight. There were those like King George V who stuck by the top hat, considering bowlers a country hat for "rat catchers," but it nonetheless became one of the most successful hats ever designed.

It was my father's hat. I always thought of it as a funny hat, because of Charlie Chaplin who wanted everything to be a contradiction, baggy pants, tight coat, large shoes, small hat. But for my father, it was a deadly serious hat. If the deerstalker was his serious country hat, this was his serious city hat, as serious as a London banker. No doubt you have seen the famous painting by René Magritte called *The Son of Man*, with a man in a bowler hat and a green apple all but covering his face. There was another painting done in the same year, 1964, called *Man in the Bowler Hat*, which instead of an apple has a white bird obscuring the face of the man in the suit, even his eyes. For me, this was my father. Always a bird between me and his face. When he died and I inherited this hat, I took one of the artificial doves which I had hanging on my Christmas tree that year, and fixed it to the brim, in homage to Magritte. A white bird on a black hat. Maybe it was a final act of defiance. Maybe it was a gesture of peace.

As I have said, this was the hat I was wearing when I last saw your father. I knew your father when he was young. He was a student of mine in his last year of high school. As I'm sure you know, the summer after he graduated, he went to dig gold out of the ground. I know this because he sent me a letter describing his experiences. I was impressed with his words. I had always known he was intelligent, but he struck me as lacking somehow. There seemed to be something missing from his character, grace or courage, call it what you will. But that letter was different. Partly to test the value of his words, and partly because I coveted them and the experiences that gave birth to them, I submitted his words as my own and won a prize. Most teachers cannot abide plagiarism, but I was struggling with the bitter realization that though I had always cherished the notion that I was a writer who taught, the truth was, in fact, the other way around. I was a teacher who wrote, without much in the way of experience or training or success. I was only seventeen when I began to teach in 1944. The men were all away in France, up to their armpits in blood and fear. And any courage I might have had to go out into the world was taken up by facing class after class of students not much younger than myself. And before I knew it, whole decades had dropped away from me like rocks from a cliff.

That's the way it was. Young men and women pass through your classroom and you try to teach them what you can before they pass on to adventures and families of their own. I was embarrassed by what I had done, and hoped to be able to avoid your father, thinking he would go on to university that fall, but that is not the way it happened. I was out walking and our paths crossed. "Can I walk with you?" he said. Ever the teacher, I corrected him. "May I walk with you?" I said. "Yes, you may," he replied. It was the nearest thing to humour I had ever heard from him. He was such a serious young man.

It was raining and the leaves were beginning to fall, leaving their grey shapes on the wet sidewalks. He held an umbrella over me and my hat as we walked along the banks of the

Thames, and he asked if I knew the town was originally called Oxford-on-Thames, by the town's founder, Thomas Ingersoll, though his son had it changed it to Ingersoll in his honour. I knew from the classroom that he loved trivia of this kind. Yes, I said. Did he know that Ingersoll was the father of Laura Secord? He did.

I don't know whether it was guilt over what I had done in stealing his story, or that I found his company surprisingly agreeable, but when we arrived at my door I said, "Would you care to come in for a drink?" He recognized this as an invitation that would be extended to an adult and he accepted it. Like a gentleman, he helped me out of my wet coat, but then he did something that took me completely by surprise. He reached over and lifted this hat from my head. "I always wanted to do that," he said. We both realized the gesture was as intimate as if he had reached over and unbuttoned my blouse. What happened next would not have happened if it were not for the intimacy of that gesture, and the wine, and the desire for a child of my own that had been building in me for some years since my soldier had been blown to bits in a pillbox near Da Nang.

You must remember that in 1967 it was not like it is today. One could not just go to a clinic and be artificially inseminated. In those days the bull and the cow had to come together. I knew your father was intelligent, and he appeared after that summer inside the earth to have become stronger and deeper. It seemed the mines had made a man of him. I was forty years old and done with wandering, believing it might be my last chance. I would not, indeed I could not, have seduced him if he had not been at least a little attracted to me. I explain. I do not excuse.

When I discovered that I was pregnant, I knew that I could not stay in Ingersoll. A single woman with child, who, as a teacher, was supposed to be a pillar of the community would create a scandal no one would forgive. As I have told you, when

I was younger, I was brought to Gannet Island. I recalled that the islanders had been very hospitable and thought it might be a perfect sanctuary for me while I waited for my child to be born. I was assured that the midwife on the island was a very capable woman, and that I would be in good hands. And I was. However, the baby came sooner than anyone expected, and everything went wrong. I had no idea there would be so much pain and so much blood. Had the baby been born today in a modern hospital he might well have survived, but he did not live beyond the first night, despite the midwife's best efforts.

At the time of my son's death, Gammy Green insisted I hold him at least once in my arms. "What name have you given him?" she asked.

"What difference does it make now?"

"It always makes a difference," she said. "The names we give speak the love we know."

I was filled with grief and anguish, knowing that because of my age and situation, I could not go down this road again. As soon as I was well enough to travel, I began to pack for Ontario. The midwife assured me that she would take care of everything, and she did, arranging for the burial and the tombstone. I told her the baby was to be named Bert after his father.

When I left the island, I did not go back to Ingersoll. I went to Toronto, a city into which it is possible to disappear. I taught there for the rest of my career. When I retired, I thought perhaps I would return to the lovely little island in the sea. I had walked its length and breadth while the baby grew within me. I had been astonished by the beauty and silence and the kindness of the people there during my time of trouble. A quarter of a century later, when I finally returned to the island, I was surprised to find a stone marker next to Gammy Green's own grave that said simply "BIRD" with the year of his birth and death that were one and the same. She must have misheard me, or perhaps not.

Several years later I happened to pick up a copy of the *Ingersoll Times* and saw an obituary for your father. He had seemed so unbearably young when I knew him that it was hard to imagine that he had died before me, and yet there it was. Included among the details was the phrase "survived by his wife June and his daughter Pertice." I knew then that he must have held me in part of his heart to have named his only daughter after me, as I had named my only son after him. I had always believed I had stolen from him, but perhaps he had offered what I needed freely after all. I resolved then, that if you could be found, I would bequeath my house by the sea and my beloved hats to you.

There are still hats I wish I owned, like Elsa Schiaparelli's eyelash hat (her famous shoe hat is a tad too Dali for daily wear), or Audrey Hepburn's black and white beauty from the Ascot scene of *My Fair Lady*, or Stephen Jones' "Wash and Go" hat made of clear acrylic that looks like splashing water, or any of Philip Treacy's marvellous feathered creations, but I am done with hats now. I am an old woman with the desire to put her affairs in order before it is too late. I trust that if you are reading these words you have fallen in love with the island as I did, though my hands were too full of damage to accept the gift.

> I wish you peace and passion by the sea,
> Pertice Malczewski

I knew this was the last hat to come to me because someone had tucked an obituary in with the final letter. June had said no one around Ingersoll had seen Miss M for years, but on the occasion of her death, the *Ingersoll Times* published a brief obituary because of her long service to the community as a teacher. Most of the obituaries for women said things like "beloved wife" or "dear sister" or "survived by" but hers said merely "late of Oxford Lodge," and that was it. The very same day a vicious storm was tearing apart her beloved house by the sea, my namesake was voyaging toward the undiscovered country from which no traveller returns.

Nine hats. That's all I would ever receive from the woman after whom I was named. Nine the number of the muses, those daughters of memory who reigned over epics and history and astronomy, poetry sacred and erotic, song and dance, tragedy and comedy. Nine the number of months Pertice Malczewski waited for her son and my brother to be born. Nine the number of months I had been on Gannet Island.

Some days when I wore the bowler, I felt as serious as a banker or a gunslinger or an ornithologist, and other days I felt as comic as Chaplin, who believed life is a tragedy when seen in close-up, but a comedy in long-shot. The February thaw and rainstorm that did so much damage to Honeysuckle Cottage led into a severe cold snap, but as the days lengthened you could feel that spring was on its way. Easter was a moveable feast, like Paris, and this year it fell early, on the very last day of March. Clive was home from the mainland and invited me to help with the pancake breakfast after the sunrise service at the Church of the Straits and Narrows. "I'll pick you up," he said.

I was surprised when he showed up on a motorcycle, a vintage Triumph. "Haven't been able to drive it since last summer," he said. Back before I even knew he existed. "I like your Easter bonnet," he said, taking in my black bowler with the white dove. I had dressed up for the occasion, even though I knew I'd be cooking, wearing a navy polka dot dress fitted and flared in all the right places and Es's *Starry Night* earrings.

"Maybe I should change," I said, knowing what asphalt could do to skin.

"I hate to say it, because you look great, but maybe you should, just to be on the safe side." When I came back out without my bowler, wearing jeans and a black chiffon blouse with little birds on it, he handed me his extra helmet. When I fastened the chin strap, he pulled up the rear of the helmet to make sure it wouldn't roll forward and off. Even when he was satisfied I would be safe, I still hesitated. At the rehab in the Saint John Hospital, I had met several young men who were recovering from horrific motorcycle accidents. Kip had been completely messed up and he had been in car, but those guys were broken beyond belief. "Just watch the exhaust pipe. It can get hot," Clive said, as I climbed on, using his shoulders as support. I was nervous at first, but Clive was a careful driver, and I soon began to relax and feel safe, leaning into the curves with him, my arms tight around his waist.

Just before we got to the church in Castalia, he rolled to a stop beside the tiniest road kill I have ever seen, some kind of mouse that never made it across the highway. Clive carefully lifted the dead creature and draped it over the front of the motorcycle, like hunters did with big game across the hood of their safari jeep. "Eat your heart out, Hemingway," he said. Somehow, Clive always managed to get me laughing. He never told jokes like the kind you read in books, but he was able to improvise humour out of the most unlikely situations.

When we arrived at the Church of the Straits and Narrows, I stepped into the washroom to pull myself together after the ride in the wind. It felt weird to be in public without a hat, especially on a day when hats used to be *de rigueur*. Could this be the same girl who used to complain about wearing a hairnet? When I walked into the kitchen in the annex, Clive was standing with his back to me, his shirtsleeves rolled up to the elbow, putting ingredients in a huge bowl. He had two spatulas sticking out of the hip pockets of his blue jeans, handles down.

"Reporting for duty, sir."

"Aprons are over in that drawer," Clive said. He himself was wearing a black BBQ apron with red chilies all over it. "I brought my own." While I was tying on an apron, Clive said apologetically, "It's a mix, but I add eggs even though the instructions say just add water." He had a carton open on the counter, and was cracking eggs expertly with one hand on the side of the bowl. I hadn't seen anyone do that since the Paris cooking school scene in *Sabrina* with Audrey Hepburn. "You can start mixing another batch," he said, spooning batter onto the griddles with a little sizzle. He grabbed the spatulas out of his back pockets, and twirled them around like a gunslinger. "Let's flip…" he said, as he walked bowlegged between griddles, making "ca-chink, ca-chink" sounds as if he was wearing spurs.

As we worked, I told him all about Pertice Malczewski, ending with the waterlogged copy of the *Phoenix*. "She stole my father's words."

"I guess the cottage was her act of atonement," Clive said.

Then I told him about my half-brother, buried by the shore in the year human beings first saw the far side of the moon. He paused and looked at me closely.

Suddenly the pass-through in the kitchen wall behind the counter slid up, revealing three grey-haired ladies, standing there like domestic fates watching us, one holding a pitcher of syrup, one a pitcher of orange juice, and one a saucer with butter. "S and B," Clive said by way of explanation. He looked at my face and laughed. "S and B, not S and M. Social and Benevolent Society." Hospitality for gatherings like this was the social part of what they did, but most of the benevolence was behind the scenes, caring for anyone in the community who needed care. The room where the breakfast was to be served was filled with tables covered with flowered plastic cloths. People were starting to filter in, some of them dressed in their Easter best, but many, like Clive and me, dressed casually, including Simon, who got everyone singing "Johnny Appleseed" as a grace.

After breakfast, the tables were cleared and supplies set out for the kids to make Ukrainian Easter eggs. In fact, they were emulating the designs with black markers and paint. Making them the real way with a stylus and dyes, beeswax and candle flame, was not for rookies. Simon's wife Bronwen, who had wept as the piñata gave up its treasures, was telling the Ukrainian legend of the Easter egg, how wherever blood fell from Christ's wounds, an egg appeared and those that were touched by Mary's tears became elaborately decorated. As she talked, she handed out charts with Ukrainian symbols to the older children, diamonds for knowledge, ladders for prayers, spirals for immortality, birds for wish fulfilment and fertility. The younger children were put to work decorating baskets for the egg hunt later.

"Kind of pagan, isn't it?" I said, half-joking, half-serious.

"You mean p-EGG-an?" Clive asked, laughing. "You keep what you can use."

After the egg decorating, everybody moved outside for the egg hunt. Because Easter came early, there was a raw feeling in the air, and everything was muddy rather than green, with only a few brave crocuses peeking out, and everyone expecting there would be at least one more snowstorm. It was windy, and I was glad I wasn't wearing a dress after all, especially one with a full skirt that blew up at the slightest breeze. I stood on the sidelines watching the egg hunt. Someone had hidden little foil-covered chocolate eggs in every nook and cranny of the church grounds. Clive and Bronwen were helping the youngest children by steering them towards the obvious hiding places, and stopping the greedy kids from grabbing everything. Then there was the classic egg-on-a-spoon race for the children, and for this the eggs were hardboiled. Then finally, there was the egg toss. Everybody lined up in pairs, and this time the eggs were raw. Clive stood at the far end, passing an egg from hand to hand and looking in the direction of the parking lot. Obviously he was waiting for a partner late to arrive and so, trying not to feel disappointed, I paired myself with the little girl who had no partner. As I gave the girl a little practice toss with a foil-covered egg, I looked up to see Luke, striding across the field.

"Hi, Pertice," Luke said, looking surprised, maybe because he was used to seeing me in a hat, or because I was here on Clive's turf. He wasn't taking any chances. He pulled off the X ring from his right ring finger and slipped it into his pocket. Clive had no rings to take off, but he rubbed his hands together and breathed on them. "Let the games begin," he said, winking at me.

It's always a pleasure to watch men catching. It's my favourite part of baseball, the man appearing out of nowhere with a spectacular outstretched arm, leaping against the outfield fence to prevent the ball from escaping. Sometimes you were not even sure he would come up with it, but then there would be the grin and the glove held high. You could tell by the way the brothers were throwing and catching that they knew what they were doing. Long easy tosses that found their mark every time, both men holding their hands not out front like the little kids whose eggs cracked all over their shoes, but to the side, so they could swing them smoothly past their bodies, allowing the motion to cradle the egg and counteract the pressure of the fall.

After every successful catch Clive and Luke took a step backward, getting farther and farther apart. Long after everybody else was eliminated the brothers were still tossing, now at an impressive distance from one another, Luke standing at the edge of the cemetery that bordered on the church lawn, and Clive next to the church wall. "They take this very seriously," said Simon the minister, who was wandering around handing out paper towel for people to mop the goo off their hands and whatever else had been hit, though most of the eggs had fallen harmlessly on the pale grass. "Eventually though," he said, "the sheer weight of the fall will crush the egg, no matter how accurate the aim." And that is exactly what happened. Though Clive threw the egg right on target, and Luke reached to catch it, the weight of descent caused it to disintegrate in Luke's hands. "FU..." he yelled, but remembering where he was, he said the "CK" softly, so only those standing near him could hear. He shook off the yolk and broken shells, as Simon announced, "Once again, the winners of the egg toss, the Ferguson brothers of Castalia!"

Since Simon's sleeves were pushed up because of the egg goo I could see he had a tattoo on his right forearm, a Celtic cross with all the complex knotwork and meanders forever etched into his skin. "Did it hurt?" I asked him as we walked back toward the church.

"The cross?" he asked, gesturing toward his arm. "Yes, it hurt." He paused for a minute and then said, "It's not for the faint of heart."

"Tattoos, you mean?"

"A life of faith. Not everyone has the balls for it, or *huevos*, as your Hemingway would say." He shaded his eyes and looked out toward the sun on the water. "I love it when you can't tell where the sea ends and the sky begins," he said, pointing at a horizon that wasn't there.

People were moving towards the open church doors for the morning service. In most churches you had to pass through a tiny dark vestibule like a decompression chamber, but here there was nothing between the well-lighted sanctuary and the wet green of spring. I looked around for Clive and Luke but couldn't see either of them, so I slipped into the back. In celebration of Easter, the front of the church was lined with lilies in pots, all blooming like little white trumpets. As the piano began to play, Clive slipped in beside me. I looked around before I could help myself. "Luke doesn't care for it," Clive said. I knew he meant that church-going was not to Luke's taste, but the way he said it, it sounded like Luke couldn't be bothered to nurture and tend. Clive, on the other hand, was clearly at home, tapping his foot along with the triumphant music, and singing in his deep rich voice, a weir stake holding up a shimmering net of higher voices. It occurred to me that there were few places in the modern world that allowed a grown man to sing out loud. After the hymn was over, he leaned over to me and whispered, "I love Easter." He sounded genuinely thrilled.

The sermon wasn't what I expected. Simon did not mention the stone that rolled away, or the women who came to sprinkle spice on all the stench and rot, or the empty grave clothes, or any of the things that you might expect from an Easter sermon. He talked, instead, about the Hebrew Year of Jubilee, every fiftieth year when the work in the fields was stopped, and the slaves were set free, land was returned to its original owners, and debts were forgiven. And suddenly I recalled what I had chosen in jest as my licence plate slogan while driving with Es somewhere in the middle of Quebec. "J'oublie."

"Do you realize you've lost an earring?" Clive asked when the service was over and we were coming out of the church. I reached up to my ears and found that he was right. "I must have lost it during the egg toss."

"I'll help you look," Clive said, getting down on his knees in the grass where I had been standing.

"Normally I wouldn't care," I said. "But Es gave them to me. She painted them."

"Looking for this?" asked the minister. He had been cleaning up the little pieces of coloured foil the children had dropped while eating their chocolate eggs, and he had seen the sparkle in the grass.

"Thank you," I said, putting both earrings safely in the pocket of my jeans. You didn't get the chance very often, but it was always a relief to rewind to the moment before things started to go wrong.

"Lost and found is our business," the minister said with a grin.

"I've still got to deal with the breakfast dishes," Clive said, turning back toward the annex.

"Need some help?

"Never hurts."

While we were working away at the dishes, I suddenly asked the question I had been thinking about all morning, "Don't you find it weird to run your life based on the sayings and doings of a man who died long before you were born?"

Clive climbed down from the chair he had been standing on to stack clean plates in the upper cupboard, and looked at me long and hard. "What got you hooked on books in the first place?" he asked. I looked down at the plate I was washing, but didn't say anything. "What took you to Toronto to study?" I held up my dripping hands, with a kind of a shrug. "What governed your choice of courses?" My eyes were starting to water. "What made you fall in love with cooking?" Clive kept the questions coming. "What made you finally decide to come down here with nothing more than a key as a clue?"

"Okay, okay, I get the point." It was a little embarrassing when you looked at it all at once like that.

He wasn't about to relent. "Say it."

"Hemingway."

"Yeah, and how flawed was he?"

"He was pretty flawed."

"I rest my case, and besides, my guy didn't stay dead."

And that, in the end, made all the difference. I hadn't really intended to start going to church, but that was where Clive went on Sunday mornings when he was home from the mainland, and I wanted to be with him and with Charlotte and Bronwen and Simon and Julia and other people I had met who were interesting and generous. Charlotte called it the Book club, capital B, and that seemed as good a description as any. I had never felt so at home as I did at the Church of the Straits and Narrows. There comes a point when you have to put aside your fears and take the plunge. Like Gammy Green walking between islands in the dark. Like Peter stepping out of the boat. You see the hand held out in the storm and decide it makes sense to grab hold. There were other churches on the island with fonts like bird baths for baptism by sprinkling, or dunk tanks like the ones at county fairs for baptism by immersion, but at the Church of the Straits and Narrows, people were baptized at high tide in the bay, lowered into the cold waters of the Bay of Fundy by a strong arm tattooed with a cross.

Since it was ages since we had gotten together for a real "chin-wag," as Charlotte called it, she invited me for Easter dinner. She invited Clive, too, but he didn't want it to get back to his mother that he had stayed on the island and not gone home for Easter dinner. He dropped me off at Aristotle's Lantern in North Head and kept going on his Triumph to catch the ferry back to the mainland. I was glad to go to Charlotte's because I wanted to talk to her about something I had been thinking about since I'd heard her say "Here again," standing beside Swallowtail Light, casting Will's ashes into the sea. "The more I learn, the more I realize I shouldn't be writing about Hemingway, I should be writing about Will. He's the one who really deserves a book." Charlotte was so moved she started to cry.

As it turned out, Charlotte also had surprises for me. After lunch, she put her arm around me and said shyly, "I have something to show you, Persimmon." In the middle of the sunroom where nine months ago I had told Charlotte how Japanese Persimmon Salad had changed my life, there was an old-fashioned press like something Gutenberg would have used. Charlotte handed me two etchings, one of an island fisherman in a red apron, and the other of a hermit crab crawling out of his shell. "I took the intaglio course," Charlotte said. "Just like you said I should. I wanted to get into the pottery course, but it was booked. So I took the other one." There it was again. All the delicious things that happen by accident.

"These are gorgeous," I said, glancing from one etching to another. "You have the gift."

"I guess I learned a lot from Will over the years, looking at all those paintings, looking at life itself as if it was a painting." She had told me once that she was his ears and he was her eyes. Now without his eyes she had found her own. "To tell you the truth," she added, lowering her voice as if she was about to tell a secret, "it's a lot like cooking: keep your knives sharp and your ingredients fresh." She laughed. "And it never turns out quite the same way twice." Charlotte flipped through a binder on the table with her notes from the course. "I got a great recipe for a ground. That's the solution that keeps the acid from eating everything in sight." She put on her glasses and read the ingredient list for Sugar Lift Ground out loud:

5 oz. corn syrup
4 oz. India ink
3/4 oz. Tide
pinch of gum arabic

"All ordinary ingredients but the last, and Will even had some of that hanging around for use as binder for watercolour painting." She picked up one of the copper plates she had used. "You paint your design with this right on the plate. The ground dissolves in water, exposing the metal to be etched. I am discovering that combining techniques makes for the most interesting pictures." Charlotte bubbled with enthusiasm for her subject. "The teacher was very helpful, but I figured out some things on my own. Like you have to keep the burin really sharp. That's this thing." She held up the etching instrument with its chisel-like blade and wooden handle. "You test it like this; touch it to your thumbnail. If it sticks, it's sharp enough; if it slips, it's too dull. And I also discovered it's a lot easier to move the metal plate and hold the blade still, rather than the other way around." Charlotte called these things tricks, but I realized they were not tricks really, just better ways of getting the thing done.

When I was gathering my things to go, Charlotte came out from the kitchen with a container full of leftovers. "Please take these," she said, handing them to me. "I'll never get them eaten by myself." Then she reached in her pocket and pulled out an envelope, which she also handed to me.

"What's this?"

"Tickets to Toledo," Charlotte said. At first I thought she meant Toledo, Ohio, but she meant Toledo, Spain. "We were supposed to go for our fiftieth wedding anniversary. You know how Will loved El Greco."

"You should go yourself, Charlotte," I said, handing the envelope back.

"No, I've thought about it since the funeral. I couldn't bear it without him," she said, gesturing the tickets away. "And the baby is due any day. Fay wants me in Alberta, and I want to be there to help in any way I can."

"Couldn't the tickets be postponed or something?"

"I looked into that, and it's now or never. Haven't you always wanted to go to Spain?"

It was true. Ever since my father's death had prevented my departure back when I was seventeen, I had been wanting to go. "Yes, but…"

"No buts, Persimmon. I want to thank you for getting Will's paintings back to us all. He would have been so pleased." She paused. "And for this," she added, waving at the printing press and all the works of art it would pressure into existence.

"But there are two tickets," I said, opening the envelope.

"The other one is for Clive. That is, if you don't mind." Then she told me something I had not known. Every time he was back on the island, after he was done assisting Mr. Harmon however he could,

Clive had spent hours helping Will and Charlotte with tasks around the house that they couldn't manage by themselves. What had Es said? You can tell the most about a man by what he does when no one's looking.

POSTLUDE:
LIFE IN THE AFTERNOON

Art is never stationary for very long.

~Robert Percival, *Ukiyo-e: Art for the People*

A few days before Clive and I were to leave for Spain, I was in the bedroom deciding what to pack. Charlotte had given us the airline tickets to Toledo, but the rest would be up to us. We would be camping and travelling light. Should I take a hat? Four out of the nine hats I had been given had found their way elsewhere, and the Merry Widow and the bowler were out of the question for travelling. The boater might be good to keep away the Spanish sun, and I had sewn little combs on the inner band so I didn't have to hold it down in a wind. The deerstalker was for cooler weather than Spain in May. The cloche might be too, but a felt hat could easily tuck into a corner of my backpack somewhere, and lately the ribbons with their arrowed code for love had felt appropriate. I put it on and looked in the mirror. It was one of my favourites. I still enjoyed wearing hats though I didn't feel compelled to anymore now that my deal with Miss M was done. June had done some sleuthing and discovered that Pertice Malczewski's body had been given to science, maybe in a last gesture to please her father. But her heart had been given to me. This house and these hats, and the little stone bird in the graveyard by the sea.

I was still wearing the cloche when I answered the door. It was Clive. "Frank had a scare with his heart," he said as he took off his motorcycle helmet. "He's quitting fishing. Hazel said he's selling his licence."

"Even though he knew how much you always wanted it?" I asked, remembering that day on board the *Hazel*, with Clive working hard in his father's presence, refusing to become again the little boy who was subject to his father's anger as dark as the earth and twice as deep.

"Yeah...even though." I would have invited Clive to come in, but had discovered that when he was upset, he seemed restless inside, preferring instead to talk outdoors where he could feel the wind off the water. Unlike Luke, he was never sick of the view.

"Maybe you could put in an offer," I said.

"It's a lot of money."

"Well, what are we talking?"

"Nearly half a million dollars if you count the boat and all the equipment."

"You can't be serious!"

"He said they're asking up to $800,000 for lobster licences in Nova Scotia."

"He's got everything he needs. What's he going to do with that kind of money?"

"I don't know, but he wants it anyway."

"He wouldn't cut his own son a deal?" Clive had told me that Frank had received his fishing rights from his father Matthew free and clear. Clive shook his head.

"Isn't there anything you can do to get him to change his mind?"

Clive shook his head again. He sat down on the front step and looked out to sea. He was silent for a long time, then he said, "Maybe one thing."

I looked at Clive, at the hunger in his sea-blue eyes. I sat down on the step beside him to listen as he talked. "The last time I went out in a boat with my grandpa Matthew, it was dawn at Grit. You remember, that's the name of our herring weir. At thirteen I was big enough to row the dory while he was busy 'feeling in' the weir." Clive started to explain what this meant, but I told him I already knew. PM had told me about it in her letter with the sou'wester she had been given the first time she was on this island. All those fish moving along the shore into the heart-shaped weir from which they could not escape. "After he was done, he asked me to pull alongside a weir stake and stop rowing. Gramps held on to the weir stake to keep us from drifting while he talked. 'A time will come,' he said, 'when your father won't be able to fish anymore. If you want this life, and I think you do, it will not come cheap. It pains me to say it because he's my son, but your father is not a generous man. You must save every penny against that day. If what you have is still not enough, I want you to remember what I'm going to tell you to do.'"

Clive asked me to come with him for support since he had not set foot in his childhood home since the night of his fight with Frank. I replaced my cloche with Clive's extra helmet and we drove toward Castalia. Following instructions he had been given more than a decade before, Clive pulled into the driveway of the house his grandfather built and his father still occupied. He put down the kickstand of his Triumph and dismounted, keeping his hand on the brake until the last moment. I followed him as he went up to his own front door and he knocked on it as a stranger would. Frank answered. Since the trouble with his heart, he did not look as powerful or intimidating as he once did. He looked grey: his tousled hair, his weathered skin, his hard eyes. Clive did not waste time with formalities. "Gramps told me before he died that if this day ever came, I needed to show you something." He walked past his father through the kitchen to the cellar door and I followed. At one time the whole cellar had been walls of exposed stone and an earthen floor, more like a cave than part of a house. Now one corner had been made into a laundry room, but the ceiling was too low to allow for much more than a furnace and some shelving for storage for all the useless stuff Hazel was constantly buying. Careful not to bump his head on the overhead beams that still showed the signs of the axe, Clive headed toward the wall facing the sea, with Frank following close behind.

This part of the cellar was lit only by a single light bulb turned on by pulling a chain. As his father watched, Clive cleared away several old boards and window frames leaning against the wall to expose the foundation stones. There in the middle of the wall was one black stone standing out from the grey stones that surrounded it. It was one of the black volcanic rocks that were not indigenous to the island but were used as ballast on ships from elsewhere, and then washed ashore after a shipwreck. Clive had never understood the numbers that were etched into the rock with a stone chisel, a kind of scrimshaw in reverse. It was hard to see them in the dim light. 1-7-9. Since his grandfather chose not to explain, Clive had always assumed the numbers indicated a date of some kind or maybe a lot number. He turned to face his father. "Grandpa said to show this to you. He said you would know what it means." For once Frank was silent. "I'll show myself out," Clive said, leaving his father standing alone in the harsh light of a naked bulb staring at the black rock. Once we were outside, Clive gave me a kiss. "Thanks. I couldn't have done that without you."

"Now what?" I asked as we drove away.

"Now we wait."

The day before we were to leave for the airport in Saint John, Clive showed up, beaming. "Good news," he said. "I can have the licence with the boat and the gear on two conditions." Frank had not told Clive this directly but had used a lawyer, Jim of the Ampersand, as a go-between.

"What conditions?"

"Frank wants a down payment of fifty grand and an annual salary for as long as he lives, even if he never sets foot on the boat again."

"And?"

"I'm to look after Luke."

"Meaning what exactly?" I asked.

"Meaning if the licence is ever sold, Luke gets half the proceeds. It's all laid out in the legal documents."

My first reaction was fear. Having the rights to a piece of the ocean seemed risky beyond measure. If nothing improved, maybe lobster and herring would go the way of the cod, and Clive would end up owning nothing at all. I remembered the old woman who had coveted PM's hats, whispering, "No one owns the sea." I knew the dangers Clive would face if he went to sea. Will, who had painted amazing portraits of boats abandoned on beaches, spoke of *the unromantic business of fishing at sea— its hardships, monotonies, and dangers.* The very first time I took the ferry from the mainland I had seen the map of Gannet Island littered with shipwrecks. But I also knew how well fishermen learned the bottom of the ocean, every rise and trough, every intricate bit of topography and the currents that flowed over them. They saw it as other people saw the harbour at low tide, rich and revealed. I knew Clive had done the best he could with what he had been given and now, for the first time in his life, possibilities writhed in his hands like caught fish, fins like razors against his glistening fingers. He could send them back to the secret deep or hit them hard on the head, gut them, take them home, feast.

I touched Clive gently on the arm as I had done the day he had told me about Nina's drowning, "Are you sure you want this, Clive?"

He put his arms around me and gathered me in. "I do," he said making it sound more like a vow than an answer. He took a deep breath. "I wasn't sure I was sure until I said I was."

"But what about your job on the mainland? What about the trees?" I asked, realizing as I said it that the only reason Clive had travelled light for so many years as tenant and pilgrim was because he was waiting for something to change. And now it had. Facing his father had taken all Clive's courage, but it had paid off. This would mean Clive was coming home for good.

"I want this more," Clive said. "Always have."

"What happened? Why the change of heart?" I knew from the effort to get Will's paintings into the museum how stubborn Frank could be.

"I'm not entirely sure. After everything was signed at the lawyer's office and I was about to leave, Jim stopped me, and said, 'Your father said to tell you one is the first book.'"

"What's that supposed to mean?"

"Jim didn't know. 'Don't shoot the messenger,' he said. But I've been thinking about it all the way over here, and I think I might have figured it out." Clive put his hand on the doorknob that had received the mysterious key nearly a year before, and walked into Honeysuckle Cottage. He knew I had a Bible because I had confessed to swiping the one from the hospital. I had read through quite a bit of it and was surprised at how full of scandal it was. Sex and violence in spades. Full of the weakest human beings. Blood everywhere. But also forgiveness and grace, love and choice. As I went to fetch it from my bedside table where I kept it along with Thomas's flashlight, I glanced around Honeysuckle Cottage with its windows full of ocean, the seabirds painted on the kitchen cupboards poised for flight, the art work on the walls, the Hat Trick by the door. All that had been salvaged and redeemed.

"1-7-9." Clive said. "Look it up."

I turned to Genesis, chapter seven, verse nine and read out loud: "Male and female came to Noah and entered the ark…"

Clive squinted and bit his lower lip. "Try the other first book."

I turned to Matthew, the book that shared a name with both Clive's grandfather and Clive himself, a name that meant gift. "Which of you, if his son asks for bread, will give him a stone?"

Days later, I thought of these words as we stood in the Sacristy of the Toledo Cathedral in front of *El Espolio*, the El Greco painting that had inspired Will's four great crucifixions back on Gannet Island. Reproductions could not compare to the vividness of the actual painting up close. The way the red robe of the man facing death set everything on fire. The way the carpenter and Mary Magdalene looked hard at what lay ahead, in cloaks rare as saffron, common as sun. Apparently, El Greco told the Pope that if anything ever happened to the Sistine frescoes, he could paint better ones. After the guide finished explaining how his art combined influences from the three countries he called home, the icon-like faces of his native Greece, the bold colours of Italy, and the mysticism of Spain, Clive and I talked about the influences in Will's art, the expressionism of the English painters he admired, the simplicity and natural beauty of the Atlantic provinces, and the tranquil stillness of the country of silence.

"When I get home, I'm getting started on my book," I said.

"The book about Hemingway?"

"No, a different book altogether. A book about Will." I told Clive about my plans for a book about Will's life and career, all the terrible obstacles he had faced head on, obstacles that would have crushed a lesser man. I had been working my way through the Book of Remembrance signed by all the people who had attended his funeral, gathering information and anecdotes, interviewing those on the island, and corresponding with those who were not. I had gone to Saint John for the first time since I had been in the hospital there to visit the museum where he had been curator. I was reading through articles and clippings and catalogues, whatever I could lay my hands on, and Charlotte and I had been trying to organize the uncatalogued artwork and unpublished writing he had left behind.

Clive was as thrilled as Charlotte had been. "Will's life, now *that's* grace under pressure," he said.

With the rest of the tourists we were swept out from the Cathedral into the streets of Toledo, which still looked amazingly like it had when El Greco painted it in 1597, though he had moved the cathedral spire closer to the centre of the canvas. We stopped in at one of shops with windows full of Toledo's specialty. We had been told that the Confiteria Santo Tomé was the best, and the taste of their marzipan made from Valencia almonds, thousand-flowers honey, fresh farm eggs and pine nuts, left my own marzipan in the dust, but my figures of Peter and Jesus walking on water would have held their own amongst the various fanciful shapes, including eels and dragons, and little rolls stuffed with pumpkin or custard called Saints' Bones. Snacking on marzipan, we walked together through the streets, where people were dismantling the decorations from the Corpus Christi festival, taking down the wreaths, lanterns, and antique tapestries from balconies, sweeping up flowers and aromatic herbs from the streets.

"We should go to a bullfight," I said, catching sight of a poster nailed to a lamppost, looking dramatic and incongruous against the remnants of religious pageantry.

"Not me," Clive said.

"You don't want to go?"

"I'm not interested in killing as a spectacle."

"I didn't think you were squeamish."

"Sometimes the man is killed."

"Hardly ever."

"Over five hundred professional bullfighters have died since 1700," Clive said. Clearly he had known this was coming and had looked into it. "If it just happened to be a day when the man was killed, and I had paid money to see it, I would never forgive myself." Hemingway said you never knew how people were going to react to bullfighting. It was not something you could be neutral about. Either you thought the whole thing was brutal and disgusting or you were an *aficionado*, passionately in favour of it all. Hemingway had loved it, right to the end. After he killed himself in Idaho, they found tickets he had purchased for the upcoming bullfights in Pamplona in his desk drawer.

"I owe it to Hemingway," I said.

"Well, go yourself then," Clive said.

All of the things I might say in response to this sounded more like excuses than answers, so I didn't say anything.

Clive ran his hand over his chin. He had stopped shaving since we had been camping, with hot water and mirrors in short supply, and at first his stubble had scraped me when we kissed, but now that his beard was coming in, it was softer. "To tell you the truth," Clive said, "I could use a break." Surrounded by people speaking a language we couldn't comprehend, Clive and I had been speaking only to each other. Two people who, up until very recently, had been used to spending long days alone were now together 24/7, sightseeing or eating or sleeping side by side in the tent Clive used when he was in the woods, a small green ark in the darkness. "See you back at the campground."

Even before he disappeared around the corner, I began to miss him. I had never been afraid to do things alone, even in Toronto. I went to parks and restaurants, movies and museums, so why not a bullfight? On Gannet Island I had taken pleasure in solitude to a whole new level. But something had changed. I wanted this man to share my passions even if they weren't noble. I had not realized until that moment how much I had come to count on him to hold me up like a sturdy well-built chair, to make me take delight in the world that whistled by, to make me laugh. I felt the way I did the afternoon Es left me behind that first time on Gannet Island. Bereft.

I wandered slowly back toward the campground outside the walls of the old city, stopping for a bite to eat at a café. If Clive had been with me I might have felt adventurous enough for pigs' tongues in pomegranate sauce or squid cooked in their own ink or bull's testicles, but instead I ordered *tapas*. Choices included smoked salmon, tuna and sweet red peppers, sardines, smoked Sierra ham, spiced sausage, toasted almonds and olives stuffed with anchovies, anything salty enough to make you want to drink more. I ordered *sangria*. The drink was cool and quenching, deliciously dry and rich, with a touch of citrus. It was also beautiful, the light through the carafe leaving a red shadow on the table. If I made this at home I could remember this afternoon with the red shadow, the moisture beaded on the glass, and the Spanish sun slicing through the open door of the café like a scimitar. There were probably dozens of recipes I could look up on the Internet, but I wondered exactly how they made it in Toledo. I tried to make myself understood to the bartender who was wiping glasses behind the bar. He was all darkness, dark hair cut close, dark skin, and eyes so dark they seemed almost black. Only his shirt was light, a white so bright that when he moved across the sunshine of the open doorway, it seemed to blaze. He reminded me of Romero, the bullfighter in *The Sun Also Rises*, who looked like he put on his pants with a shoehorn. He moved in his body the way Luke had. Lissom. I felt sure Luke would have gone to a bullfight. He would have been okay with death in the afternoon. The bartender finally understood. I left with the recipe scrawled across a white napkin, a recipe for the beverage of blood.

When I got back to the campground, Clive was there. If what we'd been having was a fight, it seemed to have passed. When I threw stones, they landed with a loud splash, sending ripples out and out until they eventually ran out of room, bogged down in the sand by the shore, but Clive could throw a stone in such a way that it came down into the water without a splash, so an instant later you could not see a stone had been there at all. He called it cutting the devil's throat.

"How about a compromise?" he said. "We could go in Portugal where they don't kill the bull." I didn't tell him that Hemingway hated the *simulacro*, the act of killing simulated by the placing of a rosette at the moment of going in with the sword in a *real* bullfight. I didn't have the heart to argue. Clive had spent the last two hours finding out which Portuguese town near the Spanish border was holding a bullfight and arranging to rent a car to get us there and back in time for our flight back to Canada the next day.

I would not admit it right away, not even to myself, but I felt enormous relief to be released from the necessity of looking at death without blinking. As much as I loved Hemingway and pored over *Death in the Afternoon* as if it was some kind of bible, I suddenly realized that I had not really wanted to go to the bullfight and see the wounds that horns made in a man's gut or the sword made in the neck of the bull. Even if Hemingway thought bullfighting was a tragedy and not a sport, like Clive, it was not something I wanted to pay to see.

As we headed across Spain, I was glad Clive was driving, as both the traffic and the terrain were unpredictable. You never knew when you crested a hill whether someone would be in your lane, hurtling toward you at high speed. It could be a truck or a car or a scooter loaded down with a man and woman, two children, several parcels, two chickens and a dog. As we drove through the Spanish countryside towards Portugal, we saw giant black silhouettes of bulls rising up out of the olive trees beside the highway. These, we discovered, used to be advertisements for a kind of sherry. When Spain outlawed highway advertising in the eighties, the writing was removed, but people objected when they tried to take down the bulls because they had become such a part of the landscape. The huge black bull on every horizon.

As the miles unravelled, we talked about travelling as children. June used to play "I Spy," or "Animal, Vegetable, Mineral" with me, or that one where you had to pack your suitcase with items that began with all the letters of the alphabet. Albert rarely played. He was a cruciverbalist. I had come across this word once in the *Reader's Digest* "It Pays to Increase Your Word Power." For as long as I could remember Albert had been a crossword puzzle enthusiast, finding the isolated words that went across and down, separating the darkness from itself. "We never played anything," Clive said. "If we got excited or the least bit loud in the car, Frank would crank up the radio and tell everyone to shut up."

I told him about Varsha and he told me about Wren, the only woman he had gotten really serious about. They were both in the forestry program and stayed together for four years, but after graduating, she returned to her native BC to work on dealing with the mountain pine beetle that was spreading across her province like a red tide. As much as she cared for him she could not ever imagine living on Gannet Island, and she knew that was his true heart's desire. He had been prepared to follow her out west, saying she was more important to him than home, but she was determined to move on. He was devastated. "I really thought she was the one," he said. Two years had passed, but it had taken him a long time to recover, even using versions of all the techniques for managing an infestation, pheromone baiting, snip and skid, controlled burn. "I did everything I could to get her out of my head but it wasn't until I saw you looking sexy in a sou'wester that I began to have hope again," Clive said laughing.

When we crossed the border into Portugal and arrived at the bullring, there was no debate about the kind of seats we wanted. The most expensive were in the shade, the least expensive in the sun, but we wanted the mid-range seats called *sol y sombra*, sun and shadow. This was a small-town fight with none of the pageantry and elaborate costuming of the big city. The ring itself was very plain, like a slice of

a huge oil drum set at the edge of a field, with bleachers filled mainly
with tourists. You could tell the tourists by their baseball caps.

The bull came into the ring looking dark and powerful and
angry, his blunted horns wrapped in leather to prevent him from
killing. Centuries before it had been decided that Portugal did not
have enough men to permit such waste. And a bull that cannot kill
should not be killed. Here there was no suit of lights, the elaborately
embroidered *traje de luces* of the Spanish bullfighters that cost a small
fortune. Instead, the mounted torero wore a simple black jacket, grey
pinstripe pants, and a red sash. The forcados, named for the forked
poles they once used to keep the bull from climbing the staircase to
reach the king, were also simply dressed in short jackets and pants
to the knee, both the colour of dust, with red ties and sashes. Each
man carried a green hat trimmed with a red band on his left shoulder
during the opening ceremonies.

We were supposed to admire the horsemanship, but it seemed
unfair with the man astride the swifter animal, his feet protected by
steel boxes, the bull wearied by the banderillas piercing the hump
behind his neck.

Soon, I found myself watching the shadows of the bull and riders,
rather than the real thing which was dripping with blood. Clive had
been right to say no to the killing. This was bad enough. I could not
look without blinking. It seemed much more fair when the horses
were gone, leaving only eight men standing single file without cape
or sword, without defence or weapon. Then one, the man told he will
be at the head of the line at the last minute so he had no time to get
nervous, put on his green hat and challenged the bull to charge him.

A man beside us who spoke some English explained what it
was that was about to happen. This was the *pega de cara*, the "face
catch," the main event of a Portuguese bullfight. The bull charged the
brave man in the green hat, and the man grabbed the angry half-ton
bull by the horns. He was flung over the bull's shoulders in a kind
of spectacular aerial somersault and fell heavily onto the ground. He
scrambled to his feet and the men lined up behind him for another

effort. They tried again and again. After torn sleeves, bloody noses, and lots of dust, they at last managed to surround and subdue the bull, one man holding onto his tail.

"I'm glad it's not me out there," I said.

"I'm sure they have it worked out so they usually win," Clive said.

"I've seen a few of these," the man beside us said, gesturing in the direction of the ring, "and apparently the trick is that when the man leaps between the horns it temporarily blinds the bull. Without light, he'll stop in his tracks, and the men have won." We watched the defeated bull being ushered out of the ring by trained steers. "Of course, it doesn't always work," the man added. "The Portuguese have a saying, 'Sometimes you get the bull and sometimes the bull gets you.'"

By the time we left to make our way back to the car, the crowd was dispersing. A man who looked a little like a younger, burlier version of Zorba the Greek, was walking just ahead of us with a little girl wearing a fancy pink dress. She tugged repeatedly at his sleeve, saying *Banheiros* over and over again. The man ignored the child until suddenly there was a watery noise and a dark puddle spread across the dusty floor. The man grabbed the little girl and yanked her roughly toward the exit. Clive followed them. I followed Clive but wasn't sure exactly what happened next because it transpired so quickly.

It looked like the man raised his hand to strike the child and Clive grabbed him by the arm to stop him. The little girl was crying and Clive and the man were standing against the exterior wall of the bullring yelling at each other in different languages. Then the man pushed Clive back against the wall, hard with both hands against his chest. The man was smaller than Clive but heavier and the push took him by surprise. Clive's head snapped back and struck the wall, and suddenly there was blood. The man scooped up the crying girl and ran down a narrow street. In a moment, they rounded a corner and were out of sight.

"Maybe we should find a hospital?" I asked, unnerved by the amount of blood.

"No big deal. Cuts to the head tend to bleed a lot, but once it stops I'll be fine," Clive said, as we walked slowly back to where the car was parked. He had had stitches so many times in his life he seemed to know when he needed them and when he didn't. "But I think you'd better drive." This was my worst nightmare, narrow streets, steep hills, foreign road signs, and a stick shift! I closed my eyes. Clive was wearing those pants that convert to shorts and when I opened my eyes again, he had zipped off one leg and was using it to press against the cut at the back of his head. He looked lopsided, walking with one leg long and one short.

I had been thinking that maybe we would have time to just keep driving west all the way to the coast, all the way to Cape St. Vincent, *o fim do mundo*, the end of the world. There had been a postcard at the border showing all that was left of Henry the Navigator's "college of the sea," a mariner's compass laid out in stones beside a lighthouse that looked almost like a minaret on a mosque where you could imagine a muezzin calling out prayers. I imagined this lighthouse and Swallowtail speaking to each other across the windy Atlantic, their code of light crossing like the dotted lines they used in old movies to trace the progress of the hero. But now we had no choice but to travel eastward to Toledo.

Back at the car, I draped my sweatshirt on the passenger seat to prevent any blood from getting on it, and helped Clive in. At first he was quiet so I could concentrate on driving, but when we were back in the countryside he began to talk again. "Today is Nina's birthday," he said. "About a year after she died, my mom told me she saw my father looking at Nina *that way*. She was only twelve, but already starting to curve, and wearing her hair up, which made her look older. Frank gave her earrings that said 'Daddy's Little Girl.' As far as my mother knew, that was all, just the looking, before Nina left us." I took my eyes from the road for a moment to look at Clive. "Our pain comes from only seeing a small part of the picture," he said, with a catch in his voice. We drove for a while in silence then Clive said, "She got her ears pierced for those earrings."

Suddenly he grabbed my arm. "Stop! Stop here," he said as we approached a bridge over a small river. I pulled into a rutted lane off the main road, and stopped the car, my hands unclenching slowly from the steering wheel. Clive got out and headed toward the river, unzipping his other pant leg and pulling off his bloody T-shirt as he went. I watched him plunge into the swiftly moving water. Moments later he came up clean.

Where he waded out of the water, two boys were standing on a flat rock fishing. Instead of rods they were using empty beer bottles with the fishing line wound around the neck. As they flung them forward like wands casting spells, the lines sang off the green glass of the bottle into the green glass of the river. I watched as Clive gestured to them to let him give it a try. Before long a sparkling fish was leaping at the end of his line and you could tell by their grins that the boys understood that, surprisingly, this stranger was one of them. The fish wasn't very big so Clive expertly removed the hook and let it go.

"We might as well eat since we're stopped anyway," I said, as Clive rinsed his bloodied shirt as best he could and laid it on the grass to dry. We had wonderful Portuguese bread, cheese, and fresh figs. Maybe not the Pamplona picnic Hemingway had once described, with squab, cheeses, cold smoked trout, Navarre black grapes, brown-speckled pears, marinated eggplant with pimentos, unshelled shrimps, and fresh anchovies, but delicious nonetheless in the warm sunshine, and the wine, like Hemingway's, was river-chilled. I took it upon myself to propose a toast of sorts. "This," I said, indicating the feast in front of us. "And this," I said, gesturing toward Clive. "And this." I held my glass toward the river finding its shining way to the sea. "Many doves, same hat."

"Amen," said Clive recognizing a good grace when he heard one.

Wading through Hemingway's pages and pages of death, I was always delighted to suddenly come upon a description of a Spanish picnic or an Italian celebration dinner or his favourite, an American sandwich of peanut butter and onion. Always a moveable feast. Hemingway called his book about bullfighting *Death in the Afternoon* because there was cruelty and danger and death, but when I thought about the afternoon, I thought about the slant of light on green waves, the decent weariness of a workday winding down, afternoon tea at Aristotle's Lantern. I thought about art and the people with "the gift" who made it. I thought about the mouth as a lamp, scones hot from the oven with cloudberry preserves, a picnic in the shade. The catching and not the killing—that was the true pleasure. That was life in the afternoon.

The picnic wasn't the only pleasant thing. Waiting for his T-shirt to dry, Clive lay stretched out on the grass propped up on his elbows, with his eyes closed. He had a farmer's tan, but his working man muscles were ripped for real. Even with his eyes closed, Clive must have known I was admiring him, because he patted the grass for me to come over and join him. Some people were like a stretch of grass that looked innocently empty and green, but when you got up close, lay down and put your face between the blades, suddenly you became aware of another world moving there unseen, small creatures moving to and fro, the click and hum of an unimagined empire. Then of course there was yet another layer of life below this, invisible to the naked eye, like the creatures that live in your eyelashes. I had seen magnified photos in the *National Geographic*. You couldn't think about this too much or it would overwhelm you. I felt a rush of all that had attracted me to him that day of the pie contest and since, the startling blue of his eyes, a face in which nothing was quite straight, bearing scars from being a boy and being a man, his deep familiar voice illuminating fragments of the world like a flashlight flickering across a dark path. "How you feeling now?" I asked, brushing my fingers across his bare chest.

"Fine," he said, and he did look as good as new, with all the blood washed away and his skin glistening clean and cool like the river. He closed his eyes against the hot Spanish sun. "This is bliss." We lay side by side on the warm grass in silence. Then he took his calloused right hand and slid it from my ear lobe all the way down to my heel. When I asked him what he was doing, he smiled and said, "Cruising."

Whatever that meant for another man, I knew for him it meant measuring the riches on a given plot of forested land.

"Hemingway's idea of heaven," I said, "was a big bull ring and a trout stream that no one else was allowed to fish in and two houses in town, one where he would have his wife and children and be monogamous and the other where he would have his nine beautiful mistresses on nine different floors."

"Give me the first house," Clive said, "but put it by the sea."

"Honeysuckle Cottage is a house by the sea."

Clive sat upright, and looked down at me, his face serious. "Is that a proposal, Pertice Mabel McIlveen?"

"It just might be, Matthew Clive Ferguson," I said, blushing in spite of myself. Clive had never tried to overpower or seduce me. He had just waited patiently for me to choose. He laughed. "Well, in that case, I accept." When he leaned in to kiss me long and hard on the mouth, he seemed to have forgotten about any headache he might have had.

Beyond a low stone wall near where we were sitting, some men were hacking at trees with hatchets, prying off big oblongs of bark, leaving the orange-coloured inner flesh of the tree exposed like a sheared sheep.

"What are they doing?" I asked, as we started to pack up the picnic.

"They're harvesting cork."

When Clive lost his link to the sea, trees became his passion. As a silviculturist, he had to think in decades, not moments, planting seedlings you could not be sure of until years down the road. He believed in preservation and care, maintenance and rescue. He didn't care whether anyone knew he had been involved. He was just glad that on the mainland trees were being planted, trees that would endure long after he was gone, and that back on the island only the right number and size of lobster were being pulled from the ocean floor, so the species would have a fighting chance. When talking trees, he used words like crown and girth. He believed knowing the trees of a place was to know the place, so while I pored over guidebooks and maps, he read about orange and olive, carob and cork oak. "They can only harvest cork once every nine years or it damages the tree too much," he said. "Some of these trees have survived from the fourteenth century because it's illegal to cut them down."

He stuck the cork back in the wine bottle so we could have the rest later. He would need all his concentration for the road. Now that the bleeding had stopped and he was refreshed by the swim and the picnic, he felt up to driving again. Clive stood up and put his damp T-shirt back on, wincing as he pulled it over his head. As we carried the picnic things back to the car, I looked again at the cork harvesters. I knew from Hemingway that small corks were stitched into the scarlet cloth for the matador to hold in his hands when he lifted the lower end of the heavy bullfighting cape. But I had not until now thought about the cork being cut from a living tree. "There's no such thing as unscathed," Es had said. I thought about who had decided that this was as much hurt as the tree could bear. And everyone since who had agreed to go this far and no farther, for fear of destroying the whole.

When we arrived at the Portuguese-Spanish border, I remembered how the Canadian border guard had first directed me and Es to Gannet Island via Deep Harbour, and how the sea itself had been a border between the old life and the new. Clive pulled into a shop to buy souvenirs, figuring they might be cheaper here than the tourist traps of Toledo. We wanted to pick up something marvellous for Charlotte, who had given us the gift of being here in her place. Because it was a border town there were items representing both Portugal and Spain. "Let me know if I can help," said the salesclerk who, like so many Europeans, could speak several languages.

There were red and gold flags of Spain with the crests of the old kingdoms and the motto *plus ultra*, more beyond. There were flags of Portugal, with green for hope and red for the blood of the defenders. I looked around at the little painted roosters and damascene daggers, colourful cork bags and "bota" or leather wine bottles, olive oils and tins of saffron. There were decorative tiles and ceramic plates in the

Moorish style. We had just decided on an exquisite marquetry tray with wood inlay in intricate geometric patterns for Charlotte when Clive said, "I want to get you a souvenir. I was thinking a hat."

The Hat Trick that Clive had made for me had six hooks, and of the nine hats I had inherited from Pertice Malczewski, only five remained: the boater, the Merry Widow, the deerstalker, the cloche and the black bowler with the white dove. Alice had the bergère. The pillbox had sailed over the cliff. The painted Endurable was in the Grand Harbour Museum along with Will's paintings. And the sou'wester now belonged to Clive. One more hat would make six, the exact number in that exquisite Degas painting. If the sou'wester came back to live at Honeysuckle Cottage, I could make room for it by passing on one of the others to Es, who was planning another visit if she could "stomach all the quaintness," and Jesse was willing to come with her this time. "What about this one?" Clive said, holding up a *montera*, a bullfighter's hat with two knobs like blunted horns worn by the *matador de toros*, the killer of bulls, along with his sword and suit ornately embroidered with gold. I ran my hands over the soft dark pelt. "The lambs must be under three days old when they are killed, or they lose their black color and curly fur," the sales clerk explained, bringing me a mirror in case I wanted to see how I looked. "The best pelts come from lambs still in the womb."

I passed the *montera* back to Clive. "How about this one?" I said, handing him a *forcado*'s hat — the simple knit green hat with the red band —worn by the lead man in the group who faced the bull armed only with conviction and courage.

"*Sol y Sombra*," Clive said, holding up the green hat then the black one. Sun and Shadow. To my surprise I didn't have to think about it for very long. The choice was simple now that I understood that you did not have to be the bull to fight the bull. Now that I knew there was a better way.